MW01223854

AND for the SAKE of the KIDS

or: GOD HELP US, MR. LANCASTER

by

Steven J. Conifer

And for the Sake of the Kids
© 2011 by Steven Conifer

This book is dedicated to

my brother, Phil,

and in honor of the late

Kurt Vonnegut, Jr.

"There is something wrong in a government where they who do the most have the least. There is something wrong when honesty wears a rag, and rascality a robe; when the loving, the tender, eat a crust, while the infamous sit at banquets."

– Robert G. Ingersoll

"Money is like manure; it should be spread around."

– Brooke Astor

"When I give food to the poor, they call me a saint.
When I ask why the poor have no food, they call me a Communist."

– Dom Helder Camara

PART I:

Winston

1

I first met Winston at a banquet held in his father's honor, early last summer, at a swank hotel here in Pittsburgh. That was where I first met Archie, too.

Local media were invited. I, then being a weekly columnist for the *Post-Gazette*, was a member of that elite coterie. I was excited to go, because I'd been tracking Archie's exploits in the coal industry for quite some time and was eager to score an interview with him. I realized that the chances of that were slim to none, but I'd written several articles on the man, had taken great pride in blasting him at every opportunity - I was even toying with the idea of writing an unauthorized, tell-all book on the son of a bitch - and I was itching to meet the guy, maybe get an inflammatory question or two in before he shrugged me off.

But before I could get to Archie I saw Winston, and after that the corrupt dealings of a garden-variety corporate whore lost all interest for me. After that, I was interested only in the sleazy tycoon's blond-haired, blue-eyed son, a man perhaps twelve years my junior whose face could appear in a thousand portraits and still leave artists hungry for more.

I did my best to act casual, of course. It was no easy feat, what with my hormones raging like a wildfire, with my being overcome by lust. I could scarcely remember my own name, I was so distracted.

He was standing in the lobby of the hotel, greeting guests as they arrived. Most were business associates of his father's, some relatives, others journalists or television reporters. A few of the last were snapping pictures as they walked in, hoping, I suppose, to capture an unexpectedly candid moment there in the vestibule of the city's finest hotel. Or maybe they just couldn't help themselves, were as much slaves to their professional impulse to record what they observed as I was a slave to my carnal yearnings. In any case, I shook his hand and said hello.

He looked at me, smiling not indifferently. "How are you?" he said.

"Fine," I blurted out - ejaculated, really, if you'll pardon the tawdry pun - and no doubt blushed. "I'm very well, thank you. And you?"

His smile faltered a bit. "I'm good, thanks. Are you with the press?"

"I am."

"Which outlet?"

"The *Post-Gazette.*"

His face brightened. He waved at someone behind me. "Really? That's excellent. You're a reporter?"

"Yes. Features, the occasional op-ed piece. I cover business and politics, mostly."

"Great. Well listen, we're glad to have you here, my father and I."

Without thinking I said, "My name is Terrance. Terrance Farmer."

He nodded, a little awkwardly, and smiled at a passing guest. "Good to meet you, Terrance Farmer. I'm Winston Lancaster."

And so he was. So he was.

The banquet was held in one of the hotel's opulent ballrooms and was attended by about three hundred people, the vast majority of them seated at round tables constructed of cheap pine and covered with flimsy white cloth. The exceptions were Archie, his family members, and his close business partners, who sat at a long, finely carved mahogany table at the front of the room, before the makeshift stage which had been erected so that Archie and a few of his cohorts could deliver windy speeches on the virtues of capitalism, and maybe share an anecdote or two about their golf games if the moment seemed amenable to it. Which is to say, if the guests seemed drunk enough to appreciate such hideously trivial, self-indulgent yarns.

I myself was seated with some colleagues from the *Post-Gazette* and a news anchor from a local television station. I disliked all but one of them, and exchanged only the most frivolous chit-chat with the one I didn't. Part of it was that I didn't really want to be there, except to corner Archibald Lancaster and make him squirm a little by asking him questions nobody in his exalted position was obliged (and much less disposed) to answer.

But most of it was that I couldn't stop stealing glances at Winston, who was seated at one of the ends of the long mahogany table, and every feature of whose face I had already committed to memory, and whose easy, confident laugh I could somehow hear above the raucous din of the guests, and every detail of whose inner life I ached to learn, and whose every passion and quirk and aversion and weakness I longed to know, and to study, and to cherish.

I couldn't stop looking at his face, and wondering what delightful or terrible secrets hid behind those incomparable blue eyes, what glorious dreams and ugly fears might dwell there.

Dinner was served. Chicken and artichokes, with a side of mashed potatoes garnished with black pepper and chives. Not bad, not bad.

The news anchor asked me a question, something along these lines: "Are you planning a follow-up to your story on Gerricot's expansion into the retail market? I hear he wants to open a couple of electronics stores on the west side. Sounds like a pretty wise move to me." Gerricot was the owner of a local telecommunications outfit and had been flirting with the notion of selling communications technology on a limited scale throughout the city, just to sort of test the waters and see whether consumers would bite. A few months earlier I had written a story on the tentative moves he had made in that direction, his most recent liquidations and acquisitions and so forth.

I gave an answer, something along these lines: "No, I don't think so. I'm more interested in that gentleman over there." I pointed at the man I was talking about.

The news anchor, perplexed, followed my finger. "Oh? How do you mean, exactly?"

"He's responsible for more suffering than most anyone who's ever lived," I said.

"He is?"

"Yes. And everyone at this table knows it."

He looked at me (everyone at the table did), then looked

back at the man, who was feasting on grilled chicken and insatiable hubris. "Archibald Lancaster?"

I smiled wanly at the reporter and popped an artichoke into my mouth. "The one and only."

But of course I was still thinking about Winston.

I saw him again on the way out, and waved to him. He waved back. Once more he smiled, and I was sure that he meant the smile especially for me, every corner and crease and subtle lilt. I could see his straight white teeth, savored his high, delicate cheekbones and pouting lips and round, prominent Adam's apple.

I was shaking as I got into my car. I was shaking as I drove home.

I barely slept that night, kept waking up from dreams of kissing him.

2

Let me get this out of the way right now:

I am not, as a rule, attracted to other men. As a matter of fact, in my entire thirty-four years on planet Earth, there have been only two males for whom I have felt even the barest twinge of desire. One, I confess, was a high-school classmate. The other was -

well, *is* - Winston Lancaster, son of Archibald Lancaster, the famous coal magnate and multi-billionaire. He is still a multi-billionaire, as you probably know, though he is now worth roughly twenty billion dollars less than he was just six months ago. No doubt you've heard *that* part of the story!

But what you haven't heard is the rest of it, nor the details of the portion which has been made public. This, despite the fact that Archie's recent burst of philanthropy has likely received more media attention than the assassination of John F. Kennedy, the first moon landing, and the fall of communism in the former Soviet Union combined.

Which is only fitting, really, since the former event did infinitely more to change the world than all of the latter three, or pretty much any other historical event since the crucifixion of Jesus Christ.

Ironically, speaking of Christ, some have likened the elder Lancaster to that immortal personage, dubbing him "The Modern Messiah." I say that is ironic because Jesus Christ didn't have to be bribed to die for the sins of humanity, and because, despite his seemingly enormous financial sacrifices, Archibald Lancaster is today living far more comfortably than almost anyone else on the planet.

Plus, unlike Jesus, he is beloved in his own lifetime. Also, he was never flogged in a public square and then nailed to a cross.

Minor differences, I realize.

3

Well, maybe I should tell you what Archie said in his speech. It went something like this:

"For eight years I have owned the most successful energy company in the history of the world. It has only been that because of the hard work and dedication of those who show up every day in the plants and offices around this country, which are themselves due to the ingenuity of many of the people seated at the table in front of me. The people who made Dacey Energy what it is today, and who will surely continue that fine tradition in the coming years. I am enormously proud, more proud than I could ever tell you, to head a company which serves such an important role in modern society. We employ over fifty thousand people directly, and through our subsidiaries and contractors tens of thousands more. We are a force to be reckoned with, truly, but more importantly a *benevolent* force. A force for good.

"I know there are those who dissent. I realize that we have

our detractors. Most of them are do-good environmentalists who mean well but judge on too flimsy a basis. They put their agendas before their eyes. Dacey Energy, as I'm sure most of you know, has probably the most environmentally respectable record of any energy provider in recent history. We have gone out of our way to reconcile the economic interests of our industry with the environmental concerns of both governmental agencies and private citizens, and invariably have been found in compliance with every state and federal regulation on the books. Mistakes have been made, certainly, but in every case a conscious and concerted effort has been undertaken to correct those mistakes."

He of course had but one "mistake" in mind when he said this. And it was of course anything but a mistake. Mistakes are something you don't mean to do and feel bad about later. Archibald Lancaster, so far as I could tell, had never felt bad about anything in his life.

It occurs to me that now would be a good time to impart at least the highlights of Archie's stint as Dacey Energy's third and by far most infamous CEO. This may get a bit tedious, but it's crucial information, so bear with me.

Archibald Lancaster, himself the son of an ultra-wealthy

railroad man from Waterford, Connecticut, became Dacey Energy's president and chairman in October of 1995. In May of 1996, he became its CEO as well. He was preceded in that role by Fumihiro Roshari, by all accounts a decent fellow who was drummed out of his job by American powerhouses weary of a foreigner running such a lucrative corporation. Archie, the darling of not only his father but rich white men everywhere, was the obvious replacement. Prior to that, Archie had held high-level positions first at timber and later at oil companies, and had even bought a professional football team (which, I add with a note of sour delight, has yet to make it to the play-offs).

For the first seven years of his tenure, Dacey enjoyed the largest profits and by far the most ambitious expansion of both its market and workforce in the company's four-decade history. Under Archie's stewardship, Dacey hired a full ten thousand new workers, signed some five dozen supply contracts with coal companies throughout central Appalachia, and attracted well over sixty big-name investors both whose contributions and stock yielded historic earnings. By the spring of 2003, Dacey Energy boasted annual sales of forty-two million tons of coal, had twenty mining complexes in Kentucky, Virginia, West Virginia, and western Pennsylvania, and served almost a hundred and fifty utility, industrial, and metallurgical customers around the world. Archibald Lancaster had arrived.

And then, in the fall of that same year, something went terribly wrong near a little town called Inez, Kentucky. No one died, but no one *had* to die.

What happened was bad enough.

What happened was this:

At about twelve minutes before eight on the morning of November 18, 2003, a coal tailings dam at a preparation plant owned by Eastern Kentucky Coal, a subsidiary of Dacey Energy, collapsed, releasing a torrent of tainted water and deadly coal waste into nearby streams. The water totaled nearly a third of a billion gallons, the waste over 150,000 cubic yards. Seventy-five miles of rivers and streams were contaminated, turning an iridescent black. Fish along the Tug Fork of the Big Sandy River were decimated. Whole towns were forced to turn off their sources of drinking water, lest their residents suffer the same fate. Measurable amounts of hazardous metals such as arsenic, mercury, lead, copper, and chromium were later detected in the water supply. The clean-up costs were estimated at roughly sixty million dollars, and ultimately surpassed sixty-five million. Consumers, of course, wound up footing most of the bill.

Dacey Energy and its subsidiary later declared in a court document that the dam failure was an "act of God." Evidently they thought it God's fault that the barrier between the underground mine shaft and the coal-waste impoundment from which the slurry had poured like hot fudge was substantially thinner than environmental regulations prescribed.

Evidently, God Himself had compelled Archibald Lancaster to overlook warnings from his own employees that the barrier was too thin, because God, like Archie, just hated to see money wasted on superfluous, life-preserving safeguards.

By April 2004, over six hundred residents of Inez and surrounding communities had filed claims against Dacey Energy and EKC for such grievances as damaged property, polluted drinking water, and medical problems ranging from chronic migraines to disturbances of vision. Of the roughly one hundred and fifty people who filed medical claims, nearly half remain seriously ill. The rest, though physically unharmed, spent the early part of that year repairing their homes or businesses at their own expense, clearing coal sludge from their sinks and toilets and back yards while awaiting reparations from a company whose five highest-ranking executives command a collective annual salary approximately four hundred times larger than those claimants' lifetime earnings combined. Reparations which, of course, they were likely to never receive.

Meanwhile, there had occurred three smaller but similar failures at two other preparations plants owned by subsidiaries of Dacey Energy (one in Kentucky and one in Virginia), each resulting in damages and injuries less extensive but no less serious than those arising from the Inez catastrophe. Dacey Energy has maintained its innocence with regard to these subsequent failures just as vigorously as it has denied charges of impropriety at Inez, and continues to prevail in the courts.

Three months after the spill, the U.S. Mine Safety & Health Administration concluded that the maps supplied by Eastern Kentucky Coal for the impoundment at Inez showed "no substantial error in their estimate of the rock-barrier's width," despite a finding by an independent engineering outfit that the barrier was no more than ten feet thick, about sixty feet thinner than projected by the maps. In a suit brought by a citizen rights' group on behalf of those affected by the spill, the Third Circuit Court of Kentucky sided with MSHA, which has since contradicted its original position and stated that EKC was unambiguously at fault for the spill. The courts seemingly have paid this conspicuous reversal no mind whatever.

In May 2004, shortly before Archie's banquet at Pittsburgh's most luxurious hotel, the federal official heading MSHA's latest investigation into the collapse of the Inez plant's coal-waste reservoir was asked to resign his post. The source of the pressure? Why, the White House, of course!

Less than a month after the disaster, and long before the MSHA team had even issued its preliminary findings, EKC had sought approval from the administration to resume dumping coal waste into the seventy-two acre impoundment at Inez. Within forty-eight hours, MSHA had granted the request.

So, yeah, I have an agenda in writing this book. But it isn't about the indifference of big coal companies toward the environment, nor even particularly about the evils of corporate America. If anything, it is about the perils of human greed and the virtue of selflessness. But not even that, really. That theme is much too hackneyed to merit another book-length treatment. And I don't want this to be a political statement, either, much less a leftist diatribe vulnerable to exploitation by college kids in search of a new literary justification for majoring in the liberal arts.

No, this story is about something larger, more fundamental: the pliability of the human spirit, and the resilience of the human mind. Or maybe it's the other way around. No, wait, never mind: it's about the capacity of the human heart both to absorb magnificent triumphs and to cope with agonizing defeats. The same as any profound work is about, I guess – and may I be forgiven, kindly, for the sin of deeming my own work profound?

But the truth is, I don't know *what* this goddamned book is about, at least not on a symbolic level. Literally, it's the story of an obscure, almost-middle-aged newspaperman who falls in love with the barely-twenty-something son of a prominent, super-rich industrialist whom the newspaperman despises and yet, somehow, ends up befriending.

Ah, there you go: this book is about the very different yet equally traumatic experiences of loving someone you don't want to, and of loving someone you're not allowed to.

Yeah. Yeah, we'll go with that.

4

If you're wondering, I did get to speak to Archie on his way out of the hotel. I asked him why he didn't come clean about his involvement in the slurry spill at Inez the previous fall, why he didn't just 'fess up and reimburse his customers for their losses, either directly or by lowering the price of his product.

He told me this: "No comment."

Then I asked him why he had contributed almost two million dollars to the campaign of a candidate for the state Supreme Court of Pennsylvania who had privately pledged to rule in his favor in an upcoming case concerning a contractual forfeiture with a local mining company.

He told me this: "No comment."

Talk about your candid interviews!

5

Of course, when I told the television reporter at the banquet that Archibald Lancaster was responsible for more suffering than almost anyone who had ever lived, I was exaggerating a bit.

But then, I didn't really mean the remark literally. I meant it figuratively, as a commentary on the ruthlessly inhumane practices of people with Archie's influence and wealth. Archie was a symbol, in my mind, a prototype of the American white-collar corporate bureaucrat who reaps monetary rewards for himself, hedonistic pleasures, at the material but more importantly the spiritual expense of the powerless, disenfranchised, largely oblivious consumers who make him rich.

And Archie did fit that mold, epitomized that ignoble class as strikingly as any overstuffed mogul or pampered icon in recent memory. Put simply, I was saying this: "That man over there is the personification of unbridled avarice and unaccountability run riot, which together have caused more hardship and grief than any other combination of human attributes in the history of the world."

And probably he still would be, had what happened not happened, had fate not afforded me a most unexpected means by which to open his eyes to the inestimable joys of altruism.

Had I not had my camera on me the night that I caught him cheating on his wife in his own house.

6

The next time I saw Winston was by chance, two weeks later, at a restaurant in downtown Pittsburgh. It was a Mexican restaurant that I went to every Friday night, mostly to eat and drink but also to see the ethnic bands that would sometimes perform there. You know, mustachioed Mariachis dressed in palm-straw hats and skin-tight charro suits playing trumpets and fiddles and singing songs of undying love and passion. Who could miss it, right?

And there he was, sitting at a table near the bar, drinking martinis and smoking cigarettes like they were going out of style. I had had a couple of gin and tonics myself and was feeling ballsy, so after I finished my enchilada and refried beans I went over to his table, sat down, and grinned at him.

"Remember me?" I asked.

"No," he said. His eyes were glassy.

"I'm Terrance Farmer. The reporter from the *Post-Gazette*. I met you at your father's banquet two weeks ago."

"Terrance Farmer?"

"Yes. The reporter. Remember?"

An uncertain smile crept across his face. "Sort of, yeah. Hey, how are you?"

"I'm well." God I can't tell you how gorgeous he looked under the wan, blue-green lights of the bar! The way his face glowed, the way his eyes shimmered, the way... I can't tell you. "How are you?"

He shifted his gaze to the band, which was belting out a Mexican ballad louder and more furious than any I'd ever heard, and then reluctantly back to me. My heart sank like a brick. "Okay. So what's up?"

"Not much."

He cupped his hand behind his ear.

"Not much," I repeated. "I enjoyed meeting you at the banquet."

"Uh huh."

"Maybe your father told you that I gave him a hard time."

"Huh?"

I shifted in my seat and smiled awkwardly at him. "Maybe we can talk later. Once the music dies down."

He smiled, confused, and lit another cigarette. "Sure, sounds good."

So I went back to my table and waited. When he paid his check and left the restaurant, I followed him into the parking lot.

A blast of cold air hit me on the way out. The temperature had fallen by at least ten degrees in the space of two hours. I saw Winston button his blazer (cream-colored over a maroon shirt, very stylish) and wished I'd worn a jacket myself. The wind ruffled his flaxen hair and a few unruly whorls tumbled over his forehead like drunken dancers. Everything about him was stunning, just exquisite, beyond belief. He made his way to a beige Cadillac, which he unlocked with his key fob (of course - as if a fellow like Winston Lancaster would own a car with manual locks!).

"Winston," I said from behind him.

He turned and faced me. "Oh, hi. Terrance Farmer, right?"

I blushed. I couldn't help it. "Yeah. But you can call me Terry if you want. My friends do." How moronic and inarticulate I sounded! How trite! I reminded myself of a teenage girl in the throes of puppy love, which, except for my being a then-thirty-three-year-old man, I guess I was.

He nodded and smiled. My heart was beating wildly. I kept waiting for him to say something, but he only went on nodding and smiling. Finally I said, "We met at your father's banquet, remember?"

His smile turned apologetic, a little guilty even. "Right. Of course. How are you?"

"I'm fine, thanks."

"You're the reporter, right?"

"Yeah. From the *Post-Gazette.*"

He nodded again. "Yeah. I think I've read a couple of your articles."

"Really? Which ones?"

"Um. Did you write one about that Internet guy? The one from Boise who started his own software firm?"

"Dennis Lipscomb. Yes. That was almost a year ago, though."

He chuckled. The sound was boyish, innocent, beautiful. "Well, I usually stick to the *New York Times*. Local news tends to bore me. But yeah, I've definitely heard of you. You're a good writer."

"Thanks. I don't suppose you've read any of my articles about your father, have you?"

His smile withered. "No. You've written some?"

"A few, yeah. They're not very flattering, though, I'm afraid." Suddenly I was struck by a brilliant idea. "Hey, would you like to join me for a coffee? We could go to the Blue Cat. If it's not too late, I mean."

"You mean the place on 7th and Grove?"

"Yeah."

He appeared to debate the idea, then acquiesced. It was a small miracle, I tell you. "Yeah, sure, I guess I could do that. But it'll have to be quick. I've got an early start tomorrow."

I beamed. I had forgotten all about the wind on my face, the chill in my fingers and toes and earlobes. Between my pleasant, gin-induced buzz and the stupid but lovely anticipation in my loins, I was at that moment quite possibly the happiest man in the world. "Are you kidding?" I said. "I drink coffee even faster than I drink liquor."

He laughed. "Then I'll meet you there in ten minutes."

"Ten minutes it is."

I waved to him as he got into his Caddy and started the engine. I watched him drive off. I stood there, sighing inwardly, paralyzed by a longing so desperate and intense that I knew it could never be fulfilled.

Nothing, I had learned long ago, eludes a man so artfully as the thing he wants most.

The Blue Cat Café is a quaint little joint in South Hills with a fifties decor: long formica counter with red vinyl stools in front; black and white tiles on the floor; ceiling fans with clunky wooden paddles; assorted themed paraphenalia on the walls; and, of course, a monster juke box teeming with classic rock-and-roll tunes. Over the past few months I had grown oddly attached to the place, frequenting it almost daily and even working on some of my articles there. It was cozy, you know? Homey.

Winston and I sat in a booth by the picture window overlooking some of the city's priciest real estate, exchanging nervous glances and fidgeting with our utensils (unnecessary, all of them). Neither of us said much at first; I don't think either of us fully understood what we were doing there. We sipped black coffee and picked at some Danish and made inane conversation about sports and the weather. (I had to bluff quite a bit with my remarks on the former; I have never been much of a sports fan, though I do casually root for the Pirates on those rare occasions that they make it to the play-offs.) He seemed relieved when the waitress came by to check on us, and I have to admit that I felt somewhat relieved myself. I had not anticipated such awkwardness, what with how swimmingly we had gotten along in the parking lot of the Mexican restaurant.

When the waitress left I heard myself, at last, utter something substantive: "So you're a student, or...?"

He let out a deep breath and nodded gratefully, as if he had been waiting all night for me to ask a question, any question, that would advance the conversation beyond idle chitchat. "Yep, sure am."

"You go to Pitt?"

"I do."

"Senior?"

"Sophomore. Well, junior next year. The semester ended last week."

I laughed. "My God," I said. "When I saw you drinking at the restaurant, it never occurred to me that you were doing it on a fake

ID."

He smiled. My heart went: *thump, thump, thump.* "I wasn't. I know the owner. I mean, my dad knows the owner, so -"

"One of the perks, huh?" The words were out before I could choke them back. He looked at me, no longer smiling. I blushed fiercely and lowered my head. "I'm sorry," I said. "That came out wrong."

"It's okay." He sighed. "It's the truth, anyway, I guess."

Slowly, I met his gaze. My cheeks remained a deep crimson, I am sure. "That's beside the point. It was cruel, what I said, true or not."

"Can't be cruel if it's true, can it?"

"Of course it can. Anyhow, please, forgive me."

"It's okay. Really."

I swallowed thickly, remembered my coffee and took a sip. "So you're nineteen?"

"Twenty. My birthday was last week."

I attempted a congratulatory smile. "Well, happy belated birthday."

"Thank you."

And then, because there lives within me some great evil bent on wrecking my happiness - because, that is, I could not help myself - I said: "Was the Caddy a present from your father?"

Bewilderment, incredulity swept over his face.

I held my breath for a moment, then said, "I'm kidding, Winston. It was a joke. I was playing off what I said a minute ago."

Comprehension slowly dawned on him. He burst out laughing. "You're a devilish lil' sonofabitch, aren't ya, Terry?"

I joined him in his laughter, relieved beyond measure. "I'm known to get that way from time to time."

He lit a cigarette and wagged his finger at me. "I'm gonna have to keep an eye on you."

Please do, I thought. "Reckon you might," I said.

"You don't mind if I smoke, do you?"

"'Course not."

He gave me a thumbs-up (corny, juvenile, and totally adorable) and dragged deeply on his coffin nail. "Wanna hear something funny?" he asked, completely at ease now.

"What's that?"

"The Cadillac *was* a birthday present from my father."

We both cracked up again, and at that instant I knew there wasn't going to be any "early start" the next day for Winston Lancaster.

"A concert pianist? Really? I'm impressed." We were headed to a bar on the East Side, a popular nightspot called The Carousel. We'd share a pitcher of beer, he'd said, and then part ways; six hours' sleep should be enough. He had neglected to tell me what it would be enough *for*, and I hadn't asked. I had told myself it was because I didn't want to pry, but really I just hadn't wanted to hear the answer. I had feared it might arouse jealousy in me, a worry which would soon prove justified.

"Well, I've been playing since I was five years old. My mother forced me to."

"You didn't like it?"

"No, I did. But she would have made me do it even if I hadn't."

"I see."

He flicked his cigarette outside and rolled up the window (and I do mean *rolled* up; forever behind the times, I had not yet invested in a car with power windows). The temperature had been dropping steadily all night, not quite breaking records but certainly unseasonable for May. "I can't do it full-time, of course, because of school, but I play locally whenever I can."

"With an orchestra?"

"That's pretty much the only way you can play concert

piano, isn't it?"

I laughed. "I don't know, Winston. I'm not very knowledgeable on the subject."

He smiled. "Well, it is. I play with the Pittsburgh Symphony."

"You're joking."

"I'm not."

I gaped at him, awestruck. What incalculably fortunate woman, I wondered bitterly, would the gods one day see fit to bestow upon this paragon of beauty, this model of brilliance? What ignorant, undeserving bitch would know the exquisite thrill of lying down with him, and take for granted the singular honor of bearing his children? I turned my head and winced.

"Something wrong?" he asked.

"No, I'm fine. I'm just... amazed, is all."

"It's not as difficult or glamorous as it might sound."

"Such modesty," I said, clenching my teeth.

The bar was crowded, unsurprisingly, mostly with college kids. Winston, therefore, fit right in. I, by contrast, stood out nicely. That I attended him only compounded the general disquiet, which I'm sure existed more in my imagination than in reality. At any rate, we did draw at least a few curious glances, none of which Winston seemed to notice. Or, if he did, he made no indication of it.

I had been to this particular establishment only once and hadn't cared for it, had found it unpleasantly rowdy, squalid and seedy but without any redeeming charm, and within a minute of our arrival I was struck by the same reaction, only stronger this time, more visceral - a reflection of my age more than anything, I decided, and at once felt a pang of equal parts guilt and remorse: I did not belong here, was too old for such foolishness, and I certainly had no business being in such a place with a kid still almost a year away from his first legal drink.

"Get us a table?" he shouted over the roar of the patrons. He gestured at a door on the other side of the room. "I have to use the bathroom!"

"Sure thing!" I yelled back, and the feeling intensified. My stomach lurched sickeningly, like a boat far off course, in waters choppy and uncharted.

I found us a relatively quiet table in a corner, near one of the pool tables, and ordered a pitcher of Miller Lite from the bar. By the time Winston returned I had drunk two large cups of the stuff (I could not recall the last time I had consumed beer from anything but a bottle, and tried without much success to draw nostalgic pleasure from the act). Once again mildly intoxicated, I felt better, more relaxed, but still a mite uneasy. Judging by the expression on Winston's face, I was not alone in my discomfiture.

"They didn't even ID you," I said. "Does your dad know every bar owner in town?"

He smiled complacently and sat down. "Yeah, pretty much."

I nodded. "Do you come here often?" *Oh, Christ, here we go again.*

"Sorry, what?"

"I asked if you come here often."

"Sometimes," he said. He lit a cigarette, poured himself a cup of frothy beer, and ogled a young girl at the bar. "See her?"

I pretended not to. "Who?"

"That girl at the bar. In the red skirt."

"Oh," I said. "What about her?"

He laughed and swigged his beer. "Think I could get her?"

"Winston," I said, "I have no doubt that you could."

But he made no attempt to get her. Perhaps he thought such behavior unseemly, at least while in the company of a newly acquired (and substantially older) friend. Or perhaps it had something to do with his engagement the following evening. Whatever the reason, he stayed where he was, at the table, and gulped what was left of his beer. "You okay, Terry?"

"Yeah," I said. "I'm fine. Why do you ask?"

"I don't know. You just seem a little distracted."

I smiled. "Must be the chick in the skirt."

He lit a fresh cigarette and nodded, laughing. His eyes wandered back to the shapely brunette at the bar, summarily appraised her legs. "Can't blame you for that, man." He shook his head, still gawping at her. "Damn, I say!"

I cleared my throat, eager to change the subject. "So how long have you smoked, if I can ask?"

"Huh?" He yanked his gaze away from her as if with a great effort and looked at me. He blinked, puzzled. "Oh. Um... a couple years, maybe?"

"Couple years," I echoed. "Long time."

"You never smoked?"

"I did, actually. When I was your age."

He smiled guiltily. "Bad habit, I know."

I nodded and refilled my cup. "Yeah, well, so is this."

"Very true."

"Winston?"

He puffed his cigarette and leaned in a little. "Yeah?"

I shook my head. "Never mind. I forgot what I was going to

say."

"Oh." He crushed out his cigarette in a tin ashtray and topped off his beer. There was nothing left in the pitcher but suds. "Is this cool?"

"Yeah." I had never felt so sad or adrift in my life. "No problem. Listen, I think we should go after you finish that."

"That's fine," he said, a little startled. "I'm pretty tired myself."

I summoned a wan smile and drummed my fingers on the table. "No need to rush," I said.

We had ridden together to The Carousel because we both lived a few miles southeast of The Blue Cat, in Shadyside. The journey back was mercifully short and, for the most part, uncomfortably quiet. It had been a strange evening. We had gone from bare acquaintances to best friends and then back again, or perhaps even further, to total strangers. I regretted ever having met him. I was jubilant to be near him. "Winston?" I said.

"Yeah?"

"Can I ask you a somewhat personal question?"

"Well," he said, looking out the window, "I don't see why not."

I breathed deeply and tightened my grip on the steering wheel. "How do you feel about what your father does?"

For a long moment he was silent. Then he said, "I'm not sure what you mean."

"I mean, are you okay with it? With how... with the way he makes his money?"

"Selling coal?"

I glanced at him, skeptical. "No. Not selling coal."

"Well, that's what he does, basically."

"That's a bit of an oversimplification, don't you think?"

"I said 'basically.'"

I nodded. "That's true. You did." My mind protested: *Leave him be!* My mouth said: "But there's a lot more to it than just selling coal. I mean, there are a lot of people who suffer terribly because of the actions of large corporations like your father's. There are-"

"What people?" He was growing defensive.

"What do you mean, what people? Just... people. The employees, the customers, the customers of the customers. All the millions of people whose lives are in one way or another affected by the practices of such outfits."

"My dad wasn't responsible for those coal spills."

I jerked in my seat, honestly floored. "Winston, I didn't-"

"No, but you may as well have."

"Look, I think you misunderstood me. I wasn't accusing anybody of anything."

He sighed, kept his eyes trained on the darkened scenery beyond his window. "You think you're the first person to confront me with this shit? You think I'm just some naive, spoiled, carefree billionaire's brat who laps up luxury off a silver plate and never gives a second thought to where it comes from? If that's what you honestly think, Terry, then I think I misjudged you. And I don't think I want to know you, either."

I felt sweat rising on my forehead and in my armpits. My stomach flopped again. "It isn't what I think, Winston. I don't think that."

"Then why did you ask me those questions? What were you getting at?"

I signaled right and turned into the parking lot of the now closed Blue Cat Café. I pulled up next to Winston's Caddy and cut the engine. "Look," I said. "I asked you those questions because... well, because I was curious to know how you felt about the inequality of wealth in America."

He looked at me, disbelieving, and convulsed in a paroxysm of laughter. Once he'd caught his breath he said, "Oh, my God. You

40

can't be serious. Are you serious?"

"I'm serious." I was blushing again. I was wounded, baffled. I had forgotten his age, his station in life, his mindset.

"Sorry," he said, fighting to stifle his smirk. "I'm sorry, Terry. I don't mean to seem flippant."

"So you think it's okay for one person to control more capital than is owned by millions less fortunate?"

"Who says they're less fortunate? Maybe fortune has nothing to do with it. Maybe it's about hard work and dedication. Resourcefulness."

I looked at him. "Do you really believe that?"

He began to nod, then stopped and averted his eyes. "I have to go. I have to drive to New York tomorrow. Today. Whatever."

"New York? Why?"

"That's where my girlfriend lives. Well, she's not really my girlfriend, but I'd like her to be. She used to go to Pitt. That's where I met her. Now she's in med school at NYU."

"Wow."

"Good night, Terry. I had a good time tonight. Up until the end, anyway."

I mustered another feeble smile. "Same here. Night, Winston."

He got out of the car, started to close the door, hesitated. He bent down and looked at me. "I'm ambivalent," he said.

"Ambivalent?"

"About the inequality of wealth in America. About what my father does."

"Oh."

He smiled gorgeously and closed the door. I thought of the high-school classmate of mine at whom I'd once made a pass in the boys' room. I felt ashamed, nauseated.

I started the car and drove home.

7

I had two articles due by mid-week and one by Friday: one on casino-gambling legislation recently introduced to the state senate, one on the explosion of food-additive stock, and one on a new college-scholarship program spearheaded by the governor and members of the Education Department. By Tuesday, I had written the first paragraph of one of them.

I was distracted, of course. Distracted by thoughts of *him*. And I wasn't sleeping well, either. Five or six hours a night, if I was lucky. I kept waking up from dreams, most of them to do with Winston, most of them transparently symbolic of my infatuation with him.

In the most recent of these, I was wandering around my apartment, scouring closets and drawers and cabinets for an unknown object of great value. But of course I couldn't find it anywhere, and the longer I searched the more frantic I grew, until I was ripping drawers from their tracks, tearing cupboard doors off their hinges, and generally seething. At the end of the dream I was squatting on the kitchen floor with my face in my hands, rocking and sobbing. My pillow was damp when I woke up (the sun had not yet risen), but whether from tears or perspiration or both I couldn't tell.

When I returned from lunch on Tuesday afternoon, one of my colleagues, Mitch Dolan, asked if I was under the weather. He said I didn't look very well at all. Mitch was then head of the paper's obit department, so it was unclear whether he'd meant his remark as an expression of concern or whether he was simply inquiring into a possible addition to his impending workload. After a moment's deliberation I settled on the former, more charitable interpretation and reassured him that I was fine, I just hadn't been sleeping well and may have eaten some questionable salmon for lunch.

Mitch chuckled his grating, vulgar chuckle. There were

potato chip crumbs in his mustache. "Sounds a little fishy to me."

"I'll pretend you didn't say that."

He frowned, hurt, and waddled back to his desk. I had never met anyone weirder or more inexplicably sensitive than Mitch Dolan, nor anyone who told cornier jokes (most of them simply unimaginative puns).

I sighed, surveyed the clutter accumulating on my desk, and terminated the screen saver on my computer. On the screen, in the primitive word-processing program installed by men so frugal they sewed their pockets shut just as a precaution, was the first paragraph of my article on the gaming bill before the state senate. It was adequate but uninspired. For perhaps the thousandth time in my career as a journalist, I reminded myself that inspired news-writing was bad news-writing. *So sayeth the gurus, so dictate the gods.*

I indented for a new paragraph, typed three words, and lifted my fingers from the keys. I looked at my phone.

I picked up the receiver and dialed a number.

Dacey Energy's corporate headquarters was (and remains) located in Richmond, Virginia, but because the Lancaster family made its home in Pittsburgh, the company maintained executive offices at a professional building here in the city. It was out of these offices that Archie normally worked, though once or twice a month he would fly down to Richmond just to keep up appearances. He could not, given his position, afford to develop a reputation as an otiose, hands-off figurehead with little interest in the day-to-day operations of his corporate empire. In other words, he could not afford for people to develop an accurate impression of him. (Which is not to say that his eye ever wandered from the bottom line; no CEO as successful as Archibald Lancaster ever lost sight of *that*.) On that particular Tuesday afternoon, according to his secretary, Archie was *en route* to the Richmond headquarters. What lousy timing I had!

"Well," I told her, "this is Terrance Farmer. I'm a writer for the *Post-Gazette*. I'm sure you're familiar with our fine rag."

"I've heard of it," she said evenly.

"Lovely. Anyhow, I met Mr. Lancaster at a banquet last week and he promised me an interview. I was hoping that could be arranged before the end of the month."

Pause, then: "I don't believe Mr. Lancaster has any openings in his schedule quite that soon. What exactly would be the nature of this interview, Mr. Farmer?"

"Um. General purpose, I suppose. Good old-fashioned

investigative journalism."

"I see. And what, exactly, are you investigating?" Her tone was turning colder by the second.

"Well," I said, stalling. "The impact of Dacey Energy on the local community. How the company affects everyday people."

"Everyday people," she echoed.

"Yes. How it helps them, and how, potentially, it... doesn't help them."

"Mr. Farmer," said the secretary.

"Yes?"

"Mr. Lancaster doesn't discuss the company's environmental policies unless it's at a press conference, or else otherwise on his own terms. He certainly won't grant an interview to some muckraking reporter seeking only to berate him."

"Berate him? Ma'am, I think you've got this all wrong. I haven't any axe to grind with Mr. Lancaster. I simply want to provide the general public with a better, fuller understanding of his contributions to Dacey Energy and his vision for the company's future."

Longer pause, then: "Yes, well, as I told you, Mr. Farmer, he's on his way to Richmond and won't be back until Thursday. Perhaps you could call back then."

"All right. Would you kindly -"

"Good-bye, Mr. Farmer."

She hung up. I smiled. For the moment, anyway, I had forgotten all about Winston and his impenetrable blue eyes.

But then I got home, and found a message on my answering machine from none other than the junior Lancaster himself: "Hey, Terry. It's Winston. Lancaster. I didn't figure a newspaper writer would have a listed number, but I guess you like to be accessible to your readers. Or maybe this is the wrong Terrance Farmer. Anyway, if this *is* the right number, I just wanted to let you know that I had a good time the other night. We should do it again sometime." He left his number and bade me farewell.

I reached for the phone, then drew my hand back. I went into the kitchen and made myself a Caesar salad. Drank a glass of red wine. Pondered, pondered.

By the time I had finished my salad and my second glass of wine, I'd decided that I would never speak to Winston again.

"Winston? It's Terry. I got your message."

He coughed. "Oh, hey. Hey, Terry."

"You okay?"

"Yeah, I'm fine. Just a little head cold."

"Sorry to hear that."

"It's okay. So what's up?"

I was pacing back and forth in my living room, biting my nails. "Nothing's up. I mean, nothing worth reporting. I'm just returning your call, is all."

"Oh." He coughed again. "Oh, well, I was gonna see if you wanted to go out tonight."

"Tonight? Oh, gee."

"Just for a couple drinks."

I hesitated, wiping my hand across my brow. It was suddenly very sweaty. "I really ought to work on some articles I have due. And you have that cold."

He laughed. My heart soared, my goddamned heart, and my brain, my brain was a jumble of loose wires and faulty circuits. No sense was getting through. All reason had shut down. "It's really nothing. But if you have to work -"

"Where did you want to go?"

"Well, I was thinking The Carousel, if that's cool with you. You seemed to enjoy yourself there on Friday."

"Um." I glanced at a painting hanging on one of my living room walls, an astonishingly faithful reproduction of a Hieronymus

Bosch triptych called *The Garden of Earthly Delights*. Somehow, the painting decided me. "Yeah, of course I did. What time did you want to meet there?"

"I was thinking around nine."

I smoothed the hair behind my hairs. "Sounds good," I said.

"Cool. I'll see you there, then."

"Nine sharp."

"Later."

"Bye. Later."

I hung up the telephone and closed my eyes. *Pathetic,* I thought. *You're pathetic.*

And so I was, so I was. But I was smiling, too.

8

He had never looked so good. Burgundy sweater over an open-collared, baby-blue dress shirt, tan corduroys and black Skechers on bottom. Hair raked back, still damp around the edges from his evening shower. Eyes sparkling. Face unblemished. Smile coy, elusive, infectious, inimitable. Either I would have him tonight or I would die, those were the only two options, have him or die -

"Terry! What's up, man?"

"Winston," I said, taking a seat next to him at the bar. There was no crowd tonight, mercifully. But for Winston and me, the place was virtually deserted. "Hey, how are you?"

"Couldn't be better, man. How you doin'?"

I laughed. The sound was, to my own ears, feeble and vague and hollow. "Oh, shit, I'm okay. I'm good."

"Cool, cool."

"How was your trip to New York?"

He chortled, urbane and noncommittal. "Uneventful," he said.

"Really? How so?"

He laughed again. He was clearly intoxicated. A half-empty bottle of Heineken sat on the bar before him. "You want a drink, man?"

"Sure. I'll have a gin and tonic."

"As you wish, sir."

He summoned the barkeep, a lanky thing barely older than Winston, and ordered my drink. Then he turned back to me. "You're an interesting guy, Terry."

"I am?"

He laughed for a third time. My drink came. I drained it at two draughts. "Yup. You want another?"

I shifted on my stool, smiling awkwardly. "Sure."

He nodded to the bartender, who promptly delivered another gin and tonic. This one I sipped. Winston lit a cigarette (home-rolled, by the looks of it), exhaled a thick plume of smoke out the corner of his mouth, and rested his chin on his hand, his elbow on the bar. "You really hate my father, don't you?"

I coughed, nearly spat out what little of my drink I'd begun to imbibe. "What? No. What?"

Winston laughed uproariously. "You don't have to lie, man. It's cool. I know you hate him."

"No," I said. "I really don't. What gave you *that* idea?"

"What you said the other night, for starters."

"Oh, no. Not *that* again." I raised my glass to my lips, then lowered it. "For starters?"

"I found a couple of your articles about him on the net, in the *Post-Gazette*'s archives. The ones you mentioned to me last time."

I raised my glass again and took a long drink. "You did?"

"Yup. The one about Inez, and the one about Benjamin Grent." Ben Grent was the candidate for the Pennsylvania state Supreme Court who, as hearsay had it, had privately vowed if elected to help exonerate Dacey Energy in its upcoming court battle. Neither article had been scathing, exactly, but neither had recommended Winston's father for sainthood, either.

51

"Oh," I said, not looking at him. "Those ones."

"I'm not mad, Terry."

"You're not?"

"Of course not. You were only writing the truth as you saw it."

"As I saw it?"

"Well," he said, grinning wryly, "that part about my dad's conscience being as much in doubt as the United States' justification for the war in Iraq was kind of a cheap shot." He laughed.

I groaned and tossed off the last of my drink. "Maybe that was a tad harsh. But I won't lie to you, Winston. I *do* take strong exception to a lot of what your father has done as the CEO of Dacey."

"No shit? Could've fooled me."

I laughed obligingly and cleared my throat. "Why don't we just get this out of the way right now? You want to?"

"It's your ball game, Terry."

I wasn't quite sure how the "ball game" had suddenly become mine, but figured I'd humor him. I signaled for the bartender to bring me another gin and tonic, took a deep breath, and spoke without meeting his eyes. "From what I can gather - and that part is key, since I'm not omniscient with regard to the facts of the case and I'll concede from the outset that while I've done my homework as best I can, as a mere mortal I can't be absolutely, metaphysically certain that I haven't overlooked a detail or two along the way - but *from what I can gather*, your father, at least in his professional capacity, has little or no concern for anything save maximizing the profits of his company and by extension his own.

"What's worse, he seems woefully oblivious of the consequences of such reckless, unprincipled gluttony, of its devastating impact on real people, flesh-and-blood human beings who for the most part mind their own business, play by the rules, and struggle just to survive. Folks who bust their asses every day at shitty jobs they can't stand and yet have almost nothing to show for their labor. People who are screwed so hard and so often that they've grown numb to the pain and just resigned themselves to lives of perpetual misery and disappointment. Somebody with your father's money and power could single-handedly transform millions of such lives, reshape the economic face of the entire world, for better or ill. And in his own mostly inconspicuous, low-profile way, I guess your dad has made a start at that. Unfortunately, at least from where I'm sitting, his endeavor thus far has been almost exclusively for ill." I finally looked at him. His face was blank, unreadable. "With all due respect, I mean."

He killed his beer and kept silent, his eyes roaming the bar.

"Are you going to say anything?"

Frowning, he motioned for another beer. "What do you want me to say? You obviously think my father's the scum of the earth. I'm not about to change your mind, am I?"

"Dammit, Winston, I didn't... no, no, just forget it. I knew this was going to happen. I shouldn't have said anything."

"I asked you to say something."

"Yes, you did."

The bartender brought his beer. He guzzled perhaps a quarter of it. "Oh, fuck, maybe you're right. Maybe he *is* a greedy, no-good son of a bitch."

I think my jaw gaped a little. "Winston?"

"No, no." Incredibly, there were tears welling up in his eyes. "Let me... just let me say this."

"You're drunk."

"I know I am. So what?"

I shook my head. "Sorry. Never mind. Go ahead."

"I don't know how to feel about what he does. I'm ambivalent, remember?"

"Yeah. I remember."

"But I love him. You can understand that, can't you?"

"Of course I can."

"You said something, though, something I thought was pretty stupid."

"When? On Friday?"

"No, just now."

I gestured for another gin and tonic. At some point I couldn't quite identify (one could seldom identify such moments, I had discovered), I had resolved to get drunk, every bit as obscenely and shamefully sloshed as the boy next to me, the unfinished articles be damned, the ineluctable dawn and attendant alarm clock be damned. "And what was that?"

"You said, 'Your father, in his professional capacity, only wants to make a profit for himself and his company.' Or something like that. Remember?"

"Sure."

"Well, what the fuck *else* is he supposed to do in his *professional* capacity? Try to *lose* money for himself and his company?"

I took a swig of my fresh drink. "Point taken. But you know what I meant. Some business people, even *qua* business people, actually give a damn about things other than the amount of black ink in their account books. They care about the communities of which they're a part. They care about the safety and well-being of their customers. They care about doing the right thing as well as the lucrative thing. Maybe it's all ultimately directed at boosting their revenues, a kind of phony munificence, but it sure beats the hell out of blatant, unabashed rapacity. Doesn't it?"

He polished off his beer and ordered another. "Yeah. I guess." He laughed meekly. "You sure use a lot of big words when you're drunk, Terry."

I chuckled. "I'm not drunk yet, pal. Getting there, though."

"Terry?"

"Yeah?"

I love you.

"Did my father really approve that rock-barrier, even though he knew it was too thin to withstand the weight of the coal sludge?"

"All evidence points in that direction, I'm afraid."

"What evidence?"

"Well, for one thing, the head of the Inez plant showed him maps - never released to MSHA or any other governmental agency, of course - indicating a grossly deficient barrier-width, about ten feet or so, and asked him if he ought to suspend the plant's activities for the next ten to fourteen business days. By the end of that period, this guy explained, the barrier could be sufficiently buttressed to bring it into compliance with federal regulations, to make it safe, in other words. Of course, the interruption would be extremely costly, and the plant's employees none too happy about the loss of pay. Not that the latter made much difference, of course: Dacey has been non-union from day one."

"And my father told him not to do it?"

"Not only did he tell him not to do it, he told him not to bother augmenting the barrier at all."

Winston's jaw dropped, literally. "What? Why?"

"He didn't think it was necessary. He thought it would be a waste of money and manpower."

"How do you know this?"

I knocked back what was left of my drink. "Because I interviewed the guy who ran the Inez plant about three weeks after the spill, and he told me."

"He told you? Why would he admit that? Wasn't he afraid of what would happen to him? Wasn't he afraid he'd lose his job?"

"First of all, he'd *already* lost his job. Your dad fired him three days after the spill. Well, as far as the general public knows, he voluntarily stepped down and took a lower-level position at another Dacey subsidiary, citing personal reasons, but in actuality

57

he was terminated. And secondly, everything he told me he did so on condition of anonymity, so he couldn't be implicated. He was pretty pissed off at your dad, understandably. He *wanted* to rat him out. Just not at a pinch to his pocketbook."

Winston cringed. "Jesus Christ."

I ordered my fifth gin and tonic of the evening. I wasn't totally in the bag yet, but after this one I would be. "Yup. Welcome to my world, Winston."

Puzzlement surfaced in his features. "Wait a second."

"Yeah?"

"If this Inez guy told you all that stuff in confidence, then how come you wrote about it in your article?"

"I didn't *write* about it, Winston. I *alluded* to it. I never divulged the man's name. I wrote, 'According to one anonymous source.' Oldest journalistic trick in the book."

"Seems a touch underhanded to me."

"Well."

He took a big gulp of his beer. "My father's a prick," he said.

I laughed. I couldn't help it. "Hey, now. Nobody called him a prick. I merely suggested that perhaps his scruples are less than impeccable ."

"Same thing. 'Person whose scruples are less than

impeccable' is just a euphemism for 'unethical prick.'"

"Well," I said, "yes, I suppose it is."

"But it's not my father you're really after, is it?"

I belched, rather loudly. "Excuse me. What do you mean?"

"I mean it's not really my father you've got it in for. He's just a pawn in a larger game."

I began to laugh, and then to cough uncontrollably. "Sorry," I said. "I think I need to slow down a little."

"I hope I didn't give you my cold."

"I doubt it. I haven't heard you cough or sniffle once all night."

"It's the beer," he proclaimed confidently. "Best cough medicine you can buy."

"To that," I said, and raised my glass. We toasted to nothing at all. "Now, what did you mean by that 'pawn in a larger game' comment?"

"Oh, nothing. Just that your real enemy is capitalism itself, not my father or Dacey Energy or any other particular entity. You said so the other night, didn't you?"

"I did?"

"Well, you said something about the inequality of wealth in America."

"Ah. So I did."

"Is what I said true? Are you anti-capitalist?"

"Am I a communist, do you mean?"

"However you want to put it."

I sipped my gin. "No, Winston, I'm not a communist." I snickered. "I'm a people-person."

"What's *that* supposed to mean?"

"That I give a shit about people. I can't say that I like them much individually, but in the abstract I do. In the abstract I *love* them. And I care about them. I want to see them prosper."

"And that's why you hate people who make money?"

I sighed. He was too bright to be asking such asinine questions. "I don't hate people who make money. I hate people who make money and refuse to share it."

"Share it with who?"

I gave him a long, hard stare. "With other people," I said.

"Imagine," I said, "a society in which the Oprahs and Bill Gateses of the world routinely criss-crossed the globe, just doling out huge wads of cash. What a glorious place to live that would be!"

"People like that give to charities. My dad even gives to charities."

"The people most in need of charity are the ones least likely to get it."

"Huh?"

I threw back my sixth gin and tonic. "Charity money goes to orphans and war veterans and old people with rare diseases. Those people need assistance, sure, but so do the three or four billion people who live in poverty, mostly through no fault of their own. What about *those* people? Should we just write them off because their disadvantages aren't visible enough, or because they don't complain loudly enough?"

Winston shrugged. "There's welfare."

"Please. People on welfare pretty much deserve what they get, unless they have some legitimate excuse for not working. It's not people like that whom I'm concerned about. It's the people who work their tails off and are honest and decent and still get the short end of the stick."

"Well, they chose jobs that don't pay well. What did they expect?"

I sneered. "What the hell are you talking about, Winston? They didn't choose shit. Most people can't afford to go to college, or else aren't genetically equipped to do so. They lack the prerequisite intelligence, because they didn't inherit it. They don't have any control over that."

"Maybe they're just lazy."

"No doubt some of them are, Winston, no doubt some of them are. But all of them, or even most of them? I highly doubt that. Lazy people don't show up at gas stations and factories and fast-food joints and grocery stores every day just to put food on the table and make ends meet. That's not the behavior of lazy people. It's the behavior of desperate people who have no other choice."

He took a swig of his beer. It was perhaps his twelfth. "Well, Terry, Jesus Christ. If rich people just gave away their money, the market would be flooded. There'd be inflation. Prices would sky-rocket."

"Why would they? There would be no more money in the system than there is right now. It would just be more evenly distributed. If businesses jacked their prices way up, the whole economy would suffer, and thus so would the businesses themselves. The whole point of capitalism is for everybody to get rich. So if the consequences you envision would truly destroy free enterprise, then capitalism is self-defeating. Right?"

He shook his head. "Fuck, dude, I don't know. I'm *drunk*."

I studied his face, his confused, comely, sinless face, and though I wanted to weep, I first smiled and then broke into rambling, hysterical laughter. I drew a wary, reproachful look from the bartender and with an effort restrained myself. "Me, too," I said. "Me, too, Winston."

"But doesn't there *have* to be a lower class? I mean, isn't it inevitable? If somebody's gaining, somebody else is losing. Right?"

"Well, yes, to a point. There's always a yin-yang element to it. But it needn't be so drastically out of whack as it is in *our* society."

"Out of whack?"

"Unbalanced. Unfair. Lopsided. You know?"

"Yeah."

I did away with my drink and licked my lips. I wanted another one but didn't dare place an order. I didn't need one, anyway: I was five shades of hammered. Winston drew a tin box from the pocket of his cords, opened it, and produced a short, home-rolled cigarette. He lit it with a match and ogled the bartender.

"You roll your own cigarettes?" I asked.

"Yeah, sometimes."

"You got another one?"

His eyes narrowed. "Yeah, sure. You want one?"

"I think I do, yeah."

He gave me one and I lit it, immediately started coughing. It was the first cigarette I had smoked in eleven years.

Winston laughed. "You sound like me six hours ago."

"I haven't smoked in a long time," I said.

"Then what made you want one?"

"I don't know," I said. I rubbed my eyes. They felt hot and dry and irritated. "I just did."

"Terry?"

"Yeah?"

"What are we going to do?"

I shook my head and smoked. I was beginning to experience some of the old satisfaction. "I don't know, Winston." All at once I was overcome by exhaustion, both moral and physical. "I don't know."

9

We staggered out of the bar, holding each other up. We were laughing, belching, goggling at the night sky. It was a beautiful sky. Every star in the firmament shone with improbable brilliance, or, to our inebriated eyes, at least seemed to.

"Look at the stars," I said.

"I am. They're amazing."

"They're so *bright.*"

"I know."

"I don't think either of us can drive."

"Me, either."

We had set out for an unknown destination, lurching more sideways than forward. I had a vague suspicion that we were headed in the direction of my car and said so. "We could just hang out and smoke and listen to the radio till we sober up enough to drive."

"Okay."

"You wanna get a coffee or something first?"

He shook his head and halted in mid-stride. He bent at the waist, clutching his knees. "I think I need to throw up."

I nodded matter-of-factly. "All right." As a pointless afterthought I added, "I'll just wait over here."

"Okay."

He retched a little but didn't vomit. He rubbed the back of his hand across his forehead, as if wiping away sweat. "I don't need to throw up," he said.

"Good," I said. "I didn't wanna see that."

He gave a booming, drunken laugh and righted himself. "Let's go."

We went.

My car was parked in a lot three blocks from The Carousel. I had no idea where Winston had parked his and didn't ask.

"It's no Caddy," I said, unlocking the driver's-side door (with a key, of course - as if a fellow like Terrance Farmer would own a car with automatic locks!). And indeed it wasn't: it was a '96 Buick Regal. Not the flashiest set of wheels in the world, not by a long shot, but dependable? Jesus Christ, they ought to have called that particular model The Buick Immortal ("The Car That Just Won't Quit!"). "But it'll do."

I climbed in, reached over, and unlocked the passenger's-side door for Winston. He fumbled with the door-handle, as if he had never encountered such a baffling device. Mistaking his difficulties as evidence that I had not in fact succeeded in unlocking the door, I leaned over again and pushed the latch in the opposite direction, thereby re-locking the door.

"Try it now," I said through the closed window.

He gave it another shot. "Still won't open."

"What the hell?" I studied the latch and realized my error. I roared with laughter. "Sorry," I said, unlocking the door. "Now try."

This time he got it open on his first attempt, and half-sat, half-collapsed in the seat. "I couldn't get that damned thing open," he said. His hair, well groomed at the start of the evening, was now tousled and lank, a confused mess of velvety blond quills. His cheeks were flushed from the wind, the skin on his neck milky and delicate in the faint light of the parking lot's sodium-vapor lamps. I wanted to touch his face. God help me, I was *going* to touch his face. "It was sticking."

"There was some confusion there," I said. "I accidentally locked you out."

"Huh?"

"Never mind. You wanna listen to some music?"

"Sure. Put on 106.4."

"106.4?"

"Yeah. Classic rock station."

"I know. I listen to it all the time."

I turned the dial to 106.4. We caught the tail end of "Sympathy for the Devil." Mick Jagger's high-pitched squawking gave way to Jim Morrison's anguished, boozy crooning on "Love Her Madly." Cruel, I suppose, but fitting. I did my best to ignore the lyrics and enjoy the music. Drunk as I was, the task posed little difficulty: there was nothing so splendid to an intoxicated mind, I had found, as an old song long cherished.

"You like The Doors?" I asked Winston.

"Yeah. Kinda. I like their earlier stuff."

"Oh, that's the best."

"Yeah."

"You got any more of those cigarettes?"

"Yeah, sure." He reached into his pocket and removed the tin box, opened it. He stared into it for a while, as if not comprehending its contents, and then looked at me with rueful, tragic eyes. It was at once the most untellably endearing and disarming expression I had ever beheld. "There's only one left," he said.

"Oh."

He grinned, his eyes flashing wickedly. "And it's a little more potent than your average cigarette."

"Oh."

He laughed. "Wanna smoke it?"

I stammered, debated, hedged. "Um. Shit, I don't know, Winston. It's been a long time since I did that."

"Terry," he said, poking me in the arm, "before tonight you hadn't smoked a cigarette in eleven years. Why hold back now?"

I chuckled, probably blushing. My penis, I noted with absent surprise, was completely erect. I shifted uncomfortably in my seat

68

and gave a small shrug. "What the hell," I said. "Light 'er up."

He laughed again, harder this time, and smacked the dashboard with a heavy fist. "All right! Now that's what I'm *talkin'* about, motherfucker!"

"Calm down, Winston." I scanned the parking lot for lights, people, anything. There was only empty night. "You gonna light it or what?"

"Yeah," he said, still laughing. "Of course."

He lit the cigarette (this one fatter than the others, I noticed, and rolled in cigar papers), took a deep drag, and passed it to me. I held it for a moment, inspecting it for God knows what, and took a quick, shallow draw on it. I immediately started coughing. Winston broke up again.

"What?" I said, my eyes watering. "I told you it's been a long time. Since you were in diapers, almost."

"Sorry," he said. "It's just funny."

"Yeah, yeah."

He took a couple hits and handed it back to me. I puffed once, held in the smoke, coughed a little, and took a second, longer draw. "This stuff is strong," I said, wheezing a little, my eyes watering. I passed the joint back to him.

"I know it is. It's expensive as fuck."

"Oh, yeah?"

"Five hundred bucks for an ounce."

"Holy shit."

"Tell me about it." He took three quick tokes and offered it to me.

"No, thanks," I said.

"You good?"

I blinked. "Good at what?"

He doubled over with laughter, thrashing around in his seat.

"What?" I sounded hurt. I guess I kind of was. "What'd I say?"

He collected himself, apparently at great pains. "It's an expression, man. It means, 'Are you cool? Have you had enough?'"

"Oh. Sorry. I guess my age is showing."

"It's all good."

I hesitated. "Another expression meaning 'Don't worry about it'?"

"Yeah." He smiled. "Damn, you *are* outta touch with the youth, aren't you?"

I nodded. "I don't watch a lot of television."

He took another drag. "I can't blame you for that. Most of it's crap."

"*All* of it's crap. Especially that reality shit."

He giggled. "What, you don't like *Survivor*?"

"Please."

I watched him smoke and lowered the volume on the radio, venturing that we had both heard "Pinball Wizard" one too many times. I opened my mouth, closed it again. I rubbed my Adam's apple. "Winston?" I asked.

"Yeah?"

"I've never heard you talk about your mother."

His face grew serious, reserved. "We only met a few days ago," he said.

"Yeah, I know. But still... it just seems odd that you've never mentioned her." I paused, glanced out the windshield. "Sorry if I'm being nosy."

He dragged on the joint. "It's cool."

"Well?"

He rolled down the window and tossed out the remains of the cigarette. I thought about saying something but kept my mouth shut. I wanted to hear what he had to say. And then a terrible idea occurred to me. "Oh, fuck, Winston, I'm so sorry."

"For what?"

"She's dead, isn't she?"

He laughed and shook his head. "No. She's alive and well."

"Divorced?"

"No. She and my dad are still married."

"Oh."

He coughed and scratched his nose. "She isn't around much. She and my dad don't get along very well."

"Does she work?"

"She did. At the tourist bureau here in Pittsburgh."

"But now?"

He frowned. "Now she spends most of her time in Chicago. She has a job there, with some government agency or another. Parks and Recreation, or something. Whatever she does, she really seems to like it. It's all she ever talks about."

"You don't seem very happy about it."

He smoothed a furrow in his shirt collar. "I was happier when she and my dad were together."

"You don't think she's having an affair, do you?"

He shrugged. "How the fuck should *I* know?"

"Sorry."

"It's okay." He looked at me. "How about you, Terry? I know nothing about you. Where are you from? Where did you go to school? Do you have any brothers or sisters?" He paused, glancing at my right hand. "I'm guessing you're not married?"

I sighed. I was hardly in the mood for an in-depth conversation that required more than a token involvement on my part. But I had asked about *him*, so what choice did I have? I had to comply. "I *was* married, but I've been divorced for three years. It was an amicable separation, and we're still on good terms, my ex-wife and I, though we seldom talk. She lives near her parents now, in New Hampshire. Her name is Linda.

"As for the other stuff: I was born in Providence, Rhode Island. I went to school at Rutgers in New Jersey, majored in journalism. I have one older sister. She's thirty-five. She's a teller at a bank on Long Island. Her name is Denise."

He smirked. "That was concise."

"I'm a news-writer. It's ingrained."

He turned the radio up. Tom Petty was halfway through "Don't Do Me Like That." Winston yawned. "I love this song," he said.

"Me, too." I licked my lips. "Hey, Winston?"

"Yeah?"

"Do you have any *normal* cigarettes?"

He snickered, his eyelids drooping, and reached into the left pocket of his cords. "Of course I do," he said, unveiling a pack of

Malboro Lights. "Want one?"

"Yeah."

He gave me one. He lit it for me and reclined in his seat. "I'm gonna rest for a second," he said.

"Okay."

I smoked and watched him fall asleep. I was mildly stoned but sobering up. "Living Loving Maid" came on the radio. Winston began to snore, very quietly.

How could I want to touch such an innocent creature?

How could I sit there and not touch him?

Not knowing what else to do, I took him back to my apartment. I figured he could sleep on my couch and I'd drop him off at his car on my way to work in the morning. Provided that I *made* it to work in the morning: it was a little after midnight when we arrived at my apartment, and my alarm was set for seven o' clock. I have never been the sort of person who functions well on less than eight hours' sleep, and with a hangover to boot, I'd be lucky if I was up by ten.

Now, let me say up front that I had no lascivious intentions whatsoever when I decided to let Winston sleep over. I had no plan, no plot, no scheme, nary an impure thought. Besides, the kid was

74

soused. What was I going to do, molest him in his sleep? Tempting, maybe, but not happening. No, I'd just take him home, lie him on the couch, tuck a pillow under his head, cover him with a blanket, and turn in. Nothing complicated, nothing salacious.

On the drive, though, I did some thinking. I started to wonder whether my feelings for the boy weren't at least somewhat mutual, whether a part of him didn't harbor a certain taboo longing of his own. A latent yearning to experiment, we'll say, to try something new. Why else would he have invited me out tonight? What reason could he have for seeking my company other than being attracted to me, however dimly or subconsciously? Might his affection be purely platonic, the stuff of friendship merely? But I was substantially older than he, had nothing clearly in common with him, might even be considered a staunch adversary of his father's. What could he possibly want with such a man, if indeed he felt nothing for him? The situation mystified me.

When we got to my building I woke him and told him to follow me inside. I had initially planned to carry him in, but soon realized that I lacked adequate strength for such a feat. He woke up slowly, and, naturally, was exceedingly groggy, but he got out of the car obediently enough, muttering a little but not asking any questions, and plodded up the stairs behind me. We both entered my apartment on watery legs, though his were far feebler than mine, and had I not caught him he would have collapsed in the kitchen.

I hauled him into the living room and lay him on the threadbare sofa I had bought when I'd first moved in, eight years earlier, before Winston had even made it to high school. He fell back to sleep immediately. I went to the closet in the hallway, retrieved a spare blanket and pillow, and carried them back into the living room. I slid the pillow under his head, as planned, and spread the blanket over him, as planned, and then started toward my bedroom, as planned.

And then I turned around, not as planned.

And went back to him, also not as planned.

And knelt beside him, and looked at him, and ran my hand through his hair, so thoroughly and completely shattering any plan I'd devised as to merit some kind of award for the Most Unplanned Series of Actions Ever.

Then he opened his eyes and looked at me, without really seeing me. "Terry?" he mumbled.

"Yeah?"

"We should start a band."

I laughed. "Okay."

"I play the piano, you know."

"Yeah. Yeah, you told me." I paused, licked my lips. My heart was pounding. There was sweat all over me. "Winston?"

He was falling asleep again. "Yeah?"

"Can I... can I kiss you? On the mouth?"

"Yeah, sure."

So I did. And then he woke up more fully, and stared at me, wide-eyed and befuddled. "Terry?"

"Oh." I backed away from him. "Oh, shit. Winston, I'm sorry."

He sat up a little, his eyes narrowing. "Did you just kiss me, Terry?"

"Yes," I said. "I did."

"Why?"

"Because you said I could."

"I did?"

"Yes."

He lay back down. "Oh. Well, I'm pretty drunk. You shouldn't listen to me when I'm drunk."

"Okay."

He began to snore. I sat on the floor of my living room and cried, rocking a little, gnawing on my knuckles to muffle my sobs. After a while they abated, and I rose, and went to bed.

The next morning, when I awoke at nine-thirty, Winston was gone, much as I had expected he would be.

10

Thereafter, at least professionally, my life rapidly went to hell. I was chewed out for being three hours' late the morning after my ill-conceived outing with Winston, I turned in only one of the three articles I'd owed the paper that week (the one on casino gambling), and for the ensuing month my job performance was generally erratic and the quality of my writing inconsistent. Such behavior was highly uncharacteristic of me, and my boss, the editor-in-chief of the *Post-Gazette*, quickly took note of it.

One afternoon, about two weeks after said outing, he summoned me into his office and asked me if everything was all right. I told him everything was fine, I just wasn't sleeping well and had been having some problems at home. The first was certainly true, the second debatable, depending on how one defines "problems at home." Does pining for the company of a young man you barely know and kissed without his explicit, sober consent qualify as a "problem at home"? If so, then I wasn't lying. If not, then I was. In either case, I said what I did, and my boss, an eccentric and aloof man who guarded his personal life from his employees as habitually as most of us urinate, seemed satisfied with my explanation. He dismissed me, with the admonition that future infractions might involve more serious consequences. I took the admonition to heart, and left.

I didn't call him, Winston, because I couldn't. What would I say to him? "Sorry I tried to make out with you when we were drunk"? Please. And I called Archie's office only twice more, because on my third attempt his secretary made it abundantly clear that he was never going to grant me an interview: "Mr. Lancaster has asked me to inform you that he won't be participating in any media events until further notice, and requests that you cease attempting to contact him. He is unavailable for comment, and will remain so for the foreseeable future. Please try back in a couple of months. Thank you." Or something along those lines.

Nevertheless, I had begun to write (and intended to complete) another feature article on Archibald Lancaster, this one about his alleged arrangement with Benjamin Grent. It was based mostly on hearsay and a couple of articles published in area newspapers, with just a dash of civilized hyberbole thrown in for good journalistic measure. Still, to make it newsworthy, I needed an interview with him. A couple of memorable quotes, however evasive and generic and noncommittal. I needed words from the mouth of the devil himself.

But the devil was unwilling to see me, of course, and in his absence I floundered, a man with a mission he could not complete. And a mission he didn't entirely *want* to complete, insofar as its completion might wreck his nonexistent chances of winning the affection of the devil's son.

Talk about your dilemmas!

For the month before I saw Winston again, I was miserable. I had terrible nightmares, excruciating migraines, hardly slept, barely ate, and wrote shoddy articles scarcely worthy of a first-year journalism student. They passed muster, though, I guess, because nobody said anything about them. I was ashamed of them nevertheless. When I saw them in the paper I winced.

I resented Winston deeply during that time, because he was the cause of my anguish and my inability to practice my profession to best of my ability, and because, if I'd never met him, I never would have known any better, wouldn't have known what it's like to want something so fully and desperately and stupidly and hopelessly as to ask aloud, "How could You put this thing before me, when I cannot have it?"

And to ask that, when you doubt that you're being heard in

the first place, is particularly humiliating. But you're driven to it, find that you have no choice, because your longing is that intense. Because you want the thing that badly, and know not where else to turn, or what to do.

I remember:

In the first week of June, a few days before I was reunited with Winston, I rented a movie on the way home from work. I don't remember what it was, or even what it was about, or who was in it. I just remember that I drank a bottle of wine as I watched it, and smoked two or three cigarettes, and was bawling by the time the end credits started to roll. It reminded me of something, some spark, some liveliness that had once infected me, some profound and ridiculous compulsion to live. God it hurt me, that pain, that great, humongous aching that swelled in my breast as my eyes swept across my unremarkable domicile and perceived, registered, the vast desolation that gathered there. It was such a common, basic pain, I surmised, and yet it very nearly killed me. I went to bed that night half-convinced that I would not wake the next morning, so abysmal was the void inside me.

I awoke the next morning, forty-five minutes earlier than I needed to.

And then, wouldn't you know it: Winston called me on the tenth of June and invited me to a party at his father's house.

11

"Terry?" he said.

"Winston?" I said. I was at home, in my kitchen. I had ravioli cooking on the stove.

There was silence for a moment, then his voice again: "Hey."

"Hi."

"How are you?"

I coughed, half-deliberately, and already I could feel beads of perspiration rising on my forehead and on the nape of my neck. "Oh, I'm fine, I guess. How are you?"

"I'm okay."

I transferred the pan of ravioli to one of the back burners, letting it cool down for a minute. I had cooked it too long. "Glad to hear it," I said, turning off the front burner. "So what's up?"

"Not much." Long pause. "It's been a while."

"Yes, it has. About a month, I think." *Thirty-two days and nineteen hours,* I thought. *If you want to be exact about it.*

He sighed. It was a tense noise, ponderous and unsteady. Beneath it, I could hear him groping for words, finding none that seemed suitable. "Terry, listen-"

"Winston, you don't have to say anything. I apologize for what I did." I closed my eyes and slumped against the sideboard, dreading his reply and the conversation to follow.

"You don't have to. I'm not mad at you. I know you were drunk. You weren't thinking straight. Right?"

"Right. I mean, of course I wasn't." I opened my eyes, took the pan of ravioli from the stove, and emptied its contents into a bowl. The ravioli was slightly burned and still steaming a little. "I never would have done that if I'd been sober. I don't know what possessed me."

He sighed again, this time with palpable relief. "Thank God. Because I thought maybe..." His voice trailed off.

"You thought maybe I was gay?"

He laughed nervously. "Yeah," he said. "I did. I mean -"

"I'm not gay, Winston."

"I believe you."

"Okay." I got a fork from the drawer by the stove and speared a chunk of ravioli with it. "How'd you get home that morning, anyway? Did you call a cab?"

"Yeah. I had to be somewhere. A concert rehearsal."

I chewed the piece of ravioli as quietly as I could. "With the Symphony?"

"Yeah."

He was lying, of course. "You must have felt pretty rough."

He laughed, mostly at ease now. "Oh, man, you have no idea. My head was fucking *pounding*. I almost threw up on the piano."

I mustered a good-natured chuckle. "Yeah, no doubt. How many beers did you drink that night? Fifteen?"

"Something like that."

A brief silence ensued. I could think of nothing to say, precisely nothing. So I resorted to that old failsafe, "So what's new?"

"You already asked me that, Terry."

"I did? Sorry."

He laughed. "It's cool. Anyway, there's not much to tell. I broke up with that chick from New York."

Oh, happy day! "I didn't realize you were dating her."

"Well, I was. Sort of."

"What went wrong?"

He cleared this throat. "Everything. Nothing. I don't know. It just wasn't feasible to date her, what with our living so far apart."

"Yeah, long-distance relationships seldom last."

"True, true." He paused. "Hey, there is *one* thing of note going on."

"Oh, yeah? What's that?"

"My dad's having a little get-together at his house on Friday night. Friends, neighbors, some people from work. He said I could invite a few of my friends over, if I wanted."

I was lifting another glob of ravioli toward my mouth, and my arm froze in mid-air. "What's he celebrating?"

"Nothing in particular. He often throws parties for no reason. He's rich, remember?"

"Yeah," I said. I siphoned the ravioli from the fork. "I do seem to recall that."

"So you wanna come?"

All at once my throat closed up like a fist, the chunk of ravioli squarely lodged halfway down. I was choking.

"Terry? You there?"

I gasped for air, felt panic bloom in my chest. I dropped the phone on the counter, stuck my head under the tap on the sink, and guzzled water. From a thousand miles away, I could hear Winston saying my name and asking if I was all right. I stood upright, clumsily giving myself the Heimlich, and staggered around the kitchen like a stew bum. At last, after untold eons, I felt the ravioli budge a little, and a tiny stream of precious air hiss through the opening thus formed. My lungs gulped it greedily, clamored for more. I returned to the sink and guzzled more water. The piece of food was disintegrating faster now; I could breathe again, think again. Winston was saying my name over and over, and there was real concern in his voice. I was touched, dimly but sincerely.

I coughed, my eyes watering, and reached for the phone. "Sorry," I wheezed. "I almost died just then."

"Jesus Christ. What happened?"

"I choked on a piece of ravioli."

There was a long silence, and then he laughed riotously. "Ravioli?"

"Yeah. God. That was pretty scary."

"Do me a favor?" he said.

"Yeah?"

"When you come to the party, don't choke on anything."

"So I'm coming?"

"Yes, you are."

I twined the phone cord around my fingers. "Winston, I have no business being there."

"Sure you do. I've invited you. You want an interview with

my dad, don't you?"

"Well, yeah."

"Then you have two good reasons for coming."

"What's the second one?"

"You want to see me again. Don't you?"

"Of course I do."

"Then come."

"Your dad isn't going to give me an interview at his party, Winston."

"He will if he's drunk. He'll do almost anything when he's drunk."

"He drinks?"

"Like a fish. So are you coming?"

"I don't know."

He sighed. "Just come. Okay?"

"Okay."

"And bring your camera."

"Why?"

"You'll want to take a picture of my dad after you interview him, won't you?"

"Winston, it's not going to hap -"

"Just bring it."

Something in his voice made me relent. "Okay, I will. What time should I be there?"

"Eight or nine. Whenever."

"What kind of attire?"

"Oh, whatever. Formal, semi-casual."

"Should I wear a tux?"

"Only if you want to."

"Okay." Pause. "Hey, Winston?"

"Yeah?"

I looked at my fridge, my hand gripping the phone so tightly that my knuckles were paper-white. "Nothing," I said. "See you on Friday."

"Okay. Bye, Terry."

"Bye."

I hung up. I looked at the bowl of ravioli on the counter. "What the fuck," I said, and took another bite.

12

Archie's was a sprawling Victorian mansion on Penn Avenue in Point Breeze, with copious ivy crawling up the sides and a long brick path winding through the front yard, flanked by pink azalea bushes. The grass was neatly cut, every blade of identical length, green and lush and lovingly nurtured, doubtless rife with some specially engineered fertilizer available only to the rich and famous. A tall, wrought-iron fence encircled the perimeter of the lot. The house itself was located about three blocks from where the old Heinz mansion had once stood, which, as every local history buff knows, Heinz burned down in the latter part of the nineteenth century to protest the implementation of a property tax. The protest, unlike Archie, was unsuccessful.

I turned into the semi-circular driveway at the side of the house and drove up to the portico, where a gangly teenage valet in a powder-blue tux signaled for me to stop. He told me he'd park my car for me, and I asked him where. On the street, he said. I told him I could do that myself. He insisted that I let him do it for me. So I cut the engine and handed him the keys. "Don't lose it," I told him. "I'll need it back."

He assured me that he wouldn't lose it, and that my keys would be waiting for me when I was ready to leave. "Just go around to the front of the house," he said, "and through the gate, then follow the path to the door." The man's fortune, I reflected dourly, was predicated on bureaucracy. Why, then, should I expect getting into his house to be anything less than a perfect ordeal?

The inconveniences did not end with the asinine

coordinates of the driveway relative to those of the main entrance, nor with the meandering course of the brick path. No, waiting for the intrepid adventurer at the end of said path were a half-dozen zig-zagging flights of concrete steps, atop which, finally, lay a stout oak door shaped like an upside-down "U," with a gargoyle knocker. Panting a little, I knocked three times and straightened the knot in my tie. A gaunt Hispanic man opened the door. His tuxedo was well pressed, his pencil-thin mustache finely groomed. He was, in every respect, a fully animate cliché. "Hello," he said, and gave me a big, supercilious smile. His accent was diluted but perceptible. "How are you this evening, sir?"

"I'm fine, thank you. And you?"

"I am very good," he said. "May I have your name?"

"Terrance Farmer."

He ran his eyes down a tablet on a small cherrywood table by the door. "I do not see your name," he said.

"You don't?"

"No, sir, I do not. I am sorry."

I forced a polite smile. "My name is Terrance Farmer. Winston invited me."

"Winston?"

And then he appeared, behind the servant. He was wearing a

gray flannel suit over an Oxford blue shirt. He looked marvelous. "It's okay, Juan Carlos. I know him."

I waved at Winston, the situation growing ever more surreal (*Juan Carlos, that has to be a joke*). The servant favored me with an apologetic smile and stepped aside. Winston came to the door. "Hi," he said, his eyes bright, voice rich and giddy. "Thanks for coming."

"Glad to." I tapped the wide-angle Nikon roped around my neck. "I brought it, since you asked."

"Good deal." He gestured for me to step into the foyer. "Come in, please."

I looked up at the stars - there were hundreds of them that night, thousands even, white and radiant and dazzling - and stepped inside.

"I guess your dad doesn't much like visitors," I said. We strode through a wide, plushly carpeted hallway and into an expansive, blindingly white kitchen whose dimensions dwarfed those of my entire apartment.

"Why do you say that?"

"Because it's harder to get into this place than Fort Fucking Knox."

He puzzled for a moment, then laughed. "Oh, right, the path."

"And the steps."

"Yes, there are quite a lot of them, aren't there?"

I smiled. I felt better than I had in months. Or at least since I'd last seen him. "Eighteen, to be exact."

He nodded. "Can I get you something to drink? We have beer, wine, champagne, liquor, anything you want."

"Oh, gosh." I scratched my chin. "You know, I've been drinking a bit too much lately."

"Really?"

"Yeah." I hesitated. I meant to ask for a Coke, but heard myself say this instead: "So I'd better stick to beer tonight."

He laughed his vibrant, scintillating laugh and clapped me on the shoulder. "Terry," he said, "I've really missed you."

And I you, Winston. I you.

He fetched a couple of Heinekens from the fridge, opened them, handed me one, and told me to follow him into the den. "We'll have some privacy in there," he said. "I thought maybe we could talk for a bit before we joined the party. That cool?"

"Sure. It's cool." I sipped my beer as he led me through a doorway on the opposite side of the kitchen from which we'd entered. The doorway opened onto a narrow hallway with a hardwood floor and a short, steep staircase at the end. There hung a painting on either wall, the two prints facing each other like men preparing to duel. Both were abstract expressionist pieces, and quite subtle.

One of them looked vaguely familiar to me. I stopped and pointed to it. "This... this isn't an original DeKooning, is it?" I had minored in art history at Rutgers and had been fascinated by the surrealists, especially Dali, as well as the abstract expressionist crowd, Pollock and DeKooning being my favorites. I figured that, with his money, Archie probably could have afforded to buy the whole fucking Louvre; an original DeKooning, then, would have set him back about as much as an expensive meal or a pair of designer shoes would have lightened the average American's wallet.

Winston chuckled. I could tell he was already half in his cups. "No," he said. "It's an original Lancaster."

I shook my head in amazement. "You? Really?"

"Did it a couple years ago."

"So you paint, too?"

"Too?"

"Well, you play the piano."

He snickered. "Oh, right."

"You're a real Renaissance man, aren't you, old buddy?"

He blushed. My love for him was born anew. "Nah. I'm not that great at either."

"Winston, you play with the Pittsburgh Symphony!"

"Only now and again."

"Modest, schmodesty," I said, and followed him upstairs.

The room was spacious, of course, with a high ceiling and an octagonal window on the far wall. There was a Turkish rug in the middle of the floor, with dark colors to offset the egg-shell carpet. More paintings hung on the walls, some of them presumably Winston's and others reproductions of famous works, most notably Edward Munsch's *The Scream*. A big-screen TV sat in one corner, a stereo system in other. Against the wall to our left was a couch upholstered in mauve-colored silk, probably Italian. Flanking the couch were marble pedestals polished to a gleaming mirror-shine, each sporting a round tortoiseshell ashtray. The arrangement of furniture seemed designed to underscore the expanse of the room, as if its owner worried that guests might look down upon it as contemptibly small.

"Have a seat," Winston said, gesturing at the couch. I lowered myself cautiously onto one of the cushions, terrified that I might harm it somehow, and watched as he crossed the room and opened the window. It opened outward rather than vertically, of course, adding that elusive touch of class to a room which otherwise might have seemed only mildly extraordinary.

"We're allowed to smoke in here with the window open," he said, taking a seat on the opposite end of the couch. He drew his tin box from the breast pocket of his suit, popped the lid off, and fixed a cigarette between his lips. Then he produced a pack of matches, lit one with his thumbnail, and fired up the smoke. He offered the box to me. "Want one?"

"Yeah," I said. By that time I had begun smoking pretty regularly again, as much as half a pack a day: not as bad as when I'd smoked in my teens and early twenties, but close. I was sure I'd eventually get back there if I kept at it. I had yet to decide whether I resented that, and, if so, whether I blamed Winston for it. "Thanks."

He lit the cigarette for me with the same match, blew it out, and dropped it in the ashtray beside him. "You can put your camera on the stand there," he said, pointing to the pedestal on my right. I had forgotten all about the thing, despite its considerable weight, and looked at it as if I had never seen it before.

"Oh, right." I removed the camera and gingerly placed it next to the ashtray. I turned back to him, smiling sheepishly, trying hard to think of something to say and coming up with precisely naught. Fortunately, a moment later he relieved me of my burden.

"So come on, Terry," he said, smiling piquantly, his eyes aflame with all the mad, directionless ardor of youth. "What's new, man? There's gotta be *something*." He gave a skeptical little chuckle.

"There really isn't," I said, going to cross my legs in my usual one-thigh-over-the-other fashion, then quickly correcting myself and placing the ankle of my right leg on the knee of my left. With a tickle of self-consciousness I put my left hand over the ankle, relaxed my shoulders, and devoted all my energies to appearing casual. "My job's going okay. My ex-wife is fine. I don't have any pets."

He laughed. "Not an animal person, huh?"

"No, no. I actually love cats. And dogs. But pets aren't allowed in my building." In truth, I had always been quite loath to canines, deemed them sycophantic and dull-witted if occasionally useful. "Say, what's the deal with Juan Carlos? Is that his real name?"

He laughed again. "Of course it is. Why wouldn't it be?"

"I don't know. It just seems so... stereotypical. Everything about him seemed that way. How many servants does your father have?"

"Servants? They're not *servants*, Terry. They're... help."

"Same thing. How many?"

"I don't know. Two or three. Why?"

"Just curious."

He took a long gulp of his beer and looked at me, a peculiarly crooked grin half-realized on his face. He was taunting me, I could tell, good-naturedly but sophomorically. "You're not really sure what you're doing here, are you, Terry?"

"No, I'm not." I smoked and returned his gaze. "Care to let me in on the secret?"

He cracked up. "There's no *secret*. You're here because I wanted to see you, that's all. That's a good enough reason, isn't it?"

"Sure," I said. I felt more awkward than ever, and had no concrete idea why. My gut just told me that something was awry here, something major. "So where is everyone?"

"Down in the parlor. And the dining room. Most of them are still eating. You hungry?"

"No, I'm fine, thanks. I had something before I left the house. The apartment, I mean."

"You want another beer?"

I glanced down at my Heineken. It was three-quarters' full. "Winston, you just gave me this one."

More laughter. Yeah, he was definitely well on his way to

Boozy Town. "All right, all right. Just asking." He took another greedy swig of his own beer, dragged on his cigarette, and fixed me with his eyes. "Anyway... I've been doing some thinking."

"Oh, yeah? What about?" *The kiss? You liked it? You want to try it again, maybe, this time for real?*

"Just all the stuff we've talked about. You know, about my dad and his money and... the inequality of wealth in America."

I nodded thoughtfully. My penis had stiffened a little and now softened again. "What about it?"

His face grew serious. "I'm starting to think you might be right about it."

"Right to object to it, you mean?"

"Yeah. I mean, I don't think it's fair for you to single out my father and try to make an example of him, but-"

"I don't single him out, Winston. I'd just as soon target any other billionaire in my articles, if he or she were of local interest and implicated in the same kinds of shady deals as your dad. And let's not forget that Dacey Energy has been on the *Fortune* 500 for the last six years, your father himself in the top ten of *Forbes'* 400 Wealthiest People in the World for the last five. To call people on that list 'rich' would be like calling a serial killer 'anti-social.' Rich people can buy Rolls-Royces and homes in the Caribbean. Your dad

98

could buy a couple of underdeveloped countries and his own private fleet of space shuttles. That isn't wealth, Winston; it's quasi-omnipotence."

He shook his head, frustrated. "Okay, okay, I get the point. I understand that my dad is *particularly* well-off."

"Only Bill Gates, Warren Buffet, that Saudi prince, and one of the Walton kids are worth more."

He glowered at me. "Terry, dammit."

"Sorry."

"The point is, sometimes you make it sound like he's the devil himself."

I lowered my head, genuinely ashamed. "I'm sorry. I certainly never intended to. Sometimes I just... well, sometimes I just get carried away."

"It's okay."

I looked at him. "So what brought you around to my side of this, anyway? Did your dad do something, say something? Have you been reading *The Communist Manifesto*?"

He laughed a little. It was a quiet laugh, tender and self-aware, the polar opposite of his usual, boisterous guffaw. It was mature and restrained, a window into the modest part of his soul that already belonged to an adult. "No, no," he said. "Nothing like that."

"Then what?"

"Stuff," he said absently. He was staring vacantly at the blank screen of the television.

"What kind of stuff?"

He sighed. "Promise you won't laugh?"

"Sure."

He shifted on his cushion and polished off his beer, crushed out his smoke, immediately lit another. "Well, I was watching TV the other night, one of the late shows, and the host was interviewing some superficial celebrity... is that redundant?"

I laughed. "Virtually, yes. Go on."

He paused, considered. "Well, I just got to thinking about how unbelievably lucky this actor was, to have pretty much been in the right place at the right time, which he even admitted. I'm not saying he isn't a good actor or anything, or that he didn't struggle for a while before he became rich and famous, but I couldn't off-hand see any reason why, mostly as a result of pure luck, he should have so much and almost everyone else so little. What makes *him* so goddam special, you know? There are thousands, maybe millions of people, just as talented if not more so, who have done basically all the same things he has, explored all the same avenues and exhausted all the same resources, but who spend their days teaching school or waiting tables or pumping gas instead of making millions to laugh or cry on cue, just because they didn't catch a break. Just because *their* talents happened to go unnoticed.

"As far as I could tell, that was the only difference between the guy on TV and most of the performers in our local actors' guild, or the comedy troupe at my college. Lots of those people are just as skilled, just as ambitious, just as dedicated as any celebrity. But the celebrity is rich and famous and they're not. Why? Because, by sheer chance, somewhere along the way the celebrity got noticed and the rest of them didn't. And that's it. That's the only difference between them."

I glanced down at my cigarette and saw that the tobacco in it had almost completely burned away. I had taken but two draws on it. I stubbed it out in the ashtray beside me and replaced my eyes on Winston. He was looking at me nervously, expectantly. "Winston," I said. My voice trembled a little.

"Yeah?"

"That was beautiful, man." I laughed heartily. "I couldn't have put it better myself. Not if you'd given me two weeks to work on it."

He blushed and grinned with childish, giddy delight. My

penis stiffened again. "Really?"

"Really."

"Well, thanks."

"You're welcome. And you know something? I've had very similar thoughts myself while watching celebrity interviews or skimming a magazine article about some bloated government fat cat -"

Archie appeared at the top of the steps, clad in a tuxedo and leather shoes at whose price tag the likes of a Terry Farmer would have surely reeled. His platinum hair was swept neatly back on his head, his face clean-shaven, his posture straight as a rod, his smallish potbelly all but imperceptible. Except for the snaps of red in his eyes, he might have been preparing to get his picture taken for the cover of *Time*. He looked first at me and then at his son. "Winston," he said. "You're wanted downstairs."

"By whom?" I stole a cautious glance at Winston, flummoxed by his diction. He extinguished his cigarette.

"By my guests," replied Archie. There was a hint of indignation in his tone, but only a hint; the rest simmered under the surface like a great, unhappy stew. "They'd like to hear a few songs on the piano."

"Oh," said Winston. "Okay. I'll be down in a minute."

Archie shot a perfunctory glance at me, smiled a fast, mock smile, and returned his attention to his son. "Well, aren't you going to introduce me to your friend?"

Winston looked at me as if he were surprised to see me sitting there. He was flustered, embarrassed. It was a disposition I had never seen him exhibit, and never would have associated with him. I, in turn, was disconcerted by it. "Yeah, sure. Dad, this is Terry Farmer. Terry, this is my Dad. Which I guess you already know." Winston swallowed and looked timidly at his father. "Terry's a reporter for the *Post-Gazette*."

This time Archie gave me a bigger, more deliberate and perfectly derisive smile. "Ah, yes. Mr. Farmer. I believe you've called my office a few times, have you not?"

I tried to speak but could not. My tongue was glued to the roof of my mouth. My brain was numb, empty, a white void of panic. It was easy to be belligerent when you were sitting safely behind a computer screen, I realized, easy to be captious when you were surrounded by dozens of people in the lobby of a hotel and your flurry of incendiary questions were bound to go unanswered. It was *not* so easy, however, when he was standing right there in front of you, the fifth wealthiest man in the world, with no one else around but his fretting son, and in his own home to boot. In that

103

one endless moment all I could think was this: *He could squash you like a bug, and wouldn't hesitate to do it.*

"Are you all right, Mr. Farmer?"

"Yes," I said. The word came out on its own, a purely instinctive reaction. "I'm fine. I just... excuse me."

"So you *are* the one who's been after an interview with me?"

"Yes, sir. I'm the one." *Sir? You called him "sir"? What's wrong with you?*

Archie cleared his throat audibly, hardened his gaze. "Tell me, Mr. Farmer: what exactly is it that you'd like to ask me about?"

"Oh," I said, my words still running on auto-pilot. "Just this and that."

"This and that?"

"Dad," said Winston, my hero, my savior. "Maybe you could talk to Terry later, after he's had a chance to unwind a little and meet some of the guests."

Archie's smile melted. "You'll be sticking around for a while, then?"

I looked at Winston. He gave me a reassuring little nod. "Well, I guess I could hang out for a couple of hours, if it's all right with you folks." I spoke through a clod of wet sand.

"Of course it's all right," said Winston at once. "Isn't it, Dad?"

104

Archie gave his son a sweet, paternal grin that said simply: *Oh, you smart-assed little bastard.* "Sure it's all right. The more, the merrier. That's what I always say when I throw one of these parties, isn't it, Winston?"

"That's what he says," Winston told me.

"Winston?" said Archie. "You're coming down now?"

"Yeah, I'll be right there."

Archie humored me with a nod. "A pleasure meeting you, Mr. Farmer."

"Likewise, sir." *You did it again, asshole.*

The senior Lancaster departed.

13

In 2002, Gus Capito, then owner and president of Capito Mining, had sued Dacey Energy for fifty million dollars and won. A jury in Allegheny County had found Dacey liable for forfeiting on a contract with Capito Mining, as a result of which one hundred and fifty miners had lost their jobs. With interest, by the summer of 2004 that verdict was worth more than sixty-one million dollars.

In August of 1997, Capito Mining had signed a ten-year contract with Bellmore Coal, a Virginia-based concern which for the next two and a half years had served as Capito Mining's chief source of mining projects and therefore its chief source of income. Then, in February of 2000, Dacey Energy had bought up both Bellmore Coal and its parent company, Mid-Atlantic Power. Within a matter of weeks, Dacey had re-allocated to its own non-union mines ninety-five percent of the work previously assigned to Capito Mining, thereby effectively terminating the contract.

Two months later Capito Mining had filed for bankruptcy, and a month after that filed suit against Dacey Energy in Virginia's Fourth Circuit Court. The court had ruled in the plaintiff's favor and awarded a $6.1 million verdict "for bad faith and breach of contract." The Virginia Supreme Court had refused to hear Dacey's appeal. In November 2000, Capito Mining had then filed its Allegheny County lawsuit, charging that Dacey and its subsidiaries had "tortiously interfered with Capito Mining's contract with Bellmore, as a consequence of which Capito Mining was forced out of business." Capito won, as I said, and was awarded damages in the amount of fifty million dollars.

On March 17, 2004, about a month before I met Archie and Winston, Dacey Energy had filed papers appealing the decision to the state Supreme Court of Pennsylvania. By the first week of May the court was slated to hear the case in early 2005, shortly after reconvening. Indeed, had Dacey not withdrawn its appeal just last month, the justices would be reading the lawyers' briefs right now. And Archie, no doubt, would be preparing to testify on his company's behalf. Instead, Gus Capito will keep every penny of his well-deserved sixty-odd million dollars.

There was, as it happened, only one incumbent justice up for re-election last year. His name was Wade Grady. He was a Democrat. He was pro-labor, pro-union, and very much anti-Dacey. Grady's opponent in the general election, Benjamin Grent, was a staunch conservative. He was anti-labor, anti-union, and unequivocally pro-Dacey. Three of the court's other six justices, including Chief Justice Phillip Niles, were of ideologies at least roughly in line with Grady's. The remaining three were as conservative as Ben Grent, one of them perhaps more so. The outcome of the contest between Grady and Grent was thus of colossal importance, not only to the future of both Capito Mining and Dacey Energy, but to the economic and political future of Pennsylvania generally.

By the time I met Archibald Lancaster in May 2004, he had already personally donated more than $1.7 million to a dummy organization called "And for the Sake of the Kids." The sole objective of this group, despite its official veneer as a citizen-action coalition engaged in protecting the future of Pennsylvania's youths, was to help defeat Wade Grady and elect Ben Grent in his place.

Upon hearing of the donations, Gus Capito said, "I had no idea that Mr. Lancaster cared so much about children."

15

What the Lancasters called their "family room" was really a ballroom, occupying perhaps nine hundred square feet in the east wing of the mansion. The floor was a terrazzo, the walls barren save for a couple of twelve-by-fourteen murals of the city (painted, I supposed, by a local artist commissioned expressly to execute such works). A massive crystal chandelier hung from the ceiling. Four mammoth, brown-leather sofas girdled a low glass table in the center of the room. In the far left corner, upon entering the room from the parlor, was a gloss-black Baldwin grand piano, its lid serenely raised.

Winston took a seat on the matching bench, raked his eyes across the thirty-odd politely attentive faces in his audience (lingering on mine for just a second, I was sure of it), and launched into the most magnificent rendition of Beethoven's "Fur Elise" I had ever heard, finer than even Beethoven's itself.

And then an even more sublime rendition of Mozart's *Symphony No. 40*, and then a still more breathtaking rendition of

Beethoven's "Moonlight Sonata," and, finally, the most orgasmically divine rendition of Debussy's "Clair de Lune" ever achieved by human fingers. Each performance was greeted with thunderous applause from the guests.

By the time he stood and took a bow, there were tears in my eyes.

He approached me cautiously, as if uncertain how I had received his music. "What did you think?" he said. He was beaming, clearly proud of himself, but his eyes were sad, almost contrite.

"It was beautiful," I said. "Absolutely gorgeous. Nothing less. I'm... honestly, Winston, I'm stunned."

He laughed. "Thank you."

I leaned in a little, lowered my voice. "Do you always play that well when you're half-lit?"

He looked at me, smiling perhaps the most resplendent, winning, guileless smile ever to cross a human face. "That's when I play *best*," he said.

I saw her as Winston led me into the kitchen: a tall, dark-haired woman in a low-cut, rose-colored dress. She was hanging on Archie like a cheerleader on a high-school football captain, fawning and flirty and brazenly obsequious. Archie seemed as pleased by it as he did uncomfortable with it, and made only a token effort to rebuff her advances. He was, as Winston had essentially predicted he would be, thoroughly shitfaced.

"Want some whiskey?" Winston asked me.

"Um."

"It's good stuff. Glen Garioch. One of the finest brands in the world."

"Oh. Wow. I've never even heard of it."

Winston laughed. "It's almost three grand a bottle."

I nodded. "Then that would explain why I've never heard of it."

We went into the kitchen and he filled a tall glass about three-quarters' full with the absurdly expensive spirit. "I assume you want it straight?"

I actually preferred Coke with my bourbon, but I didn't want to seem vulgar. "Yeah. That'll be fine."

He handed me the drink. "There ya go. That oughtta put some hairs on your chest."

"Aren't you having one?"

He opened the fridge and plucked a Heineken from the bottom shelf. "Nah. I'm gonna stick with beer for tonight. Did you really like my piano-playing?"

I took a sip of my drink. To call it stiff would have been a wild understatement. But to call it anything less than heavenly would have been equally dishonest. "Yes. Very much. You're amazing, Winston."

"Thank you."

"You're welcome." I sipped my drink and looked at him, waiting for him to say something. He didn't. "Listen, Winston -"

"Hey, you want to meet some of the guests? There are some semi-famous people in there, you know."

"Really? Like who?"

"Well, um." He drained half of his beer. "Ever heard of Tom Sheiffer?"

"The guy who runs First Mutual Savings & Loans?"

"That's the one."

"He's in there?"

"Yup."

"He's almost as rich as your dad."

Winston frowned. "Come on," he said, starting toward the ballroom. "We've been pretty anti-social up till now. Let's mingle a little."

"Okay," I said, following, always following. "Let's mingle."

Winston introduced me to about nine guests in five minutes, only half of whose names I caught and most of whose faces are now just a blur in my memory. They were all haughty and plastic and chicly dressed, the women painstakingly made-up and adorned with gaudy jewelry, the men vigorously scrubbed and shaven and stinking of pungent colognes. Diamond rings were flaunted, Rolexes flashed, mink coats caressed, hair product a universal fixture. There were fake smiles, affected laughter, inconsequential conversation, humdrum questions asked and answered out of strained politeness.

There was present, indeed, every ingredient of a thoroughly and unblushingly meaningless social function. And there were investment bankers, book publishers, corporate executives, corporate lawyers, heart surgeons, art dealers, politicians, local celebrities, socialites of every imaginable stripe, a university president. I met perhaps a quarter of them, one by one, nodding and shaking their hands, caring not one whit who they were or what they did, smiling as convincingly as I could, wondering what in the hell I was doing there.

One of them, a fifty-something stock broker with a handlebar mustache, seemed to recognize my name. "Are you the

Terrance Farmer who writes for the *Post-Gazette*?" he asked me.

"Yes, that's me."

He released my hand abruptly and stepped backward. "I'm rather surprised to see *you* here, what with the sorts of things you've had to say about Archie over the past few months."

"Well," I said. I looked around for Winston but didn't see him anywhere. "I'm somewhat close with his son."

"With Winston? Really?"

"Yes."

"One can only imagine how," he said.

I blinked. "Oh? What exactly do you mean by that?"

"Nothing at all," he said, taking his wife's hand. She was a pale, emaciated woman, silent and brooding. "It was a pleasure meeting you, Mr. Farmer."

"I'm sure." I nodded to the man and, my drink now half-drunk, went to find Winston.

He was with his father, by the piano. They were deep in conversation, something to do with his schooling (I thought). I waited for a break in the dialogue, and then went to Winston, meaning to tell him that I had had a wonderful time and would be heading off now, thanks very much, good seeing you again, keep in touch.

But he caught me, of course. He knew exactly what he was doing. "Terry," he said. "How you holding up?"

"Oh, I'm good," I said.

"Still want that interview?"

"Huh?"

"Still want that interview with my father?"

I looked at Archie.

"It will be quick," he said sternly, "three minutes tops, and no questions about Inez or Grent or anything of the sort."

I looked at Winston. "Maybe I should just go."

"Terry," he said. "Don't be ridiculous. You've been trying for this interview for months now. This is a golden opportunity. Why would you pass it up?"

I pulled Winston aside. "No," I whispered. "Not like this. I won't do it like this. Not with him toasted and me halfway there. It isn't right. This is stupid. I'm not doing it, Winston."

"Terry," he said, his eyes like polished rocks. "Do it. Trust me on this. Do it and ask any questions you want."

"Winston," I protested.

"Terry, if you've ever trusted anyone or anything in your life, trust me about this. *Do it.*"

I turned to Archie. "Where would you like to do this?" I asked.

"Come with me," he said.

I followed him into the parlor.

"Mr. Lancaster," I said, squirming in a flower-patterned, wing-backed chair with a yawning fireplace on one side and a gemstone floor globe in a gold-plated stand on the other. I hadn't brought a tape recorder, but Winston had furnished me with a pencil and notepad. "What is it like to be the fifth most affluent man in the world?"

"What is it like," he asked, "to be the tenth most affluent man in the world? The hundredth? The forty-nine thousandth? I am a man like any other."

"But you're not," I said, still squirming. "You're not, sir, inasmuch as you control more wealth than nearly anyone else on the planet. Few men know that feeling."

"I possess no special powers," he said. "I just have money."

"Money is a special power unto itself."

"Perhaps." He stood, went to the hearth, and opened a humidor made of Spanish cedar. "Cuban?"

"No, thanks." I waited for him to sit and light his cigar, then asked, "How much was your father worth at the time of his death?"

Archie puffed, exhaled. My eyes began to water. "I don't recall the exact amount."

"Roughly," I said.

"Eighty-nine million dollars."

"Did you inherit all of it?"

"The bulk."

"But you were motivated to work, nevertheless?"

"Of course I was," Archie said. "I was never shiftless, never a loafer. I despise loafers."

"Do you hate the poor?"

"Of course not."

"Do you give to them?"

"I give to charities."

I scribbled on my notepad. "What kind of charities?"

"Literacy, education, medical. All kinds."

"When did you become the CEO of Dacey?"

"May of 1996."

"What do you know about Gus Capito?"

Archie frowned. "Didn't I advise you against such questions?"

"How do you mean?"

"No questions about Inez," he said. "Remember? And no questions about Ben Grent."

I scribbled something, debating how best to proceed. "I'm only curious, Archie, whether you expect your company to win the case it has brought before the state Supreme Court."

He nodded, exhaling a massive cloud of cigar smoke. "I have every confidence that we will prevail."

"With or without Ben Grent on the court?"

He sneered. "You just aren't going to give up, are you?"

"Sir?"

"Of course we can win the case without Grent on the court. Justice has no party affiliation, no ideology, no agenda."

I jotted that down verbatim. It was highly quotable, and just the kind of sentimental, lofty-sounding bullshit you'd expect from the mouth of a man for whom justice, or at least his own warped version of it, was a commodity like anything else. "So then your recent donations to the group supporting Grent's candidacy," I proffered hesitantly. "'And for the Sake of the Kids.' They suggest nothing about any ties you might have to the Grent campaign?"

Archie leveled me with his eyes. "If you're asking whether I want Benjamin Grent to be elected, then the answer is yes. However, if you're asking whether my donations were designed, circuitously or otherwise, to buy my company a desirable ruling in the upcoming case, then the answer is no. I repeat: I do not need to tip the court in my favor by dishonorable means, for my company is innocent of any wrongdoing."

I looked into his eyes and was astonished to discover that, more likely than not, he actually bought his own buncombe. "Why, then," I asked, "do you suppose that the jury in Allegheny County felt differently?"

He puffed his cigar, squinting behind the smoke. "Perhaps they fell victim to a certain prejudice prevalent among ordinary people: the assumption, woefully unfounded, that people of great means are ultimately, collectively responsible for all great evils. It's the old proposition: wealth begets avarice, and avarice dishonesty."

"Money is the root of all evil?"

"As the expression goes."

I scribbled. "So you concede, then, that what happened to Gus Capito was a great evil?"

He smiled, his eyes awash with disdain. "I believe your three minutes are up, Mr. Farmer."

14

It was only later, when Winston mentioned it in passing,

that I remembered the camera, and the whole point of my having toted it to the party. "Dammit," I said. "I forgot all about the blasted thing."

"Well," Winston said doubtfully, "do you still want to get the picture? I could ask my dad if he'd mind giving you another minute or two."

"No, no. Forget about it. I'm sure I can dig up a photo in the paper's archives, if I decide I want to include one."

He nodded. He looked, I thought, deeply unhappy, drunk and preoccupied and conflicted. "Well, it's still up in the den. The camera, I mean. You want me to get it for you?"

"No, that's okay. I'll get it myself here in a minute, before I leave."

"You're leaving?"

"Winston," I said, "it's almost midnight."

"Yeah, but it's Friday. You don't have work tomorrow, do you?"

"Well, no."

"Then what's your rush? Come on, just hang out a little longer. There's plenty more Glen."

I laughed. I was touched by the frankness and seeming urgency of his plea, or what I took to be such. But I was also a little perturbed by it, and by the loneliness, the neediness from which, ostensibly, it had sprung. This was not the self-assured, carefree, at times even detached Winston to whom I had grown accustomed. This was a Winston I had never met.

"Is something bothering you?" I asked him. We were sitting in the parlor, he drinking another beer and I still nursing my tumbler of whiskey. Most of the guests had departed. "You seem a little unsettled. A trifle glum."

He snickered, but his eyes remained morose. "I love it when you talk like an old British person," he said. I was unaware that I ever so talked.

"Come on, Winston. I'm serious. What's up? *Something's* on your mind."

"It's nothing," he insisted. "Honestly. I just get a little blue sometimes, late at night, after I've been drinking. What would a writer like you call it? 'Pensively introspective'?"

I smiled. "Something like that, yeah. You sure you're okay?"

"Yeah," he said. "I'm okay. Will you have one more drink with me before you go?"

"Of course I will." What else could I say, do? How could I abandon the boy to his woe, however fugitive or niggling? "But please," I said, "make this one a beer."

120

So we went into the kitchen, and he got us a couple of Heinekens, and we drank them at the kitchen table. We talked about music, art, religion, politics. We talked about what he wanted to do after he graduated from college (he wasn't sure, but liked the idea of starting his own business, maybe a piano store or a record company). We talked about my spur-of-the-moment, finally ill-conceived interview with his father.

The conversation lasted for maybe half an hour, and at no point did I suspect him of chicanery. Even now, despite his admission of guilt, I am not entirely convinced that the remainder of the evening was planned, that he had consciously plotted what was about to occur, the dazzling and life-altering denouement. I think it was as much a product of chance as it was the actualization of a massaged and nuanced scheme.

Whatever the truth, when I had finished my beer I told him that I'd best be going, the hour drew late and I grew weary. He proposed that I was over the legal limit and might consider sleeping on the couch in his den. I declined, knowing better and wanting to sleep in my own bed. "However," I said, "I do need to piss. Where's the nearest bathroom?"

He took a swig of his beer and reached into the right inside-pocket of his jacket. "There are two down here," he said, training his eyes on the floor. "But we're redecorating both of them, so they're kind of cluttered right now." He dug deeper into his pocket and produced a small brass key, which he laid on the table. "Here, use the one upstairs. The doors in this place are real old-fashioned, still open with keys. The bathroom door has a tendency to lock itself. Just go up the stairs, take a right, and it's the last door on your left."

I took the key. "How do I get to the stairs?"

He grinned. For the first time all night, he looked happy. "Just go into the foyer and they'll be on your right." He pointed to the doorway leading into the foyer. "That way."

"Thanks."

I palmed the key and started toward the foyer. Then he called to me: "Terry!"

I turned. "Yeah?"

"Hold on a sec." He leapt out of his seat and ran through the hallway, up to the den. A moment later he returned with my camera. "Here," he said, handing it to me. "Didn't want you to forget this."

Startled, I thanked him, bade him good night, and made my way upstairs. My bladder was quite literally on the brink of exploding.

The staircase was spiral, of course, and climbing it fairly winded me. I blamed the cigarettes, silently cursing myself for picking them back up (what mad things love can make us do!), and slogged down a dark hallway in pursuit of a bathroom not to be found.

Did I hear a faint moaning behind the door I came to? Yes, I did. Did I use the key and open it, anyway? Yes, I did. Why? Oh, shit, I don't know. Fate? Curiosity? Some inscrutable combination thereof? One of those, I guess.

And what did I find on the other side of that door? Why, Archie in bed with the dark-haired woman formerly clad in the rose-colored dress, now bare-assed naked and straddling the elder Lancaster like a veteran call girl!

Reflexively, I took three photographs of them in rapid succession, and then the woman screamed. At which point Archie, pausing only to don his robe, cursing a blue streak, his face contorted into the most lurid expression of ire imaginable, scrambled out of the bed and charged me.

I turned, fled, and flew down the stairs, through the front door, down the steps, through the gate, up the street, and slowed only when I reached the portico. The valet saw me coming and, dismayed, surrendered my keys immediately.

"My car?" I gasped. "Where's my car?"

He stammered and gestured vaguely toward the street.

"Where?" I shouted. "*Where*, goddammit?"

He pointed east. "That way," he said, his face a rictus of terror. "Half a block!"

I went, racing, and while I have no idea whether Archie chased me beyond even the foyer of his mansion, until I arrived home I was absolutely certain that he was behind me, stalking me, bent on relieving the world of my odious presence. I didn't feel safe until I was inside, with the door locked securely behind me. And even with all the alcohol in my system, I lay awake for almost an hour that night, tossing and turning, conjuring the various grisly fates to which I might be doomed, asking myself again and again what had possessed me to snap those pictures.

Imagine, then, the abysmal dread which devoured me next day, when I learned that Archie's mistress was none other than Vanessa Grent, wife of the candidate for state Supreme Court.

PART II:

Archie

15

I found out from Winston.

Inexplicably terrified to be alone in my apartment, and thinking the fresh air might ease my hangover, around ten o' clock on Saturday morning I ventured out to the library, where for six or seven hours I sat and read magazines and paperback crime novels. Of course I retained only a fraction of what I read, what with the ten-pound cement block in my stomach and the steady throbbing in my temples.

But it was safer, I felt sure, to be out among people than to be on my own. There was no telling what might happen to me if Archie or one of his hoods found me holed up in my apartment, what obscene forms of revenge they might exact upon me. All the while, the incriminating celluloid lay buried under a stack of old bills in a shoebox in my bedroom closet. I had almost taken the film with me, but decided it would be better to leave it at the apartment; if somebody got to me and I had it on me, things could turn very ugly.

When the library closed at five o' clock, I went to a pizza parlor downtown and lingered over the crusts of three slices of pepperoni and olives, until the guy behind the counter starting giving me funny looks. The pizza was the first thing I had eaten all day and it tasted good. I felt better after I ate, steadier. I had the courage now, I thought, to go home.

So I went home, and when I did I found nine messages on my answering machine. The first three were from Archie, the fourth from my sister in Long Island, and the sixth a "courtesy call" from a credit card company I had told on three separate occasions to fuck off. The fifth and seventh were hang-ups (Archie again, I suspected). The eighth was from Winston. The ninth was by far the most fascinating, so hilariously ironic that when I heard it I literally laughed until I cried: an automated call from the Benjamin Grent campaign urging me to vote my conscience on November 2nd and "restore dignity to the state Supreme Court."

This last bit was an allusion, I assumed, to Grent's oft-repeated allegation that Wade Grady had voted fifteen years ago to allow a convicted sex offender to work as a janitor at a local grade school. The truth of the matter, from what I could gather, was that Grady had voted to overturn a ruling by a lower court that a decades-old statutory rape conviction was in itself insufficient to bar the defendant from employment in a setting where children were present - controversial, perhaps, but hardly the work of the Dark Forces.

Archie's first message, received shortly before ten-thirty, went something like this: "Mr. Farmer, this is Archibald Lancaster. I believe you and I need to talk. Please call me immediately." He left his phone number and hung up. He sounded awful.

His second, received about forty-five minutes later, proceeded along these lines: "Mr. Farmer, it is absolutely urgent that you call me the moment you get this message. There's something we need to discuss, as I'm sure you must realize. Please, call me back as soon as you possibly can." He left his phone number again. He sounded only slightly recovered.

His third, received just after two, went roughly as follows: "I'm not the sort of man who enjoys playing games, Mr. Farmer. We both know what you've done. I'm sure we can reach some sort of agreement amenable to us both. There's no need to make this hard on yourself. These things can be forgiven, Mr. Farmer, even forgotten. Please, do the right thing. Do the *smart* thing." Short pause, then: "I look forward to hearing from you." He didn't leave his phone number this time, and he sounded vastly more alert, infinitely more affronted. In the thirty-six hours to follow, I would find myself returning again and again to that vaguely baleful warning, "There's no need to make this hard on yourself." Translation: "Don't make me hurt you, Farmer."

Winston's message caught me totally off guard, and after I'd listened to it a third time my legs turned to wet sponge: "Terry, it's me. Winston. We have to talk. But not on the phone. Whatever you do, don't call my dad's house. I repeat: do *not* call my dad's. Meet me at the Squirrel Hill entrance to Frick Park at eight-thirty. And don't... don't bring anything. If you can't make it, call me on my cell phone." He left his cell phone number and hung up.

I collapsed on my couch, my jaw in my lap. *Don't bring anything.* What would I bring? An umbrella? My arrowhead collection? The photos I had not yet developed, might *never* develop? Of course he'd meant the photos. But why would I bring them? And how in the hell did he know about them in the first place?

That's when it dawned on me that the whole thing had been a setup, Winston its lone, ingenious architect.

Ruddy sunlight dappled the treetops, splintered on the windshield of my Buick as I drove south on Murray Avenue. Then I turned east onto Hobart Street and the setting sun disappeared behind me, sliding with turtle-like speed down the western rim.

A moment later I saw him, sitting on a bench near the open wrought-iron gates at the park's entrance, his head down and arms crossed over his chest. There was no fancy apparel today, no modish blazer or button-down shirt. Just a plain white tee and blue jeans, and moccasins on his feet. I didn't see his Caddy anywhere. I parked at the curb in front of the bench and got out. Providentially, we found ourselves alone.

"Winston," I said.

"Terry."

"You look terrible."

He laughed feebly. "Thanks. You don't look so hot yourself."

I sat down beside him on the bench. "It's been a very long day."

"Not half as long as mine."

"I'm sure that's true."

"You didn't bring them, did you?"

"The pictures? No. I haven't even had them developed yet."

"Good. Because I don't want to see them."

"Then why did you have me take them?"

For the first time, he looked me in the eye. His face was that of a fifty-year-old man, his forehead a busy snarl of worry-lines and jowls slack with exhaustion. He looked in that moment far too much like his father. "So you figured it out."

"Well, my mind was already headed in that direction, I think, but the message you left on my machine kind of pushed it over the edge." I lit a cigarette and stamped an impulse to brush his hair out of his eyes, to comfort and dote on him. "Why'd you do it, Winston?

Because you want the world to know how ethically bankrupt your father is? Did you think I'd publish the photos in the newspaper or something?"

"I don't know."

I sighed. "Winston."

His head had begun to droop, and now he raised it again, and again made eye contact with me. Only this time it was tenuous, marginal, that of a scolded child not wanting to face his parent but too frightened to look away completely. "I don't *know*. I was angry at him. I still am. As a matter of fact, I hate the piece of shit." For just a second he looked me square in the eye again. "Terry, I hate my father."

"Because he's having an affair?"

"Yes. And because he doesn't care about me, or anyone except himself and maybe his mistress. He's exactly what you've said he is all along: a corrupt, self-indulgent philistine. I don't know if it's inherently wrong to make a shitload of money, and I don't know if adultery is always inexcusable, but I do know that my father would be a better, happier man with a tenth of what he's got and that my mother never did anything to deserve an unfaithful husband."

I proceeded with extreme caution. "Winston, I don't mean to

133

stoke the fires of your unrest here, but... that night in my car, after our little talk at The Carousel, didn't you sort of hint that your mother might have a little something on the side in Chicago?"

He lit a cigarette of his own and shook his head. "No," he said. "I don't recall that at all. Why do you bring it up, anyway?"

"Never mind. I just... I'm just not sure how fair it is to portray your father as Satan incarnate when there may be things you don't know. Things between your parents, I mean."

Skepticism played on his features. "My mother has nothing to do with this, Terry. This is about my father and me. Are you sure you're not just feeling guilty somehow for turning me against him? Because if you are, let me set your mind at ease: this has nothing to do with you, either. I mean, you definitely made me aware of some pretty shady shit he was involved in, but no, I began hating my father long before I ever met you. You were just sort of the... the catalyst that brought my feelings to the forefront, I guess."

"Great," I said wanly. I felt impossibly tired. "I've always wanted to be a catalyst." I flicked my cigarette onto the street. It was squashed a moment later under the brawny tire of a blue pick-up truck. The day's last threads of sunlight wove their way through the elms on the opposite side of the street.

"So what *are* you going to do with the photos?" he asked,

134

watching the traffic.

"I don't know. What would *you* have me do with them?"

"I guess that's up to you."

I lit another cigarette. "So you knew they'd be in the bedroom when I went upstairs? How?"

"I knew Vanessa would be there, and I knew my dad would be drunk by the time the party started winding down. So it was a pretty reasonable guess." He paused, considered. "Didn't you hear them before you opened the door? You must have."

I dragged on my cigarette, summoned a hazy memory of the night before. "I guess so. But I was a little drunk. Disoriented."

He gave me a listless, dubious smile. I smiled back. I couldn't help it.

"Okay," I said. "I was *very* drunk. And intrigued, I admit."

"I figured you would be."

"You gave it that much thought, huh?"

"Some."

We suspended our conversation while a bony, white-haired man with an iPod jogged past us on the sidewalk. A fiery band of purple-orange twilight, like a fresh bruise, siphoned into the elms the parting whispers of dusk. When the jogger was out of earshot I said, "Who is she? This Vanessa woman, I mean. Do you know?"

"Of course I know." He looked at me, disbelieving. "You mean you don't?"

"How could I?"

"I just thought you would, given who her is husband is and all."

"Who's her husband?"

"Ben Grent. The guy running for state Supreme Court."

It would be a wild understatement to say that I was fairly jolted by this news.

Winston told me he had walked to the park from his father's house and I offered to give him a ride home. He tightened the laces on his moccasins and shook his head. "No, thanks. Might not be a good idea. If he sees you he'll kill you."

I started to laugh, taking his remark as a joke. Then I saw the disquiet in his eyes and my laughter dried up fast. "He's that pissed?"

"Yeah. He's that pissed."

"Has he talked to you?"

"Only to ask how I know you, and why on God's earth I invited you to the party."

"What'd you tell him?"

"That I met you last month at his banquet and you're interested in the piano and we just sort of hit it off, and that I didn't think he'd mind my inviting a friend."

"To which he replied?"

"'How the fuck did he get a key to my bedroom?'"

I swallowed hard. My mind was reeling. "And you said?"

"I said that I didn't know and that I didn't want to look at his big fat cheating face."

"Jesus. You said that?"

"Yeah."

"You're lucky he didn't kill *you*."

He nodded absently. "I should get going. Call me on my cell phone when you decide what you're going to do with the pictures. "

Suddenly I found myself enormously frustrated with him. "Winston, I told you, I haven't even gotten them developed."

"You will," he said, and then he was gone.

My appetite was gnawing at me again on the way home, and I hadn't done any grocery shopping in almost a week, so I stopped at a sit-in deli in Oakland for a turkey and bacon sandwich. A copy of that day's edition of the Pittsburgh *Tribune-Review* (the *Post-Gazette*'s rival publication) was lying on the table where I sat, and the lead on the bottom half of the front page leapt out at me: "MID-ATLANTIC POWER, ALLEGHENY COAL TO FORM MULTI-MILLION DOLLAR MERGER."

I ate my sandwich slowly, reading the first four paragraphs of the article:

> AP - The Cleveland-based Mid-Atlantic Power and Pittsburgh based Allegheny Coal have signed a $129.6 million merger, Darren Sedgewick, president of Mid-Atlantic Power, announced Thursday. The merger will take effect on July 1 and is expected to benefit holders of stock in both companies.
>
> "This is big news," Sedgewick said in a telephone interview this morning. "It's very exciting to think that both companies' services will be strengthened by this, and more readily available to consumers as a result." Sedgewick would not comment on what the merger might mean for the cost of his company's product, but hinted that he does not foresee any significant hikes. "This merger is less about boosting profits and

more about boosting quality and efficiency," he said.

Archibald Lancaster, president and CEO of Mid-Atlantic's parent company, Dacey Energy, has reportedly agreed to con-\tribute over $100 million in cash and indebtedness to Allegheny Coal at the time of the merger in exchange for 40 million shares of the company's common stock. The merger will result in current shareholders of Allegheny Coal owning approximately 50 percent of the new Allegheny and the current shareholders of Mid-Atlantic, of whom Lancaster is the foremost, owning approximately 50 percent of the new Mid-Atlantic.

"We are delighted to combine these two companies into a powerful industry player," Lancast-er said in a statement issued by his Richmond, VA office. "The combination of Allegheny's mines and strong balance sheet with Mid-Atlantic's ambitious new infrastructure and three new Pennsylvania plants will create a well-financed, senior energy producer with cash costs in the lowest quartile of world production. The new Mid-Atlantic Power will be the elevated platform from which both concerns might continue to pursue their aggressive growth strategy."

Here my concentration was broken by the onset of a quarrel between a customer and the girl behind the deli counter. "I called ahead twenty minutes ago," the customer was barking, his timbre perhaps two octaves below a shout. "It's only five sandwiches! How long can it take to make five sandwiches?"

"Sir," the girl countered, "I told you it would take at least half an hour. We're pretty busy, as you can see." She was right: there were about eight people in line and another half-dozen or so waiting on their food. I had had to wait ten minutes for my own.

The customer sighed, his indignation giving way to hauteur. "Well, next time I'll be taking my business elsewhere. This is an outrage."

The deli girl blinked. "An outrage?"

"Yes! It is!"

"I'm sorry you feel that way, sir."

"Don't patronize me!"

The girl, God bless her, fought hard to keep her cool. "I'm not patronizing you, sir."

Now an angular, unhappy-looking man, presumably the deli's manager, emerged from the kitchen and told the girl he'd like a word with her in private. Timidly, she followed him into the kitchen. I watched the grumbling customer, watched his face light up as he pondered the just deserts the girl would presently face, and felt a gargantuan contempt for him. I hated him, truth to tell, could scarcely quell my urge to strangle the life out of him. A minute later, the girl stalked silently out of the kitchen, her mascara already running, her apron shed and hair now liberated from its oppressive bun. She was quite beautiful, as I recall.

The man smirked as she darted past him, then turned and saw me glaring at him. For a brief instant his eyes seemed to register the profound smallness of what he had just done, to evince some damp flicker of shame, and then the manager kindly exonerated him with an assurance that his order would be ready shortly. "Thank you," the man said, shifting uncomfortably on his feet. "I appreciate that."

My sandwich half-eaten, I rose and followed the distraught young woman outside.

"I saw what happened," I said as she bent to unlock the driver's-side door of her decrepit Chevy Corsica. "With that asshole customer, I mean."

She opened the door but did not get inside. There was a dim wariness in her eyes, but mostly just hurt and bewilderment. "Oh yeah?"

"Yeah. I'm really sorry."

"Not half as sorry as I am," she sniveled. "My boyfriend was laid off three days ago."

"I'm sorry. Where did he work?"

"McJurgen's. It's a shipping warehouse. Ever heard of it?"

"Yeah, I've heard of it."

"Looks like we won't be renewing the lease on our apartment." She appeared on the verge of breaking down again. "We worked really hard for that, too."

I went to her, thought about hugging her and then decided she might take it the wrong way, what with my being a perfect stranger and all. Instead I just patted her on the arm. "I'm sure you'll find another job. A better job."

Her eyes swam with dread and the beginnings of a familiar, finally baseless hope. "Yeah, maybe. Or maybe we'll go on welfare."

"Jesus," I said. "Is it really that bad?"

She wiped her nose on her sleeve. Ordinarily the act might have been unseemly, but under the circumstances it only compounded my pity for her. "It's always that bad," she said.

Without really thinking I reached into my back pocket, removed my wallet, and plucked out a fifty dollar bill. "Here," I said, handing it to her. "I know you don't know me from Adam, and I don't know you from Eve, but... take this, please. It's not much, but it'll help with the little stuff for the next couple of days."

She made no move to take the money, her suspiciousness (or perhaps her pride) momentarily stronger than her survival instinct. "Oh, gee. I... I don't think I could do that, mister."

"Take it," I repeated. "It's not working for me." She was still hesitating, so I gave her one last prod: "Don't worry, I'm not crazy or anything. I'm actually a reporter for the *Post-Gazette*. Familiar with it?"

"Yeah," she said, and now she started to reach for the money. "My dad reads it all the time."

"In that case, he's probably read hundreds of my articles. So I sort of owe him this, as thanks."

Her hand closed around the bill. "Thank you," she said quietly. "God, thank you so much. I won't forget this."

"Don't mention it."

Then she collapsed in my arms, weeping violently, and by instinct I stroked her hair, endeavoring at length to calm her.

By the time I got home I was exhausted, physically and mentally. Relieved to find no more messages on my answering machine, I went straight into my bedroom, undressed, turned out the light, and crawled into bed. An hour or so later, growling with frustration, I threw the sheets back and groped around on the bedside table for the remote control to the 17" TV I kept on a little stand in the corner of my room. I was tired, yes, but unable to sleep. I kept thinking of that roll of film in the shoebox in my closet, and of the girl at the deli, and of my abortive interview with Archie.

So I turned on the TV, and, finding nothing I could stand to watch, went into the kitchen to fix myself a bourbon and soda. After two gulps I felt much better, and took the rest of it back to bed with me. I was about to switch off the television when I saw that a repeat of the previous night's *Late Show* was coming on. Long a devout fan of Mr. Letterman's, I figured I'd watch the monologue while I nursed what was left of my drink, then try again to grab some shuteye.

But when the monologue was over, and my glass emptied, I felt strangely more awake than I had all day. So I got up, refilled my glass, and went back to bed to watch the "Top Ten" segment and the first celebrity interview. The latter was with a very popular young actress whom I had seen in a few films and liked, but found myself resenting, typically enough, as the interview wore on. At one point Dave made a crack about how much money the actress had commanded for her last picture (a sum, twenty million dollars to be precise, so astonishingly astronomical as to dwarf the annual salary of the nation's most prominent brain surgeon), in reply to which the actress giggled sheepishly and shrugged her shoulders, as if to say: *Hey, I'm not the one who decides these things! Go talk to my agent.* I thought of Winston, of what he had told me at his father's house, and when the show went to commercial I changed the channel.

Now I found myself watching a sports show, in which two well-groomed, clean-shaven men in dark suits sat behind a kidney-shaped desk and argued volubly about whether some college basketball star was overrated and what his prospects might be in the NBA. "Todd Hanes has a very bright future," one of the commentators said, "no matter what team he decides to play with. And you can bet he'll fetch a very attractive sign-on fee, Brian." Brian did not demur, and, indeed, seemed every bit as comfortable as did his co-host with Todd Hanes' collecting millions of dollars for playing a game he had presumably once played for free.

I changed the channel again, was now watching a game show hosted by a geeky red-haired guy in a Hawaiian shirt and tweed coat the color of egg yolk. "Sarah," he boomed at one of the female contestants, "if you answer this question correctly, you win the Ford Explorer. Otherwise, Sam will get a shot at it." The camera panned to the shiny new truck, then back to an ecstatically screaming Sarah. The host continued: "Sarah, name one of the two Japanese cities on which the United States dropped an atomic bomb at the close of World War II." Sarah's expression was that of a woman who had just been asked to recite the periodic table from memory. After a tense five seconds she blurted, "Tokyo!" The host shook his head, admirably concealing his shock at the contestant's stupidity. "No, Sarah, I'm sorry, that's incorrect." The audience expressed its sympathy with a collective "Awwww."

The host now turned to Sam, a fat man in a New York Knicks jersey. Tufts of his armpit hair were appallingly visible. "Sam," asked the host, "are you ready to win that Ford Explorer?" Sam bellowed his agreement, applauding perhaps only to horrify viewers with an even clearer shot of his profuse pit-hair. "Okay, Sam: who was the vice president of the United States under Jimmy Carter?" The host had barely posed the question when Sam began

146

to shriek Walter Mondale's name over and over. Bells and whistles sounded. Confetti fell from the sky. Sam the Armpit Man had won a twenty-nine-thousand-dollar vehicle for knowing a piece of trivia familiar to many ninth-graders.

Disgusted, I killed first the last drops of my bourbon and then the TV. Within five minutes I was asleep. I had a dream that night, an incredibly vivid dream, and by the evening of the following day a plan was pretty well formed in my mind. But it was the bombshell of Monday morning that transmuted this plan from idle fantasy to concrete aim.

On Monday morning I was fired.

16

My boss, an officious asshole whose parents had had the gall to assign him a name so innocent-sounding as "Kyle," called me into his office about two minutes after I sat down at my desk. What's more, he actually came and got me himself, rather than, as was his custom, relegate the task to some lowly assistant. So I knew right from the start that it was something serious.

Kyle Barnes was a stocky man who carried himself stiffly and generally behaved as if he were in great pain. He seemed particularly uneasy when he sat, continually contracting and expanding himself as though testing and finding inhospitable the space he occupied. He sighed, he fidgeted, he repeatedly folded and unfolded his hands. But, more than anything, it was his decidedly unattractive habit of crinkling his nose and twitching his eyebrows when he spoke that nettled his employees. He was in top form that morning, merging all of these quirks with a precision and diligence I found nauseatingly surreal.

"Terry," he said, his tone obligingly ceremonious, eyes flitting about the room like a newly uncaged bird. "This isn't going to be easy." Already I knew what was about to happen, if only in the dusky reaches of my subconscious. I think I was too scared to know it otherwise.

"It isn't?" My voice sounded as if it were coming from several light years away. It was timid, gutless, a child's voice. I was ashamed of it, loathed it.

He shook his head somberly, still averting his eyes. "No. Not one bit. I like you, Terry. I think you know I like you."

"I prefer to believe so, yes." I passed a slick palm over one of my pant legs.

"And you've done excellent work for us, on the whole."

"On the whole?"

"Well, some of your recent pieces haven't been exactly

stellar, particularly that article on Weirton Steel's new low-carbon and free-cutting division." His eyes finally found mine, held there for a moment before sliding to his desk blotter. "Which, if you remember, you turned in almost a full week late. You've also developed something of a proclivity for tardiness."

"Yes," I said at once, convinced that manufacturing an air of rare maturity and accountability was my best chance of staying employed. "That's true. All of that is true. And you're right that the quality of my work has been slipping a tad of late. But, as I believe I recently told you, sir, I've not been sleeping well, and -"

"Yes," he cut in, probably to forestall the litany of flimsy excuses I would have otherwise unleashed upon him. "I recall your saying something to that effect. I'm sorry to hear there's been no improvement in the situation. And I have no doubt that, whatever the reasons for your... lapses of professional deportment, they're both legitimate and extenuating. Nevertheless..."

Always, I thought morbidly, *always there is a "nevertheless."*

"Ours is a business like any other," he went on, "and in my capacity as editor-in-chief, I am obligated to act in its best interests."

"One of which is firing me?"

He nodded gravely, folding his hands on the blotter. "I'm

afraid so, Terry. Please, don't think that I made this decision lightly."

"No," I said flatly. I was on another planet, one in which coherent thought forever succumbed to gut-wrenching pain. "I wouldn't dream of it."

"I can hardly believe the words myself, even as they spill from my own lips."

"You're not alone there, Kyle."

"Here," he said, reaching into a drawer. He produced a plain white envelope which he slid across the desk. "Take this."

I opened the envelope and removed a check for fifteen thousand dollars, which was about three months' pay. Three months for eight years of service. "What's this?" I asked, knowing full well what it was. And still my voice sounded to me as though it were emanating from deep space.

"Severance pay," he said. He forced a bland smile. "It's in addition to your pension, of course."

"There won't be much of *that*. And I won't see a dime of it for another thirty years."

"Yes, well." He gave a mild shrug, barely distinguishable from one of his repertoire of twitches.

I leaned forward in my chair. I spoke now as if I were

possessed, as if I had no fear at all and nothing to lose. And I guess I didn't. "Say, Kyle, this wouldn't have anything to do with what happened this weekend at Archie Lancaster's house, would it?"

His eyes narrowed as he leaned forward in his chair. "I beg your pardon, Terry?"

"You know, the pictures I took?"

Kyle blinked. "Pictures? Terry, I have no idea what you're talking about."

I smiled, cautiously on the outside but resplendently on the inside. "You know, the pictures I took of Archibald Lancaster cheating on his wife with Vanessa Grent."

Kyle gasped. "Jesus Christ, Terry! What the hell are you on about?"

"I think you know," I said. "I think you do, Kyle."

"Well, I don't. Anyhow, if you're willing to accept the check, we'll have HR draw up a contract -"

Now I was leaning so far across the desk that my face wasn't more than a foot from his. "I think he called here this morning, that's what I think. Not more than a minute after you sat down behind that desk, I'll bet. Offered you a king's ransom to get rid of me, made it sound like an act of charity, like you'd be doing the world a favor. And you bought it, of course, bought it hook, line, and sinker, because you're every bit as money-hungry and depraved as all the rest of them. Christ, there's no justice. Thanks for proving that to me, Kyle. Thanks for being a splendid and graphic incarnation of everything I hate about this world. You've done me a great service, you really have, sir. Because now I know what I need to do, and exactly how to do it. So yes, thank you. Thank you, Kyle."

I stood, check in hand, and stormed out of the office.

My erstwhile boss sat silently, momentarily rendered mute.

I went home, stashed the check in a kitchen drawer, retrieved the film, and took it to a store downtown to get it developed. I moved in a mental fog, not really thinking but just acting, acting in accord with the scheme I had hatched. To kill the hour it would take to get the film developed, I drove to the Blue Cat for an early lunch. My favorite server there, a kind-faced forty-something named Tonya, brought me a glass of milk and a grilled cheese sandwich. Sensing my despondency, she asked if there was anything wrong.

"Oh," I said, "not really. Just got fired from my job for taking pornographic pictures of a multi-billionaire coal tycoon and now intend to use them in the most far-reaching act of extortion ever known to humankind." I looked at her, smiling languidly. "You know: same old, same old."

She smiled back and tucked her pad into her apron. "Just holler at me if you need anything else," she said.

I hadn't planned to look at them until I got home, thinking it best to examine the evidence in private, but found I couldn't help myself. My car, I decided, was private enough. I had to see them, had to see whether my plan had any chance of success. It took me about five seconds to determine that it did. That, as a matter of fact, it had virtually no chance of *failure*. Grinning madly, I stuffed the negatives into my trousers' pocket and the photos themselves into the glove compartment.

Then I drove to the building that housed Archibald Lancaster's Pittsburgh office.

It was a twelve-story glass-and-steel job on Fort Duquesne Boulevard, near the bridge. I parked around back, went in, and asked the biddy working the lobby desk on which floor I might find Archie's office.

"The ninth," she said. "But you need an appointment to see him."

"That won't be a problem."

She looked at me with mild disfavor and went back to reading her book (a Mary Higgins Clark yarn - what else?). I went to the bank of elevators on the far side of the lobby, pressed the call button, and whistled while I waited for the car to arrive. A young man in a navy-blue suit appeared beside me (and, of course, pressed the already-lit call button). I smiled at him. He did not smile back.

"Pleasant weather we're having, isn't it?" I asked him.

He nodded and mumbled assent.

"I'm about to blackmail the fifth richest man in the world," I said. To emphasize the insanity of the affair I added, "For as much as a hundred million dollars."

He appraised me through cool, narrow eyes, his red lips tightly pursed. "All right," he said.

I chuckled. The car arrived and the doors opened. We got in. "You'll understand what I mean when you read tomorrow's paper," I said. The doors closed and we started to move. "Or the next day's."

"Hello," I said to Archibald Lancaster's secretary. "I need to see Mr. Lancaster."

"Do you have -"

"An appointment? No. No, I don't. But I don't need one. Just tell him it's Terrance Farmer from the *Post-Gazette*. He'll want to see me right away, I'm sure."

She looked at me levelly, her expression a veritable carbon copy of the lobby receptionist's. She pressed a button on her intercom. "Mr. Lancaster?"

"Yes?" Archie's voice came through. He sounded tired, harried. I was not surprised.

"There's a..." She took her finger off the button and looked at me inquiringly.

"Terrance Farmer."

She pressed the button again. "There's a Terrance Farmer here to see you, sir."

Short pause, then: "Send him in."

"He'll see you now," his secretary said, as if I hadn't heard him.

"Thanks." I gave her a hearty, shit-eating grin and entered the lucullan office of one Archibald Lancaster.

"Archie," I said. "How are you?"

The walls were stained-oak panels, the couch black leather, the desk mahogany, the carpet the color of plums. A floor globe, this one maple (no doubt hand-carved and hand-painted), sat in the far left corner, a bonsai tree in the far right. A wall-length window behind his swivel chair looked out on the Pittsburgh skyline. "Terry," he said weakly, pointing to the couch. "Please, sit."

I sat. I said nothing.

"I called you over the weekend. Several times."

"Yes, I got your messages."

"But you didn't return my calls."

I cleared my throat. "I needed time. To think about things."

He squirmed in his chair, opened a desk drawer. "And you have? Thought about things, that is?"

I nodded slowly, watched him pluck a cigar from the cedar humidor on his desk and light it. "Yes," I said. "I have."

"Good. That's good, Mr. Farmer. I'm glad to hear it." He puffed on his cigar, exhaled, and gestured at the humidor. "Care for one? They're Cubans."

"No, thank you."

"You're sure?"

"Yes."

He nodded, forced a little smile. "So you've come to your senses, then? You're willing to turn over the photographs and the negatives?"

"Sure I am," I said. I sounded affable, malleable, reasonable. I was, of course, anything but.

"That's excellent." He gave a tense, wavering laugh. "That's a huge relief, Mr. Farmer."

"But of course I'll need something in return."

His jowls slackened. All his false jocundity fled. He took a momentous breath, his whale of a torso heaving pregnantly. "Of course you will. I expected as much." He reached into a drawer and removed a checkbook. He tore off a check, took up his fountain pen, and leaned in to write. "Twenty-five thousand will do, I trust?"

I shook my head. "No," I said. "No, it won't."

"You're looking to play hardball, aren't you, Mr. Farmer?"

I smiled. "Oh, go ahead and call me Terry. By the time we're through here you will be, anyway."

He put the pen down and reclined in his chair, puffed his cigar. "Do you have the photos with you?"

"Maybe."

"Could I see them?"

"You don't need to. All you need to know is that they show everything. Clearly."

He sat up and put his cigar in a hexagonal crystal ashtray. "They do, do they? Even Vanessa's face?"

"One of them does, yes."

157

"One of three, is it?"

I nodded, worked out a crick in my neck. "Yes, three extremely revealing, graphic photographs."

He scratched his chin, tapped his cigar. "If you think you're getting more than fifty thousand, Terry, you're deluded." He reclined again.

I leaned forward, maintained flawless composure. "I wouldn't take less than a million for the pictures, Archie. But the pictures may actually be the least of your worries."

He rocked in his chair, arched his eyebrows. Through the window I spied a clear-blue, high-noon, cloudless summer sky, and drew from it an odd and invincible courage.

"I have a tape," I lied. "Of you on the phone to Ben Grent."

Archie laughed. "My ass you do."

"Okay," I said. "I don't."

"Of me saying what, allegedly?"

"Essentially, that he can't lose. Not with you on his side."

He shook his head, grinning. "How could you possibly have taped such a conversation?"

"You think journalists can't have lines tapped?"

His grin faded, but his incredulity held its own. "I call your bluff," he said.

"I'm not bluffing. But, hey, if you doubt the existence of the Grent tape, you might be curious to hear the Cunningham tape."

He set his cigar in the ashtray. "The Cunningham tape?"

"You know, Andrew Cunningham. Your man at the Inez plant. The man you fired." I shifted on the couch, crossed my arms. "You do remember him, don't you?"

"Of course I do."

"Yeah, well, so do I. I also remember calling him after the spill. And offering to help him, to help him expose you."

"Oh?"

"That's right. I wired him. I have every word of it on tape."

Archie swiveled in his chair, kneaded one of its arms. "I can't believe you," he said. "And I can't not believe you, either."

"Well, you ought to believe me. I don't bullshit, Archie. Unlike you, I can't afford to."

He stubbed out his half-smoked cigar. "Would a million satisfy you?"

"You got me fired, didn't you?"

He blinked. "Excuse me?"

"You know, from the newspaper. You called my boss and got me fired. Did you just pay him off, or did you make up a story about me? Something really nasty, maybe, to ease his conscience?"

"I don't know what you're talking about."

"Of course you don't."

He sighed. He retrieved another cigar but didn't light it, just laid it on his desk beside the plastic cup holding his nylon American desk-flag. "Well, look, whatever you have on me, I'd be happy to settle this whole thing for a million."

"I'll take a million for myself," I said, "but everyone else will need a lot more than that. Ninety-nine million, say. That's good enough to start, at least."

Now his face was that of a man who had seen someone raised from the dead. "Everyone else?"

"All the people," I said, "that you never think about. The poor, the sick, the lonely and forgotten. The voiceless. The disenfranchised. The unempowered. You know the lot. You've heard about them on the news, I'm sure."

"What the hell are you talking about?"

"The little people," I said. "You know the bunch I mean. They comprise eighty, eighty-five percent of the country's population."

Finally he lit his fresh cigar. I don't know why he didn't simply relight the other one. Maybe he was just rubbing the extravagance in my face, reminding me just how much clout he carried, how heavily his fist would fall if he decided to bring it down on me. "The little people?"

"Yeah," I said. "The people who have shit-nothing. The people without college degrees, fancy homes, fancy cars, jobs they aspired to or aspire to keep. The ones who flip burgers, dig ditches, push papers, lift hoods, hang power lines, move furniture, and... and mine coal. Come on, Archie, you know the ones. Don't pretend you don't. You see them every day without seeing them."

He took three quick puffs on his Cuban. "And you want me to give them ninety-nine million dollars?"

"Seems fair, yeah. A million to me, ninety-nine million to them."

"And how, exactly, do you propose I do that?"

"You come with me," I said. "Around the country, doling it out, bit by bit. It'll take three months, six at the most. Then you can have the photos, the negatives, and the tapes. And I'll leave you alone. For good."

He smirked. "You're out of your mind."

"Maybe." Now I was leaning in so far my elbows were practically on his desk. "But you know I have the pictures, and you know I just might have the tapes, too." I paused. "And it's not as if you didn't have the money."

For a long time he said nothing, just went on puffing his

cigar. Then he said, "Give me forty-eight hours to think about it, will you?"

"Sure," I said, "if you need them. And please, feel free to call Grent and ask him whether the guy who has pictures of you fucking his wife might have the two of you on tape, discussing his campaign. Also, give Cunningham a call and ask him if the reporter who helped nail your sorry ass really did wire him up on the day you fired him. I'm sure he'll be more than forthcoming, Archie."

Archie scowled, incensed beyond measure. "Why didn't you come forward sooner with these tapes, if you really have them? What were you waiting for?"

"Why," I said, standing up, "a moment like this, of course."

17

How to describe the tension of that evening, the inner turmoil and unrest, the way the hours crawled like crippled refugees seeking shelter from a cruel tyrant? Well, I can't. All I can tell you, with any certainty, is that I sat in a darkened apartment with the door locked and the curtains drawn, smoking one cigarette after another and drinking glass after glass of bourbon, awaiting word not only on my own future but that of both a corporate deity and thousands of financially and emotionally starved nobodies. I did not, in those viscous and introspective hours, fancy myself a saint or humanitarian, not once for even a moment. I deemed myself, rather, a desperate man who had embarked on the only course which, at least in his own mind, might redeem him and set straight the follies of his past.

Whether because of Archie or my own miscues or some combination of the two, I had lost my job. Even if Archie had had nothing to do with my being fired, finding another job in the newspaper business would be anything but a painless task; and, if Archie *had* played a role in the affair, then it would be next to impossible. Thus, I was potentially looking not only at the loss of my livelihood but at that of my apartment and car as well, not to mention my dignity: basically every recognizable element of the life I had built for myself, everything from which I then derived my sense of self-identity. With all that at sake, I had acted purely on unthinking and unreasoned instinct, the barest and maybe truest thing a man can claim as his own, the final arbiter of all human affairs.

After four or five bourbons, as the sun went down at last, a resigned and superficial calm fell over me, and, in its cool if dubious shade, I phoned Winston.

"Come over," I pleaded. "You have to."

"Why?"

"Because," I said, "I'm falling apart."

"Oh, Jesus."

"Tell me about it. Winston, I'm at my wit's end here. I need someone to talk to. You're the only person who could possibly understand."

"It's that bad, huh?"

"It's that bad."

He sighed. "Okay. Give me directions. I'll be there as soon as I can."

I gave him directions, and fifteen minutes later he knocked on my door.

"Come in,come in."

He came in. I directed him to the couch in the living room. He sat down. I offered him a drink. He said, of course, that he'd take a beer. Luckily I had two Bud Lights kicking around in the fridge, and brought him one. He twisted off the cap and guzzled a quarter of the bottle. Slightly more relaxed now, he settled into the couch, watched me take a seat in the rocking chair by the window, and buried his eyes in mine. For the first time since I had met him, I

164

barely noticed his beauty.

"You saw him, didn't you? My dad?"

"Yes. He told you?"

"No." He took a gulp of his beer. "But I can see it on your face."

"Well, yeah, I saw him. Right after I got fired."

"Oh, fuck."

"Yeah."

"You think he did it?"

I shook my head. "I don't know, Winston. I don't suppose it really matters at this point."

"Well, what did you say to him? What did *he* say? Did you show him the pictures?"

"Slow down." I stood, went to the kitchen, fixed myself another bourbon, and returned to the living room. "Did he come home tonight?"

"Yeah. A little after six, same as usual. I didn't say anything to him, though. I'd be surprised if we ever spoke again." He took another swig of his beer. "After that I went to meet some friends for a pizza."

"Did I interrupt that?"

"No, I was just getting into my car when you called."

"Okay."

"Well?"

I sipped my bourbon. "Well, I told him I had the photographs. He knew that, of course. I also told him I had tapes of him on the phone with Ben Grent and Andrew Cunningham, the man in charge of the Inez plant. The man he fired after the spill."

"But you don't, do you?"

I nursed my drink, lit a cigarette. "Of course I don't."

"Did he believe you, though?"

"Hell, I don't know. I couldn't tell. He might have. He might not have."

"So what'd you do? Did you ask for money?"

"Yes."

"How much?"

I ashed my cigarette in a vase on the windowsill. "A hundred million dollars."

Winston literally stood and cheered. "All right! Sonofabitch! You ballsy piece-a shit!"

Grinning despite myself, I motioned for him to sit down. "Calm down," I said. "I didn't request it for myself."

Confusion washed over his face. "Then who'd you request it for?"

"Them," I said, jerking a thumb toward the window behind me. "All the sorry bastards out there."

"What do you mean?"

I took a drink. "You know," I said, "all the people who *aren't* on TV. The non-celebrities, the non-gurus, the non-moguls, the non-anybodies. Everyone your father isn't."

"I don't get it."

"I told him I wanted a million for myself and ninety-nine million for them. I told him we'd go around the country, handing it out little by little. It's always been a dream of mine. Except, in the dream, I always did it with my own money, and without having to blackmail anyone."

"Holy shit."

"Yeah."

I got up. My drink was empty, and so was his beer. "Want another one?"

"Sure."

I poured myself yet another bourbon, quite drunk now, and plucked the second, last Bud Light from my fridge. I had never felt quite so weird or lost or excited in my life.

"What do you think he'll do?" Winston asked me.

"I think he'll ask to see the photos."

"Will you show them to him? I mean, do they show enough to... to give you leverage?"

"Yeah," I said. "They do."

"You can see her face?"

"In one of them you can."

"Then he'll pay," he said. "He'll do it."

"You think so?"

He drank off the head of his beer. "Yeah. I do."

"You think he has a hundred million to spare?"

Winston laughed. "You should have asked for a billion," he said.

I smiled and sipped my drink.

"Terry," he said, "you're one crazy son of a bitch."

"No," I said. "I'm just jobless and sick of people getting screwed. You know?"

"Yeah."

"I don't see what else I could have done."

"I'm glad you did what you did."

"It's insane, though. He'll never go through with it."

"What choice does he have?"

I sighed, coughed, lit another cigarette. "He could have me

killed, I guess."

"He'd never do that."

"He's never been in a position like this before. Has he?"

"Not that I know of."

"Then there's no calculating his next move."

He downed his beer. "I can't believe you were fired."

"Me, either."

"I'm sorry."

"So am I."

He bit his bottom lip, cleared his throat. "Can I come with you?"

"Come with me where?"

"On your trip around the country, with my dad. Giving away his money."

"Winston."

"I'd really enjoy that."

I polished off my drink. "Let's just see what he says, okay? It's way too early to be worrying about things like that."

"Okay."

I smiled at him and rattled my glass, which now contained nothing but ice. "You really calmed me down tonight. I was on the verge of losing it." I hesitated, starting to notice his beauty again.

169

"So, thanks."

"No problem."

I looked at the clock. It was close to ten-thirty. I was drunk and ready for bed. "I think I'm going to turn in, Winston."

"Right," he said. "Sure."

I led him to the door. For a moment we looked at each other, and I was certain, *positive* there was something in that look, something besides mere friendship. Nevertheless, I could not bring myself to kiss him, was not quite drunk or stupid or fearless enough, and simply hugged him instead. He did not resist my embrace but did not exactly return it, either.

"Good night," I said.

"Good night."

I closed the door behind him and, finding myself severely depressed, went directly to bed, seeing little point in brushing my teeth when my very fate was hanging in the balance.

The phone woke me up a little after seven-thirty the next morning.

The ringing, muffled through the quilt I had wrapped around my head in the night, was the first thing I registered; the second thing was the hatchet buried between between my eyes,

170

thunderbolts of exquisite pain radiating through my forehead and temples. My eyes themselves had been transformed overnight into amphibian goggles, grotesque magnifiers through which appeared a world of hideously bright objects in sickeningly stark relief. Three or four bottles of mouthwash, I figured, and I'd barely even notice the taste of cat shit currently saturating my tongue.

I beat away the quilt and scrabbled about for the phone on my bedside table. I croaked a "hello" barely distinguishable to my own ears.

"Terrance Farmer?"

I sat up a little, coughing. "Archie?"

"Yes, this is Archibald Lancaster. Listen, I apologize for calling so early in the morning, but the situation before us is unusually urgent, as I'm sure you can appreciate. And I have a hunch that neither of us has been sleeping particularly well of late, anyhow."

I shook my head as if to clear it and rubbed my eyes with the balls of my thumbs, digging out sleep. "Actually, you woke me up."

"Oh. I see. Well, my apologies. Shall I call back later?"

"No, no, that's fine. I'm awake now." The emphasis I put on the last word was scarcely detectable, but I imagine Archie detected it, just the same.

"Good, because I think it's time you and I finally put this unpleasant business to rest."

I sat upright completely now, doing my best to ignore the hatchet; I knew it would be several hours and three cups of coffee before it started to loosen. "I believe I've already stated the terms of any such agreement, Archie. Do we need to review them?"

"Well," he said, clearly startled by my tone, "I don't suppose so. But I will need to review the documents."

"The documents?"

"The photographs."

"Oh, right." I carried the phone into the bathroom and filled a cup with water from the faucet. "I guess that could be arranged."

"When?"

I downed the water. "When are you available?"

"Now."

"Don't you have work?"

"I'm taking the morning off. I think this matter is rather important enough to warrant it."

"Okay. Where?"

"My house. I assume you can find your way back?"

"Yes."

"Then I'll see you in an hour."

I refilled my cup. "Better make it two."

I guess my hangover peaked around the time I knocked on Archie's door, because I almost swooned when Juan Carlos answered it. My vision went fuzzy, my stomach did a spectacular somersault I hadn't seen coming, and the next thing I knew I was down on one knee, torn between throwing up and passing out. A manilla envelope containing the photographs was clasped loosely in my right hand.

"Sir?" Juan Carlos asked (with what sounded like genuine concern). "Are you all right, sir?"

I gave a feeble nod and tried, to little avail, to erect myself. In a surprising and somewhat touching gesture, Juan Carlos put his hands under my arms to assist me. He held on until I appeared steady, then slowly released me. "Is it the heat, sir?"

"Partly." It was, viciously enough, the hottest day of the summer, the temperature topping eighty degrees by a quarter of ten. "Plus I have a condition."

"Condition, sir?"

"Yeah," I said. "Can't you see the hatchet sticking out of my head?"

Blank stare. "Hatchet, sir?"

173

"Uh, never mind, Juan Carlos. I'm here to see Mr. Lancaster. My name is Terry Farmer."

"Yes, Mr. Farmer, I remember you."

I looked expectantly at him. "May I come in?"

"Oh, yes, yes, by all means."

At last he stepped aside, and I, into the blessedly cool foyer of the Lancaster residence.

Within seconds Archie appeared at the top of the grand staircase, looking freshly scrubbed but poorly rested. He descended the stairs effortlully, as if weighed down with cement blocks, silently and with his head down. His right hand clutched the rail the whole time, perhaps lest vertigo strike. Dressed in a polo shirt and slacks, he might have been embarking on a weekend golf outing. Instead, he was readying himself for what undoubtedly promised to be the most intensely unpalatable encounter of his life.

"Terry," he said. "Thanks for coming on such short notice."

"Well, now that I'm unemployed I find that my schedule is pretty flexible." If this little barb caused Archie even the remotest shred of embarrassment, he didn't show it.

"Right, well, why don't we go into the kitchen and talk?"

"Yes, let's. Is Winston here?"

He halted in mid-stride, turned, and looked at me. His expression was half reprobation and half curiosity. What, exactly, did I want with his son? What, exactly, was going on between the two of us? "He's asleep. He stays up late."

"Ah."

"Mr. Farmer?"

"Yes?"

Archie nodded at Juan Carlos, who promptly retired to a room adjacent to the foyer. "I'd appreciate it if from now on you kept away from Winston. He doesn't need the likes of a blackguard like you meddling in his life, playing with his emotions. He's a very sensitive boy, and very impressionable. God knows what crazy ideas you've been filling his head with. Just the other day -"

"We're friends," I said instinctively. "We've become friends. Much because of his own doing, I might add."

"Friends? The two of you are friends?"

"That's right."

"Yes, well, you aren't anymore."

"Sir?"

"Come," he said, and I went.

He led me into the kitchen, told me to have a seat at the

great white table in the center of the room. He offered me something to drink. I heard myself almost ask for a beer (*sure would take the edge off that headache*), then told him I'd take a cup of black coffee. "But a glass of water first, please."

I saw him steal a glimpse at the manilla envelope I'd laid on the table. "A water and a coffee." He moved to one of the cabinets, opened it, brought down a glass, and filled it from the tap. I bet myself the water would be lukewarm. He walked over to the table and set the glass down.

"Thanks." I took a sip. It was lukewarm.

"I gather the photos are in there?" he asked, pointing to the envelope.

"Yes, they are."

"May I see them?"

I looked at the coffee maker on the counter. "What about my coffee?"

"Your coffee," he said through his teeth. "Of course."

He went to the coffee maker, poured water into the basket, scooped in a few heaps of coffee grounds, and flipped the switch. "One black coffee, coming right up."

"Thanks." I drank some more of my lukewarm water. I found that, my throat dry as it was, the temperature of the liquid scarcely mattered; the moisture alone was enormously gratifying. Still, I resented its being lukewarm, was convinced it was a deliberate slight.

He returned to the table and sat down. "Now, may I see them, please?"

"Sure," I said. "Knock yourself out."

He opened the envelope, turned it upside down, and let the photos slide out. He grabbed them up quickly, arranged them in a stack, and went through them with an obsessive, meticulous care. At one point he actually gasped. Even with my hangover I had to struggle not to laugh. The coffee had begun to percolate by the time he'd set them down and announced, "Those certainly are something." He looked at me, skittish and outraged. "Tell me again exactly what it is you'd need for them. Along with the negatives, of course."

Inwardly, I rejoiced. "Yes, I'm keeping those elsewhere. In a secure, undisclosed location, as they say."

"How much, dammit? A hundred million?"

I shook my head. "Not for me. Just a million for me."

"And ninety-nine million for *them*?" He waved a hand toward the front of the house, toward the street. "For people you don't even *know*?"

"Yes. That's right."

He stuffed the photographs back into the envelope and pushed it aside, glaring at me. "Why, goddammit? Tell me why. And no bullshit."

"Because," I said, "I care about them."

He barked a nasty, cynical laugh. "Oh, gimme a fuckin' break! What kind of bleeding-heart liberal claptrap is this? Are you part of some New Age cult or something? Honestly, Terry, give me a fucking *break!*"

I shook my head. "No. You don't deserve a break, Archie. You've already had a million more breaks than most people dare dream of." I drew the envelope toward me. "Besides, it's the truth. Hard as it may be for someone like you to believe it, *I actually give a shit.* I actually give a shit about people I don't even know, because... because I do, and because I'd might as well *know* them, if I know any of them. Because they're all the same, at least in one regard: due to circumstances almost entirely outside their control, they're doomed to lives they didn't ask for and basically don't want. They're broken, Archie, broken, abused, unhappy ciphers.

"Or, if they *are* happy, and *don't* feel abused and trod upon, it's a testament to their strength of character, the resilience of their spirit. Because God knows they don't have much *visibly* to be happy

178

about. They've just made the best of a difficult and unpleasant situation, have found a way to smile in the face of their hardship. You, on the other hand... well, with all due respect, sir, but it seems to me that more often than not you frown in the face of your good fortune. I mean, a man with all that you've got, every conceivable luxury at his fingertips, is so dissatisfied with his life that he seeks affection outside his marriage? That's incomprehensible to me."

Archie exploded, slamming his fists on the table. "You piece of shit! You haughty, judgmental, presumptuous piece of shit! What the hell do you know about me? What the hell do you know about my life, or my reasons for doing what I do? You don't know me! You don't know *anything* about me! Now you'd damned well better apologize, or I'll bury you *and* your fucking photographs as deep as my shovel can dig!"

I flinched, blinked, cleared my throat. "Jesus. Calm down, Archie. Look -"

"No! Don't you tell me to calm down, you pasty little weasel! I want an apology! I want a fucking *apology*!"

"All right, all right, I apologize!"

He nodded, his cheeks deeply flushed. "Okay, then. That's better."

Cautiously, I pointed to the coffee maker. "Um, sir? I think the coffee's ready."

He looked over his shoulder. "Right."

He stood, got some mugs from one of the cabinets, and poured us both some coffee.

"What's your angle, then?" he asked me. "Big-hearted journalist tortured by the plight of the poor? You wanna make a story out of this?"

I shook my head and sipped my coffee. "No, sir. Not the poor *per se*. The poor comprise all sorts of people, many of them lazy and willfully destitute. My concern, rather, is for the *working* poor. The people who earn a pittance for grueling, thankless labor, the kind of work that would break the likes of you and me inside of a week. The people who go home of a night, and survey their shoddy quarters, and think to themselves, 'Were I prettier, were I cleverer, were I luckier, I might own a decent home and have fewer blisters on my thumbs, and fewer corns on my feet. I might know some rest, some peace, some tranquility and real pride. But as it is I am a slave, sturdy but unrewarded, steadfast but unknown.' Those are the people I'm concerned with, Archie. And no, I have no interest in making a story out of this, though I can only imagine what flattering publicity *you'll* enjoy during our adventures." I paused.

"Seeing as I'm no longer a working journalist, I have no professional interest in what I'm proposing."

"You're full of it," Archie said. "You want the publicity for yourself, probably to launch a career in television. Though with the million dollars I guess you won't exactly need the work."

I shrugged. "Believe what you like. Now, what say you? Want the pictures?"

"Of course I want the pictures."

"Then deposit a million dollars in my bank account by nine o' clock Friday morning." I drew from my breast pocket a business card on the back of which I had jotted my account number and slid it across the table. "And get your bags packed. We'll leave at that same time."

"You just can't be serious."

"I just am."

He sipped his coffee and looked at me.

"Archie," I said, "you really ought to be thanking me."

"How's that?"

"Well, your reputation isn't exactly spotless these days, you know. What better way to make it over than with a long, humanitarian odyssey? The media will eat it up like candy. You'll be the darling of every major news outlet in the country. You can't buy PR like that. Only, you sort of *will* be. Indirectly, as it were. And what will it cost you? Nothing, really. With all your stocks and bonds and sundry holdings, you'll make up in interest every penny you give away, and then some. And who knows what it'll do for Dacey's profits? It certainly won't hurt it, that's for damn sure. So, look at it as a highly unorthodox form of image repair. 'Reputation restoration,' as it were."

I could see the wheels turning in his head. There was a sudden, calculating glint in his eye. "And what do I tell the board of directors? The stockholders? My employees?"

"Tell them you're going on a brief sabbatical. Tell them you're feeling inordinately generous. What does it really matter? You own the goddamned place. And it's not like you couldn't run things from the road. This is the Information Age, Archie! It's become almost unfashionable to communicate face-to-face."

"Well," he said, putting his mug to his lips, "I suppose that's true. Or I could appoint a proxy. Tim Ballmer, vice chairman of the board, would do a fine job, I'm sure."

"Glad you've seen the light."

He took a deep breath. "I still think you're insane."

I shrugged again. "Maybe I am. But, crazy or not, I'm holding

182

all the chips." I hardened my gaze. "Aren't I, Archie?"

He stood and carried his mug to the sink. "All right, Mr. Farmer. Give me another twenty-four hours to think it over." He turned to me. "All right?"

"Fine," I said, getting up myself now. "But twenty-four is all you're getting. If I haven't heard from you by noon tomorrow, I'll take the pictures to every newspaper in the state. The tapes, too."

"Tapes my ass," he muttered.

"I'm sorry, Archie, I missed that. Come again?"

He stood with his hands gripping the counter-top, staring vacantly out the window. "You can show yourself out."

And so I did, bidding Juan Carlos a good day and assuring him that things would be better soon.

18

My door frame was cracked. The jamb was splintered, as if someone had taken a crowbar to it. And the door, which I had locked before leaving, opened smoothly, no key required. Obviously, someone had broken in.

I immediately took stock of my possessions and found nothing missing, nothing out of place. Nothing even *touched*, from what I could see. But, yes, a foreign body, or bodies, had definitely trespassed here. And, clearly, the person or persons in question had not gone to great pains to conceal the fact.

It was Archie's doing, of course. He'd sent some hoods over to search for the negatives, or some dirt on me, or both. Probably both, I decided. I considered calling the police, but what would I tell them? That Archibald Lancaster, local multi-billionaire, had commissioned some goons to ransack my apartment in a misguided hunt for damning proof of his infidelity? Hardly.

I checked my kitchen cabinets and drawers, the chest of drawers in my bedroom, the medicine cabinet and drawers in my bathroom. I scoured the bookshelf in my bedroom where I had hidden three hundred dollars in cash and assorted valuables, most notably a gold bracelet with my name engraved on its underside, which my father had given me for my thirtieth birthday. Nothing was disturbed, so far as I could tell. I went back to the door jamb and inspected it again. There was, as I had initially concluded, unmistakable evidence of a forced entry.

I stood in the doorway for a moment, indignant and scared, alarmed and confused. Then I went around back to the hanging flower pot in which I had buried the negatives.

Thank great and merciful Zeus, they were there, the plastic

in which I had wrapped them still sealed with masking tape fully intact. They had not been found. Of course they hadn't been: a fucking photo-sniffing dog couldn't have found them. I'd heaped six inches of soil over them, hung the pot on the highest hook, moved a heavy grill in front of it to deter any would-be snoops. I had taken every feasible if not conceivable precaution, and it had served me well.

I took the negatives into my apartment and returned them to the shoebox. Then I called Archie.

"Have you *no* conscience?" I barked into the phone. "No sense of decency, no honor, no scruples *at all*? No respect even for the *law*?"

"What the hell are you prattling on about, Mr. Farmer?"

"Call me Terry, goddammit!"

"All right. What are you prattling on about, Terry?"

I took a deep breath, endeavored to calm myself. "You know full fucking well what I'm talking about, Archie! You had someone break into my apartment, I assume to look for the negatives! But why? What was the point of it? I have the photos, and they're quite sufficient to take your sorry ass to the cleaners!"

"I did no such thing!" retorted Archie with perfect, self-

185

righteous hauteur.

"In your words, Archie, 'gimme a fuckin' break.' Don't deny it! My door jamb is cracked like an egg! Someone fucking jimmied it with a crowbar! Are you telling me that's a *coincidence*?"

Archie coughed. "Hell, Terry, I don't know. But I sure as hell had nothing to do with it."

"Liar! Goddamned fucking *liar*!"

"Watch your tongue, Farmer!"

"Terry!"

"Watch your tongue, Terry!"

"Admit what you did!"

"I did nothing!"

I took another long, shivery breath. My chest was hitching. I was shaking all over. "Fine. Whatever. I don't give a shit anymore. But you don't have twenty-four hours to decide, not now. You have until six tonight. Got it?"

There was a long pause. I was about to ask whether he'd heard me when he said, "I don't need until six. I'll go along with your ridiculous idea. I'll comply."

Floored, I found myself incapable of responding. I guess that, until then, I had thought the whole quixotic scenario a kind of pipe dream. His willingness to help realize it rendered me momentarily speechless.

"Terry? Are you there?"

"I'm here."

"I said I'd take part in your little... experiment."

"Very good." I fought hard to keep my voice steady. "I mean, that's excellent news. I'm so glad you -"

"We're to leave on Friday?"

"Right."

"And where will we go?"

"Everywhere," I said.

I hung the phone up slowly, in a potent stupor, and then spent five or ten minutes just wandering about my apartment, looking at things without seeing them and thinking thoughts I could hardly decipher, they came so fast and inchoately.

Eventually I poured myself a glass of whiskey to celebrate. I said to myself, "Holy shit." And then I drank the whiskey, grinning like a fool.

A week or so earlier, I had begun reading E.L. Doctorow's *The Waterworks*. I was about halfway through it when I called Archie and demanded a confession he would not make. For the two days thereafter, I did little but finish reading that novel, drink coffee (before five) and beer (after five), and wonder at the fabulously deranged course upon which my life had embarked. I left the apartment only once, to buy some groceries and cigarettes, and spoke no more than four sentences to anybody. I was scared to do anything else or say anything more. I was, during those blurry and maddeningly anticipatory forty-eight hours, scared of almost everything.

On Thursday night I started packing, still not entirely believing in the reality I had been given yet nonetheless praying that the dream might persist. And it did, with one brief interruption: when Archie called me just before ten o' clock and expressed some reservations about my proposal.

"It occurs to me," Archie said, "that this whole thing is absurd."

"Well, yes," I said, "of course it is. It's nothing one would expect or predict or could easily envision. What's your point?"

"My point is that it is woefully wrongheaded. The whole design smacks of poor foresight and an arrant disregard for detail." He paused, and before I could respond he added, "A thoroughly unfounded and laughably corny idealism."

"What do you mean?"

"Well, you're suggesting I just hand out stacks of money, is that it?"

"Or personal checks," I said. "I'm sure you're good for them."

"Yes, well, in any case, it's moronic. Handing five thousand dollars to a street urchin is like flushing it down the toilet. It's useless. The recipient can do nothing *with* it, except perpetuate the hopelessness of his present circumstances."

"I can see you've given this a lot of thought."

"Well, yes... yes, Terry, I have."

"I'm glad."

"Well, am I confused somehow?"

"Sure you are."

"How so?"

"Well, the recipient can certainly pay off some bills that have been piling up. He can lessen his debt, make his life a little easier. What else would he do?"

"Something stupid," Archie said. "Something utterly asinine, like buy a new car or a year's supply of drugs or a vacation to someplace exotic. Wouldn't that defeat the whole point of this enterprise, contradict the very philosophy and sentiment behind it? Which is, I assume, to illustrate the needlessness of indigence and the permanent impact of small sums on the daily lives of the poor, how relatively little money can forever alter their lives for the better."

"Well," I said, "you raise a good point. Maybe I'll need to think about that."

"Think about it?" said Archie scornfully. "We're supposed to leave tomorrow!"

"Well, we're doing it, one way or another. But I promise to give some thought to what you've said."

"Where are we going to meet?"

"I'll be at your house at nine."

"Nine?"

"Yes."

"Fine."

I went to the window and peeked through the curtains."Oh, and Archie?"

"Yes?"

"Just so you know, a confidant of mine is aware of my plan and has doubles of the photos. Naturally, this person has been instructed to release them to the media in the event that something should happen to me."

"What are you implying, Terry?"

I let the curtains close. "Good night, Archie."

I hung up. I sat in my chair, smiling a satisfied little smile, nursing a beer.

I was just turning out the lights in my apartment when Winston showed up. I opened the door without removing the chain, cautiously, half-expecting the visitor to be one of Archie's henchmen (packing heat, of course, and sporting a big, malicious grin). When I realized it was Winston I loosed the chain and opened the door wide.

"Winston?" I said. "What are you doing here?"

"I just wanted to talk to you," he said. "Can I come in?"

I nodded and permitted his entry. He took a seat on the couch. "So you're leaving with my dad tomorrow?"

"Apparently," I said, and though I had had only two beers that evening and had planned to drink no more, I suddenly found myself fixing a whiskey and soda. "Do you want a beer or something?"

"Yeah, I'll take a beer."

I got him a beer from the fridge and took it to him, my whiskey and soda in my other hand. "Here you go."

"Thanks."

"Why exactly are you here, Winston?"

A hurt look came over his face and immediately I felt a pang of regret. "Should I go?"

"No, no. I'm just not sure what... I'm just wondering what I can help you with."

"I can't just visit you as a friend?"

I sighed, slumped into my chair. "Of course you can."

"Then okay. That's why I'm here. As a friend."

I raised my glass to him in a meaningless toast. "Good to have you here."

Winston took a gulp of his beer, stretched, rearranged himself. "My father had someone break in here today?"

I sat up quickly. "He told you that? I mean, he admitted it to you?"

He blushed. He put his beer down on the coffee table. "No, no. I just overheard your conversation with him, on the phone." He paused. "I mean, you *think* that's what happened, right?"

I sipped my drink. "Yeah," I said, my mind awake again. "Yeah, that's what I think."

"Jesus. That's insane. You think he was looking for the pictures?"

"No," I said. "I think he was looking for the negatives. The pictures I had on me when I saw him. I showed them to him."

"Oh." He quaffed his beer. "Oh, okay."

Slowly, an idea occurred to me. "Winston?"

"Yeah?"

"You didn't have anything to do with that, did you? The break-in, I mean."

Expectedly, his eyes grew wide, his cheeks grew red, his face twisted into a portrait of choler. "What the fuck? No! Of course I didn't!"

"Okay, okay," I placated him. "I was just making sure."

"Why would you think that, Terry?"

"Just your showing up so... randomly, that's all."

"I shouldn't have come."

"Winston."

He finished his beer at one draught. "Obviously you don't trust me."

"I trust you."

"Funny way of showing it."

For a long time we were both silent, and then he lit a cigarette. "Are you going to expose him after it's all over? After he's given away all the money, I mean?"

"Are you asking if I'm going to renege on our deal?"

"Well, yeah."

"No," I said. "Of course I won't. I'm a man of my word. His giving away all this money will be a genuine and extraordinary penance. Why would I extort him further? I'm not in this for kicks, Winston. I'm in it for the principle of the thing."

"But..." He trailed off.

"But what?"

"He deserves it. He cheated on my mom. He's basically buying off an election. He has no morals at all."

"He has morals enough to go through with this thing."

"Those aren't morals. Those are self-preservation instincts, survival tactics. He's only doing it because he can afford to and it will save his career. Even enhance it."

"Yeah, well. The guy's doing it, isn't he?"

"Why are you suddenly defending him?"

I put a dent in my drink. "I'm not *defending* him, Winston. I'm just saying, for him to go along with something like this is pretty marvelous, and he deserves some credit for it."

"What other choice does he have?"

"I don't know," I said. "I guess none."

"Right, exactly, none at all."

I finished my drink. "Winston?" I said. "When did you

become such a ruthless critic of your father?"

"I don't know," he said, getting up. He looked at me coldly. "When did you become such a staunch ally of his?"

"Oh, Winston, come on. Don't be an idiot. I'm not -"

But then he was gone, and I was left with an empty glass and a lot of thoughts I didn't care to think.

Part III:

I n e z

19

The morning was bright and beautiful and filled with possibility. There was nary a cloud in the sky, every birdsong was sweet, the sun shone implacably and with a rare magnificence. Traffic was unusually light, as if motorists were somehow aware of the momentousness of the occasion and dared not impede my journey. I found it almost impossible not to whistle, and every tune on the radio seemed to lift my spirits higher. The ATM receipt in the compartment under the armrest showed a balance of one million, fifteen thousand, nine hundred twenty-six dollars and seventy-four cents.

Yes, it was a glorious morning indeed.

I pulled into Archie's portico about five minutes before nine and knocked on the side door, refusing to tackle again the rigors of reaching the main entrance. After a minute or two Juan Carlos answered the door and indicated that it was a pleasure to see me again.

"A pleasure to see *you* again, fine sir!" I exclaimed, and immediately produced a thousand dollars in cash from my wallet. I rolled up the bills and tucked them into his coat pocket. "Just a little something to make your summer sizzle, give it that extra bang, you know?" I smiled.

His features were pure disbelief. "Sir?"

"Enjoy it, Juan Carlos. God knows you deserve it."

He stammered.

"Do you have a family, Juan Carlos?"

"Yes, sir! A wife, two boys, and a girl!"

"Buy them something nice," I said. "And something for the little lady."

"Thank you, sir!"

I took three hundreds from my pocket and put them in his trembling hand. "And Juan Carlos?"

"Yes, sir?"

"Get something for yourself, too."

Archie was dressed casually (or as casually as I could imagine him), in a knit shirt and khakis. Surprisingly, he looked well, relatively calm, relieved. I guess it was knowing that, so long as he met his obligation to me, he would be home free, the world never to learn of his shocking crimes against society and his estranged wife.

"Archie," I said. "How are you?"

"Fine." He instructed Juan Carlos to transport his suitcases to my car. Juan Carlos complied cheerfully, ensconced in a trance whose splendors I could only imagine. "Listen, Terry, is there any way we could wrap this up in a month? I don't think Dacey could go much longer without my direct involvement in its affairs."

"Well," I said, "I doubt that, Archie."

"Christ," he grumbled. "What difference does it make whether I give a hundred grand to each of a thousand people or twenty grand to each of five thousand?"

I turned and watched Juan Carlos haul the luggage outside, load it into my trunk. I turned back to Archie. "All the difference in the world," I said.

"Terry," Archie said. "Follow me into the kitchen. I'd like a quick word with you in private."

I looked at my watch. It was eight past nine. "Archie, we really ought to get going. We have a lot of ground to cover."

"Not until we discuss what we need to discuss."

Obligingly, I followed him into the kitchen. "It's the pictures, right? You want the pictures?"

"And the negatives. I'm not stepping foot outside this house until both are in my possession."

"You'll get neither," I said firmly, "until you have completed at least half of the transactions. Then you can have the negatives.

200

You'll get the photos when the mission is completed."

He shook his head. "I'll need more assurance than that, Terry."

"What kind of assurance? Shall I sign something?"

He frowned. "There wouldn't be much point in *that*. No, I want to know the location of both items. And I insist that, whatever their location, they remain there until... this thing is over."

"They're in one of my bags," I said. "I'll show them to you before we leave. When we're together, they'll remain in the bag. When we're apart, they'll remain with me. That's non-negotiable."

Resignedly, he nodded. "Let's go."

I had awoken that morning rather expecting to find some mention of Archie's imminent expedition in the newspapers. I had not. "Didn't you alert the media?" I asked him, merging onto the freeway.

"About what? This?" he asked.

"Of course this."

"I alerted my staff."

I looked at him. "Don't tell me you intend to *avoid* publicity during this excursion?"

"I intend neither to seek it nor to avoid it."

I chuckled. "I think you'll get it, in any case."

"I have no control over that." He fiddled with his seat belt. "Where are we *going*, Terry?"

"First stop: Inez, Kentucky."

He jerked in his seat, perfectly mortified. "Inez? Why in hell?"

"We're starting where your conscience left off," I said.

"You're a major-league asshole, do you know that?"

I smiled. "Lie back and get some sleep, why don't you? We have a long ride ahead of us."

He turned away, watching small hills slowly give way to mountains.

Fifteen minutes later, half-dozing, he muttered, "Who are you, Terry?"

I looked at him, creasing my brow. "Who am I?"

"Yes, who are you?"

I said, "Just... someone."

"Someone who what?"

"I don't know." I looked at the road, then back at Archie. "Someone who likes to think he enjoys a large perspective on things."

202

"And extorting me?"

I glanced at the fuel gauge and saw we needed gas. "It's an offshoot of the perspective," I said. I spoke slowly, uncertainly.

"Convenient," he mumbled. "Real convenient." He sighed, shifted onto his side, and fell asleep, his snores at once resonating throughout the car.

I got off the freeway at the next exit and drove to the nearest gas station, stealing periodic glimpses at the man slumbering next to me.

He slept for about an hour, stirring as we encountered some heavy congestion near Morgantown, West Virginia.

"Where are we?" he asked groggily.

"About fifteen miles outside Morgantown."

He scanned the traffic. "What's the holdup?"

I rolled my window down and lit a cigarette. "Couldn't tell you. I can tell you what it's *not,* though: it's *not* a football game."

"How astute of you."

I smiled. "Must be an accident. We'll be rolling here in a few minutes, don't worry."

"Do you have to smoke in the car?"

"It's my car. And you smoke cigars."

"Not if it bothers people."

"Well, it bothers me. I really wish you'd give them up."

"You're a real smart-ass, aren't you, Terry?"

"Can be." The traffic began to budge a little. "Is it really bothering you?"

He sighed and waved a hand at me. "Just smoke the goddamned thing."

"Thanks." We were up to twenty miles an hour now. "You know, Archie, we're going to be spending a lot of time together over the next few months -"

"Must you keep reminding me?"

"- so it's important that we learn to tolerate each other."

"You don't hear me insulting you, do you?"

"I'm just making a point, is all."

"And the point is taken."

I slid my cigarette through the gap in the window and rolled it up. "So here's what I'm thinking." I waited for him to reply, but he didn't. I went on, "You'll give four thousand, nine hundred and fifty bucks apiece to twenty thousand people. They'll consist of coal miners, factory workers, gas-pump jockeys, shipping clerks, burger-flippers, carpenters, cashiers, anyone employed in a menial, particularly blue-collar capacity."

"Don't doctors work hard? And lawyers? And CEOs?"

"Doctors and lawyers, yes. CEOs, that's arguable. In any case, people employed in such fields are nearly always duly compensated for their efforts."

"People are compensated proportionately to the level of skill required by their jobs."

"Skill isn't everything, Archie. Plain old-fashioned muscle is as essential to our economy as any book-learning or technical dexterity. Besides, skill is mostly a function of genetics, over which people have no control at all."

"'From each according to his ability, to each according to his need'? Is that the Marxist bilge you're promulgating here, Terry?"

"In a nutshell, yes."

I jockeyed the Buick into the passing lane to get around a slow-moving van. A young boy traveling in the backseat had his face pressed against the tinted side window, his lips puckered and cheeks puffed out like fish gills. Archie scowled at the whelp with raw antipathy. "That," he said, pointing to the lad. "*That's* what you want to enrich with my money? With the money I've *earned*, irrespective that you apparently disapprove of the method?"

I looked at the kid, gave him a big, toothy smile. He giggled gleefully. "Yeah," I said. "What's so wrong with that?"

"You'd understand if you walked a mile in my shoes," he sneered.

"I don't want to walk in your shoes for even a meter." I glanced down at his loafers. "They look uncomfortable."

"I thought about what you said, though." We were coming up on Fairmont now, about three and a half hours from our destination. "About the potential futility of the experiment, I mean. How the people are apt to fritter away the money on useless crap."

"And?"

"I devised a solution."

Intrigued, Archie sat up a little, gave me his full attention for perhaps the first time all day. "I'm listening."

"You have lawyers at your disposal round-the-clock, don't you?"

"I do."

"Did you bring a cell phone?"

"Yes."

"Ah, never mind, you'll never get decent reception around here. Wait till we stop for lunch, then call one of them. Have him draw up a contract."

"A contract?"

"Yes. Well, more like a template for multiple contracts. We'll need thousands of copies of it, naturally."

Archie was baffled. "What kind of contract? What are you talking about?"

"I'm talking about a contract which legally binds the recipients of your generous gifts to certain parameters within which the money can be spent. It will stipulate that twenty percent of each charitable donation, or nine hundred ninety dollars, is to be either placed in an interest-bearing savings account, inaccessible for one year, or else paid toward a specified end, to attenuate a specified debt. For instance, a mortgage or car payment. The remainder can be used by the recipients however they please."

Archie appeared to mull over the recommendation. "I have no idea if that's even legal."

"How could it not be? It's your money. If you give it away, you can set whatever conditions you like on how it's used."

"It just doesn't seem practical to me."

"Why not? It would be an extremely basic, straightforward document. No fine print, no tricks, no catches. And the people will agree to it, I'm sure, without exception. Nobody in his right mind would turn down five grand just because he can't blow it all on Ho Hos and beer."

Archie snickered. I was stunned. "Archie," I said, "I don't think I'd ever heard you laugh before. At least not good-naturedly."

"Ah, well, that just tickled me."

I glanced at him, saw he was smiling. My mild shock persisted. We had passed Fairmont now and the traffic had thinned out considerably. The curves in the interstate grew increasingly sharp, the slopes gradually steeper. The scenery was gorgeous. Charleston lay a hundred and forty miles to the south. I figured we'd stop there for lunch. "Yes, well, amusing as it was, what I said is also *true*, isn't it?"

"I suppose so. As for the question of legality, I guess my lawyers could settle that."

I adjusted my seat. My right leg was getting numb. "Yes, they could. But do you *like* the idea? Do you think it makes sense?"

"I like the idea, yes. I'd certainly feel more comfortable giving away all this money if I knew that at least some of it would be used wisely. But I can't exactly envision explaining the damned contract, however simple, to twenty thousand stupefied souls, collecting twenty thousand signatures. It just doesn't seem feasible. Where on earth would we store all the forms?"

"We'd have bundles of them, say a couple of hundred at a time, mailed to whatever hotel we were lodging in at the time, and then mail them back, completed, before receiving the next bundle. Piece of cake."

Archie nodded. "Yeah. Yeah, I guess that could work." He paused, gave me an intent, almost admiring look. "You've thought very hard about this, haven't you, Terry?"

"Yes, I have."

"Why is this so important to you? What part of you responds to it so powerfully?"

"I don't know," I said. "The nice part, I guess."

I pulled off at the rest stop near Flatwoods, needing to pee. Archie was absorbed in a biography of Henry Ford which he had extracted from a duffel bag he'd dumped on the backseat.

"Do you want anything? Chips, soda, a candy bar?"

"No, I'm fine."

I got out of the car, pausing only to drink from the water fountain inside the lobby, and made my way into the men's room. Standing at the urinal beside me was an abdominous man, grizzled-but somehow convivial-looking, in a checkered red-and-black flannel shirt and dusty jeans, bright blue suspenders strapped snugly over his shoulders. "This place smells like dog shit," he ventured. The bathroom indeed reeked of a canine-like feces.

"Sure does," I said.

"Where you headed?"

"Inez, Kentucky."

"My grandpappy's from there. From Kentucky, I mean."

"Is he?"

"Yessir. Ashland. Thirty-two years in one of them chemical plants."

"Jesus Christ."

"Tell me about it."

"That's no easy chore."

"It's a helluva thing!"

I flushed the urinal and zipped my fly. "How about you? What line of work are you in?"

"Timber."

"Oh, yeah?"

"Yessir. I'm a logger in Jane Lew. On my way back from Clendenin. My folks live down there."

We went to the sink, washed our hands. Afterward, I stretched out mine and he shook it. "Terry Farmer," I said. "From Pittsburgh."

"Keith Childers, from Jane Lew."

"Pleasure to meet you."

"Same." He snapped his suspenders. "What's your business in Kentucky, if you don't mind me askin'?"

"Well, let me show you," I said, gesturing toward the door. "Follow me."

I led Keith out to the car and introduced him to Archie. "Keith," I said, "this is Archibald Lancaster. Archie, this is Keith Childers."

Reluctantly, Archie extended his hand. Keith shook it enthusiastically. "Pleased to meetcha, sir," he said.

"Likewise," said Archie.

"Archie," I said, "Keith is a logger from a little town here in West Virginia."

"Is that right?"

I nodded, smiled at Keith. "That's right."

Archie mimicked my smile. "That's wonderful, Keith. I was once in the timber business myself."

"You was a logger?"

Archie blinked. "Well, no. I... ran, helped run, a company called, uh... Franklin Timber."

"Keith," I said, turning to the man, "you probably don't have a whole lot to speak of, material-wise. That is to say, plain folks

211

such as yourself don't have the easiest time getting along in this world. You know what I mean?"

Keith gave a puzzled little nod. "Well, nossir, I don't reckon we do. I got me a nice little house, though, almost paid off."

"That's lovely," I said. "But you deserve more, don't you?"

Keith blinked, thought a moment. "Well, I suppose you might look at it that way. But I ain't complainin'."

"Do you recognize Archie's name?" I asked.

Keith shook his head. "Nossir, I sure don't."

"Archie is an extremely wealthy man."

"Oh yeah?"

"That's right. And he wants to show his gratitude for his good fortune by presenting you with three hundred dollars." Keith's jaw dropped. So did Archie's. "It's just a small token of his appreciation for how good life has been to him, how well fate has treated him."

"Nossir," said Keith, "I don't reckon I need no charity."

I shook my head. "No, no, this isn't charity. This is a *reward*, a show of thanks. You've earned it." I looked at Archie. "Why don't you give Mr. Childers the money he's earned, Archie?"

Archie, flummoxed, reached into his back pocket and pulled out his wallet. "Of course," he said, manifesting six fifty dollar bills.

He handed them to a disbelieving, dreamily euphoric Keith Childers. "Here you are."

Keith held the money in his right hand and goggled at it, as if it were the currency of some alien nation. "Thank you, mister! I mean..." He looked at me. "Who *is* this guy?"

"He's Santa Claus," I said, and burst out laughing. Involuntarily, I embraced this flannel-clad stranger. "He's Santa Claus in the flesh, Keith, and you're the first lucky kid to sit on his lap!"

"Well, Archie," I said when we were back on the road, "how did that feel?"

"Giving three hundred dollars to a perfect stranger? How did *that* feel?"

"Yeah."

Archie shrugged. "Quite pointless, actually."

"Pointless?" I asked, shocked. "How so?"

"Well, what's he going to do with it? Honestly?"

"Oh, we're back on that kick, are we?"

"No, no, I'm not suggesting the man is going to go out and buy drugs with it or anything like that. But it's three hundred bucks. What's it going to get him? A new muffler on his car and some flowers for his wife?"

"And if it does? If that's how he chooses to spend it?"

"Drop in the bucket," Archie said, obstinate. "Like spitting into the ocean."

I shook my head. "You really see it that way, don't you? You've genuinely lost the ability to comprehend the magnitude of what just took place, haven't you? To comprehend just how much three hundred dollars means to somebody like Keith Childers, and to envision just how far a man like him can stretch it?"

"Please," Archie grumbled, looking away, "spare me your 'Mother Theresa of the Working Man' routine. I'm fed up with it already, and we've only just begun. You act like you're John Lewis, for Christ's sake."

Deliberately, I lit a cigarette without rolling the window down. "I'm surprised you've heard of him," I said, and relished the sourness in my own tone.

"Catty bastard."

I smiled. "Three more hours, Archie. Three more and we're there."

We arrived in Charleston, West Virginia a little after twelve-thirty. We had exchanged few words in the previous eighty minutes. We lunched downtown at a little restaurant called The Blossom Dairy, which specialized, appropriately enough, in dairy products. Their ham-and-swiss sandwich, I discovered, was particularly delicious, ambrosial when taken with a carton of their whole milk. Archie picked at a tuna salad.

"What are your intentions when we reach Inez?" he asked me, very matter-of-factly. He took a sip of his tea and stared at me, his body stiff, expression indecipherable. I had begun to wish the fucker would smoke a joint or something and loosen up.

"We'll repeat what we just did, only on a larger scale. And with contracts to distribute."

"So you don't have anything planned for tonight?"

I took a hefty bite of my sandwich, spoke around the food. Interestingly, I had no qualms whatever about this solecism. I was, in fact, completely at ease. My mind felt clearer than it had in years. "I may find a bar and drink some beers," I said.

"But you don't plan on giving away any more of my money?"

I laughed. "No, that can wait until tomorrow. Tonight, I'm a millionaire on the town!"

"On the town of Inez, Kentucky," said Archie churlishly.

"Every village has its charms, mate."

He frowned and pushed around his salad with his fork. "This

is one big game to you, isn't it?"

"Well, yes and no. Yes, in the sense that it's a dream come true, albeit in a vastly different form than I'd ever fantasized about. But no, in the sense that I'm taking every second of it as seriously as any human being could take anything. One of these days you'll realize just how monumental this whole thing is to me, Archie."

"Maybe." He speared a piece of lettuce with his fork and chewed it methodically. "God, I hope so."

Naturally, a brilliant idea struck me as we were finishing our meals. "Archie," I said, "why don't you give a couple hundred to the gal behind the counter?"

He pushed his half-eaten salad aside. "What?"

"You have a couple hundred more on you, don't you?"

He fidgeted, stammered. "Well... yeah."

"Go give her whatever you have left, assuming it's less than five hundred. I don't want to go totally hog-wild just yet, before we get those contracts."

He leaned into the table, flabbergasted. "Give her whatever I have *left*?" he said.

"Yeah," I said. "Why not? She probably makes six, seven bucks an hour, tops. She could use the money to pay her next month's rent. Shell it out, Big Stuff."

"I thought I was supposed to give five thousand dollars apiece to a bunch of coal miners?"

"Yeah, well, the whole thing's at my discretion." I swallowed the last of my sandwich. "Isn't it?"

He looked at me.

"Isn't it?"

"Jesus Christ," he said, and stood up.

"Here you go," he said to the towheaded sandwich-fixer and cashier, placing four bills on the counter. "Three hundred and twenty dollars. There's your tip."

She laughed hysterically. "Real funny, mister. Can I get you a refill on your tea?"

Archie turned and looked at me. I smiled and gave him a reassuring thumbs-up. He turned back to the girl. "No, really, you can have that. That's for you."

Her laughter died. She turned pale. "You're giving me three hundred and twenty dollars? As a tip?"

"Yes," Archie said. "Um. You deserve it."

"There ya go, man!" I hollered.

The girl reluctantly collected the cash, but hesitated to put it in her apron pocket. "Why are you giving me this?" she asked.

Archie looked at me again.

"He can afford it!" I yelled.

He turned back to her. "I can afford it," he said.

Compulsively, she laughed again. "Who are you?"

"He's Archibald Lancaster, fifth richest man in the world!" I yelled. I felt drunk. My whole body thrummed like the strings of some divine guitar. I was outside myself, omnipresent, transcendent and flooded with benign power. I was floating on clouds of pink cotton, riding in a golden chariot, rolling on a bed of feathers with my head propped up by lavender pillows. I was Archie Lancaster with a sense of humor, a sense of adventure, and a healthy dose of empathy. I was everything I had ever wanted to be.

"I can't take this," the girl said, and laid the money on the counter.

Archie came back to the table. "She won't take it," he said dejectedly.

"Sure she will," I said. "Just leave it there. Just leave it there. She'll take it." I chugged the last quarter of my milk. "She'll take it, don't worry."

20

When I had called my family to apprise them of my

impending journey, I had mentioned nothing about being fired. I had just said that I'd grown somewhat close to Archie and had persuaded him to join me on a kind of "charity trip" around the country. "Mr. Lancaster is going to make a series of small donations to American workers to show his support for their tireless efforts," I had said, "and I'm going to cover the story as a journalist. At the end of the excursion, I'll write a series of articles about it, and maybe a book."

They inquired, with not-insubstantial worry in their tones, whether my job would be secure during my absence. "No question about it," I had reassured them. "I got a full go-ahead from the powers that be. Kyle Barnes, my boss, was particularly delighted with the idea. It bears his unreserved stamp of approval. The paper will even give me a stipend to live on while I'm gone, just as if it were a sabbatical." This, fortunately, seemed to set their minds at ease.

But how, they wondered, did this whole thing come about? How *exactly*? "The details are really pretty mundane. I interviewed Archie a couple weeks ago and broached the notion, admittedly fantastic, that a man of his wealth might engage in some kind of large-scale humanitarian enterprise. To my utter shock, his reaction was one of unbridled glee. He said he'd always been fascinated by the prospect of such a charge. And thus the endeavor was born."

My sister, Denise, wanted to know what Archie was like in person. Without faltering, I gave her the following answer: "He's a very sweet man, actually. I know you'd never think it, what with all the scurrilous attacks on his character so pervasive in the media - yes, including my own - but, yeah, there's a lot to recommend the guy. I think he knows he's made some serious mistakes in the past and sincerely wants to atone for them. It's really quite inspiring."

My sister mused over this for a moment, chewing on it with audible skepticism and surprise. "Wow," she said finally. "Maybe people really *can* change."

21

We crossed the border of West Virginia and Kentucky at two-thirty, and were in Inez at ten minutes of four.

Back at The Blossom Dairy, Archie had called one of his lawyers in Pittsburgh and pitched the contract idea to him. Incredulous but compliant, the lawyer, whose name was Kenneth Stevens, had promised Archie that he would have the document ready by six o' clock. Mr. Stevens had been unable to say with absolute certainty that such a contract was even valid, but noted that he could think of no reason why it shouldn't be. Before getting down to work, he would be sure to consult a few of his colleagues with more experience in the field of contract law. Provided there were no snares, legal or otherwise, Archie could call after six with the address to which he would like the first three hundred copies of the contract sent. Mr. Stevens would have them shipped overnight.

Now, as we were hauling our luggage into the Inez Sleep Away ("Clean Rooms at an Affordable Price!"), a certain doubt arose in me. Given its weight, it rather distressed me that it had not occurred to me earlier. "Archie?" I said.

He was grimacing at the weight of his two elephantine suitcases. "Yeah?"

"How are we going to *enforce* these contracts?"

He stopped and put the cases down on the asphalt, panting a little. "Enforce them?"

"Yeah. Like, after the people have signed them, and we've given the money away, how are we going to verify that the recipients have fulfilled the terms of the contract? How are we supposed to monitor the way they spend the money?"

He blinked, bit his bottom lip. Suddenly, his cheeks flushed with a deep, petulant crimson. His eyes blazed. "Well, goddammit, Terry! How the hell am *I* supposed to know? This whole contract business was *your* idea, not mine!"

"Yeah, but you're the corporate guy! I'm just a lowly journalist! So this is really *your* domain, isn't it?"

He shook his head, perfectly unamused, and picked up his bags. "I'm going to check in," he said. "You can stay out here and give it a few hours' thought, if you'd like. Let me know when you come up with something."

Suitcases swinging at his sides, Archie stalked into the lobby of the motel, I following closely on his heels.

The solution hit me as Archie was signing for his room key. "Call your lawyer back. Tell him to add a clause to the contract."

He glanced at me sidelong and spoke quietly, as if not wanting the clerk to overhear our conversation. "Stipulating?"

"That the twenty percent of each gift designated as untouchable for one year must be placed in a new savings account whose balance shall remain the exact amount of the gift, that is, nine hundred and ninety dollars, until one year following its receipt. Furthermore, any of your lawyers shall be legally entitled to confirm the balance of the account at any time during the one-year period. Should it be found to be off by even one cent, the owner of the account shall forfeit its contents *in toto*." I paused, marveling at how smoothly I had delivered the spiel. "Hey, that was pretty good, wasn't it? Maybe *I* should have been a lawyer."

"Yeah," said Archie, frowning. "I think you would have made a fine one."

So then we were separated, in our own separate rooms with our own separate agendas for the remainder of the day. First on Archie's was grabbing an afternoon nap. First on mine was taking a hot shower and then a quick dip in the kidney-shaped puddle that passed for the Inez Sleep Away's swimming pool.

I asked Archie, before he retreated into his room, whether he might like to join me for dinner. I had no particular hankering to dine with the man, but, with his being my indentured servant and all, felt obliged at least to offer. Fortunately, he declined. "This may be a vacation for you, Terry," he said plainly, "but for me it's a chore. A business trip. And I'd just as soon leave it at that, if it's all the same to you."

I told him I understood completely, that I'd meet him in the lobby at eight o' clock the next morning, and went off to take my shower.

The pool, initially, was deserted. I imagined that the motel's having a total of about five guests had something to do with that. (It couldn't have had more than ten guests, because it only had ten rooms.) I was relieved by this, and immensely so; I'd no desire to share the tub with a stranger, much less the fat, hairy brand of stranger most likely to be encountered.

The water was very cold, which was also agreeable. At four-thirty on that cloudless June day, the temperature was a scorching eighty-nine degrees. I remember, because from the pool I could see the sign for the Ninth Street Bank, the current time and temperature alternately displayed. Beyond that was a McDonald's (I supposed Archie and I would visit it in the morning before heading out to the mines), and, beyond that, still azure sky rimmed by infant mountains dressed in green. The view was idyllic, in its own way, and as I swam a few laps in the tiny pool, the steady equanimity I had enjoyed since morning amplified itself dramatically. I could not recall a moment in my life when I had felt more serene or more simply contented.

Upon completing my sixth lap across the pool, I reared up from the water and saw a young woman, perhaps no more than thirty, opening the gate between the patio and the parking lot. She had a red-and-white striped towel draped over her arm. Her hair was sandy, her eyes sad, her figure fine. She wore a blue bikini bottom and a white cotton tee. She walked meekly across the patio, dropped the towel on one of the lounge chairs, and doffed her shirt. Her breasts, as had been discernible at once but was now amply confirmed, boasted the sublime buoyancy of youth. Apparently she had not yet seen me.

I propped my elbows on the side of the pool. "Hi," I said. I gave her the most wholesome and unthreatening smile I could muster. I was, of course, fiercely aroused.

She started, then laughed. Blushing, she reflexively covered her chest with her arms. I admired her modesty. "Oh," she said. "Hello, there."

"Howdy." I tried to think of something else to say, but couldn't, so just went on smiling. She smiled back, awkwardly, and stood frozen in place. After a moment of this uncomfortable silence I heard myself ask, "Staying at the motel?"

She blinked.

"That was a stupid question, wasn't it?"

She laughed again. "Yeah, kind of."

"Sorry." I probably blushed a little myself. "My name's Terry."

"Susan," she said. She reached out a hesitant hand and I shook it. "How's the water?"

"Cold," I said. "Pleasantly so."

She dipped a toe in the pool and immediately jerked it out. "It's freezing!"

I laughed. "Only at first. You get used to it quick."

"Well," she said, sighing amiably, "only one way to find out if you're lying." She ambled over to the deep end of the pool, raised her arms in perfect diving form, and plunged in. When she emerged a moment later, her eyes were aflame with playful outrage. "Oh, Jesus! It's like the Arctic Ocean! I'll kill you!"

I cracked up. I had not thought it possible for my mood to improve; I had been wrong. "Well, why do you think that penguin was shivering in the lobby?"

Bemused stare. "Penguin?"

I shook my head, still laughing.

"Oh." She rolled her eyes and swam nearer to me. "Ha ha. So where you from, Terry?"

"Pittsburgh. You?"

"Washington, Pee-A. Small word, eh?"

"Washington? Really?"

"As I live and breathe."

"And what brings you to these parts?"

"My brother's a coal miner at the Big Branch pit. I'm in

visiting him and his wife for the weekend. But they don't have much space, so... this is where I shack up when I come down."

I nearly choked on the pool water. "Coal miner?"

"Yes. Since he was sixteen."

"Wow. That's hard work."

"Bet your ass it is!" She blushed again. It was impossibly cute, her blush. "Sorry."

"No, no. It *is* hard work. *I* sure couldn't do it."

She shook the excess water out of her hair. We had floated into the shallow end of the pool. "So what *do* you do, Terry?"

Without giving it a second's thought I said, "I'm a journalist. A newspaper writer." I realized that what I had said was technically untrue, and a pang of sorrow coursed through me. I think I may have actually winced. "For the... the *Post-Gazette*, in Pittsburgh."

"Oh, wow. That's something."

"It is," I said. "It's definitely something."

"And what are *you* doing in Inez?"

I paused, considered. "That's kind of a long story."

Mercifully, she did not press the issue. "Have you worked for the paper your whole life?"

"Pretty much, yeah. After college I did some freelance work for magazines for a few years, then got a job at a small-town rag in

New Jersey. That's where I went to school."

"So that's where you're from originally?"

"No, I'm originally from Rhode Island."

"Yankee boy, eh?"

"Through and through."

She stretched her arms out and swam toward the edge of the pool, doing the breaststroke. "Me, I'm a southern girl." She cast a friendly, almost inviting glance over her shoulder, the evening sun dancing in her eyes. And out of nowhere I thought, *I could love those eyes, I could love them very easily.* "Born and bred."

"Hey, listen," I said, and it wasn't me talking anymore. It was a richly splendid mixture of my lust and curiosity, and that relentless, low-key euphoria which swaddled my brain. "I don't suppose there's a motel bar, but I'm sure we could find a place to get a drink and maybe have some dinner. I mean, if you can spare a couple of hours. You interested?"

A knowing grin touched her lips. "Am I interested?"

"Yeah. Are you interested in... having a drink with me?"

She ducked her head under the water, and when she came up her grin was fully, exquisitely etched. "Yeah," she said. "I'm interested."

I nodded, trying to compose myself. Inside I was trembling,

228

and thanking a God whose existence I had often doubted. Somewhere in my congenitally cynical mind there lurked the caution, muffled but adamant, that this run of inconceivably good luck would soon end, perhaps disastrously. That experience would have me keep my expectations to a bare minimum, especially where human nature was involved: no high so sweet as this could last for long. Still, my giddiness showed great resilience to reason.

"Good." I was still nodding, like a puppet with a broken wire in its neck. "Gosh, that's great."

The only restaurants in town were a Pizza Hut, a truck stop, and a place called Grandad's Diner. Susan and I opted for the last. She had a chili dog and onion rings, I a hamburger and fries. I asked for a beer, was told they didn't serve alcohol, and got a Coke instead. Susan contented herself with a glass of milk.

"If after the meal you still want a drink," I suggested, "I'm sure we could find a bar somewhere."

She nodded and ate an onion ring. "Yeah, we'll see. My brother gets off work at eight, and I'd like to be there when he gets home."

With that, I thought it wise to let the subject alone. "Well, Susan, I know what *he* does for a living, but how about *you*? I wanna say... eighth-grade math teacher?"

She snickered. "Oh, God, do I really seem that boring?"

"No, no. You just seem like the teacher type. The math part was just a blind guess."

"Well, you weren't even close. I'm a paralegal."

I tried a fry. It was greasy and delicious. "A paralegal, huh? Well, that's..."

"Insufferably prosaic?"

I laughed. "I was going to say 'challenging and rewarding.'"

"I think that's how it was described in the classified ad."

"That's how *every* job is described in the classifieds. 'Looking for an exciting career in food preparation? Enjoy working with emotionally troubled children? Regularly long for intimate contact with meatloaf? The cafeteria at Bellevue Elementary School is waiting for you!'"

Susan was mighty tickled by this, almost snorting milk through her nose. "That's so true," she said. "It really is, though!"

"Yes, I know. I spent three months in classifieds when I first got hired on at the *Post*."

She tasted her hotdog, chewing it with great care and thoroughness. At last she announced that her palate found it acceptable: "This is actually really good."

"Is it?"

"Yeah."

"Did you expect it to suck?"

She swallowed, licked her lips, and gave me a big, *ain't-you-silly* smile. "Terry, you're a goof."

"Hmm." I was smiling again, compulsively. "Sometimes. Sometimes."

The conversation waned as we ate our meals. I wish I could say that my burger was as good as Susan's chili dog, but I'd be lying if I did.

Both because of her seeming decline in enthusiasm for the whole drink idea, and because I had found appreciable merit in that gloomy admonition about all good things' having to end, I had all but reconciled myself to the likelihood that my evening with Susan would conclude with our meal. Once again, I was wrong.

"Still want that drink, Terry?" she asked when the check came.

"Oh, yeah. Absolutely." I tapped the check. "But only if you let me pay the tab."

"Why don't we split it?"

I shook my head and held up a hand. "No deal. But if it'll

make you feel better, you can buy me a beer at the bar."

She smiled. "All right," she said. "You win." She stood and slipped the strap of her purse over her shoulder. "I'll meet you outside. I need a cigarette."

"You smoke?"

She nodded guiltily. "Yeah, but not very much. Only after a meal, or with a drink. It's still bad for me, I know."

"Well, you're in equally unhealthy company. Maybe even *unhealthier*. I smoke about a pack a day."

"*That's* a relief!"

I watched as she made her way outside, deciding that she looked almost as good going as she did coming. I paid the check with cash and left the waitress a tip of two hundred dollars.

We found a bar near the truck stop, on what I imagined the locals might facetiously call "the outskirts of town." For reasons unclear to me (and probably even to its owner), the name of the establishment was The Silver Dollar. Three of its four patrons that evening appeared to be truck drivers, if their beer bellies and John Deere caps were any indication. The fourth might have belonged to any occupation at all, or to none; all that could be inferred from his demeanor was that he was six shades of lit up.

"Quaint, isn't it?" I whispered to Susan as we took our stools.

She whispered back, "I suddenly have an overwhelming urge to cut a man's throat with a broken bourbon bottle."

I chuckled under my breath and turned to the barkeep, a surprisingly spindly woman with suitcases under her eyes and a sizable wart on her right cheek. Dull-eyed and sallow-skinned, she moved with the laborious air of one who was heavily sedated. A cigarette, perhaps forgotten, burned in an aluminum ashtray on a cabinet under the shelves of liquor bottles.

"Gitcha sumpin?" she rasped.

"What do you have on draft?" I asked her.

"Bud Light." Pause. "And Miller Lite."

"Choices, choices."

She cocked an eyebrow: *You gettin' smart with me, boy?*

"Um, I'll just take a Dos Equis in a bottle if you have it."

She turned to Susan. "You want somethin', honey?"

"The same... is fine. Thanks."

Little Miss Listless retrieved our drinks. The drunk guy at the end of the bar hollered something unintelligible at her (it sounded a bit like, "Lola, I's shee got t'bleeds now"). She ignored him. "Five-fitty," she said to us.

"Let me," Susan said, producing a ten dollar bill from her

purse.

I tipped my beer to her. "Thank ya, ma'am."

She laughed and handed the bill to the barkeep. "Trying to blend in with the locals, Terry?"

"When in Rome," I said, and took a long, deep swig of my beer. It was ice-cold heaven. I felt my body, hardly tense to start with, immediately relax further.

She lit a Virginia Slim and sipped her beer. "Cheers," she said, and held the bottle up.

I touched mine to hers. "What are we toasting to?"

"To new friends," she said.

"To new friends," I echoed.

"You know," I said, "when I first saw you at the pool you looked kind of down. Was I just imagining that?"

She shook her head. Her beer was half-gone. I was on my second. "No, you weren't."

"Well, what was wrong, if you don't mind my prying?"

She turned her eyes away, frowning. She spoke quietly, lugubriously: "Jimmy, my brother... well, he might be sick. They think he might have cancer."

"Oh, Jesus. I'm so sorry."

234

She smiled wanly but did not look at me. "Thanks."

"What kind of cancer?"

"Lung."

"Oh, shit."

"Yeah."

"How old is he?"

"Thirty-seven. He's been smoking since he was fourteen."

I put my beer on the bar. I had been preparing to light a cigarette and now discreetly returned it to the pack. "That's..." I trailed off, let out a deep breath. "Have they run any tests?"

"Just the preliminaries. Chest x-rays and all that. He's waiting on the results of a biopsy he had done this week. He's supposed to hear something back on Monday."

"So that's why you're in town?"

"That's the main reason, yes."

I thought of a million comforting observations ("There's always room for hope," "God will see you through this," "Some people beat it," etc.) and rejected them all as offensively trite, factually bogus. Anything truthful I might say would be disheartening, and anything positive a disrespectful deceit. So I elected to say nothing, and sensed in her a profound gratitude for my silence.

"Just to make matters worse," she went on, "his health insurance won't pay any of the hospital bills because the company says it's a pre-existing condition."

"Well, how long has he had a policy with them?"

"Three months. See, Eastern Kentucky Coal - that's the company that owns the Big Branch mines - switched carriers back in March because this new carrier's premiums are cheaper, or something like that. So all their employees were forced to take out new policies, or else pay the previous carrier's premiums out of their own pockets. Obviously none of them could afford to do *that*, and so now my brother's screwed. The whole thing was really shady."

I picked up my beer and drained it in three gulps. I ordered another and, bridling my urge for a cigarette, faced the pretty, despondent lady beside me. For a long time I just looked at her, very intently, my brain racing. Finally I said, "Susan, does the name Archibald Lancaster mean anything to you?"

We got back to the motel at five minutes of eight, agreeing to meet in the lobby at eight o' clock sharp the following morning. It had taken me about half an hour to convince her, first of all, that I wasn't a crackpot, and secondly, that I would indeed be able to

236

effect the kind of scenario I had described. Suffice it to say that I had never in my life witnessed such total astonishment or such effusive appreciation. Nor would I in the four weeks that I spent on the road with Archie, not for all the boundless incredulity and elation I was to encounter.

"Terry," she said as she got into her car. It was a white Honda Civic, dusty and well-worn. "Are you an angel sent from heaven?"

"No," I said matter-of-factly. "I'm a journalist from Pittsburgh."

She laughed, then started crying again. I went to her, hugged her. "Hey," I said. "I'm only doing what any other decent human being in my position would do. I'm no saint, Susan."

"You are to me," she said through her sobs.

I hugged her tighter. "Well, I graciously accept the title, okay? But remember what I said: I'm not doing this to get something in return. I expect nothing. You owe me nothing. Got it?"

She nodded, her face nestled in my chest.

"Your gratitude is reward enough." I planted a tentative kiss on her forehead. She did not recoil, or even flinch. "Not to mention your beauty."

22

Not long after Archie and I had departed The Blossom Dairy in Charleston, West Virginia, a reporter for that city's evening newspaper, the *Daily Mail*, entered the restaurant and took a seat at the counter. His name was Jonathan Friedman. He was an habitué of the establishment. After taking his order, the young woman upon whom Archie had bestowed the sum of three hundred and twenty dollars broached the subject of her recent encounter with the multi-billionaire. Of course, she didn't *know* that he was a multi-billionaire.

But John Friedman did.

"He was this chubby, white-haired guy," she told Mr. Friedman, still reeling from Archie's inexplicable largess. The four bills which Archie had given her were fanned out on the counter, as tangible evidence of her fantastic claim. "Not bad-looking, though. He was with a younger guy, also not bad-looking. I don't think they were business partners. I don't really know *what* they were. They seemed like a pretty unlikely pair."

"And what did he say, exactly? The chubby one, I mean?"

"Nothing, really. He just handed the money to me and told me I deserved it for working so hard."

Friedman snickered. I imagine that the penchants of his palate were not the only explanation for his frequent presence at the restaurant. "Well, he had a point there."

"I guess. I mean, hell, I *do* slave my butt off."

"Damn right you do. So did you catch his name?"

"Um." She struggled to remember the occurrence, which now seemed to her a distant, charming dream. "Yeah, the younger guy said it. He said, 'That's Archibald Lancaster, fifth richest man in the world!'"

Friedman's jaw dropped. "Say again?"

"Archibald Lancaster. That was his name. What, is he famous or something?"

Friedman nodded, very slowly. "Yes," he said. "You could definitely say that. What about the other guy? Any idea what *his* name was?"

"No, it was never mentioned."

"And where were they headed? Did they say?"

"Oh, shit," said the girl.

"What?"

"Hang on, I'll remember. The guy who gave me the money was talking on his cell phone, and he said the name of the town."

"And what was it? What was the name of the town?"

She closed her eyes, concentrated. It started with an "I," didn't it? Yes, it did. But it wasn't Indianapolis, no. And it wasn't Ithaca. It wasn't a well-known town at all. It was -

She opened her eyes. "Inez," she said. "Inez, Kentucky."

23

That night, I sat for a long while on the edge of my bed, in my motel room, and thought. I thought, for one thing, that I could use another drink, and that I had been drinking too much lately, thought too much about alcohol and when I'd next be consuming it. I also thought about Winston, and how he figured in all this, what he might be doing at that moment, a whole mansion to himself. I wondered how often he thought about me, whether my periodic conviction that he felt something for me was but wishful thinking. I thought about my family, and why I had not been totally forthright with them.

And, finally, I thought about Susan. I had not been totally forthright with her, either. I had told her what I had told my family: that Archie's involvement in my "little experiment" was entirely voluntary, that he was doing it out of the bigness of his heart. In each case I had lied for the same reason: I saw no point in doing otherwise, in divulging the truth of the matter. What good would it serve? Besides, I had made a deal with Archie that, provided he satisfactorily discharged the duties he had undertaken, I would hold his scandalous conduct, both personal and political, in strictest confidence. And there was, to be certain, indisputable logic in my thinking. Yet, nevertheless, I felt guilty. I felt sneaky, underhanded, manipulative.

I guess that night, my first night on the road with the man who was to forever alter umpteen lives, was the first time I began to doubt the morality of my scheme.

I knocked on Archie's door at quarter of eight.

"Who is it?" His voice was gruff, almost hostile.

"It's Terry. Let me in, please."

"You said to be in the lobby at eight. It's quarter till."

"Well, there's been a development. A slight change in the weather. Open up."

He opened the door. He had pants and a shirt on, but no socks or shoes. The lower half of his face was a veil of green shaving cream. His eyes were dull and bloodshot, anchored fast in abject self-pity.

"Change in the weather?" he said, a prisoner who had just received word that his usual breakfast of eggs and toast was to be replaced by dry oatmeal and a cup of lard.

"Just a slight one," I said, and stepped inside.

When we emerged ten minutes later, Archie had his checkbook in his hand and a severe frown on his face. It was not, he had said, that he did not sympathize with the circumstances of Susan and her brother, but rather, that he did not feel it his place to intrude into their personal affairs. He felt it presumptuous to make the offer I was requiring that he make, dismissed as folly my assurance that they would be greatly appreciative of his generosity.

"Perhaps *she* will be," he had said, "but I have a hunch that *he'll* resent the hell out of it." He had not even bothered with an attempt to defend the insurance company's refusal to pay her brother's claim, nor Dacey's failure to somehow remedy the situation. I supposed he had known that such would be pointless.

As promised, Susan was waiting for us in the lobby. Her brother, on the other hand, was nowhere to be seen. "Where's Jimmy?" I asked, momentarily forgoing introductions.

"In the car," she whispered. She was, I noted in passing, one of those rare women who make jeans and a halter top look elegant. "He wouldn't come in."

I motioned for her to step aside. "Why not? What's wrong?"

"He won't talk to him," she said, stealing fitful glances at Archie.

"Why not? Principle of the thing?"

"Precisely."

"Well, will he take the money?"

"Only if it comes from you. He said that... that Mr. Lancaster can reimburse you if he wants, but he won't take the money directly from him. I know it seems silly, but that's the only way he'll do it."

"I guess he wasn't much impressed with Archie's conversion, huh?"

She bit her bottom lip, gave a little shrug. "I guess not."

I nodded. "Okay," I said. "I'd sort of expected this. And it's fine. It's fine. We can work around it."

She took my hands, pulled me closer. "No," she said. "We won't take a penny from you."

"Susan, he'll give me the money. Don't worry about it."

"Then let me see him do it. He has his checkbook with him, doesn't he? Tell him to write you a check. Right here, right now."

I turned around, made brief eye contact with Archie (his face was stony, uninterested), and turned back to her. "Okay," I said. "All right. We can do that. Why don't you come over and meet him? You don't have to shake his hand or anything. Just meet the guy. I promise he won't bite." I tried a smile and found it unfitting.

"Okay."

I took a couple of steps, then realized she wasn't following me. "Susan?"

"Yeah?"

"Are you coming?"

At last she budged. "Yeah, I'm coming."

"Archibald Lancaster," I said, "I'd like you to meet Ms. Susan Reynolds."

He went to extend a hand, then pulled it back. Much to my chagrin, his intuition about the reluctance of Jimmy Reynolds to accept his recompense had been vindicated, and his split-second judgment, now, to withdraw his hand bespoke a surprising sensitivity. I began to sense, rather uncomfortably, that Archie was far more in control of this situation than I, and somehow more emotionally in tune with his beneficiaries-to-be. "Ms. Reynolds," he said, "a pleasure."

She manufactured a polite smile. "Nice to meet you, sir."

"Terrance here informs me that you and your brother have fallen on hard times, and I deeply regret that. Now, I realize that charity is never easy to accept, but it would be my honor-"

I kicked him lightly on his shin. "Archie, it seems that Ms. Reynolds and her brother, for reasons we need not explore, would prefer that I myself confer the funds upon them. If it's all the same to you, of course."

Archie shot a perplexed look at me, then flashed a smile at her. It was the quintessential politician's smile, slick and opaque and well-proportioned. "Of course. Whatever you fine folks are most comfortable with. I'm quite flexible."

"He's not kidding," I said. "Sometimes, if he tries hard enough, he can get his head all the way up his ass."

There was shocked laughter all around. Even my own laughter was shocked; I had not intended to make any such remark, nor was fully able to believe that I actually had. (What had prompted it, exactly, was an even deeper mystery.) Archie, I could tell, was inwardly livid. But on the outside he kept smiling, and said this: "Well, Terry, shall I write you a check so that you can assist this young lady?"

So he wrote me a check for twenty-five thousand dollars. Jimmy Reynolds's medical bills did not even approach that figure, but I had convinced Susan the night before that, given the huge uncertainty surrounding her brother's future (medical and otherwise), such an amount would be quite suitable. Besides, I had added, he deserved that much for his inconvenience, for how abominably his employer had treated him. They both did.

I put Archie's check in my wallet (I would probably just tear it up later, I figured, and spring for the twenty-five grand myself), then wrote Susan a check for the same amount. She thanked Archie perfunctorily, and me profusely.

And there, again, was that guilty feeling.

While Archie was on the phone with his lawyer, confirming that the contracts had been shipped overnight to the Inez Sleep Away, Susan led me outside to meet her brother.

"I'm really sorry about that," I said to her, as the lobby door swung closed behind me. "About how that... went. If I'd known your brother was going to feel awkward about taking -"

She silenced me with a kiss. "Terry," she said, tears pricking the corners of her eyes, "how on earth can you be apologizing after what you just did for us?"

I stammered, blushed. "Well."

"In the space of ten seconds you completely changed our lives."

I shook my head. "No," I said. "*Archie* did. Mr. Lancaster did."

"Yes, because of *you*."

"It's his money, Susan, not mine."

She laughed, wiped her eyes. "Dammit, Terry, can't you just accept my thanks?"

"I accept it," I said.

"Good. Now come with me."

Jimmy Reynolds was a big guy, though not quite as big as I had expected, with stern eyes and a rugged visage. He wore two or three days' stubble on his chin, and his hair in a ponytail. There was a partially visible tattoo on his left bicep, though too much of it was hidden by his shirtsleeve for its design to be identifiable. He looked to me more like a mechanic or a construction worker than a coal miner, one of those surly, taciturn, beer-drinking types who hide under cars all day or swathe themselves in the brainless whir of a jackhammer. Certainly I was not prepared for the timid, soft-spoken man who greeted me with a gentle handshake and a cautious smile.

"Jimmy," he said. Perhaps, I reflected absently, the taciturn part was right.

"Terry Farmer. Pleased to meet you, sir."

"You know my sister." He phrased this as a statement, but clearly meant it as a question.

"Yes, sir. I met her yesterday, at the pool." I started to point, then, for fear of seeming patronizing, lowered my hand.

"You're friends with Archie Lancaster?"

"Well," I said, shaking my head, "I wouldn't say *friends*."

"He's inside?"

"Yes, right inside the motel there."

He nodded, very slowly and very calmly. Equally calmly he said, "I wouldn't give that piece of shit five minutes of my time. Not five *seconds*. You can tell him I said so."

"I completely understand, Jimmy. Sir. And I'll be sure to pass that along."

"And neither would any of the fellas I work with down the pit." He looked not at me as he spoke, but at the dashboard of Susan's car.

I nodded, smiled at Susan. She smiled back, as if to say, *That's Jimmy for you!*

"My sis tells me he's a new man now, says you done showed him the light."

"Well, Jimmy, he *has* undergone a certain transformation."

"Shit," he scoffed, "now you sound like Susan, slinging them

248

fifty-cent words around." A faint grin touched his lips. Susan laughed.

"Yeah, bad habit of mine."

The grin, barely there to begin with, vanished instantaneously. "Sonofabitch put a whole buncha good men outta work not too long ago."

"Yes, I know about that."

"Wouldn't piss on the bastard if he was on fire."

"I don't blame you, Jimmy. But he really has -"

"Jimmy," Susan interjected. "Remember what we discussed last night? About the money?"

Jimmy nodded, scowled. "I said I'd take it from your friend here, but not a cent from that no-good scum bag Lancaster."

Susan presented the check to her brother. "That's exactly what we did, Jimmy. This is from Mr. Farmer. From Terry. He wrote it himself."

Jimmy frowned, wheezing a little. He appraised the check cursorily, with seeming indifference, and did not move to take it. "I still don't like takin' no pity money."

"This isn't pity money," I said. "It's just what Archie, Mr. Lancaster, owes you."

"There ain't no sum in the world that'd... that'd cover *that*."

"Well, I hope this will make an acceptable start."

Just then a violent coughing fit beset him. He clutched the armrest, doubling over.

"Jimmy?" Susan asked, alarmed. "Are you all right?"

He managed a weak nod, his coughs tapering. "I'm all right." He looked at me, his eyes hard and serious. "Yeah, it'll do. And after that snake cuts you a check to cover thissun, I strongly recommend you cash it and run like the mill-tails of hell. Just pretend... pretend you never knew him."

I looked at Susan, then back at her brother. "Yeah, Jimmy. Yeah, sure, I'll give that some thought."

"As for you -" He hoisted himself out of the seat, took the check, and embraced me. I was so startled that I merely stood there, limp and frozen. "You're doing a hell of a good thing, buddy, and I thank you from the bottom of my heart."

"You're welcome," I said, and my voice sounded curiously like his, reedy and constricted. "You're welcome, Jimmy."

"Come to the mines with us," I said. "With Archie and me. We're going to make history today. I want you to witness it for yourself."

"No." She paused, thought, shook her head. "I wouldn't be

comfortable with that. I don't even think you should do it, Terry. It's a bad idea, believe me. I mean, you saw how Jimmy reacted to this whole thing. His feelings toward Mr. Lancaster might be a little more extreme than the other miners', but not much." She sighed. "It just isn't going to work, Terry. Stick to your grocery stores and bottling plants."

"Not a chance," I said. "Those miners, and the residents of Inez generally, are the people to whom Archie owes the most. Your brother was just a beginning, a symbol of the larger campaign, as it were."

She looked at me doubtfully.

"Look, if they start throwing tomatoes or try to run him over with a bulldozer, I'll get him out of there, okay?"

She smiled dimly. "Okay."

Without really meaning to (at least, *I* had not meant to), we had traversed the parking lot and now found ourselves at the pool, where a seemingly eternal fifteen hours ago we had met. "Will I see you again?" she asked. "When you get back to Pittsburgh?"

"Of course," I said, and for some reason thought immediately of Winston. "If you'd like."

She nodded, smiled again. Her eyes were at once wistful, hopeful, dampened by thoughts perhaps of some distasteful eventuality. "I'd like that very much, Terry. How long do you think you and Mr. Lancaster will be gone?"

"A few months. Four, six at the outside."

"How can I reach you once you're home?"

"Got a pen and paper handy?"

"I'm afraid not."

"Got your cell phone on you?"

She shook her head. "I left it back at the house. I didn't get much sleep last night, so I was kind of moving in a fog this morning. Sorry. Do you have yours? You could put my number in it."

I grinned. "We're quite the pair, Susan. I don't even *own* a cell phone. I'm... well, hopelessly behind the times, I guess. A true curmudgeon."

She laughed. "Nothing wrong with being a little old-fashioned."

"Except in moments like this," I said, laughing with her. "But anyhow, just look me up. I'm in the book. Believe it or not, there are only three Terrance Farmers in Pittsburgh, and the other two are both married. Their wives' names are listed alongside theirs."

"Were you *ever* married, Terry?"

"Once," I said. "But it's been over for three years now. You?"

"Never," she said. "Always wanted to try it, though."

252

I stuffed my hands in my pockets, feeling oddly encumbered by them. "You know, you'd almost think you and your brother belonged to different families. Where's *your* accent?"

She giggled. "I guess I lost it when I moved up north. And, yeah, Jimmy and I are very different, but we're also very close. He's not exactly an intellectual, but he's the sweetest man you could ever hope to meet."

"He seems very nice, yes. Very genuine."

"He is. He's a really great guy." She enclosed her hand around my arm. "And so are you."

I sighed. My pink cloud had burst, and all at once I felt terribly sad. And, somehow, very much alone. "Thanks," I said. Then: "Well."

"Yeah," she said, licking the corners of her mouth. "Well."

There was a long, wordless moment in which we exchanged thoughts too onerous and poignant to voice, and then, with only fleeting hesitation, I kissed her.

24

While hardly the expert on Archibald Lancaster's corporate life which I had become in my waning days as a journalist, John Friedman was nevertheless well acquainted with the general flavor

253

of the Lancaster dynasty. He had read my articles, I would later learn, on Dacey's feeble response to the coal spill at Inez and Archie's staggering contribution to the Benjamin Grent campaign.

He had also done a little independent research on the man's history in the business world, his lineage, and the incredible wealth he had accumulated over the previous two decades. The young reporter was quite naturally intrigued, therefore, by the idea that the world-famous coal baron might be involved in some radically benevolent cause.

To the end of satisfying both his personal and professional curiosity, and having a free weekend, Mr. Friedman had thus taken the liberty of tracking his lead, courtesy of Miss Blossom Dairy, all the way to Inez. Fortunately for his efforts, but more his career, there was (and, so far as I know, remains) only one motel in the town. That motel, of course, was the Inez Sleep Away. Possibly he would have made the trip on that basis alone, but thanks to the loose-lipped day clerk to whom Archie's name doubtless meant exactly nothing, this ambitious and quick-thinking newsman was spared having to make such a decision.

And so there he was at eight forty-three in the morning, sitting in his ice-blue Dodge van in the parking lot of the motel, sipping coffee and patiently awaiting the exit of America's

Corporate Prince.

Wisely, he did not make himself known to us as Archie and I emerged from the lobby. Had he done so, it seems quite likely that Archie would have insisted on a modification of the day's itinerary, so as to eschew Mr. Friedman's meddlesome clutches. And I probably would have gone along with such an adjustment; I had no greater desire that Archie's obligatory acts of charity be publicized than did Archie himself. Why, precisely, Friedman chose to bide his time is still unclear to me. Perhaps he had anticipated the futility of interrogating Archie there in the parking lot, or perhaps his curiosity, the very impetus which had brought him to Inez, superseded his journalistic instinct to ambush at the first opportunity his unsuspecting prey. Whatever the reason, he stayed in his van, out of view, and quietly followed my Buick to the McDonald's at which Archie and I stopped for breakfast.

"Let's go inside," I said, parking the car. "We'll sit and eat like civilized human beings."

"And give some more of my money away?"

I smiled. The contracts would not arrive until noon or so, but Archie was already vividly aware of their essential dispensability, that their principal purpose was simply to appease him. "Well," I said, "the thought *had* crossed my mind."

"I only have five hundred in cash. That's all the ATM would give me."

"Which ATM was that?"

"The one I visited on my way to dinner last night."

"Grandad's?"

"How'd you guess?"

I laughed. "Come on," I said. "I have a few bills on me. I'll help you out with this one."

We went inside, and John Friedman followed.

The restaurant was fairly empty, of course, since most of its working patrons had already come and gone. There were, in fact, but three souls in the dining area: an old lady in a lime-green house-dress, a boy of perhaps twelve with mud smeared on his hands and face, and a middle-aged man in grimy coveralls. They were quite a trio, but no match for the employees. These latter consisted of a morbidly obese black woman, an overweight young man who next to the black woman resembled a length of fishing line, and a gawky fellow, likely the eldest of the bunch, who was evidently the shift manager (the stripes on his shirt gave him away).

Archie and I approached the counter, and the two cashiers snapped to attention. I went to the black lady's register, Archie to her Caucasian and substantially skinnier counterpart's. They said almost in unison, "What can I get you, sir?" I felt the eyes of the patrons on my back, boring into it. I gave her my order (two Egg McMuffins and a black coffee, I can still remember that), Archie gave his to the white guy (what *it* was I *cannot* remember), and they punched their buttons with the pictures of hamburgers and milkshakes and chicken salads.

I recall thinking, as I often had, how mechanical and impersonal was the whole scenario, how distinctly robotic it made me feel. With six and a half billion people on the planet, it came as no surprise to me that the larger part of modern life was increasingly so constructed. These were not new or revolutionary thoughts - that, with the technological explosion of the late twentieth and early twenty-first centuries, human beings for decades had been steadily dehumanized, perfecting the art of emotional paralysis, had become almost platitudinous. But they were nevertheless a powerful reminder of why I had undertaken this expedition in the first place.

Other, that is, than my profound if perhaps excessive thirst to help shrink the ever-widening income gap in a country with a

257

surplus of seemingly everything but integrity and perspective. I wanted - and do please forgive the howlingly idealistic ring of this - to break down those ridiculous, artificial barriers and, well, bring people together. And what better way to bring people together than by meting out giant clumps of free, no-strings-attached cash?

"Ma'am," I said to the morbidly obese woman behind the register, "how much do you make?" I think I heard Archie groan.

"'Scuse me?"

"How much money does this job pay you? Six bucks an hour? Seven?"

"Um." She reluctantly revealed that her job paid exactly five dollars and eighty-five cents per hour.

"Five dollars and eighty-five cents an hour," I echoed.

"That's right."

"That's despicable," I observed.

"Say what?"

"I say it's *despicable*, is what I say!"

"Hell yeah it is!" volunteered the fat Caucasian.

I turned to my exasperated hostage. "Isn't it despicable, Archie?"

"I can think of few more egregious crimes in the history of mankind," he said. His tone was even, his face perfectly deadpan.

"I heard that," said the black woman, who had, indeed, appeared to hear him.

Perhaps fearing a mutiny, at this juncture the gawky shift manager, whose name tag identified him as Greg, valiantly intervened. "Is there a problem here, fellas?" he asked, congenially enough.

"No problem," I said. "I was just having a conversation with -" I looked at the woman's tag - "with Marsha here about how obscenely underpaid she is."

"Yes," Greg said. He had a slight lisp. "I overheard that part."

"Well, Greg, do *you* think it's fair, how meagerly she's compensated for her labor? Indeed, how meagerly folks of her ilk generally are compensated?" I glanced at the other cashier's tag and saw that *his* name was Mike. "That includes you, Mike."

"Um, sir," said Greg, "I really don't know. I'm just the shift manager. I'm not in charge of payroll or anything."

I nodded, saw out the corner of my eye that Archie had his head down. I was almost beginning to feel sorry for him. "You know, Greg, I suspect that *you're* not paid what you're worth, either."

He shrugged sheepishly. "Well."

"Well nothing! What do you pull in? Seven, maybe eight

bucks an hour?"

He floundered. "I really don't... that's none of your business!"

"Fair enough," I said, freeing my wallet from my back pocket. "It's a rather personal question I asked you, and I respect your wish to keep the answer private." I thumbed twelve hundred dollars in fifties out of my wallet. "But it's a shame you're not more open about it, Greg, because unless you make more than twenty cool ones an hour-"

"Seven-twenty!" he blurted. "That's all I make!"

"Damn, that *is* a pittance." I counted out four hundred dollars and pushed the bills across the counter. "Here you are."

"Hey!" barked Mike, gesturing to his co-worker. "What about me and Marsha?"

"Yeah," she trumpeted proudly, "what about us?"

I laughed. "Geez, gimme a second! I was just *getting* to that." I started to count out four hundred for Marsha, then stopped after the third bill. I looked at Greg. "Wait a second... give me fifty of that back."

"What?"

"Give me fifty of it back. You said you make seven-twenty an hour. That's one thirty-five more than Marsha and Mike make."

"So?"

"So it wouldn't be fair to give you as much as I'm going to give them."

Greg snarled. "Hey, come on! You can't do that! What are you, an Indian giver?"

I reached across the counter and snatched one of the fifties in his hand. "Thirty seconds ago you would have been happy to get twenty bucks! Now gimme that!"

"No! You already... hey!"

Thus ensued a feverish and decidedly juvenile battle for the fifty-dollar bill, which ended a moment later when it tore in half. Greg issued an anguished moan. Marsha gasped. Mike looked on in horrified disbelief, his considerable jaw agape.

"Oh, Jesus Christ," said Archie, removing his own wallet. He dug out a fifty and shoved it at Greg. "Here, just take one of mine." He shook his head in disgust. "You're pathetic, the lot of you! You'd think you hadn't eaten in days!"

From behind us the old lady in the lime-green dress said meekly, "I'll settle for twenty."

But of course she didn't have to, because Archie gave her a full one hundred and fifty dollars. He gave the same amount to the boy and the man in the coveralls. (He was rather chary of entrusting such a large sum to a child, but I prodded him, exhorting the boy to give the money to his parents; he assured me that he would.)

After we had made the rounds, I addressed everyone in the restaurant. I said this: "You have just experienced that rarest of human behaviors: altruism. It consists of performing charitable acts, kindnesses, especially to strangers, without being legally or socially obligated to do so, and without any expectation of reciprocation. That is, you do nice things for people, even people you don't know, without expecting anything in return, and even though you needn't do so to avoid incarceration or alienation from your peers. It is a wonderful and highly underrated concept, and I suggest that all of you investigate it just as soon as you possibly can, if you haven't already. You may find that putting it into practice makes for a very rewarding hobby, and that the satisfaction it gives you is worth incalculably more than whatever material assets you give away in its pursuit. Also, the more you give away, and the more in need the recipient, the greater the spiritual reward.

"Now, the altruism from which you have benefited here today was not an isolated incident. On the contrary, it is, or will soon become, just one of a very long series of such incidents, some of which you may eventually read about in the newspaper or hear about on television. I suppose, therefore, that I had might as well reveal, without further ado, the identity of the engineer behind this crusade, the man behind the mask, as it were, who will be orchestrating these systematic if ostensibly spontaneous contributions to the common welfare." I smiled and gestured flourishingly at Archie, whose face was caught in a fierce comic battle between embarrassment and ire. "Ladies and gentlemen, I give you Archibald Lancaster!"

By the time I had finished delivering this speech, both the patrons and the employees were staring at me with utterly blank expressions, dumbfounded perhaps beyond recall. What they didn't know, of course, was that the night before, while lying in bed at the motel, I had mentally composed the speech and, by silently reciting it a half-dozen times, committed it to memory.

S-l-i-c-k!

Our tiny audience broke into stunned, uncertain applause (I guessed that none of them was familiar with Archie's work), at which point John Friedman, who had skillfully hidden himself at a table behind a row of flowerpots on a ledge, rose and himself vigorously applauded this exalting vision of panoramic goodwill.

"Hear, hear!" he cried, laughing (not quite contemptuously, but not exactly cheerily, either). "That sounds thoroughly refreshing, gentlemen! Any chance you might have a little something left over for yours truly, before you continue on your way?"

Archie and I looked at each other, as if both wondering if the other somehow knew this man. When it became apparent that neither of us did, I looked at Friedman and said, "Who are you?"

He came around the ledge, grinning, and put his hands to his chest, feigning modesty. "Me? Why, I'm just passing through, thought I'd stop in for a cup of coffee before I ran my morning errands."

"Where's your coffee?" I asked.

His grin faltered. "I haven't ordered it yet."

I reached into my pocket and turned up seventy-four cents, mostly in dimes. Although I hadn't the foggiest idea who he was or what he was after, for some reason I already hated this fellow. I guess he was just that obviously a no-good prick; or maybe it's that, after you've interviewed hundreds of people, you develop an uncanny ability to spot the pricks long before they've exposed their rottenness to you. I went over and put the coins in his hand, closing his fingers around them. "Here you go, buddy. That's for your coffee."

Now his grin withered completely. "For my coffee," he said. "Yeah."

"Everyone else got over a hundred dollars."

"Well," I said, "everyone else didn't ask."

He blinked at me, then went to Archie. "John Friedman," he said, extending his hand. Archie did not shake it. Seemingly unruffled, Friedman lowered it and casually brushed one of his pant legs. "I'm a reporter for the Charleston *Daily Mail*. In West Virginia."

Archie looked at me. "Ever have *deja vu*?"

"Only when I don't want to," I said. Marsha tittered. She was really growing on me, that girl.

"How'd you find us?" Archie asked John Friedman.

"You stopped by The Blossom Dairy yesterday, did you not?"

"You saw us there?"

"No," said Friedman, "but Gina did."

Archie motioned for me. "Let's go, Terry. Our business here is finished, is it not?"

"It is," I said, and joined him at the door.

"Hang on just a second, fellas," Friedman persisted, following us outside. "I just want to ask Mr. Lancaster a couple of questions."

I turned and glared at him. "Look, buddy, Archie isn't giving any interviews, and you don't need to bother chasing this story, because I myself am a reporter for a newspaper in Pittsburgh, and I'll be covering the whole thing. So, please, begone."

Naturally, he ignored me. "Whose idea was it?" he pressed. "To give away all this money? Was it your own, Mr. Lancaster?"

Likewise ignoring Friedman, Archie and I hurried to my car. But still he was not deterred. (Reporters, alas, are about as hard to deter as serial killers, and twice as irksome.) "How much do you plan to give away? Will it only be here in Kentucky? How many people do you expect will profit from your alms?"

We got into the Buick and I started the engine, rolled the window down. "I'll try this one more time," I said to Friedman. "Fuck off!"

He pulled back a little. "Who are *you*, anyway?" he said.

"The Dalai Lama," I said. "Didn't the haircut give me away?"

I put the car in reverse, gave Friedman the bird, and squealed the tires as I turned out of the parking lot.

The Inez McDonald's, as well as the Inez Sleep Away and the Ninth Street Bank, are actually about two miles outside the "city limits" (these bounding an area of perhaps seven-tenths of a square mile). At the junction where Ninth Street intersects with Main Street, there is a sign which reads, "Welcome to Inez: Where Community Comes First!" Unless the sign has been replaced or restored in the past eight months, spray-painted below it, over the "600" in the words "Pop. 600," is the numeral "466." Apparently somebody conducted an informal census and found the original estimate of the town's population inordinately optimistic.

As we passed this sign, I pointed it out to Archie and said, with real glee in my voice, "Hey, look, we're finally here!"

He shot me an incurious look, then faced the window.

"I'm sorry about that reporter," I said. "You don't think I had anything to do with that, do you?"

He shook his head. "No."

"Well, you don't seem very happy."

"Why *should* I be happy, Terry? Would *you* enjoy being held against your will, and dragged all over God's green earth, and forced to slowly squander your life's earnings on a bunch of backwoods hicks?"

I laughed. He really could crack me up sometimes, that nutty multi-billionaire. His take on things was, if nothing else, charmingly novel, and risible in the narrowness and rarity of the experiences from which it arose.

"Archie, please. Ninety-nine million dollars is less than one two-hundredth of your entire net worth. Your giving it away is the equivalent of the average American's giving away a hundred dollars." I did not mention the fact, because I found it almost revoltingly obvious, that the average American would have to work for about thirteen hours to earn a hundred dollars, whereas Archie made two or three times that much in the time it took him to blink.

He faced me now, with an expression of stark incredulity. "That can't be right," he said.

"Are you even aware, Archie, that the average American makes about twenty thousand dollars a year?"

"Well, yes."

"And has virtually nothing in savings?"

"He has assets."

"Yes, a house worth perhaps fifty thousand dollars the mortgage to which will take him about thirty years to pay off. And a car worth, say, seven thousand which he might own outright by the time his kids graduate from high school. And that's about it. No yacht, no real estate, no expensive jewelry, no stocks or bonds in the bank. Just a house he can barely afford and a piece-of-shit car he half-owns." I stole a glance at him. "What are *your* assets? Are they even included in the twenty-two-point-five billion you're supposed to be worth?"

He was facing the window again. "Look, I don't want to fight about this, all right? I just want to get it over with as quickly and painlessly as possible. And by the way, Terry, I've seen no evidence of your recording any of the transactions I've made thus far. By *my* calculations, I've already parted with one thousand, one hundred and twenty dollars."

"I don't doubt that you've got it pinpointed to the cent."

"And we've not even used the contracts yet! Isn't that going to foul up your formula?"

"I'll figure it out, don't worry."

To his credit, he did not appear to be particularly worried.

Big Branch Road forks off Main Street about three miles east of Inez. Between it and the western edge of the town, there is a string of empty storefronts, ramshackle double-wides (pink insulation stippled with soot burst from the sprung corners of one of these, which I might have thought abandoned if not for the "JesUSaves" quilt hanging in one of the windows, a sheet of duct-taped plastic where the pane of glass should have been), a pawnshop, a row of tidy-looking one-story homes with big, asphalt aprons, and a sandstone courthouse. Nearly all of the modest yards have dog pens, the preponderance of them housing bony pit bulls. Boat trailers are parked in fully thirty percent of the driveways, often alongside inexplicably expensive vehicles. At the time Archie and I drove through the town, which was in the third week of June 2004, there were no visible signs of the disaster which had struck seven months prior. Where thick black sludge had once oozed, smothering all life in its path, there now sprouted the smiling, lush green grass that is the marriage of hydroseed and mulch.

Roughly parallel to Main Street, with the exception of a half-mile segment which circumscribes a nest of trees before doubling back, runs Coldwater Creek, the body of water hit hardest by the slurry spill. It is at the confluence of this tiny tributary and another, Wolf Creek, that Big Branch Road inconspicuously originates. Flanking the mountainous artery itself are snaking corridors of maples, spruces, and dogwoods, periodically punctuated by craggy shelves of limestone or shale, and clearings littered with junked car parts and discarded furniture. In one of them I saw the decrepit, rusted skeleton of an entire flatbed truck, and wondered how long it had sat there, and how much longer it would sit there.

"Archie," I said as we passed the truck, "tell me something, and please tell the truth: Did you have anything to do with Eastern Kentucky Coal's switching insurance carriers? With Jimmy

Reynolds's illness not being covered under the new plan?"

He shook his head. "No. Dacey owns the plant and the mines, but they operate quite autonomously. We - I - don't participate in such decisions. We're not in the business of micromanagement."

I don't think I entirely believed him at the time, but I do now. I have come, it seems, to believe a lot of the things he'd said that I had initially dismissed as barefaced propaganda.

I have gotten to know the man.

The fence surrounding the mine-site emerges, to the unready motorist, like a great steel monster from a dense fog, its million or so hollow, diamond-shaped eyes peering out at an alien world. Its mood is uneasy and unsure. It is sneaky, furtive, and abrupt. It is tall and wide. It might well encircle the grounds of the world's oldest and most secluded castle. In fact it girds one of the oldest and probably the most notorious bevy of pit mines on the face of the earth. That the site should be so well hidden from public view did not, frankly, surprise me much; I had known enough about the workings of the coal industry to expect it, and had long appreciated the dark symbolism of their physical remoteness: whereof one is blind, one finds no cause for alarm.

"I assume," said Archie, "that you have a plan."

"A plan?"

"To get us in."

I looked at him, appalled. "What are you talking about? You own the fucking place!"

"Oh, okay. And what shall I tell the guard? That I'm just dropping in for a visit with my buddy from Pittsburgh?"

Flabbergasted, I slowed the car to a near stop. Dirt kicked up around the tires. The blacktop had petered out some hundred yards back. "Jesus Christ. If this was going to present a problem, Archie, why didn't you say something sooner?"

"Because," he replied with indisputable logic, "I assumed you had a plan."

"Haven't you ever *been* here before?"

"Once," he said. "Six years ago."

"And what was the purpose of your visit?"

"To discuss a supply contract with the president of Eastern Kentucky Coal, who was here discussing it with the mine supervisor."

"Well, might the president be here today?"

Archie laughed grimly. "On a Saturday?"

I growled and slammed my fist against the steering wheel. (Truth be told, I already wanted a drink.) "Goddammit!

272

Sonofabitch!"

"Calm down, Terry. I'm sure we can come up with *something.*"

"Got any suggestions?"

He thought for a moment. "Yes," he said. "I do have one."

We pulled up to the gate. I had already rolled down the driver's-side window of my car. A mechanical wooden arm with orange and white stripes obstructed our path. A young guard, no more than twenty-five years old, occupied the squat white booth. He poked his head out of the paneless window. "How you doin'?" he asked cheerfully, in the native accent. "Can I help you with somethin'?"

"Hello," I said. "My name is Terry Farmer, and this -" Archie leaned forward on command. "This is Archibald Lancaster."

Whether it was Archie's name or face or both I cannot say, but, whatever the trigger, the guard straightened at once and conjured a look of sober deference. "Sir," he said, "how are you?"

"Fine," said Archie, with a nod. "How are you?"

"I reckon I'm all right," said the guard. "Thanks for askin'!"

"Listen," I said, "I apologize for Mr. Lancaster's and my showing up unannounced like this, but we're in the middle of a

273

spur-of-the-moment tour of all the Dacey Energy mines, kind of a half-PR, half-rally-the-troops sort of thing, and we just happened to be in the area today. Archie, Mr. Lancaster, intends to visit all the mines in eastern Kentucky over the next week or so, giving pep talks to the miners and thanking them for their service to the company. Big Branch, you'll be proud to learn, is the first on our list. Are there many men down in the pit at the moment?"

The guard nodded briskly. "Oh, yeah," he said. "Saturday's probably the busiest day here! There must be fifty or sixty fellas down there just now!"

"Excellent," I said. "Well, Mr. Lancaster deeply regrets that you won't be able to attend the gathering, what with your having to tend your post and all, but..." I turned to Archie. "Sir, would you care to have a few words with your faithful employee here?"

"Certainly," said Archie.

I turned back to the guard. "What's your name, pal?"

"Doug," he said.

"Doug, Mr. Lancaster would like to shake your hand and offer you a small token of his gratitude for your hard work here at the pit."

Archie got out of the car and went to the booth. Doug emerged, smiling and chummy. Archie offered his hand and the guard accepted it enthusiastically. They exchanged a few pleasantries, and then Archie wrote him a check for five thousand dollars. For a moment Doug just held it with both hands and gawked at it, swaying as if about to faint. Then he grabbed Archie's hand and shook it again, so violently that I feared he might snap it off. I watched all this in silent rapture, and then my eyes wandered to a large sign bolted to the chain-link fence, high up on the right-hand side of the gate.

The sign read, in green letters on a white background, "HELP KEEP OUR ENVIRONMENT BEAUTIFUL! PLEASE PUT LITTER IN ITS PLACE."

How Friedman had managed to follow us to the mines without our knowing it is something I may never figure out, but which vastly altered the course of events over the next four weeks. I suppose that he stayed far enough behind us to evade notice, but close enough not to lose sight of my Buick. Besides, I had not expected him to follow us (my naiveté, I realize in retrospect, was inexcusable, especially with my being a journalist, or ex-journalist, myself), and so had not paid much attention to the cars that appeared in my rearview and side mirrors. In any event, not only did he make it to the mines unnoticed, but, through sheer cunning, was able to penetrate the main gate.

I would later learn just how he accomplished this near-miraculous feat: by telling Doug, the guard on duty, that he was with Archie and me. When the guard pointed out that Mr. Lancaster had said nothing about a third visitor, Friedman, a consummate actor, countered that Mr. Lancaster didn't *have* to say anything about a third visitor, because Mr. Lancaster didn't have to do *anything*. "If you value your job," Friedman had gently prodded, "then it would certainly be in your best interest to open the gate." He had known well enough of the poverty that engulfed places like Inez, that to the denizens of such towns there was no more frightening prospect than unemployment (death, of course, was far less opprobrious), and shamelessly exploited the fact. And why not? There was dangled before him, like cheese before a famished rat, the kind of story by which whole careers are made, and journalistic legacies established.

The guard may not have been the brightest bulb in the chandelier, but nor was he too stupid to realize who signed his bosses' checks. So he opened the gate, and in drove John Friedman, no doubt salivating at the thought of the spectacle he was about to observe.

25

An open pit mine is, truly, a sight to behold. To an aerial observer, I suppose it would resemble an inverted cone with concentric grooves of decreasing circumference spiraling around its walls (like the helix in the eye of a hypnotized cartoon character), and a blanket of black silt collected at its point. The grooves are the benches, which are basically ledges formed of sundry rocks and metals, and the blanket of silt is the coal bed. In order to enable the travel of rotary drills and draglines between the benches, flat ramps called "access roads" are plowed at forty-five degree angles to the benches, so that a machine can move freely from one to the next. The pit can range in depth from just a few dozen feet to several hundred. The one at Inez is almost five hundred feet deep.

Given the dimensions of the pit, the equipment is by necessity colossal itself. The draglines can reach heights of forty or fifty yards, with buckets large enough to hold several mid-sized automobiles. The drills, trucks, shovels, bulldozers, and so forth are comparably humongous. A typical dump truck at a large mine is six times the height of the average man and can carry two hundred and fifty tons of freight. (Still, from the elevation at which I stood the equipment near the bottom of the pit looked scarcely bigger than the toys in a small boy's sandbox.) I had read of such monstrous machinery but never actually seen it. Now that I stood at the edge of the pit, gazing down in surreal wonderment at these giant, almost mythical creatures (and, not too far in the distance, an ocean of harmless-looking sludge), I was quite literally in awe, speechless and numb. It was probably the closest thing I had ever known to a religious experience.

Archie, naturally, was less impressed.

"So what now?" he asked me. "Shall we interrupt their work so they can hurl insults at me while I try to write them checks for five grand apiece?"

"Archie," I said, "don't be so cynical. Why do you expect such a universally hostile reaction, anyway? Surely you have a supporter or two down there. You've been feeding and clothing these people and their families for close to a decade now." I looked again at the scores of men operating the various machines, boring into thick seams and dumping the overburden into the slag pit. They were, of course, completely oblivious of our presence.

"They're still smarting from what happened here," said Archie. "I don't blame them for that."

"But Dacey wasn't at fault for the spill, remember?" I raised an eyebrow, suppressed a smirk.

"True, it wasn't. But that's beside the point."

"The point being?"

A strong wind rose, and he squinted against it. "In the eyes of these men," he said, "I have perpetrated so much wrong, some of it real but most of it imagined, that no good I might do could ever redeem me."

"How do we get their attention?" I asked Archie.

"That's a good question."

"Is there a mine supervisor?"

"There's always somebody serving in that capacity, yes."

I surveyed the fifty-odd men, mere specks in the gargantuan cabs of their playthings. "Any idea who's serving in it today?"

Archie looked at me with such pure, untarnished contempt that my only defense was heedless laughter.

"Well," I said, "let's find out." I pointed to a long, pale-green building on the other side of the pit. An inoperative conveyor belt coiled its way from a pair of mine shafts in a nearby hillside, through a silo perched on a berm, and finally to the plant. They were the shafts, I expected, through which the slurry had poured into Wolf and Coldwater Creeks after the pond collapsed. "That's the treatment plant over there, is it not?"

"Yes."

"Will there be someone in there today?"

"Of course."

"Will he know who's running the show?"

"Well," said Archie, "let's find out."

So we found out. The plant supervisor, a frail, semi-coherent old man, did not appear to know who Archie was nor to care in the slightest. I'm not even sure that he knew who he himself was. I got the distinct impression that Archie and I could have introduced ourselves as members of the president's cabinet and ordered him to shut down the plant, and his only response would have been, "Oh, all right."

He did not have a clue who presently might be charged with the responsibility of overseeing the mines. He did, however, suggest a way that we could easily command the attention of all the miners. The plant was equipped with sirens, he informed us, which, when activated, signaled that the men were immediately to disable their machines and cease all activity. The sirens normally were sounded only in the event of an emergency, but the plant supervisor saw no reason why they wouldn't serve our purpose just as well.

So he turned the appropriate key and pressed the appropriate button, and the sirens commenced to wail. Within seconds, all noises and movement in the pit came to a grinding halt, as if the earth upon which the miners toiled had been swallowed by a fast-moving glacier. Man and machine alike fell still.

The old man, who never did tell us his name (and wore no badge to identify himself), furnished us with a bullhorn. "This is how we communicate with the fellas down there," he told us. "But you still gotta use your lungs on account of the wide open."

We thanked the gentleman for his time and assistance, and then started toward the door through which we had entered. At this point he surprised us by revealing that, far from being a doddering idiot, he knew substantially more than he had initially let on. "It ain't right what you done, Mr. Lancaster," he said from behind us. We turned around, Archie holding the bullhorn. I suppose we both assumed that he was referring to the corporate irresponsibility and negligence, of which Archie was the most visible symbol, widely regarded as the cause of the coal spill. If so, we were both mistaken. "Not paying all that workers' comp."

"How's that?" asked Archie.

"My brother, my grandfather, my uncle. You turned your

back on all of 'em, sir. Or your company did, anyhow. And not just them, either. They was just three in God knows how many. Denied 'em what they had a rightful claim to. You think it's all right to treat folks like that when they broked their necks for you to live like you do? Forty-six million dollars, that's what I read. Not one penny of it paid. These is people who hurt theirselves on *your* time, Mr. Lancaster."

I whispered to Archie, "What's he talking about?"

"I don't know," said Archie.

"Oh, you know," said the old man. "You know just as plain as those fancy shoes on your feet, and I can see it on your face. Excuse me, sir."

He turned and disappeared around a corner. Archie's complexion had blanched by seven shades. I felt tired, confused. My mind turned again to alcohol and its vain, bewitching promises. "How about that one?" I said languidly. My voice echoed softly off the high cement walls. "Is it real or imagined?"

Archie handed me the bullhorn and continued toward the door. "Somewhere in between," he said. "But closer to real."

I was at that moment overcome with a panicky certainty that I was somewhere I did not belong, engaged in something I could not control, and would soon regret ever having met

Archibald Lancaster, the broken shell of a man I now watched slogging through a wide, empty corridor.

It was cold in there, but it was not the cold that made me shiver.

The miners were in disarray, the sirens having ceased and there still being no obvious reason why they had come alive in the first place. Dragline, bulldozer, and shovel operators had vacated their cabs and were now standing around on benches of varying depths, speculating on what might be happening. A handful of men were climbing one of the ramps, as if perhaps meaning to ascend the pit on foot. It was impossible to know what the miners were saying or to see the expressions on their faces, of course, but I did not get the sense that they particularly welcomed the interruption of their work.

I held out my hand and spoke to Archie without looking at him. "Let me have the bullhorn, please."

He gave it to me without argument or question. I put it to my lips and pitched my voice as loudly as I could: "Good morning, Big Branch employees! My name is Terrance Farmer! I am a journalist from Pittsburgh, and have with me a very special guest who would like to address all of you! Please make your way to the top of the pit! Thank you!"

How well the men could make out my words, I don't know. But all or nearly all of them at least must have heard my voice, for a moment later they piled into their trucks and embarked on the slow, convoluted journey up the side of the massive bowl. No doubt they thought something calamitous had occurred. I could almost feel the heavy, familiar dread blossoming in their stomachs, the searing memories rushing to the surfaces of their minds, as now they themselves rushed to the surface of their gaping colliery. Wounds which in nineteen months had but scarcely closed, I imagined, had in an instant been sundered afresh.

A few minutes later, the men had parked their trucks and were trudging wearily, anxiously toward us. I was able to count forty-six of them; I suspect I missed at least half a dozen. As they got close enough to see our faces, several of their number froze in mid-stride. They recognized Archie, of course, and questioned whether they might be hallucinating. Or maybe they knew he was really there but were afraid to come any closer, lest he inform them that their next paychecks would be their last. After a moment's doubt, having no other choice, they resumed their timid march onward.

When they had all gathered round, I raised the bullhorn to

my lips again. This time, having no need to shout, I spoke at a normal volume. I said: "Gentlemen, it is my great privilege and pleasure to introduce to you Mr. Archibald Lancaster."

There was no applause. In fact, for a second or two there was no sound of any kind. Then a couple of the miners hissed and booed. Another told them to shut up. And then there was silence again.

I continued: "Gentlemen, the man who stands here before you today is not the man I suspect most of you believe yourselves to know. He is, on the contrary, a different man altogether. He may look the same and sound the same and dress the same, but please, let none of those outward appearances deceive you. For he is, I repeat, not the same man at all.

"I am a journalist from Pittsburgh. Through my work I have had the opportunity to become closely acquainted with Mr. Lancaster and the fine industry in which he plays such a pivotal role. Last week, while graciously submitting to an interview I had asked to conduct with him, Mr. Lancaster volunteered to accompany me around the country in an effort to alleviate the economic burdens of working men and women like yourselves. Logically enough, he has chosen to start with the folks to whom he is most indebted. Those are his thousands of tireless employees, especially those who, like most of you, have remained loyal to his company through some trying and turbulent times.

"And now," I concluded, "I give you Archibald Lancaster."

Unlike the speech I had delivered that morning at the Inez McDonald's, the one I had just given was entirely ad-libbed.

Hesitantly, Archie took the bullhorn from me, spoke into it. "Hello," he said.

"Hi," said a few of the men. A few others hissed and booed again, and again someone told them to be quiet. The rest continued to listen in silence, with equal parts curiosity and apprehension.

"As Mr. Farmer just told you, I'm Archie Lancaster."

"Hi, Archie Lancaster!" yelled one of the miners. "Go to hell, asshole!" shouted someone at the back of the throng. Presumably the same man then demanded, "Why'd you hit the sirens? Don't you want that pool in your living room?"

Nervous laughter ensued. Archie blushed, recovered, and forged ahead: "What my friend Terry said is very true: I have undergone some remarkable changes in recent days."

"Coulda fooled us!" hollered someone.

I seized the bullhorn. "Please," I said. "Give the man a chance to speak." A couple of the miners toward the front seconded the motion, and the fellows promptly settled down.

"I realize," Archie continued, "that many of you take issue with certain policies of Dacey Energy, including some for whose implementation I am largely if not exclusively responsible. I also realize that most of you, maybe even all of you, have honest differences of opinion with me on other, more peripheral matters of business. Probably some of you flatly object to my leadership just on principle, whatever that principle might be. But I hope that faction is small in number. I hope that the great majority of you are more reasonable, more fair-minded than that. Honest disagreement is one thing; dogmatism, blind hostility, is quite another."

One of the miners cried out, "Why don't you speak English, man? None of us ever learned Bullshit too good!" There was more jittery laughter. Rather to my chagrin, I heard my own voice among it. Archie's cheeks reddened again.

"Look," he said, "I'm trying to shoot straight with you. I promise you this is leading somewhere. Please, bear with me." The crowd simmered down, and Archie went on: "What happened to this town in November 2003 was a tragedy. I was, and remain, the first to admit it. Perhaps most tragic was that decent folks like yourselves took much of the rap for it, even while your own homes and families suffered its most salient consequences." Perhaps he saw the uniformly blank faces in his audience, for he quickly revised, "Even while your houses and the people you love bore the brunt of the thing.

"I apologized for the spill when it happened, and I'll apologize for it again right now. But I maintain, and I hope that all of you would join me in the sentiment, that nary a man in the service of Dacey Energy could have even foreseen, much less forestalled, that disaster. It was very much what the company described it as at the time: 'an act of God,' as unavoidable as it was unfortunate."

Now perhaps half of the miners voiced dissent, some of them groaning, others broadcasting colorful epithets. Archie looked at me as if for moral support, which I could not offer. He turned back to the men. "Gentlemen," he said. "Gentlemen, please, hear me out."

"We'll hear you out when you quit treatin' us like fools!" announced the brave soul in the back.

"Now, look," Archie began, and then trailed off. What could he say? That neither he, nor any other top official at Dacey, had seen the maps provided by the president of Eastern Kentucky Coal, with their accurate projections of the perilously inadequate rock-barrier's width? That his decision to take no pre-emptive action had been the result, not of greed or carelessness, but of ignorance? He was no stranger to denial - for years, I now hypothesize, he had successfully convinced himself, through a combination of ego and alcohol and tortured logic, that his moral shortcomings were as few and as frivolous as those of the average man - but he was no lunatic, either. So he did the only thing he could: he lowered his head as a sign, if not of shame then of concession, and quickly changed the subject.

"My purpose here today," he said, "is not to discuss business, nor past events, but to extend an olive branch, so to speak. To attempt a reconciliation for sins perhaps only vaguely identified." With this he paused, as if surprised by his own eloquence. "I suppose that goal could be achieved in various ways, some of them more abstract than others. I could, for example, simply offer again my heartfelt apologies for this and that, and be on my merry way. But words, as I'm sure you'd all agree, pale beside actions. In themselves they carry little weight. So today, to show my gratitude for your eternal toil and uncomplaining allegiance to the cause, I shall make a very concrete gesture. I shall present you with a very tangible gift."

He looked at me again, this time seeking approval more than

support, I think. I nodded, prompting him to go on.

He said: "I shall write each of you a check for ten thousand dollars."

Half the men laughed. The other half smiled dazedly and looked around, as if expecting to find themselves on camera.

When Archie broke out his checkbook and called the first man forward, a few tentative cheers went up. But the atmosphere remained one of great doubt, skepticism engraved on the leathery and sun-burnt faces of fifty-odd men with no reason to trust good fortune.

"What's your name, sir?" Archie asked the miner.

"Hershel Mullins," the miner replied.

"Perhaps it would be more practical," I interjected, "to simply write a check to the plant for, say, six hundred thousand dollars. The plant supervisor could then evenly distribute the money among the employees, himself included. Not all the men who work at this mine are present today, correct?"

"That's correct," said Mullins.

"Well, that's fine with me," Archie said, "if it's fine with everyone else." He put the bullhorn to his mouth. "Would it be all right with you folks if I simply wrote one big check to the plant, and let the man in charge parcel out each of your shares, perhaps as a supplement to your next paychecks?"

The men expressed general agreement.

"Okay, Hershel," Archie said, patting him on the arm. "It was nice meeting you."

Slightly deflated, and positively confounded, Mullins rejoined the men. One of his co-workers joked about his tough break. Another clapped him on the shoulder and told him to keep his chin up, his check was in the mail and Sears wasn't going to run out of glow-in-the-dark hubcaps anytime soon. This was met by brawling laughter all around. Even Archie snickered. My earlier disquiet, that unplumbed morbidity which had seized me in the plant, was lifted instantaneously.

What will all my mood swings of late, I had begun to question my sexuality all over again.

Archie inquired who was supervising the pit that day. A man toward the center of the crowd stepped forward to claim the title, introducing himself as Jerry Snodgrass. Archie quickly shook his hand, asked me to turn around, rested his checkbook on my back, and, perhaps inwardly wincing, cut the check. I saw that he had written it for eight hundred and fifty thousand dollars.

"Will this yield at least ten thousand dollars per employee of the pit?" he asked Snodgrass, handing the check to him.

Snodgrass examined it, his eyes turning into tea-saucers, and nodded emphatically. "Oh, yes," he said. "Yes, this should do it."

"And you'll see to it that it's evenly divided among them?"

"Absolutely, sir!"

"All right, then."

At that moment Archie turned to me, pallid and seemingly dazed by the considerable monetary weight he had just shed with a few flourishes of his pen, and then a bulb flashed. It wasn't bright; the sky had grown overcast, with a thunderhead or two on the horizon, but there was no real shortage of light. To this day I am uncertain why Friedman used the flash at all.

A second flash quickly followed, and then a third and a fourth. Archie and I turned in unison toward their source. Most of the miners were too distracted by the check to notice what was happening, but a couple in the front row paid casual heed. Probably they concluded, if anything, that it was all part of the show, something their newly enlightened boss and his mysterious journalist friend had arranged.

There he stood, the tenacious reporter from West Virginia, snapping pictures of Archie and me, a grin the size of Texas plastered across his face.

26

"Mr. Lancaster," he said, replacing his spent roll of film with a new cartridge, "how much was the check for?"

Stunned, Archie said nothing. I, too, was silent. Friedman raised the camera to eye-level and started snapping pictures again.

"What prompted you to do this, sir?" Friedman asked, moving closer to us. "Was it a crisis of conscience?"

Behind us, the miners were passing the check around, squealing with delight. The vast majority of them remained wholly oblivious of the scene unfolding before them.

Ever the gadfly, Friedman pressed on with his endless fusillade of questions: "When did all this charity work begin? Is this the first mine you've visited in your new role as social reformer? Do you now renounce capitalism as a wellspring of greed and corruption?" And on and on.

"Archie," I said, "why don't you let me handle this?"

"Be my guest," he said.

I approached Friedman as calmly as I could. "Put the camera down," I said.

He did not immediately comply. "What newspaper is it that

you work for, exactly?"

"You followed us," I said.

He slowly lowered the camera to waist-level. His eyes wandered to Archie. He hadn't, of course, the slightest interest in talking to me. I was not a news-maker; I was incidental to the situation, an insignificant detail of an exquisite painting. I was the mote of dust on the king's great, jeweled crown. "Right. Why is he so reluctant to talk to me? Is he trying to keep this whole thing a secret?"

"Well," I said, "just maybe he is. And what of it? Why should he want to be public about it?"

Finally I had the man's attention. He gave a shrill, disbelieving laugh. "What, are you kidding me? Don't tell me he's doing this out of the goodness of his heart!"

"And if he is?" I asked.

"If he is," said Friedman, "then this is an even bigger story than I initially thought."

I nodded. "Ask me the three questions you'd most like answers to. I'll give you straight answers to all of them, on the condition that we never see or hear from you again."

He glanced at Archie. "I want to ask *him* the questions."

"I can speak for him."

"Are you his personal assistant or something?"

"No, I'm a journalist, like yourself. I believe you already know that."

He frowned and deposited the used roll of film into his pocket, as if afraid I might try to confiscate it. A powerful wave of *deja vu* swept over me. "I'm going to publish the pictures, you know. They're going to be all over the papers. This is going to be international news. So he'd might as well just answer my questions now, to avoid having to do it later, when another reporter asks them."

"Three," I repeated. "Three questions. You have two minutes. Proceed."

Here are the three questions he asked me: Why was Archie doing what he was doing? How much did he intend to give away? Where did he plan to go next?

Here are the three answers I gave him: First, he felt it his moral obligation, being so fortunate as he was, having readily achieved the American Dream while so many others struggled just to make ends meet. Second, he was unsure how much he might dish out. Third, he had no idea where he was going next.

"Okay," I said, "that's it. Thanks for coming. Have fun with the article."

"Wait!" he cried.

I turned, annoyed. "Yes?"

"What's *your* role in all this?"

"I'm his beautician," I said. "After taking my bachelor's degree in journalism, I spent six weeks in cosmetology school. That's not to be confused with cosmology school, which is where they teach you the fine art of making universes."

"You're a goddamned smart-ass, whoever you are," said Friedman.

"Likewise."

In the op-ed piece printed in Friedman's newspaper on Monday, the factual details of which were essentially reprinted a day later in the fifteen hundred daily newspapers affiliated with The Associated Press, Friedman actually quoted me as saying that I was Archie's beautician, noting that "the health of his mind is as uncertain as his relationship to Mr. Lancaster." The title of his article was this: "Multi-billionaire Energy Mogul Repenting for Sins of His Past?" The subtitle: "Head of corporate giant Dacey Energy seeks to foster egalitarian utopia." Somehow, even these ostensibly innocent capsules pulsated with a faint snobbery.

Indeed, the tone of the whole piece was snide, dismissive, detachedly smug. Friedman expressed nothing but contempt for the project, and nothing but incredulity at Archie's purported motives. "Because he has so readily achieved the American Dream?" he scoffed at one point, after quoting my answer to his first question. "One scarcely achieves that which he is born possessing. Besides, Lancaster has controlled roughly the same fortune for decades. Why this sudden change of heart? One cannot help but wonder how many layers to this story time will reveal, and how ugly will be the bottommost."

Earlier in the piece, he quoted miners whom he must have interviewed following Archie's and my departure from the pit: "'I don't exactly know why he's doing this,' said Frank Levine, an employee of the Big Branch mines for over twelve years. 'I sure can use the money, though.' Perhaps Levine's answer suggests the real explanation for Lancaster's overnight metamorphosis into the patron saint of the working poor: much as drug dealers are known to seduce new customers with outrageous discounts on their product so as to ensure future dependence, might Lancaster be plying those on whom his profits finally depend with a potent if subtle narcotic of his own? I am here speaking, of course, of that harsh drug we call 'approval.' With the kind that could buy every member of his vast workforce a new automobile, the CEO can rest comfortably certain that even his lowliest underlings will develop a fast immunity to dissension. Or maybe a still darker theory will prove better founded: some unsavory, pathological element of his overblown ego draws pleasure from exploiting the weak, the helpless, the alienated; he gets off on rubbing his power in the faces of those he reputes to pity. Whatever the true explanation, it is all but certain that it has little to do with a mid-career epiphany, or a sudden compassion for the longsuffering of the ever-toiling pauper."

Not only was he pessimistic to his core, you see, but he was verbose, as well. A younger journalist would have had the excuse of inexperience. Friedman's only excuse, I suppose, was his infatuation with the look and feel of his own abstruse prose.

He also quoted two miners who expressed misgivings about accepting the money Archie had given them. Said one, "This seems a little like blood money to me. Or like a bribe. I don't accept blood money, and I don't accept bribes." Another opined, "Maybe it's from his heart and maybe it isn't, but I've never been one to lean on other people to get by, especially not strangers, well-meaning or not. And he's a stranger, this guy, even if he is my boss's boss's boss. If I took his money, I'd feel like the guy who gets beat up by a mugger and thanks [the mugger] for sparing his life. That sort of thing just doesn't sit well with me, much as this check would lessen the strain on me money-wise."

Everything else in Friedman's article I had been able to ignore without the smallest qualm, could reject as cynical, pretentious bile. But that paragraph, those quotes, struck a raw nerve, shook me to my very core. For they were not Friedman's voice, but that of the very individuals for whose benefit my whole plan was conceived. They were the people I meant to rescue, with Archie's help, from otherwise insoluble doldrums.

Their remarks did not bode well for my prospects. I did not construe them as expressions of ingratitude, mind you; that was not what disturbed me so about them. On the contrary, they bothered me so deeply precisely because they made such basic, undeniable sense, and because underneath them lurked a proposition I had entertained a time or two myself, while pondering my scheme, but had never allowed to fully materialize in my conscious mind. I had never allowed that because I had feared that, if I did, I might lose my nerve to go through with the thing; and a deeper part of me was convinced, perhaps beyond all reason, of its perfect, transcendent rectitude

The idea, to wax metaphorical, was that the rich could no more save the poor with their money than the sick could save themselves by swallowing more poison.

Jimmy Reynolds had not seen what Archie had done as a favor; he had seen it as an insult to his pride, an insincere apology for an indefensible crime. He had accepted the money only under the pretext that it had come from me, because somehow that had made it tolerable. Somehow that had made it all right. Apparently a few of the miners Friedman had talked to felt the same way.

And I could not blame them. And I began to wonder how many more of the same mindset Archie and I would encounter along the way, and whether I could stand to simply disregard them as excessively proud and stubborn, believing as I did that their pride and stubbornness were justified, if pragmatically foolish.

In the car, on the way back to the motel, I contented myself to suppose that I could stand all of them, so long, of course, as it meant ameliorating what was an infinitely grosser injustice than any wounded ego: the crap that most human beings had to put up with on a daily basis in the form of jobs unfit for slaves, jobs that paid one-tenth or one-twentieth or one-fifieth of what they ought to.

Yes, so long as it meant that, I told myself, I could do it for the rest of my life.

Back at the motel, there was note from Susan waiting for me, behind the front desk. I do not know when she left it, or what exactly prompted her to write it. But I do know I was extremely touched by it. I even saved it, and have it before me now. It reads as follows:

"Terry, just wanted to thank you again for what you did. I know I already told you this, but you really will never fully realize its impact on me and my brother. And if I sounded hard on Mr. Lancaster, I didn't mean to, exactly. I don't know him personally, and therefore have no right to judge him as a man. I will simply trust your judgment, and believe, as you told me, that he has turned over a new leaf. I don't suppose it really matters, because I know that *you're* a good man, probably the best man I've ever met, and if he isn't decent already then he will be after he's spent a little time with you. Kindness like yours is contagious."

There is more to the note, but it is mundane and would be of no interest to the general reader. Mostly it concerns her desire to keep in touch with me. She signed the note note, simply, "Susan," in blue ink. There is a letterhead over an insignia depicting the scales of justice. The letterhead says, "J.J. Stone, Attorney at Law." Below that are the street address and telephone number of the law firm.

I read the note in the lobby, then folded it into eighths and tucked it into one of the sleeves in my billfold. Once in a while, along my travels, I would take it out and skim it, usually over a drink, and try with all my might to persuade myself that I deserved the lavish praise therein heaped upon me.

Even with additional drinks, I could never quite pull it off.

PART IV:

Travels with Archie

in Search of America

27

The contracts were there, too, of course. The manilla envelope in which Kenneth Stephens had mailed them was about four inches thick. A note inside indicated that there were five hundred in all. Archie scanned one, seemed satisfied with it, and handed it to me.

It was written in legalese, of course, but captured the gist of what I had outlined to Archie: the undersigned agreed to place in escrow and leave untouched for one year twenty percent of his or her gift, or direct it toward payment of a mortgage, home loan, car loan, credit-card bill, insurance premium, college loan, tuition fee, medical bill, or other certifiable debt to a governmental agency or private concern. Forfeiture of any condition(s) of the contract was punishable by immediate revocation of the portion of the gift designated as "frozen," as defined previously. If less than the given amount was available for reclamation, the undersigned would be subject to civil penalties. And so forth.

The document was less than a page long, the print normal size. The language, though technical, was eminently lucid. It was nothing that could not be easily explained to anyone of even minimal intelligence, or so I thought. In sum, I was also satisfied with it, and handed it back to Archie.

"Now what?" he said. We were eating lunch at Grandad's Diner.

Blessedly, neither John Friedman nor any other members of the press were anywhere in sight.

"Now we pack and hit the road."

"For where?"

"The next town," I said.

"Which is?"

I sipped my coffee, poked a fork at my lukewarm country-fried steak. "The first town we come to when we leave Inez, going west. I don't know what it's called. We'll find out in a half-hour or so."

"And then?"

"Then we keep moving west for a while. I'll look at my map tonight and plot out the trip, day by day, town by town."

He put his face in his hands. "This really is like a prison sentence," he said.

I put my fork down, looked at him. "Archie, are you honestly going to tell me that you didn't get the slightest kick, the dimmest secret thrill, out of what we did today? You helped fifty or sixty men who maybe hadn't ever been helped in their lives, and certainly never like *that*. A very deep, very old stain was erased today, or at least diluted. Dignity and peace of mind were restored to an entire community badly scarred for a long time. What you did,

Archie, put right a hell of a lot of wrong, even if it *was* coerced. Doesn't that hold any appeal for you at all?"

He sighed, looking at his chicken fajita as if it were a dog turd.

"Archie?"

"It was humiliating," he said.

"It was what?"

"Humiliating."

"What was humiliating?"

"Being reproved like that. Being assailed!"

"Who reproved you? Who assailed you?"

He put his face in his hands again. "Those *miners!*"

"Well," I said, "you expected that, didn't you? You knew how most of them felt about you."

"Yes, but to actually experience it was something altogether different."

"It really bothered you?"

"Wouldn't it bother *you* to know that scores of people you've never met would be delighted to see you tarred and feathered in a public square? The way they looked at me, Terry... their venom... it was palpable, like razor blades slicing through my arteries."

"You're being a little dramatic, don't you think?"

He hammered the table with a fist. "You weren't the one they wanted crucified, were you? No! No, you weren't! So just..." He realized that he was drawing stares from the other patrons and lowered his voice. "Let's just drop it, okay? I'm really not in the mood."

"I'm sorry," I said, sincerely. "I didn't mean to upset you. I just thought... I mean, I figured... you know."

He ground his teeth. "Yes, Terry, I know what you thought. I know what you figured. You thought, you figured, that I'd get such a huge charge out of doing what I did, such an enormous and spectacular *bang*, that I'd throw my arms around you and blubber my fulsome thanks to you for showing me the light! Well, I saw no light, I have no reason to thank you, and all I got from the experience was a headache and a bad case of nausea.

"Yes, I'm thrilled that those men will find a good use for the money, and I wish them all the best, but I was not born to be a humanitarian and the role fits me awkwardly, if it fits me at all. I get no real excitement from it, as you do. This sort of thing just isn't in my genetic make-up. Business, that's what's in my blood. I can't help that. And this isn't some movie where the bad guy learns by example the joy of being good, because I'm not bad in the first place, and while perhaps you're more altruistically constituted than most, you're no better or worse in any objective sense of the terms. You just are what you are, and I am what I am, and that's it. And that's..." He swallowed, flushed and apparently close to tears. "And that's it, all right?"

"All right," I said. I smiled. "But I'm not giving up on you yet."

For a moment I thought he was going to force his fajita down my throat.

We were packed and out of Inez by one o' clock. Fifteen minutes later, we stopped for gas at a Shell station in a tiny town called Boons Camp. (It was a village, really, probably even smaller than Inez.)

"Come in with me," I said. "And bring one of the contracts. I want to try this baby out."

"At a gas station?"

"Why not? Was there a particular kind of place where you wanted to unveil it?"

He considered. "No, I don't guess so."

"Then come on."

The boy behind the counter was seventeen years old. He was skinny, freckled, auburn-haired. All of his teeth were present.

He was clean and neatly dressed, wore a navy-blue smock over a tee-shirt bearing the AC/DC logo. His eyes were intelligent and alert and friendly. He greeted Archie and me with a courteous nod and asked us how we were.

"I can't speak for my friend here," I said, "but I myself am doing fine."

The boy looked at Archie.

"I'm okay," he said.

"Did you want to pre-pay for your fuel?" asked the boy.

"Don't you have to?" I said.

"No," said the boy, with a grin. "Of course not. This ain't no big city, like!" His was obviously good-natured mimickry of his neighbors.

"Well, that's refreshing," I said. "Isn't that refreshing, Archie?"

"Like a cold beer on a hot day," said my hostage. How keenly I appreciated his simile!

"We need twenty bucks' worth," I told the boy.

I coaxed a twenty from my pocket and plunked it on the counter. The kid punched a button on his register, deposited the bill, and closed the drawer. "You're all set."

Seeing that his smock was badgeless, I asked his name.

"Rick," he said.

"Pleasure to meet you, Rick."

I extended my hand. He shook it with no visible hesitation at all. "Well, this is highly irregular, my getting along so well with a customer!" He gave a riant laugh.

I smiled. "You don't normally care for the clientele, huh?"

"What, the likes of that lot?" he asked, jerking a thumb at the window. He laughed again.

"You seem like a pretty bright fellow, Rick. Might I ask how old you are?"

"You might. I'm seventeen."

"Seventeen! You hear that, Archie?"

"Of course I do," Archie said. "I'm standing right here."

"He's a little ornery sometimes," I confided in Rick.

"Ah."

"You like AC/DC?"

"No, I just wear this to look hip." He winked at me, brayed more laughter.

"It works," I said. "Well, how long have you worked here, buddy?"

He closed his left eye and pursed his lips, calculating. "Not quite ten months?"

"Weekend job?"

"Weekends and after school, yeah."

"You plan to go to college?"

"No offense, mister, but... are you interviewing me for a reason?"

I chuckled. He was a wily lad, to be sure. "As a matter of fact, I am. But it's not for my benefit." I pointed to Archie. "It's for this man's."

"Oh. Well, who is he?"

"Ask him yourself."

The boy looked at Archie. "Who are you, sir?"

Archie fumbled for words, as if asked something embarrassing or foolish.

"Just tell him, Archie," I said.

"Well," said Archie, "my name is Archibald Lancaster."

Recognition, shock, and disbelief registered simultaneously in the cashier's features. It was a pretty comical expression. "No way!"

"He is," I said.

"The guy who runs Dacey?" asked the boy.

"Yes," said Archie. "I am he."

The boy looked at me, still unblinking. "Does he always talk

314

that way?"

"Usually," I said.

He returned his attention to Archie. "What the hell are you doing down *here*?"

"I'm traveling with this man," said Archie, nodding at me. "Around the country. On a, uh... on a kind of, uh..."

"We're on a huminatarian mission," I said.

"A huminatarian mission?" asked the boy.

"We're giving away money," I said. "Large sums of money to people we've never met."

"Holy shit!" He looked at Archie again, then back at me, the blood rushing out of his cheeks in a great exodus. I fancied that I could nearly hear the thud of his heart. "But... why?"

"To be nice," I said. "And because Archie here can afford to do it."

The kid shook his head. "Well, yeah, but... *why*?"

I laughed. Archie appeared to be inspecting the rack of *Playboys* behind the counter. "I just told you," I said. "To be nice. To be kind. It's an unimaginable rarity these days, I know."

"So you're trying to put a positive spin on all the negative publicity his company's been getting lately?" asked the boy.

"Yeah," I said. "Basically."

"Oh."

"What do your parents do for a living, Rick?"

He shrugged his shoulders, as if he'd forgotten he had such a thing as parents. "Oh, um... my dad's a railroad engineer, and my mom works here during the week."

"Do you keep the money you make, or give it to your parents?"

"Give most of it to my parents," he said. "But they do let me keep enough to buy cigarettes and go out with my friends once in a while."

"So you're not saving for college or anything like that?"

He chortled cynically. "I wish, dude! The way it's going, I won't even get to *go* to college because I won't be able to afford to repay the loans. Not if I majored in music, anyway, like I'd want to."

"Perhaps you'll qualify for a scholarship," Archie offered. Now he was examining the candy bars on the shelf under the lottery machine.

"Doubt it," said Rick. "My parents don't make much, but they probably make too much for the government to consider me underprivileged or whatever."

"Yeah," I said. "It's kind of a catch-22, isn't it? The only way you can afford higher education is if you're either flat broke or rolling in it. There's no place in the classrooms of our universities for the hardest working members of society."

"Heck," said the kid, "that's pretty much how it is with *everything*, not just college."

"How do you mean?" I said.

"Well," he said, "if you're dirt poor you can get help from the government: food stamps, welfare, all that. And if you're rich you're already set, you can't really help but get richer, unless you're a total idiot, in which case you probably wouldn't be rich in the first place. But if you're stuck in the middle somewhere, sandwiched between the haves and the have-nots, you're... well, sirs, pardon my bluntness, but you're pretty well fucked."

"So what're you saying?" asked Archie, the conversation now sparking his interest. Perhaps he felt defensive, felt some need to justify his affluence. "You'd rather be dirt poor?"

"Maybe," Rick said. "At least then my family and I could survive without having to break our backs to do it, and we'd live almost as well." He paused, a brash little smirk elbowing its way onto his lips. "But I'd just as soon inherit a nest egg like yours, sir." At this he blushed and averted his eyes. He was fast becoming my hero.

"Some of the poorest people in history," declared Archie,

317

"have become rich beyond their wildest dreams. Now how do you explain that, if the system is so terribly and inherently unjust?"

"Luck?" said the boy.

"Luck," Archie echoed, floored. "You've got to be kidding me."

The kid, laudably quick on his toes, observed that for every rags-to-riches story, there were a hundred thousand stories of rags-to-rags.

Archie's retort was as clumsy as it was inane: "Yes, well, the joy lies in the challenge. If everyone could do it, it wouldn't be so remarkable. Such extraordinary cases give all of us something to strive for."

"Fruitlessly," I added. "In virtually every instance."

A moment of silence followed, and then I asked this of the boy: "Could you walk us through your day, Rick? Give us some idea of what it's like to work this job of yours?"

"Well," he said, "I could, yeah, but it's pretty boring stuff."

Just then a customer entered the store, a barrel-shaped old man with an unkempt white beard and sharp blue eyes set deep in their sockets, around which crow's feet radiated like spokes. I could not see his hands, but I imagined that the skin on them was rough as bark, a motley of ancient calluses and fresh blisters atop older

318

blisters yet unhealed, the disfigured legacy of decades spent welding or sawing or stripping crops. He brushed past me and went to the counter. "Pack-a Pall Mall filters 'n' a can-a Skoal Long Cut Wintergreen."

"Pall Mall filters in a box?" asked Rick.

"Don't matter," said the old man.

Rick retrieved the fellow's cigarettes and snuff, rang them up, and slid them across the counter. "Take it easy."

"Yep," said the man, and was gone.

As the door closed, Rick said to Archie and me (well, at least to me), "That's eighty percent of the job right there. Fetching smokes and snuff and occasionally a pouch of pipe tobacco. And selling beer, of course. Beer, candy, and soda. Mostly beer."

"Natural Light?" I said.

He grinned. "Or Natural Ice."

"Cheapest beer you got?"

"Yup. Unless you count the malt liquor."

I nodded. "And the other twenty percent of the job?"

Rick crooked the forefinger on his right hand and gestured for me to follow him. "Let me show you," he said.

"See those boxes?" he said, pointing to a pile of cardboard

319

boxes beside the trash can.

"Yeah."

"Every night, after closing, I have to break those down and carry them out back to the dumpster."

"There must be three dozen of them," I observed.

"Oh, easily. Always takes four or five trips." He paused, thinking, then pointed to the ashtray in the lid of the garbage can. "See that ashtray?"

"Uh huh."

"Gotta empty that every night, too. It's usually pretty full, as you can see." It was indeed overflowing with crumpled butts.

"Yeah. Gross."

"And then of course I have to haul out the garbage and throw *it* in the dumpster. Along with the inside trash, which is one behind the counter, one under the coffee station, and one in the bathroom."

"I see."

"And those ice chests," he said, wagging a thumb over his shoulder. "Hafta restock those each night and lock 'em up."

"Right."

"And sweep the parking lot. There's a trash can right in front of the store, but do you think people use it?"

"No way," I said. "It's more fun to just throw your crap on the ground."

"Exactly." He motioned for us to follow him back inside. "Now for the *really* fun stuff," he said.

He led us into the storage room at the back of the store. Inside was a mop and bucket, a broom and long-handled dustpan, an assortment of cleaning products, a collection of plastic jugs, and an array of boxes containing, I supposed, such items as napkins, straws, and paper cups.

"Every night," Rick told us, "I have to restock all the crap at the coffee station, refill the smoothie machine, and then sweep and mop the store."

"I bet that mop bucket doesn't always cooperate, either," I said.

"You kiddin' me?" said the boy, with a knowing scowl. "Tryin' to move that bastard's like tryin' to walk a dog with three legs. It's worse than those shopping carts that swerve to one side. And getting it over that hump on the floor -" He pointed to the raised slat that lay across the floor in the doorway. "Shit, every goddamned night I splash myself with water up to my ankles trying to maneuver this fucker over that thing."

I laughed. I could relate. I had once worked in a convenience store myself, during a summer in college, and had similarly wrestled nightly with a mop-bucket of my own. Archie listened politely, excruciatingly bored though he must have been.

"But what pisses me off even more," Rick went on, "is *this*." He lifted the mop from the bucket and raised it about six inches from the lip, so that the mop-head was roughly level with the detachable wringer (known to many minimum-wage employees as "the cheese-grater thingy"). He jerked it up and down, as if ringing a bell in a church tower, showing how the tip of the mop-handle collided with the ceiling. "See the problem?" he said, seemingly as exasperated as I supposed he felt each night when he had to do this for real, when mere demonstrations were an unthinkable luxury.

"Yes," I said. "I do."

"Whoever designed this building obviously didn't have the mop-pusher in mind!"

"Obviously not."

"And then there's maybe the worst thing of all," he said, leading us out of the storage room and across the hall, into a long, rectangular cooler. Cartons of beer formed a tall, lean island in its center. Cases of soda, juice, and milk lined the shelves on its walls. "You'd probably think we wouldn't do much business out here in

322

the sticks, but boy, would you ever be wrong! This sonofabitch is damned near bare as a baby's backside every night, and every night - you guessed it - I have to restock everything we sold throughout the day. That right there takes a good twenty minutes or so."

"Are you paid to close?" I asked. "To do all the things you've described?"

"Yeah, right," said the boy. "The minute I lock the doors, I'm off the clock. If I can get everything done in ten minutes, great. But if it takes me an hour, like it normally does, then it takes me an hour, and that's an hour of my own time. I'm not paid for one second of it."

"That's illegal!" Archie exclaimed (and he really did exclaim it, in the most adorably, maddeningly naive tone you could suppose). "That must violate a dozen different labor laws!"

"Tell my boss that," said Rick, kicking an empty box out of his way.

"He doesn't need to," I said. I leaned my shoulder against a stack of twelve-packs of Bud Light. I considered tearing one open and grabbing myself a can, then decided that that probably wouldn't be wise. It might give the wrong impression. "Because he's going to pay you every penny to which you're legally and ethically entitled, every dime your boss has denied you, and then some."

"He is?" said Rick. Either he'd forgotten what I had told him earlier or else he'd failed to draw the obvious inference, because there was genuine astonishment in his voice, and on his face.

"Yes, he is. How much do you make an hour, anyway?"

"Five-fifty," he said.

"Five-fifty for all *that*?"

"You got it."

"Disgraceful," I said. "Utterly *disgraceful*."

He shrugged. "Yeah, well, what can ya do?"

"This," I said, and turned to Archie, and intoned: "Trot out the checkbook, O Loaded One!"

Archie took me aside in the hallway outside the cooler.

"You can't be serious about this," he said.

"Of course I am. Why wouldn't I be? You knew exactly why we were coming in here. You're holding one of the contracts, for Christ's sake!"

"He's just a *kid*!" In his upset he had raised his voice, and now blushed at the realization that Rick had probably heard him. He blushed easily, did Archibald Lancaster, I was learning. I supposed that that was one of his few traits which Winston had inherited.

"All the more reason to give him the money," I said. "His life hasn't yet been totally ruined by poverty. Besides, you heard what he said: he gives most of the money he makes to his parents. So, what we give to him, we'll really be giving to his parents, and they could *definitely* use it."

"Well." He was relenting despite himself. And I could tell that it drove him nuts. He was unaccustomed to the subordinate role he had been forced to assume, and unaccustomed to being stood down. This sudden powerlessness was as unsettling to him as it was strange. "I just didn't think we'd be including teenagers in our philanthropy."

"Archie," I said, driving the last nail into the coffin, "it's *precisely* for future generations that we're doing what we're doing. People my age, even your age, will no doubt enjoy some of the more immediate perks of the money, but it's too late for them to use it in any radically life-changing ways. They're working class and will in all probability *stay* working class. The real beneficiaries will be their kids and grandkids, for whom it is *not* too late, who still have time to make something of themselves and avoid getting caught on the merry-go-round of debt and more debt. They can go to school, get educated, move somewhere where jobs are a little less rare than circus freaks. So, that 'kid' in there, Rick, is *exactly* who we're doing this for." I grinned, savoring the superb irony of my closing sentence: "Archie, we're doing it for the sake of the kids."

I had never seen anyone look so unequivocally appalled or embarrassed as did Archie Lancaster in that moment. *Whatever else happens,* I thought, *my life is now complete.*

"Let's make this one ten grand," I said, as if to twist the dagger I had plunged into his heart's innermost chamber. "The contract doesn't specify five thousand, does it?" I knew full well that it didn't; I had paid careful attention, when perusing it, to Section 2-A, entitled "Disbursement of Gift." The section consisted of three sentences, to this effect: "The amount of the gift conferred upon the recipient shall be at the discretion of the disburser, herein designated as Archibald S. Lancaster. Disbursement of the gift in no wise obligates the undersigned to take any action(s) other than those expressly stated in Section 2-B, below. Conversely, the disburser shall assume no legal responsibility for any action(s) carried out by way of, or consequent upon, receipt of the gift."

"No," said Archie. "I don't believe it does."

"Excellent. Then it's settled." I turned, meaning to summon Rick, when Archie put his hand on my arm, as if to restrain me. I snapped my jaw shut and looked at him, confused and, oddly, a trifle frightened.

"Why not give him twenty-five grand?" he asked me. His tone was not facetious or caustic. Quite to the contrary, it smacked of sincerity. "Or, hell, even fifty? He seems like a nice kid. I feel bad for him, having to wade through all this servile crap just to help put food on the table. It sounds like his family could really make good use of the money."

"What is this?" I shook his hand off me. "What are you playing at?"

"I'm not playing at anything," he said. His eyes plead with me, cajoled me, wheedled me. At the same moment, a single bead of perspiration spilled down his forehead, skimmed along the bridge of his nose, and plunged to his upper lip. Somehow, to me, it symbolized his desperation, belied his seeming, sudden turn of disposition. It may have been the only thing that precluded my acquiescence.

"You're lying," I said. "You're just trying to expedite the process, aren't you? To accelerate your sentence, so to speak? You think by giving away more money to fewer people you can get this thing over with sooner. Not a bad idea, mind you, but it's not going to happen. I'd rather moderately assuage the indigence of many than totally eliminate that of a few."

"Goddammit," he grumbled. The deep, righteous crimson of a pampered man's scorn bloomed savagely in his cheeks. "You bullheaded piece of shit!"

I shook my head, revolted by his ignoble ruse, his craven attempt to thwart the heavy hand of justice. "Archie," I said, "you ought to be ashamed of yourself."

"So all I have to do is put two thousand of it in the bank and not use it for one year?" He was standing behind the counter, checking out customers between sentences, one eye on the contract and another on the flat-screen monitor which sat atop the cash drawer.

"Exactly," I said. "And the other eight thousand is yours, and your parents', to spend as the three of you please. You'll put a large portion of it toward your college education, I hope."

"And there's no catch? No strings? No gimmick?"

"None whatsoever," I said.

"You swear it?"

"On my mother's deathbed."

"Wow." He passed some coins to a spavined, balding woman and bade her a good day. "You really *do* mean it."

"Rick," I said, "do I look like the kind of guy who would

bullshit about a thing like this?"

He laughed. I laughed, too. Archie stood straight and stiff as a board, sweating, unsmiling, pallid and unmoved.

Rick came outside with us, wanting to smoke a cigarette. His eyes alight, his spirits in fine fettle, he moved with a brisk, childlike gait, skipping more than walking. I could only guess at the particularly lovely, hungry, color-drenched dreams budding in his imagination, at the splendid and wonderful things he surmised were now possible by dint of his newfound riches. College, of course, and perhaps a new car, if he owned one at all. Or a vacation to someplace warm and exotic, about which previously he could only mournfully fantasize, always with a bitter awareness that the sands and surf in his mind were likely the most tangible he would ever touch.

And now they were not. And now all things, seemingly, were reachable, an horizon erstwhile beyond the blurriest glimpse wrestled into sane view. Doors which for a lifetime had been securely shut were in a wild, blinding instant thrown open. I, through Archie, had endowed this boy with the key. I, through Archie, had afforded him passage into a world even whose darkest corners and most barren wastelands he had dared not spy, and whose limitless delights the great multitudes of humankind never taste.

None of this, of course, was the reality, any more than a starving man's discovery of a peach pit ensures his survival. With ten thousand dollars we had not, of course, permanently liberated the boy and his family from the bondage of destitution. But we had nevertheless emasculated their shackles, enfeebled their old and unwieldy chains. They could breathe now, and rabid night-dreams of worldly monsters would no longer encroach upon their sleep. The vise grip had been loosened; at last they could wiggle their fingers, and grope for some fair, nearby treasure.

Rick lit his cigarette, drunk on exhilaration, and inhaled deeply. I watched him, in heaven all over again, and wondered that his own ebullience should rival and even dwarf my own. I was tempted to embrace the notion that I had discovered my life's true work, my bona fide *raison d'etre*. Yet I did not; I resisted it, for dislike of how smoothly it fit the self-image I secretly, guiltily relished, how lovingly it stroked my ego. I was not at all incognizant of my susceptibility to forms of intoxication other than the booze-fueled variety, including and especially that in whose luxuriant waters I then wallowed: self-satisfaction.

Yes, I was made up for Rick and his parents, over the moon

that I had taken part in their momentary release from penury. But at the same time I was romping in a dangerously false and seductive meadow, indulging myself in the light tickles and gentle rubs of self-aggrandizement. I had been aware of doing the same thing, though with less reckless abandon, at the pit mines and at the motel, when Archie had written Susan a check for her brother. It had caused me then only the faintest flicker of alarm. Now I found myself seriously dismayed by it, having to reel in at great pains my swollen appetite for further good deeds. With the logger and the sandwich girl that appetite had been violently awakened; with Susan's brother and the coal miners it had been amply fed; now, with young Rick, it was gorging itself.

"Rick," I said, "it has been a pleasure to know you."

"Man, Terry," he said, "you're the coolest person I've ever met."

"Well, it was really Archie here who made this happen."

"Yeah," he said, "I know." He turned to Archie. "Thank you, sir."

Archie nodded graciously, if a tad impatiently. "Don't mention it."

"And now," I said, "we must bid thee farewell."

Abruptly, without any forewarning whatever, Rick the

cashier threw his arms around me. "Thank you," he said. "Thank you so, *so* much."

Looking at Archie, who had turned away, the sun making a harsh red splotch of his face, I said, "You're welcome, son. You're welcome."

28

We hit Painstville a short while later, making two stops there: the first at a Sunoco garage, where Archie wrote two checks for five thousand dollars apiece to the mechanics on duty, and the second at a mom-and-pop bakery called Lilly's Cakes & Things.

The baker, Lilly, refused to take the money until she secured her husband's permission, which she did by telephone. By the time Archie finally signed her check, and she the contract, she was beside herself with excitement. She was the first of our forty or fifty thousand donees to hug both Archie *and* me. He denied it, but his mood and body language suggested pretty unambiguously that the gesture had deeply warmed him, gratified him. No longer was I the hero and he the villain; now we were heroes both.

But, please, don't get the idea that anything like a sudden transformation took place at that point, anything like the transformation we had tried to sell, I think with some success, to those whom we had thus far reached, that Archie's behavior might be understood. I will tell you right now that no such transformation was to occur. But a very, even tortuously gradual change did transpire. The incident at the bakery merely marked its beginning, was perhaps the catalyst of the thing. The really noticeable and noteworthy aspects of the mutation were to become apparent only much later.

After Paintsville we stopped in two smaller towns, Salyersville and West Liberty. In the first we visited a drugstore and another gas station. In the second we gave a total of twenty thousand dollars to the employees of a video store (only one of them a college student, much to Archie's relief) and another fifteen thousand to a family that ran its own burger joint. I had some misgivings about this latter affair, since the owners of even the smallest business could hardly be viewed as downtrodden. But Archie argued persuasively in its favor, even wanting to give the family twice what we actually did, on the grounds that wealth spurs job creation and jobs in turn fuel prosperity. This philosophy sounded suspiciously like trickle-down economics to me, but I was both too tired and too sober to put up a fight. Besides, I reasoned, the town couldn't have more than a few hundred people, so the owners of the store couldn't possibly be worth much. I then promised myself that in the future I'd be stricter, more insistent that we stick to the kind of folks who squirrel away loose change to pay the gas bill.

In Zag, another tiny Kentucky hamlet, we gave ten grand to a couple of men working on telephone lines (they were employed by Verizon, a company Archie had once considered buying) and a whopping seventy-five thousand to fifteen guys at a lumberyard. We capped off the evening's festivities in Morehead, Kentucky, where Archie cut a dozen checks for the nine men and three women currently on the payroll of Concordia, one of the last textile mills still operating in the state. When, exhausted, we finally called it a night and checked into a hotel in Lexington, around ten o' clock, Archie had given away well over a million dollars in the course of a single day.

Before you rush out to build your own private monument to the man, please reflect that a million dollars was approximately 1/22,000 of his total net worth, roughly equivalent to one dollar of the average American's annual salary. Moreover, in the twelve hours it took him to unburden himself of the cash, Dacey Energy brought in about five times as much in revenue, of which Archie himself would keep approximately one-fifth. So, in a manner of speaking, he broke even on the venture.

Archie surprised me by agreeing to have a drink with me in the hotel bar. I knew the man liked to imbibe, but he had not slept terribly well the night before and the day's bustle had drained him. It had drained me, too, but then, I was fourteen years younger than he and I wasn't the one who'd dropped a million bucks. Plus, my thirst was far greater than his. I can't know that for certain, of course, but it's a pretty safe guess: when we walked into the bar I was all but salivating, and ordered a beer and a gin and tonic before the bartender could so much as greet us. Archie, by contrast, took a moment to consider his choices, and casually settled on a vodka martini.

I made quick work of my beer, and was on my gin and tonic like a tiger before Archie had even put his glass to his lips.

"Thirsty?" he asked me.

"Yes," I said. "Very."

"I didn't realize you were so fond of the sauce, Terry."

"I wasn't. I'm not."

He arched an eyebrow, genially enough.

"No, really. I'm not an alcoholic or anything. I just enjoy a nightcap or two, especially after a productive day like ours. As a matter of fact..." *I didn't start drinking heavily until I fell in love with your son.*

Archie looked at me, waiting for me to continue. When I didn't he said, "As a matter of fact what?"

"As a matter of fact, I rarely touched the stuff until recently."

"Well, what happened that set you off?"

"I got depressed," I said. It wasn't a lie, mind you. "And then I got fired, which didn't exactly improve my mood."

He nodded and frowned, as if to say that he took my point. "Terry, I just want to reassure you that I had nothing to do with that. Honestly."

Of course, while I believed that he had had *everything* to do with my current unemployment, I had not intended my comment as an insinuation to that effect. "That's not what I meant, Archie. And I really don't feel like discussing it, if it's all right with you."

"Of course," he said. "I'm sorry if I misunderstood."

I waved my hand in a don't-give-it-another-second's-thought gesture and devoted myself aggressively to my gin and tonic. Archie sipped his martini and surveyed the lounge. It was in that shadowy, ten-thirty limbo between crowded and empty. Our company consisted of two men and a woman in one of the booths and a couple of codgers knocking back highballs at the other end of the bar. I ordered a refill on my gin and tonic and tapped a cigarette into my mouth. I lit a match, started to lean into the flame, and then stopped and looked at Archie. "Is this going to bother you?"

"No," he said. "We're not in a car, are we? In fact, I believe I'll have a cigar."

I nodded gratefully and lit the cigarette. Archie produced a Cuban from his breast pocket, borrowed my pack of matches, and fired it up. And for a minute or two we just drank and smoked our poisons, neither of us talking. I guess we were both reflecting on our day, on its strangeness and length, and thinking ahead to the days and weeks and months to follow. Probably he felt a little weirder about sitting there with me than I did about sitting there with him, since I was the one running the show, the whole reason we were there in the first place. But I still felt weird, very much so, and recalled the night that Winston and I had gone to the Blue Cat for coffee and at first found conversation almost impossible.

I smoked my cigarette to the filter and stubbed it out in the ashtray. At last I had found a sentence worth uttering: "Well, Archie, did the day's events in any way modify your outlook on this whole altruism thing?"

He puffed his Cuban thoughtfully. "No," he said. "If by that you're asking whether I'm now glad to be a part of this campaign."

"I saw your face," I said, "when that baker woman hugged

you."

He looked at me. *Do go on*, said his eyes.

"You liked how it made you feel."

"Well," he said, drawing himself up, switching his cigar to his other hand, stirring his drink.

"Do you wish to deny it?"

He chortled. "You certainly picked the right line of work, Terry."

"How's that?"

"You talk as though you were bred to be a journalist."

"I do?"

"Yes."

I raised my glass. "Let's toast," I said.

"To what?" He tentatively raised his own.

"To the first conversation," I said, "that we've carried on for its own sake."

Our glasses clinked, and some reluctant, uneasy partnership was forged.

"What I'm wondering," said Archie, "is where you draw the line. In theory, I mean."

"Where I draw the line?"

"When you say, 'Enough is enough. We're now committing the reverse crime: unduly punishing drive and ingenuity rather than unduly rewarding it.'"

I nursed my third gin and tonic, trying to ascertain his meaning. "Are you asking me where my socialism stops, Archie? When equal becomes *too* equal?"

He clapped his hands together sharply, the noise resonating throughout the lounge. I think his couple of martinis were finally kicking in. "Exactly," he said. "What luxuries, if any, are morally permissible? Is one ethically obligated to sacrifice any possession inessential to his survival?"

"Well -"

"For instance, this summer millions of families will take expensive vacations to upscale resorts and stay for two weeks or a month in gilded hotels brimming with every conceivable comfort and amenity. Is such behavior immoral? Will they, by such act, violate some rule of ethical conduct, anger the gods of justness and equity?"

"I don't -"

"You own a television, don't you? Do you need it to live? Of course not. You don't even need your car, or your bed, or the carpets on your floors." Then he went too far: "Or those gin and

339

tonics you're swilling down."

I motioned for him to quit jabbering, indicated that he had made his point. I lit a cigarette. "May I respond now?"

"Yes, of course. Please, go right ahead." He coughed, took a draw on his cigar.

"First of all, I don't know. I don't have an answer to any of your questions. At least, no direct or completely satisfying answer. I do not claim - and this important, so hear it and remember it - I make no claim that I have, or have even attempted to formulate, anything like a precise or rigorous or comprehensive system of thought, formula, whatever, for dealing with questions such as you've posed. I concede from the outset that they are, individually, *bona fide* dilemmas, and perhaps insoluble. But I do have something of a ready if generic reply to all of them, as intuitively and indisputably *sufficient* as it is crude, primitive, and instinctual. It takes the form of an analogy. You listening?"

"Terry, sir," he said, summoning the barkeep, his thirst now decidedly piqued, "I *am.*"

"You've accidentally put too much salt on a meal, haven't you?"

He nodded and ordered another martini. "Of course."

I, too, nodded, and drew rapidly on my cigarette, my heart

thumping robustly, feistily in my chest. I was mildly buzzed, intellectually stimulated, and emotionally relaxed: an ineffably exquisite combination. "Okay. Now, at such times, could you have said *exactly* how many grains of salt would have been ideal? What number of grains, in other words, would have yielded the optimal degree of flavor?"

He began to answer, fell silent. He grinned, sipped his drink, considered. The thrust of my analogy, its rhetorical if not its logical force, dawned on him piecemeal, like the solution to a superficially difficult math problem. "Well, no."

I smiled back at him. "Likewise with the imbalance of economic resources," I said. "Q-E-D, Archie, Q... E... D."

"I'm reminded," said Archie, "of what Potter Stewart once said: 'I can't define obscenity, but I know it when I see it.' Is that the sort of idea you have in mind here?"

"Sure," I said. I extinguished my drink. I would order a fourth and probably a fifth, but not until Archie was gone. I told myself that I just wanted some time to myself before turning in, and that was true enough. But the deeper truth was that I didn't want him to see me get drunk. "But I like my salt analogy better. It brings out the underlying point with maximal clarity: you don't have to know how much of something would be ideal in order to know that there's too much or too little of it. The difference isn't really quantitative, anyway, so much as qualitative. That the rich have too much and the poor too little is as obvious to most as a turd in a punch bowl."

He laughed. "Fair enough." His cigar was smoked. He crushed it out in the ashtray. "So, where are we going tomorrow?"

"I figure we'll head north to Frankfort, then see what towns we hit on the way to Cincinnati."

"And then?"

"I don't know," I said. "We'll go northwest for a while, I guess. Make our way to the Great Lakes, the Plains States, the Deep South, the West Coast, and back again."

"What about New England?"

"We'll get there, if the cash supply holds up." I lit a cigarette, appraised him. "You worried we might leave someone out, Archie?"

"No," he said. "I just don't believe in geographical discrimination."

I laughed. "In this case it would almost be justified. New Englanders are proportionately much better off than folks in other regions of the country, West Coasters possibly excepted."

"You have a point there, I suppose."

342

He pushed back from the bar, stood up. For a moment I thought he might extend his hand and offer me some kind of truce. But instead he just nodded and told me good night, and asked what time I wanted to be up and out the next day.

"I think we've both earned a good night's rest," I said. "We're in no great hurry."

He looked at me, his hands behind his back.

"Nine o' clock should be fine."

He nodded, turned, and left.

I watched him go, then turned to the bartender, smiling. I wrapped a hundred-dollar bill around my glass and slid it across the bar. "Make this one a double," I said.

29

The next morning found us first at a laundromat in downtown Lexington, where Archie parted with another ten grand, and then at a shopping mall, where all told we gave away something like ninety-five thousand dollars. The manager of a bookstore, unable to believe our account of what we were doing there and intolerant of the disruption to his business, asked us to leave. So Archie wrote a check to the store for thirty thousand dollars and put it on the counter, telling him to split it evenly among his employees. "If you don't," I said, "and we find out about it, the next day you'll be looking for work." I felt uncomfortable making a threat like that, albeit hollow - it struck me as rather unseemly - but it appeared I had no choice in the matter. Obviously I have no idea if the manager complied with my directive, but I like to think he did. I find it hard to accept that he should have simply pocketed the check, as two mesmerized employees witnessed the exchange.

From the mall we traveled west to a couple of suburbs, where we padded the pockets of some construction workers and enriched a bevy of pipe fitters to the tune of sixty thousand dollars. The pipe fitters were so moved by Archie's renunciation of corporate supremacy that they insisted on having their picture taken with him, which they pledged to frame and hang on one of the walls in their union hall.

After that we headed back into the city, lunched at a Chinese restaurant (the waiters and cooks couldn't understand the contract, so we just gave them five grand apiece and urged them to stuff a few fifties into some fortune cookies, so as to spread the wealth), and then sprang some rogue checks on the stunned clientele of a temp agency. "These things are so slippery," I announced with mock trepidation, "I fear I can't hold onto them

344

much longer!" And, indeed, a moment later they escaped my clutch, the lubricious devils.

Thence we drove north, to Frankfort. We arrived a little after three, and went first to a grocery store. There we conveyed the usual sums to the baggers and checkout crew, somewhat to the chagrin of the general manager, whom we could offer only handshakes and polite conversation. (Please note that we did inquire as to his salary, which he disclosed to be around sixty thousand dollars a year - far too high to warrant a check for any amount. But I might have taken mercy on him and slipped him a few hundred bucks if he hadn't foolishly revealed that his wife was a pediatric nurse, and so inadvertently confessed that his and his spouse's combined earning power vastly exceeded the nation's median household income.)

Upon receiving his five thousand dollars, one of the younger baggers immediately cast off his apron and tendered his resignation, explaining without provocation that his was merely a summer job taken for the sole purpose of buying himself "a Fender and a new set of wheels." I laughed heartily at this, while Archie simply nodded and smiled, probably wondering what the hell a Fender was (or perhaps what kind of car one might purchase for less than five grand).

345

And then we were off to Cincinnati, making only one stop along the way, in a little town called Florence, near the Ohio border. There we visited a cinema, a tiny theater with three screens and a single refreshments counter, manned earnestly and alertly by a solitary vendor named Chip. He and Debra, the girl who occupied the ticket booth, were all of maybe nineteen, both of them college students. But, as I reiterated to Archie, youth did not exempt one from need, and generally ensured it. Besides, they were law-abiding citizens and taxpayers (we assumed), and, more importantly, America's future.

So we gave them each five thousand dollars, and in their exuberance they embraced, jumping up and down as first they hugged and then kissed. Sometimes I wonder whether perhaps Archie's gifts to them galvanized a budding affection between them, and led them to date or even marry. Maybe one day they'll have a kid of their own, Chip and Debra of Florence, Kentucky, and name him after Archie. (Then again, I remind myself, the name "Archie" has fallen rather out of favor these past few decades, quite apart from Mr. Lancaster's doings.)

I asked Archie if he wanted to take a two-hour break from playing Saint Nick and soak up a film.

"What's showing?" he asked Chip.

Chip ticked off the titles of the movies currently playing at the Florence Cineplex & Arcade.

"The Tom Hanks sounds good," Archie mused.

"It's pretty funny!" agreed Chip.

"And, um, heart-warming," added Debra.

"Two for the Hanks picture it is," I said, and offered Debra a twenty dollar bill.

"Don't worry about it," she said, printing out the tickets. She plucked them from the machine and handed them to us. "These are on the house."

Chip darted over to the concession stand. "Hey," he shouted, grabbing his metal scoop, "who wants free popcorn and Snowcaps?"

The movie was good, funny and heart-warming indeed. Chip and Debra had not misled us. Archie and I departed the theater in full agreement that, had we been made to pay to see it, the entertainment would have been worth every penny of the fifteen bucks.

I asked Archie if he had taken a moment to reflect that, where Greedy, Callous Corporate Executives would unblushingly charge their own mothers twenty-five cents for a stick of gum, two kids of doubtless exceedingly modest means had thought to reciprocate our charity without a moment's hesitation. "It's a certain mindset," I told him, "a certain unspoken but deep-seated moral code which the super-wealthy as a whole once knew and conscientiously practiced, but somehow gradually forgot as their purses ballooned and their contact with ordinary people grew less frequent and meaningful."

Here was Archie's reply: "Must you always beat me over the head with your tiresome sermons?"

I apologized, and we drove to Cincinnati mostly in silence.

Once there, we ate at a seafood restaurant, dumped fifty or sixty grand on the help, and checked into a hotel downtown. I saw that there was a twenty-four-hour electricians' place across the street, called Burke Bros. Electric Company, and suggested that Archie and I make it the culmination of the day's Good Samaritan work. He consented willingly enough, but, to my inexpressible shock, proposed that we first drop in on the gallant midnight soldiers at the Kinko's next-door.

So we did, and even had fifty copies of the contract made while we there, at no charge. The five employees each received a check for the standard amount. None of them objected to the terms of the contract, or even requested clarification of them or inquired as to their philosophical justification. In fact, no donee so far had done any of those things.

With every transaction I gained further confidence in my forecast that we would come across no one so bold as to look the proverbial gift horse in the mouth, that all the recipients would be so elated that a sizable chunk of their financial worries had been wiped out in one fell swoop as to be disinclined to even the most fiddling doubts. (At some point I would convey this certitude to Archie by way of the following analogy: one of the donee's questioning the contract would have been like someone's asking the guy who prevented an anvil from falling on her head why he had used one hand to shove her out of its path instead of both.)

This relieved me enormously, for while I doubted that Archie cared as much about the contracts as perhaps he wanted me to believe, I knew that he drew a queer sort of comfort from, if nothing else, the ritual of circulating and collecting them. It gave him, I think, some illusion of control, was the last gasp of his ego to survive this whole affair: the contracts were his way of reconciling his identity with the bizarre reality foisted upon him.

Perhaps you're wondering what it is, exactly, that we said to all these people upon whom we heaped such extravagant sums.

How did we explain to them just who in the hell we were, and what in the hell we were doing? The answer, I suppose, is not a terribly satisfying one: our rigmarole varied in its finer points from instance to instance, but nearly always involved oblique (and usually windy) allusions to Archie's having more money than a Swiss bank and wanting to give back to the country that had made him what he was. As for me, I was just a reporter along for the ride, to cover the story and witness the miracle for myself.

But what you must realize is that nobody, and I mean *nobody*, had theretofore so much as raised an eyebrow at any of this. Nobody, it seemed, had given two shits where the money had come from or why it was being given to him. Everyone had just accepted at face value the sketchy, improbable explanation with which he was presented, apparently never pausing to wonder why some paunchy, white-haired plutocrat should suddenly decide in mid-career, quite breezily, to share his fortune with total strangers.

Which only underscores a deeper point, in many ways the whole point of this book: so bleak were the financial circumstances of those we helped, those drowning throngs to whom we hurtled life buoys often with just seconds to spare, that all reason and logic crumpled under the weight of raw need, of unutterable relief.

I, of course, had expected no less. Archie was rather more

surprised.

Only one of the electricians was present in the office that Sunday night, and it was neither of the Burke brothers. The man's name was Richard Seagram. He had worked for James and Eric Burke, of Chicago, Illinois, for sixteen years. He was, I estimated, about forty years old. He had not gone to college. He was the son of Irish Catholic immigrants, his mother a seamstress and now deceased, his father a retired cobbler. He had a wife and three children, two of college age. One of the latter attended a technical school and was himself in training to become an electrician. The other was a welder and worked part-time at a car wash. Mr. Seagram made twenty-nine thousand dollars a year.

When Archie and I entered the building at ten to nine, he was hunched over at one of the desks, inspecting an invoice by lamp-light. He was a big, broad-shouldered man with shaggy brown hair and wire-rimmed glasses, fleshy biceps and charmingly rosy cheeks. His face was kind but serious, with a subtle humor underlying his features. He smiled dimly at us as we approached him, probably thinking us not customers but creditors, and asked what he could do for us.

"Sir," I said, "today is your lucky day."

351

Within fifteen minutes, Mr. Seagram had disclosed to us that his marriage was on the rocks and his relationships with his children markedly strained. The source of the tension was primarily financial in nature. His welder son had no passion for his work, no interest in any industrial trade, and was unhappy that he could not afford higher education without taking out massive loans. His other son enjoyed technical school well enough, and was more or less content to follow in his father's footsteps, but had trouble paying his bills and was himself ensnared in an unstable marriage. He also, said Mr. Seagram, had something of a slight drug habit. Meanwhile, his wife of eight years - his *second* wife, he confessed with some misgiving - had recently been laid off from her job at a phone company and was "going through one of them mid-life crisis things."

"And business ain't been so good, either," he told us. "You wouldn't think an outfit like this would ever have a slow period in such a big city, but it doesn't always work that way. We have lags just like any other company. Sometimes I'm tempted to go smash up a few breaker boxes just to give us some extra work." He chuckled, a little darkly, and guiltily, perhaps worried that we had taken his comment seriously.

352

As he wove his tale of woe he sorted tools in a long red toolbox: pliers, crimpers, wrenches, screwdrivers, the whole gamut. I was tired, and badly wanted a drink, but I listened as carefully and understandingly as I could. (A few of the donees, particularly the bagger in Frankfort, had opened up a little to Archie and me, providing some insight into their personal lives and what they intended to do with the money, but in the Garrulous Department, Richard Seagram took the cake.)

Now and again I would glance over at Archie, and each time I expected his expression to be one of hopeless boredom and exasperation. But it never was. I can't say that the man looked particularly *engrossed* in Seagram's lamentations, but he certainly didn't look utterly deadened by them, either. I even sensed at times that he was being outright *attentive* to them, which strangely I found as disconcerting as I did encouraging. I was not quite sure how to react to it, the idea of his so abruptly giving a shit.

Seagram concluded his soliloquy with a description of an altercation he recently had with his wife over their kids and her unemployment. "She threatened divorce," he said, somber-eyed. "She didn't actually use the D-word, but she didn't have to. It was implicit in everything she *did* say, written on her face plain as daylight. Every time her voice rose, there it was. And then it would

353

retreat again, like a turtle into its shell." (Not verbatim, of course, but close enough to give the gist.) There he paused, as if suddenly possessed of the idea that all of this was a dream, that he was speaking not to two men but to two superbly realistic mirages. He looked at Archie. "You say you own a coal company?" He looked at me. "And you work for a newspaper?"

"That's right," I said. "You've never heard of Mr. Lancaster?"

He shook his head. "I don't believe so. The last name rings a soft bell, but then, it ain't the rarest name on the planet. *Should* I know who he is?"

"Well," I said.

Archie shrugged, and blushed. "Not any more," he said, "than I should know who *you* are."

"Why did you pick me?" asked Seagram. "In a city of a million and a half people, why did you pick me?"

I licked my lips. "You want the short, factual answer or the long-winded, schmaltzy answer?"

"I don't know," he said. "I guess the short one."

"We're staying at the hotel across the street," I said.

He closed his toolbox. "Ah."

I was holding one of the contracts, and now moved to hand

it off to Seagram for his consideration. Archie, in yet another surprising turn, nudged me in the side and shook his head. *Don't be so tacky*, his face said. *You disappoint me, Terry.* I was, I confess, a trace disappointed in myself. I had performed the action without due reflection. I had been hasty, in other words, probably because of my weariness and mounting thirst. I withdrew my arm quickly, hopeful that Seagram had somehow missed the whole tawdry affair.

"We'd like to make a contribution to your cause, Mr. Seagram," Archie said.

"What cause is that?" Seagram asked.

"The cause," replied Archie, "of saving your marriage, reconciling with your kids, and sleeping a little easier at night."

I looked admiringly at my hostage (though by then I was already thinking of him more as my partner, I suppose, more as a volunteer than a prisoner). *Nicely put*, I thought.

"You fellas wanna give me money?" asked Seagram, skeptical laughter in his voice, a *which-leg-are-you-pulling* glint in his eye. He used a thumb to hike his glasses up the bridge of his nose. "Why? You don't even know me."

"Nor have we known the dozens of people we've already assisted," I pointed out, kind of respecting and simultaneously

355

balking at the cool, even tilt of my voice. Why did I suddenly sound so much like an attorney? I shivered, or will here claim that I did.

"More importantly," appended Archie, and now I felt like one of a pair of Jehovah's Witnesses, steadily wearing down our mark, "we *do* know you. In the last twenty minutes we've gotten to know you quite well."

Finally the laughter in Seagram's air expressed itself audibly. "Please," he said. "Is this some kind of joke?"

"No joke," said Archie, as if following a script, and now defied Seagram's wildest expectations by actually producing a checkbook. "I'm going to write this for ten thousand dollars." He looked at me. "Or do you think fifteen would be more appropriate?"

"Go twenty," I said, jingled again despite my sobriety, lit up without the aid of a single chemical. The music in my head had been struck up; the angelic chorus was in full swing. "How's he ever going to put Mark through college on fifteen?"

"Jesus," said Archie. "I'd forgotten all about the college thing! Let's do twenty-five, so he has something left over for himself and Yvonne." He turned to Seagram. "Perhaps the two of you could take a nice cruise to the Bahamas. Or Europe. The Mediterranean is lovely this time of year, isn't it?"

"So I've heard," I said.

356

"I can't take any money from you," Seagram said, but his resolve was already crumbling. "I mean, I appreciate the gesture and all, but -"

"Nonsense," said Archie, tearing the check from his book. "We'll hear no more about it."

"We're only giving you what you'd already have in a fairer world," I added.

Seagram's protests tapered to a final, feeble whimper. "Yes, but -"

"But nothing," Archie said, and stuffed the check into Seagram's shirt pocket. "Don't even thank us. It's unnecessary."

There were no tears or anything, but I think our thunderstruck electrician friend came as close to crying as a man of his breed could, barring the death of a loved one.

Archie wrote another four checks, each for five thousand dollars, for the other four employees of Burke Bros. Electric Company. He did not try to justify the discrepancy between the amounts given to them and that given to Seagram, except to confirm that the other employees had been in the company's service for a substantially longer period and so earned far larger incomes. Plus, noted Seagram, those other guys' kids were all grown up and making plenty of money on their own.

Back at the hotel I did as I had done the night before and invited Archie to join me for a drink in the bar. This time he declined, citing weariness and a desire to call Winston.

Winston. He had barely entered my thoughts since I'd seen him last, the night before Archie and I had left Pittsburgh. Winston, who, with or without the help of providence, through the unlikeliest chain of events, had touched off this whole extravaganza. What did that mean, if anything, metaphysically? What did it mean personally? Did I owe him something? It felt at that moment as if I owed him everything, and that so did Archie and a growing number of people who would likely never even learn of his existence. But especially me, and Archie slightly less. Beyond that feeling of cosmic indebtedness, which caught me very much off guard and occasioned a sinking feeling in my stomach, I simply missed the boy. I missed his company, his drama, his mischief. I missed his face, all its resplendent and unsearchable beauty.

"I miss him," said Archie, and his words were so surreally coincidental with my reverie that I literally rocked back on my heels. Archie reached for me, alarmed. "You all right?"

"Yes," I said. "I just... got a little dizzy there for a second."

"You're tired, is what it is."

"You're probably right."

"Why don't you just skip the drink and go to bed?"

I shook my head. "I want to unwind for a little while. I'll be asleep by midnight, though, don't worry."

"We'll leave at nine sharp?"

"Seems fair to me."

He started to turn away, stopped. "You know," he said, "I have to admit that I had a pretty good time today."

I cleared my throat. I could not be altogether thrilled with the news because I was still reeling from what he'd said a moment earlier. "Did you?"

"Yes," he said. "Especially across the street. I can't say that I've acquired any measurable faith in the overall design or aim of the project, but what we just did felt good, I have to say." He gave a meek, self-conscious laugh totally unlike himself. "Good night, Terry."

"Good night."

He started toward the elevators, and I called to him. He turned.

"John Friedman's going to publish his article in tomorrow's Charleston paper," I said.

He nodded. "I assumed as much."

"Things aren't going to be the same after that."

"How do you mean?"

"Things," I said, "are going to be a lot less quiet."

He said nothing, just nodded and got on the elevator, disappearing behind the doors. I sighed, profoundly weary, and went off to find the bar.

30

I could have had no idea how true was my admonition to Archie. I thought I did, of course, thought myself adequately equipped for even the ugliest and most frenzied media onslaught my former brethren could wage. I had been one of them, I reasoned, and knew what they were capable of, the lengths to which each organization would go in jockeying for domination of the airwaves and headlines. They were, by and large, the parasitic, exploitative savages most people took them for.

Where I made my mistake was in assuming that their offensive would be relatively piecemeal, at least for the first week or so. I completely underestimated the speed at which word travels in the modern world, gave too little weight to the simple fact that People Talk. No doubt many of the hundred and thirty or so donees we had thus far reached had done a *lot* of talking in the previous forty-eight hours, and in so doing had opened wide the lines of mass communication, as it were.

Those who had heard reports of Archie's and my recent dealings were multiplying like summer locusts, and one of them was a night clerk at the Ramada in Cincinnati where we lodged on Sunday night. Somebody who had somehow caught wind of the Developing Story, soon to be a full-blown Phenomenon, had relayed it to one of the night clerk's friends, who in turn had passed it on to the clerk himself. By sheer happenstance, this clerk, whose name was Anthony Puiglia, had a brother who worked for a Cincinnati television station. Guess who Mr. Puiglia called right after Archie and I checked into his hotel?

Meanwhile, by yet another untoward coincidence, two other reporters from different stations arrived at the hotel early on Monday to cover a meat-packers' convention. (I had grown suspicious that something odd was afoot when, on my way to bed, I had shared an elevator ride with a group of men wearing shirts which read, "BEEF IS YOUR FRIEND." Drunk as I was, I had assumed that they were simply hamburger enthusiasts.)

And so it came to pass that, a full eight hours before John Friedman's article on the occurrence at Inez would see print,

361

seemingly a quarter of Ohio's field reporters had descended on Cincinnati's downtown Ramada, hoping to extract at least a juicy sound bite from the Man of the Hour, the Modern Messiah.

Friedman's article would nevertheless claim the honor of setting in motion, inexorably, the media circus to ensue. Still, I took a bitter solace in the knowledge that, largely by accident, many of his colleagues had beaten him to the all-important first punch, thus muffling the louder rumbles of his article's thunder.

I had just gotten out of the shower and was drying off when I heard a knock at my door. I assumed it was room service and shouted for the maid to come back later.

"It's me," I heard Archie say. "Have you turned on your TV?"

Intrigued, I wrapped a towel around my waist and went to the door, opened it. There stood Archie in a white shirt and black trousers, looking very concerned. "No," I said. "Why?"

"Turn it on," he said. "To one of the news channels."

"Hold on."

I grabbed the remote control from the chest of drawers the TV sat on and fired up the tube. Fortuitously, the channel was already set to one of the local stations. A tall, phonily handsome correspondent appeared on one side of a split-screen, a slightly less flawless-faced anchor on the other. "Adam," the reporter was saying, "we have yet to see or hear any signs of Archibald Lancaster, but according to several anonymous sources, including some of the meat packers convened here, he is indeed present in the hotel. Just where, and when he might emerge, are the questions everyone is asking."

I looked at Archie, wet bangs hanging in my eyes. "Holy shit," I said.

"Yeah." He stood in the doorway, ashen and sponge-legged, biting his lip. "Holy shit is right. Try another channel."

I scrolled to the next local station. Another reporter, this one older and brandishing a tameless postiche, stood in the lobby four stories under us, blundering his way through a spiel identical in its broad outlines to the first reporter's. I then flipped to the third local station: same thing (minus the toupee). I faced Archie, the strength oozing out of my own legs. "How do you want to handle this?"

"I was hoping *you* had some ideas."

"We could try sneaking out through the back."

He looked at me doubtfully. "Don't the stairs and the elevators both lead to the lobby?"

I paused, realizing I had no knowledge of the hotel's layout. "Shit, Archie, I don't know."

"Get dressed," he said, "then meet me by the elevators."

"All right."

He closed the door, and I proceeded to dress myself, another hatchet buried squarely in my forehead, another nuclear war erupted in my stomach.

As I dressed I continued to listen to the correspondent's report. The correspondent's name - and no, I am not making this up - was Dakota Washington. He worked for WCHZ, channel 13 in Cincinnati. He delivered his report from the parking lot of the hotel, a small crowd of busybodies gathered behind him. He said this:

"As we reported earlier, Adam, there have been numerous sightings of Mr. Lancaster around the tri-state area in the past few days, including several here at the Ramada on Stapleton Avenue. Many of these people have alleged that they witnessed Lancaster distributing personal checks to local residents seemingly at random, for purposes not yet clear. One of the clerks here at the hotel claimed in a telephone call made to our news bureau last night that Lancaster presented an acquaintance with a check for five thousand dollars on Saturday, and that he and an unidentified man, supposedly a newspaper writer, checked in late last night, without security or an entourage of any kind. One of the meat packers has told me that he saw Lancaster drinking with this unidentified man last night in the hotel bar, and later saw the man again in the elevator."

How the hell? I thought, now shaving clumsily in the bathroom. To say that hearing a stranger relate my most recent movements to millions of people was disorienting would be to grossly understate the case. That I hadn't the foggiest clue how my previously clandestine experiment with Archie's money had, in a matter of seventy-two hours, and apparently without any intermediate exposure, made breaking news on three big-city television stations (and would soon, I was sure, consume the cable news networks, those vile, squawking cousins of tabloids) - well, it so reinforced my bewilderment that I half-believed I'd gone mad.

I stepped out of my room warily, discreetly, as if expecting the paparazzi to materialize in the hallway and devour me with their legendary rapacity. But the hall was empty, silent save for the drone of the vending machines by the stairwell. I turned the corner with slightly more assurance, relieved to find only Archie on the other side.

"Is it safe?" I called to him.

"Is what safe?"

"The coast," I said. "Is it clear?"

He looked around, confirming what I guess was already obvious to us both. "I don't see any cameras," he said.

I went to him. "Not up here, no. But down there..." I pointed at the floor. "Down there, there are *lots* of them."

He nodded. "Any bright ideas hit you?"

"Well," I said, "there *is* the old-fashioned method of dealing with the press."

"And that is?"

"To face them," I said.

"Do you really think that's wise?"

I shrugged. "I don't think we have much of a choice, Archie. They've got the place surrounded like a swat team. Every exit is sealed off. So, unless you want to jump off the roof..."

He pressed the down arrow on the control panel. "Jesus Christ," he said.

"Yeah, He may be down there, too."

We actually almost made it. Two of the reporters were chatting with the clerk, their backs turned to the elevators. The other had apparently told his crew to take five and was lounging in one of the lobby's wing-backed chairs, flipping through a magazine and munching on a bagel he'd filched from the continental-breakfast buffet. Had he not happened to look up as Archie and I were crossing the lobby, we would have been home free.

But he *did* look up, and once he saw us it was all over. He was on his feet in half a second, his crew assembled and the camera rolling in another four. The other reporters quickly followed suit, and by the time we'd reached the doors they had swarmed us, bathing us in the harsh glare of their camera bulbs, six human eyes and three prying lenses trained on us like search lights. There was no escape.

The cacophony of questions went something like this: "Archie! Mr. Lancaster! How do you respond to reports that you've been giving money away?" "Mr. Lancaster! Is it true that you've been writing checks to people for five thousand dollars?" "Did you really give a million dollars to coal miners in Kentucky? Was it your own money, sir? Is Dacey Energy involved in this?"

I whispered to Archie, "Just ignore them if you want. They'll only distort any answer you give them, anyway."

Archie shook his head, resolute. I think he'd decided that he had might as well get this over with, as there was no avoiding it forever. He turned and faced the horde of rabid reporters, the shoal of microphones jabbing at him like rounded knives. Here, in a nutshell, is what he said:

367

"Yes, it is true that I have been giving money to people. The amounts have varied according to the particular needs of the recipients. Mine is a goodwill mission, an exercise in mass charity. I have led a life of privilege, of great financial success, and now it is time to return the favor. It seems to me that, while I could simply make a few large donations to a few reputable charities, my interests are better served, and the work far more satisfying, by going to the people themselves, the working-class folks who are the backbone of this nation's economy. Legally I owe them nothing, of course, but I have come to realize that morally I owe them everything. Without them, without their unyielding dedication to those industries and occupations in which they labor, without their indefatigable commitment to their crafts, those wellsprings of prosperity and opportunity, this country should hardly claim its status as a beacon of promise and hope, a model of democratic excellence, the envy of the world. And I should hardly have enjoyed all the bountiful rewards, wealth the least of them, which I have been so fortunate as to earn.

"The details of the endeavor are extraneous. I will not disclose where I intend to go next, how long I intend to continue the effort, or how much I intend to give away. Let me just say that I have thus far found the experience supremely gratifying, and extend my deepest thanks to all the decent, spirited, unfaltering men and women of the American workforce."

There was some stammering I have left out, and a couple of on-the-spot revisions. And I've polished his diction a bit. Otherwise, his remarks were exactly as I have presented them here.

Needless to say, the reporters were not fully satisfied with Archie's talking points. They had questions. They *always* have questions. Here were a few of them: "What does Dacey's board of directors think of all this?" "Do you have the stockholders' approval?" "Are you just doing this to boost your company's profits?" And, of course, they had a question for me, too: "Who are *you*?"

I told them, as I had told everyone who had so far inquired, that I was a journalist from Pittsburgh. I wondered how much longer I would be able to say that before it came to light, somehow or another, that I was in fact a jobless bum. And when the media learned that fact, how would it affect our experiment? Would it so damage Archie's and my reputations as to seriously imperil it? I had not prepared for such a contingency. It had not even *occurred* to me to prepare for such contingencies, as I had never given much thought to my own role in the scheme. Archie would be the star of

369

the show, I had figured, and our success in bringing about grassroots economic reform would rise or fall on his own credibility, his own skill in making the case for our utopian campaign.

Dakota Washington, the reporter for WCHZ, asked me this: "Are you going to write a book about your experiences on the road with Mr. Lancaster?

Here was my reply: "I might explore the idea, yes."

Obviously, I have done much more than simply explore the idea, although until I started writing this book I never really intended to. It sort of just happened one day, without my explicit approval or conscious planning, and had long evolved a life of its own by the time it occurred to me that perhaps it would best remain unwritten.

Which meant I couldn't kill it, no matter how tempting the notion, how taxing or unappetizing the task.

There is much my conscience can condone, but murder is not among it.

We escaped the hotel - barely.

Two of the reporters followed us to the car, apparently

dissatisfied with the ample fodder Archie had thoughtfully volunteered. They were gluttons, demanding seconds on their lobster and filet mignon, clamoring for desert. (And they didn't want just any dessert, either: they wanted something fancy and vastly filling, something on the order of baked Alaska or crème brûlée.) The other reporter, inexplicably content with what Archie had freely offered up - and it was, indeed, enough to feed the anchors back at the station for at least five or six hours, maybe a whole day if the station manager brought in business experts and legal analysts to probe every orifice of the story - stayed inside.

Archie deftly deflected the two more dogged reporters, telling them he planned to hold a news conference later in the week at which he would divulge further details of the operation. This didn't deter the reporters from continuing to bombard him with questions, but it did staunch their nosebleeds a bit, soften their jabs. As they were regrouping we ducked into my Buick, locked the doors, and took off.

"My God," Archie said. "Now I know what it feels like to be a celebrity."

"Archie, you *are* a celebrity."

He looked at me. "Since when?"

"Since we went to the mines, I guess. Or maybe earlier.

371

Maybe since I took..." The words died on my lips.

"Since you took what?"

"The pictures," I said.

He did not reply, turned his gaze out the window. I lit a cigarette, and steered us north, toward Middletown.

We spent the morning in the suburbs, where we were less likely to be spotted by camera-toting vampires. We hit a few of the usual suspects: fast-food joints, convenience stores, a hardware vendor, a bank or two. And some not-so-usual suspects: a funeral home, a strip club, and a police station. (Forgive me, but the undertaker was truly one grave bastard.) All told we spent close to six hours giving away in excess of a hundred thousand dollars.

It was at the police station that we encountered our first refusal, that is, the first designated recipient to decline Archie's gift. It was a rookie cop whose name, if I remember correctly, was something like Jackson Bentward, some highly unusual moniker. He could not have been more than thirty years old. By refusing the money he was not following the example of his elders, for all the other officers accepted their checks for five thousand dollars with little or no reluctance. (One of them, keen to the irony of a uniformed lawman unwittingly committing a crime, did ask if the maneuver was entirely legal, but when assured that it was took his check with a blinding smile fit for the saints.) In fact, the chief of police, a burly Canadian with a Yosemite-Sam mustache and tiny spectacles, made Archie an honorary constable.

"We heard about you on TV this morning," he said, "and we completely support what you're doing. Good people have been getting the shaft for too long."

"It's our honor," I said.

The chief gave me a quizzical look which cemented, for me, how small I had suddenly become, how extraneous to my own creation. "Excuse me," he said, "but who exactly *are* you?"

Why did the rookie cop turn down the money? In his words, "Knowing my luck, the IRS will audit me next year and take it all, anyway." Which I think was a polite way of saying, "No, thank you."

Maybe he didn't it feel it appropriate for a city official to accept what seemed to him uncomfortably like a bribe. Or maybe he didn't trust us. Maybe he thought it was some kind of trick. Maybe he wanted to be the one shrewd skeptic who could later bask in his vindication when the gullibility of his colleagues blew up in their faces.

But probably it was just that notorious party-pooper, that

eons-old crank called "pride."

31

It was Monday, June 20. Noon drew nigh. The edition of the Charleston *Daily Mail* in which John Friedman would effectively announce to the world that Archibald Lancaster had found religion would reach news stands in less than an hour, thirty thousand private residences in less than four. Soon our noble anonymous undertaking would come under the scrutiny of an entire planet. Meantime, we were stuck in bottleneck traffic.

"What the hell is this?" Archie asked me.

"I'm sure I don't know. An accident, I guess."

"The whole highway is jammed for miles!"

"Looks that way."

He cast a reproving eye at me. "Why don't we just fly from city to city?"

"What, and leave out the rural folk?"

He sighed.

"Archie?"

"Yes?"

"Are you upset with me?"

"No, I'm upset with the traffic."

"I'm sure it'll budge soon."

"I can't believe those reporters."

"Me, either."

"How do you suppose they found out about what we're up to?"

"I have no idea. But I think it'd be best if from now on we checked into hotels under my name only."

He sighed again, and closed his eyes, and, incredibly, fell fast asleep.

He woke up fifteen minutes later, when we came to a toll booth. The toll was one dollar and twenty-five cents. Exact change was not required, said a sign, but it was greatly appreciated.

"Archie," I said. "Do you have any change in your pockets?"

"Huh?"

"Change. In your pockets. I need a quarter."

"For what?"

"The toll booth."

He opened his eyes fully and looked around. "Oh. Um. Let me check." He checked and found his pockets coinless. "Sorry."

I pulled up to the booth and rolled my window down. "Never mind," I said. "I have a better idea."

"Oh?"

"Get out your checkbook."

"Oh, God."

"Find a pen."

"Okay." He began groping around in the cup-holder under the gear stick, came up with a black Bic smeared with grease.

"This guy spends all day on his feet in ninety-degree weather with nothing but a fan to cool him down."

"True," said Archie, "but he works for the government, so he probably makes *too* much." He gave a grim, weary laugh, saw that I was *not* laughing, and got out his checkbook.

I turned to the man in the booth and smiled. "Good afternoon," I said.

We did hold up traffic for a couple of minutes (we forewent using one of the contracts for the sake of the motorists behind us), but it was definitely worth it, if only to see the look on the toll booth operator's face when I handed him that check. Archie wrote it for thirty-five thousand dollars, so the operator could split it evenly with his co-workers. The people in the cars behind us probably thought that I was somehow negotiating with the guy, which I'm sure only added to their ire ("Cheapskate!"). Several horns had blared by the time we finally got moving.

"Hey," I said to Archie, "that was fun!"

"So the novelty isn't wearing off yet, huh?"

"Well, I thought it was. But I think what we just did breathed some new life into it." I lit a cigarette, smiling. "Did you see his expression? It was priceless!"

"Yes," he said, "it was just like the electrician's. And just like the pipe fitters'. And just like the coal miners'."

"What are you saying, Archie? That *you're* getting inured to this? I thought you were just starting to enjoy it."

"Hell," he said. "I don't know. It has its moments, I suppose, but it does strike me as fairly lame, on the whole."

"Lame?"

"Well, not terribly effective."

"Really? You still believe that?"

He nodded. "I must admit that I do."

I pointed to the radio. "Music?"

"It's up to you."

I flipped the dial to a classic rock station, savored the hypnotic rhythms of Bob Segert's "Against the Wind." Archie dozed again.

I smoked, the road ahead stretching out like an ophidian

skin, hard and ungiving, rich with promised delights.

We were in Middletown a short while later. About a mile off the exit, I spotted a gigantic factory called Butler County Glass & Steel.

"Look," I said, pointing it out to Archie. "What more perfect place to do some big-time wealth-spreading? That there's some blue-collar *shit!*"

Archie sighed. "Must you put it in such blatantly communist terms?"

I laughed. "How else shall I put it?"

"I don't know. Keep calling it charity."

"That makes it less objectionable, does it?"

"Superficially, yes."

I drove toward the factory, pointedly changed the subject. "Did you talk to Winston last night?"

His face sagged. He hesitated. "Yes, briefly."

"Is he all right?"

"He's fine." Stiff, laconic.

I lit another cigarette, afraid to pursue the topic further but too curious to help myself. "What's he up to?"

"I didn't really ask. What does it matter?"

378

"I was just curious."

"Roll your window down, please."

I did.

"Tell me," said Archie, "how exactly the two of you met."

I chose my words carefully. "At your banquet, last month. Didn't Winston tell you?"

"Yes, he told me. But I'm still not totally clear on why it is that you approached him in the first place."

"I assumed he was your son," I said.

"And?"

"And I wanted to speak to him."

"Why? You thought he might help you arrange an interview with me?"

No, I thought, *I wanted to kiss him.*

"Yes. Something like that."

"You people," said Archie slightingly, "are such *devious* creatures."

"Us people?"

"Media folk."

"I'm not a media person." I paused. "Anymore."

He made no reply.

The factory was massive, comprising over a million square feet, the length of three city blocks. It was also incredibly hot, many parts in the neighborhood of a hundred and twenty degrees. The workers who spent extended periods in these parts took salt tablets at regular intervals in order to avoid fainting. Only the offices on the second level were air-conditioned. Furnaces the size of elephants spanned the back wall on the lower floor. The factory workers (maybe twenty men and three women) wore protective face-shields as they fed giant panes of glass and sheets of steel into the ovens.

Meanwhile, the heated steel-blanks were placed on conveyor belts which passed through machines that stretched or shrank them to the desired dimensions, and then rolled into great coils bound by aluminum ties. The glass was either stacked and wrapped in plastic or refined with further, more controlled heat, then cooled and stored in a separate area of the factory.

I had never been inside such a place, and was immediately struck by the realization that I could not last one week as a servant of its machinery, salt tablets or none. I might be wrong, but I got the distinct impression that Archie could not last one day: I had never seen someone sweat so much in my life.

We had gotten inside by telling the guard that Archie had an appointment with the factory supervisor. The guard didn't doubt our story, because he had seen the twelve o' clock news on the portable Sony television he kept in his booth to pass the time between visitors. On the news they had aired the footage the three camera crews at the Ramada had shot earlier in the day.

Then the anchor had announced that, if appearances were to be trusted, the world was about to change radically.

We did indeed speak first to the factory supervisor, a lanky fellow by the name of Burt Varliss. He was delighted to see us, because he, too, had seen the newscast and so figured we would give him money. And we did, too: exactly two thousand dollars. He made sixty-four thousand dollars a year - hardly a fortune but hardly a pittance, either.

We asked Mr. Varliss who his boss was. He said, "The general manager." We asked what *his* annual salary was. "About a hundred thousand a year, I think," said Varliss. And *his* boss, we inquired? "The president of Butler Glass & Steel." We then asked how much *he* made per year. "Oh, gee," Varliss said, "probably close to a million bucks."

We didn't write any checks for the higher-ups.

Varliss introduced us to his underlings one by one. None of *them* had seen the news at noon, of course, because they had all been on the factory floor, feeding blanks into monstrous furnaces and gulping salt tablets to remain conscious. A few of them had heard rumors, however, of Archie's miraculous reformation. For the most part, they received him warmly.

"Why did you come to Middletown?" one of them asked.

"Why not?" replied Archie.

"We plan to go everywhere," I said.

"Everywhere?" the worker asked.

"Everywhere accessible by road," I said.

"That could take a while!" the worker said.

I looked at Archie, looked back at the man, and grinned. "The only thing we have more of than money," I said, "is time."

And I reflect now: Aren't the two resources pretty much interchangeable? What is money but freedom, and freedom but the time and ability to do as one wishes? That an enormous reservoir of currency was an essential requirement of our excursion is obvious; that mountains of available time were also necessary is equally significant. And is it not the height of injustice that those

382

with the means to live in luxury are the same people who have sufficient time to enjoy it, to relish all the sumptuous trappings of their decadent lifestyle? Should not those with little material wealth at least be given whole weeks or months of leisure time to pursue their inevitably inexpensive hobbies? Time and money, two rather indispensable ingredients of a happy and carefree life, and neither is obtainable without the other (unless, of course, one is content to sponge off others, which few self-respecting persons are). I would later draw Archie's attention to this screaming inequity, and he would concede it, except to note that each commodity was a logical consequence of the other, at least as things were presently structured.

"Exactly," I said. "Which is why the system needs to be changed."

"Changed how?"

"Changed," I said, "so that those who make very little are afforded huge chunks of time in which to do as they please without being punished for their fiscal inertia."

Archie laughed. "So communism with time instead of money, basically?"

"Oh," I said, "must you keep using that *word*?"

"Which word?"

"'Communism.'"

"What word would you like me to use instead?"

"Um," I said. "How about fairness-ism?"

Archie laughed again, harder this time. "That makes it less objectionable, does it?"

I looked at him. I knew exactly what he was doing, and told him so with my eyes. "No," I said. "It makes it more *true*."

A few of the factory workers regaled us with stories of their professional heroism, accented by briefer tales of personal triumphs. One woman told us how she had supported herself and her husband for six years on her modest wage, because her husband was a recovering quaalude addict with a slew of health problems (including what sounded like a pretty nasty brain tumor). He minded the kids and visited doctors and went to Narcotics Anonymous meetings while she slaved at the factory to earn their daily bread.

Somewhat more moving was an account one of the men told of how he had cared for his ailing parents since the age of twenty-six, driven a cab for two years to supplement his factory income (during which period he had seldom seen his wife, as she'd been enrolled in night school to become a veterinary technician), and raised four children one of whom was mentally retarded, all while battling Hodgkin's disease.

"Have you ever been without a job?" I asked him.

"Not once in my life," he said. "I can't imagine not having a job."

"Do you *enjoy* working?"

"It's not a question of enjoying it," he said. "It's a question of survival."

"How much longer do you expect to work?"

"I can't get my pension till I turn sixty-two. That'll be eight years from now. I guess that's when I'll call it quits."

"Suppose you could retire next year. Would you?"

This one stumped him. "I don't know," he said finally. "I don't think so." He looked at a couple of his co-workers. "What would I do all day?"

I had been troubled more than once by the idea that most people squandered the little spare time they already had, by watching television or surfing the Internet or gabbing on the phone about the giant shit their neighbor's dog just took on their lawn. I had also been troubled by the thought that, like the worker in question, many people didn't *want* more spare time, aware that they lacked any productive or fruitful means of filling it. Why, then, campaign to give people more leisure time? Why campaign to give them more *money*, which, as I have said, is more a way of buying free time than anything else? Wouldn't it be like giving a book to an illiterate?

I had no good answers to these questions, and was all too cognizant of the fact. I worried that I had naively assumed that, since *I* could find ample uses for extra time, so could the hoi polloi. Maybe, I found myself thinking now, I had been wrong to believe that most people counted themselves oppressed in the first place. Maybe most people were content with their lots, so accustomed to humble circumstances and obscure distinctions that the sudden receipt of fat capital, if they did not flout it *a la* Jackson Bentward, would have virtually no effect on them. With no novel to write or symphony to compose or cosmic secrets to unlock, they had enough trouble keeping themselves occupied as it was: one can watch only so many sitcoms before one's brain begins to devour itself. Perhaps, then, my whole project was woefully misguided.

But I could not allow myself to believe that. That, save the police officer in Cincinnati, everyone we had thus far met had taken the money offered them was one reason. Another was the general unrest I had encountered among almost all those I had ever known, a widespread if ill-defined and mostly unarticulated outrage at life's basic unfairness (this of course leading directly to the futile consumption of more crap aimed at distracting them from their disillusionment). I could not recall a time when I had not detected it, this vague, communal sense that something about the world was fundamentally awry, that humans were engaged in an elaborate and farcical game whose rules they all knew to be crooked but, cogs that they were, accepted that the machine could function, which in turn permitted them to be sane. And I had never been able to pinpoint as the source of this ferment anything but the irrefragable vagaries of wealth and power, that good fortune favored the ruthless and cruel as much as it had ever favored the honest and meek.

This, then, was how I reassured myself once more that my Great Crusade was noble and just and good.

By the time we left the factory, just after five o' clock, John Friedman's article had found its way to its readers, and all the major cable news outlets, catching wind of the siege in Cincinnati, had aired brief segments about Archie's apparent mental collapse. But the real storm would come the next day, once the Associated Press had run its own story on the subject and word of the CEO's lunacy had reached the better portion of the civilized world. Only in the last few months, as I have been plugging away at this memoir and Archie has been holed up at his mansion on Penn Avenue, has the hysteria begun to die down.

We weren't on the interstate three minutes when Archie's cell phone rang. It was the first time I had heard it ring, and was relieved that his was an unobnoxious, monotonous ringtone, with no hint of gimmickry. The conversation lasted two minutes, with the caller doing most of the talking.

"Who was that?" I asked.

"Tim Ballmer."

"The vice chairman guy?"

"Yes."

"What did he want?"

"To know," said Archie, "what in the hell I'm doing."

"Oh."

Archie reclined in his seat. "I'm never going to survive this."

"Well."

"I'd might as well just dissolve the company and make out with what I can."

I hesitated. "Or you could give it all away."

He looked at me.

"Maybe that would be going too far," I said.

Fifteen minutes later his phone rang again. This time it was Kenneth Stevens, head of his legal team and author of the soon-to-be-world-famous Contract. He said that a high-ranking official at Archie's banking institution had contacted him, alarmed by a recent spate of exceedingly peculiar and substantial transactions. "Since Friday," the official had said, "some one hundred and eighty-seven checks have been deposited against Mr. Lancaster's account, one of them in the amount of *eight hundred and fifty thousand dollars*! Altogether about four million dollars have been withdrawn from his account. We assume, based on media reports, that this is authorized, but we just wanted to double-check and make absolutely certain that there hasn't been some kind of error."

Archie confirmed what Stevens already knew: no error had there been, great or small.

We spent the night in Huber Heights, ten minutes north of Dayton and one hundred fifty miles southwest of Lake Erie. And, though we were twice that distance from where the newspaper was published, guess what I found discarded on one of the chairs in the lobby of the Holiday Inn where we stayed? Why, a copy of that

389

day's Charleston *Daily Mail*!

Needless to say, once Archie and I had read Friedman's piece, we were both good and ready to get hammered.

And get hammered we did, I a bit more egregiously than Archie. We spent perhaps three hours in the hotel bar, gulping vodka tonics which we washed down with bottled beers, nourishing ourselves with salted peanuts. We had skipped lunch, eaten burgers for dinner, and now found ourselves famished.

After eight or nine drinks Archie said to me, "I have to tell you something, Terry."

I was staring down into my glass, marveling at the transparency of the liquid. Yawning, I said, "Oh? What's that, Arch?"

"I didn't get you fired," he said, "but I helped get you fired."

I looked at him. I blinked. My fingers tightened around my glass. "What?"

"Three Rivers Media," he said, "the company that owns the *Post-Gazette*. I know the guy who runs it. He was a major shareholder of Dacey's at one time."

Smoke began to seep from my ears. The bartender didn't appear to notice.

"I called him," Archie said, "the day after... you know."

The smoke got thicker, poured out faster.

"I told him I thought... that I thought you might be cracking up. That you'd been making threatening phone calls to my house, and leveling wild accusations at me. And that you'd threatened to publish libelous articles about me, that you were waging some kind of personal vendetta against me. I thought maybe... I guess I thought it would shake you up, maybe get you to back off a little. It was irrational, I know, but I wasn't thinking clearly at the time. I was angry, confused... I guess I just -"

"You piece of shit," I said. "You unbelievable, unconscionable asshole."

He drooped his head in shame. "Terry, I'm sorry."

"No," I said. "Don't bother."

I stood and kicked my stool into the bar. For a moment I glared at him, flames leaping in my pupils, teeth clenched, lips quivering. Then I made haste out of the bar, leaving a bewildered and silent Archie in my wake.

32

If ever the world has changed overnight, it did so between the dusk of June 20, 2004 and the ensuing dawn. In the intervening hours, while Archie and I slept fitfully in the aftermath of our own private tumult, the minor tremor that was the day's news coverage in Cincinnati, and the slightly stronger shudder that was John Friedman's article, conspired to spawn an earthquake of seismically galactic intensity.

The segment about Archie and me on the noon news in Cincinnati begat similar segments on the five and six o' clock news programs across the state of Ohio, which in turn begat longer, more detailed segments on the eleven o' clock news shows around the tri-state. Friedman's article was published somewhat too late to affect the evening news broadcasts in West Virginia, but was the lead story on all but one of that state's eleven o' clock programs. However, it was not until early Tuesday morning that the ripple effects of the previous days' events finally infiltrated the national news networks, CNN being the first of them to break the story (which it did on its *Daybreak* program). Cementing the national prominence of our exploits was the piece by the Associated Press disseminated in fifteen hundred American newspapers on Tuesday afternoon. Within forty-eight hours every major newspaper in the world would have reproduced some version of this article, and the radio and television news channels in Europe and Asia would be as clogged with (mostly inaccurate) commentary on the Phenomenon as those in the United States.

392

Mine and Archie's adventure as Altruists in the Information Age had officially and irrevocably begun.

Of course, we weren't on speaking terms at the time. We ate breakfast in silence, at a Waffle House a block from the hotel. Either nobody recognized us or nobody felt it necessary to approach us, for our meal went uninterrupted by the strangers in whose company we took it.

There was a newspaper spread open on the table between us, a complimentary copy of the Dayton *Daily News* I had picked up at the hotel (mostly to get a handle on the size of the monster Archie and I had grudgingly birthed). We didn't make the headline - that was reserved for the death of an Akron marine who had been killed in Iraq the day before - but we did make the lead on the bottom half of page one: "Coal Magnate, Journalist Tour Tri-State, Dish Out Dough to Residents."

I noshed on a hunk of my pecan waffle with whip cream as I scanned the first few paragraphs of the article:

> Ever heard the old joke about the bourgeoise and the proletariat? No, not the corny one about the bourgeoise having more of everything but syllables; I'm

393

talking about the wittier one that makes a point: "Nice shoes," says a bourgeois to a laborer. "Where'd you get them?" "I made them in your factory, sir," replies the laborer meekly. Appalled, the bourgeois sneers, "Remind me to deduct them from your next paycheck."

Okay, so it's not that funny. But then, it's not so much a joke as a parable, a brief excerpt from an imaginary modern-day New Testament. So preoccupied with his bottom line is the white-collar stiff that he misconstrues his employee's heartbreaking loyalty to the company's product as an inadvertent confession of theft. Is there an audience for such Marxist glurge in today's hi-tech, Mammon-crazed society? Maybe not. But there are always people - lots of them - willing to take a handout.

Enter Archibald Lancaster, CEO of Richmond-based Dacey Energy, who in recent days has reportedly parted with several million dollars - and not for the purpose of expanding his stock portfolio or beefing up his fleet of private jets. On the contrary, according to rumors which Lancaster himself confirmed yesterday while fielding questions from reporters in Cincinnati, the native Connecticutian has been playing Robin Hood, with an interesting twist: the money he's "stealing" from the rich is his own.

The first question, obviously, is, "Why?" Why would one of the world's richest men decide, at the age of forty-eight and without any apparent impetus in his personal life, to "go straight"? Undoubtedly the truth of the matter will be dug up sooner or

```
later, but for the moment the
prevailing wisdom is as cynical as
one might expect: there's some-
thing the Pittsburgh coal tycoon
doesn't want us to know.
```

I tore my eyes away from the print - it required more effort than it should have, I thought - and gave Archie a troubled, solemn look. "God help us," I said, "Mr. Lancaster."

They were the first words I had spoken to him all day.

I asked Archie if he wanted to read the article and he said no, he was already feeling a little queasy from his eggs and sausage. Then he asked if I was still pissed at him. Can you imagine how surreal that was, to be asked such a question, not by a sparring lover, but by the father of the young man for whom I had developed my first concretely homosexual feelings? Well, then, I'll tell you: it was pretty damned surreal.

"Yes," I said. "Of course I am. You're going to need to give me a few decades to get over this one, buddy."

He nodded. "I promise to keep my mouth shut for the rest of the trip."

"We both know you won't," I said. "I doubt you could even if you really wanted to."

He shrugged. "I guess this is what you get for being honest."

I chuckled virulently, floored by his brazen attempt to turn the tables on me with such childish, passive-aggressive bullshit. "Yeah," I said. "I guess so."

I summoned the waitress and paid the check, left her an astronomical tip in whose conferral I was too angry and perturbed to take much pleasure.

"You know," said Archie as we headed back to the hotel, "I really am sorry for what I did, but you're not looking at this from all sides."

"Oh?" I said, asking myself why I was indulging his nonsense to begin with. "And what other sides are there to your getting me fired, Archie, other than the obvious one that pisses me off?"

"I didn't get you fired," he said, in the sulky tone of a four-year-old. He had his head down and his hands in his pockets, looked as if he'd slept even worse than I had.

"Please, let's not split hairs here, okay? I think we're well beyond that at this point."

"Fine," he said. "What I'm getting at, Terry, is that, if not for what happened, we wouldn't be doing what we're doing. We wouldn't be helping all these people like we are." He paused, perhaps trying to gauge how well I'd receive this next part (if so, he did it very poorly): "And you'd be a million bucks lighter."

I stopped dead in my tracks. I turned to him and looked him square in the eye. "Are you looking to get punched in the face, Archie?"

His face evinced apparently genuine surprise at my sudden hostility. "What? No, of course not. I just... why would you say that?"

"Never mind," I said. "Just come on. We have a long day ahead of us."

Still shaking his head, he complied.

Our day was longer, indeed, than either of us possibly could have foreseen. By mid-afternoon, probably half to three-quarters of the country had seen Archie and me either in the paper or on television, and we were recognized nearly everywhere we went. In a few places we were even mobbed, like movie stars so foolish or narcissistic as to stroll openly in public.

Most of these throngs were composed of friendly, kind-spirited types who supported what Archie and I were doing and wanted to let us know as volubly and dramatically as they could. (Yet few of them, I suspect, would have embraced a label with even faintly socialist connotations.) One of them, however, consisted principally of haughty, right-leaning college kids who had more than a few uncouth words for us. Archie made a rather lame if perversely touching effort to placate this latter bunch by reassuring them that his confidence in the free-market system remained unshaken; he was simply trying to show people that compassion and self-interest need not exclude one another. All I heard was, "Please, guys, don't think I've become one of those pinko left-wing nuts, because I really haven't! I'm just being held hostage by this asshole next to me! Quick, call someone!" The kids must have heard something similarly flimsy and desperate, because they didn't appear very convinced by Archie's clumsy rhetoric.

Wretchedly hungover as we were, the hours rather crawled more than walked, and were crippled further by the brutal heat wave presently sweeping the Midwest. Shortly after lunch, which consisted of chili dogs purchased from a roadside vendor (and soon thereafter expelled), we both found ourselves on the brink of exhaustion. We had given away a mere fifty or sixty grand, mostly to some secretaries at an office complex outside Dayton and a couple of delivery men who worked for a beer distributor in the city, with whom we crossed paths at a 7-11 on our way north. It was therefore with considerable reluctance, my own fatigue notwithstanding, that I ceded to Archie's mid-afternoon request that we find a hotel in Indianapolis and allow ourselves each a three-hour nap.

"We're in no shape to keep on without a little recuperation," he tendered.

I nodded slowly, wanting badly to argue the point but too weary to do so, and thus realizing that he was right. "Fine," I said. "But three hours is it. And I want to give out another fifty thousand or so before we check in."

His face dropped, his eyes so lackluster and bloodshot that he might have been cataclysmically stoned. "You mean we're gonna stop again?"

"No," I said. "We can do it once we get there. To Indianapolis."

Relief flooded his features. He wiped sweat off his forehead with the back of his hand. "Oh," he said. "All right."

"Archie?"

"Yeah?"

The radio was on so quietly we could barely hear it, but I turned it off, anyway. I spoke without looking at him: "Did you break into my apartment as well? In addition to getting me fired, I mean?"

"Huh?"

"You heard me."

"Did I...?"

"Break into my apartment." Now I looked at him. "On the Sunday before I lost my job."

He shook his head. "No," he said. "I swear I didn't. On my mother's grave, Terry, I swear to you that I had nothing to do with that."

"That's what you said about my getting fired."

"Well," he said, "in this case it's true."

I kept looking at him for a second, trying to descry something on his face, a glint or a gleam or a flicker in his eye, that would betray this new and somehow more odious untruth. But there was nothing there, nothing I could see, anyway, and I'll be damned if, in spite of everything, I didn't believe the son of a bitch.

We got to Indianapolis at quarter of four and located a Sheridan about a half-mile from the exit. There were no businesses near the hotel save the kind to whose employees we had already given amply: restaurants, gas stations, grocery stores, and the like. I was tired, and in no mood to be picky, but was nevertheless eager to expand the range of our recipients, to broaden the spectrum of workers who would benefit from Archie's increasingly less-feigned philanthropy. We had thus far donated heavily to laborers in the basic industries like mining and manufacturing, and to those in the service sector (especially those employed by retailers). Professionals and established entertainers were of course to be excluded on the basis of their gratuitous incomes. Who, then, did that leave?

As we were walking into the hotel the obvious finally occurred to me: we had yet to give anything to the very species of concern we were about to patronize. Hotel clerks earned meager wages and were certainly deserving of some unexpected relief, but the poor women who cleaned up after (usually well-to-do) lodgers were a prime candidate for it. Yet, we had not given so much as a dime to any of the help at any of the hotels, four in all, at which we had so far stayed. Here, then, was a major arm of the service sector to which our attention was long overdue: those who scrubbed the pubic-hair-littered bathtubs and wiped the shit-stained toilets of travelers who seldom saw them, and perhaps had never *seen* them.

Having unloaded his luggage from the trunk of my Buick, Archie ran his hand down his ashen face and looked at me. I looked back at him, with more sympathy than perhaps he deserved, this battle-weary wanderer of cruel and sprawling deserts, a casualty of

402

a long and treacherous courtship with Sirs Beefeater and Tonic, meek victim of arduous extortion. "So where we going?" he asked, his voice a pitiful rasp.

"Archie," I declared, smiling victoriously, "we're going nowhere."

"We aren't?"

"Nope," I said. "Our business is right inside this hotel."

"It is?"

"It is," I said, and led the charge to newfound treasures in wait.

As luck would have it, there were seven such treasures: two clerks, a concierge, and four maids on duty. The clerks we gave five thousand apiece, the maids ten. Not only did this strike me as supremely fair, but it met my goal of fifty grand with ample room to spare.

When, with a slightly trembling hand, she returned to its well the pen with which she had signed the contract, I asked one the clerks where we might find the hotel's cleaning personnel. She was a dazzlingly attractive woman in her early thirties, her appearance flawless in the minutest details - fingernails manicured, twice-rinsed blonde hair tied sensibly in a ponytail, cosmetics beyond reproach - and embodied all the perky ambition of one who secretly subscribes to the twaddle on motivational breakroom posters ("The Three P's to Success: Punctuality, Perseverance, and a Positive Mental Attitude!"). Also, she appeared not to have the foggiest idea what in the fuck I was talking about.

"Honey," Archie said, "the maids."

"Oh." She blinked, fighting the cloud which had fallen over her brain. "Them."

"Where are they?" I asked.

She leaned over the desk and pointed to an adjacent hallway. "Down there," she said.

"Thank you."

We nodded and went after the maids, those unsung wielders of toilet brushes and Windex.

33

You can imagine their faces, I am sure, when we opened the door to their dusky chamber and announced that we were there to rescue them from their invisible martyrdom. Especially since only two of them spoke fluent English.

"Who're you?" one of these two asked for a third time.

"Archibald Lancaster," said Archie.

"And Terry Farmer." *And together*, I thought, *we're the Two Amigos!*

"What do you want again?" asked the maid. She was a plump woman with unkempt hair and too much green eye shadow.

"To give you money," I said.

The maid translated this into what I took for pidgin Spanish, for the sake of her foreign colleagues, and turned back to us. "Why?"

"Because you don't make enough," Archie said. No prompting this time! I could not have been prouder.

"Not *nearly* enough," I added.

"We've already given fifteen thousand to the clerks and the concierge."

"You have?" asked the maid, reeling. The other Caucasian maid, a shy and homely stick, listened mutely.

"Yes," said Archie.

"But we want to give *you* guys ten thousand dollars each," I said.

"Ten thousand dollars?" gasped the portlier maid.

"Correct."

"Are you serious?"

"We are," said Archie.

"As a heart attack," I echoed.

By this point the other Caucasian maid had become visibly paralyzed, though her jaw was locked firmly shut. When the plump maid translated the last part of our exchange into Spanish (we later learned that she had worked alongside nearly a dozen Spanish-speaking maids in her nine-year career and had thereby acquired a moderate fluency in the tongue), her swarthier co-workers grew goggle-eyes and absently clutched one another, as if suddenly light-headed.

Archie leaned into my ear and whispered, "Contracts?"

I shook my head, and surveyed the four women, smiling. "Ladies, we'd give you cash if we could, but you can take our word for it that the checks..." I motioned for Archie to roll out the rainmaker. He had already depleted his first book and had had to obtain a new one at a bank late the previous afternoon. "The checks," I said, "won't bounce."

While Archie was autographing his latest thank-you cards (as I had come to think of them), I observed that the chubby maid with the eye shadow was wearing a wrist splint on her left arm and that the younger of the two Hispanic maids was visibly pregnant, probably well into her third trimester.

"You expecting?" I asked her, stupidly, forgetting that she could no more understand English than she could fathom why two strange white men were about to hand her a year's salary without at least demanding oral sex.

"Yeah," said the plump maid. "She is."

Confused, the pregnant maid asked her, "*¿qué él dijo?*"

"He wanted to know if you're pregnant," replied the first. Then, in a decidedly poor Spanish accent, making semi-circular gestures in front of her belly, she ventured a muddled translation: "*Él desea saber si usted embarazado.*" She looked abashedly at Archie and me, confessing, "I'm better at understanding it than speaking it."

"*Si,*" said the pregnant maid. "*Soy siete meses de embarazado.*"

"She's seven months' pregnant," translated Miss Wrist Splint.

"Isn't she eligible for maternity leave?" I asked.

Before the white maid could even begin to translate this new query, Archie interjected, "No, not until she's actually given birth. Then she gets six weeks off with pay."

"Six weeks?" I said, glancing at him. My surprise, I concede, was mostly feigned. "That's it?"

"That's it," said Archie. "Or at least, that's the standard policy in the private sector."

"And nothing prior to the birth?"

"No."

"Disgraceful," I said.

"Mister," said Wrist Splint, "you got *that* right."

"Call me 'Terry,'" I said. "Please."

"Okay," she said. "Terry, you hit that one right on the nose!"

"Los productos químicos en algunos de los productos de la limpieza son peligrosos para mi bebé," said the pregnant maid.

"What did she say?" I asked the translator.

"I'm not sure," she said. She looked at her co-worker. "Say it slower, Carlita."

Carlita slowly repeated her sentence.

"She says some of the stuff in the cleaning products is bad for her baby."

I turned to Archie. "Isn't it illegal for an employer to knowingly endanger the fetus of a pregnant employee?

He shrugged. "Maybe her boss doesn't know she's pregnant."

I laughed, and expected the maids to join in. They didn't. "He probably *doesn't* know," said Wrist Splint. "He hardly ever talks to us, except when something goes missing from one of the rooms or a guest complains about the bathroom sink."

"Who's your boss?" I asked. "What's his name?"

"Sandy," she said. "Jenkins."

"What if somebody wants extra towels?" inquired Archie. "Or more shampoo?"

"No," said the other, previously mute maid. "The front-desk staff takes care of guest requests."

"Oh," mused Archie.

"How could your boss," I asked, "possibly be unaware that Carlita is pregnant? Hasn't he *seen* her for the past two months?"

"*Él es un lechón ignorante de penes,*" said Carlita, with a sly smirk. Wrist Splint burst out laughing, her appreciable belly jiggling cartoonishly.

"What?" I asked, smiling myself. "What'd she say?"

"That he's a stupid cocksucker," said the plump maid.

And then we were *all* laughing.

"Your wrist," I said to the older of the two white maids, whose name was Irene Howser. "What happened to it?"

"Sprained it," she said.

"How?"

"Fell down."

"On the job?"

She nodded. "Three days ago." She blushed, snickering. "Tripped over a guest's bowling-ball bag."

"And your doctor," I said, pointing to her splint. "He gave you that?"

She glanced down at it, as if unaware of its presence. "Oh," she said. "No, I got this from my ex-husband, from where he hurt his wrist chopping wood."

"Why didn't you see a doctor?" I asked. "Don't you have insurance?"

She chuckled wanly. "Yeah, I got insurance, but it ain't worth a damn."

"How do you mean?"

"The deductible's five hundred bucks," she said. "How much do you think a doctor's visit would cost?"

"Three hundred?"

"If that."

"What about workers' comp?" asked Archie.

"Pshaw," said Irene. "Ain't worth a damn, either."

"How come?" he asked.

She extracted a pack of Virginia Slims from the side pocket of her green smock (almost the same shade as her eye shadow).

"You won't tell on me if I smoke in here, will you?"

"Of course not," I said. "In fact, I think I'll join you." I shot a glance at Carlita. "But what about the baby?"

"*Es aceptable,*" said Carlita. "*Mi novio fuma en el apartamento toda la hora.*"

"What'd she say?" I asked.

"Light up," said Irene. "Her boyfriend smokes around her all the time."

I did light up, but not until I'd taken a few steps back from Carlita. The room wasn't small, but neither was it so big that one could smoke in it without disturbing others. With only a small floor-fan and no windows, nor was it well ventilated

"Why were you all in here, anyway?" I asked Irene. "On a break?"

"It's almost quitting time. We were putting away the supplies."

I puffed guiltily on my cigarette, felt Archie's disapproving eyes crawl over me. "I see."

"So you're like a billionaire?" Irene, the maid, asked Archie, the CEO.

"Yes," said Archie, and I savored the guilt in his voice. I

might have been contributing ever so slightly to the mental retardation of Carlita's fetus, but at least I didn't own all the fucking money in the world!

"Holy shit," said Irene.

"Yeah," echoed her white co-worker, whose name was Kathy Fitzsimmons. (The other Hispanic maid, who called herself Agnes Moya and could not have been more than eighteen years old, had yet to utter a word. I don't think even her Spanish was very good, to tell you the truth, and I got the distinct feeling that she was functionally illiterate.)

"How'd you get all that money?" probed Irene, in a somehow inspiringly cavalier tone. "You got stock in gold?" At this she and Kathy chortled.

"No," said Archie. "I own an energy company."

"They sell energy?" asked Irene.

"Yes," said Archie, not sarcastically. There was a kind of numb, insipid resignation in his voice. "Parcels of energy."

"How much is one parcel?"

Archie looked at me. I looked back at him, shrugged. I was tickled to death by the question. "Five hundred dollars," said Archie.

"Wow!" exclaimed Irene. "And how far does that get you?"

"Seventeen miles," he said.

"That's not very far."

Now it was Archie's turn to shrug. "Well."

"It's very good energy, though," I said. "Comes straight from the earth."

"So," I said, "why wouldn't workers' comp cover the cost of a doctor's visit?"

"It was gross negligence on my part," said Irene, and I could tell that she was simply parroting something she had overheard at orientation or maybe read in the employee handbook. "I was super careless, so it don't count."

"How were you careless?" I asked. "Is maneuvering around bowling balls one of the job requirements?"

She shrugged. "I guess."

"It's irrelevant who's at fault," said Archie. His tone, oddly, was more defensive than dispassionate. "The workers' compensation system is designed to protect employees injured on the job regardless of how or why they're injured, except in rare cases."

"I musta had four rare cases," countered Irene.

"How's that?" I asked.

"I've put in four claims during my nine years as a maid," she said, "and all four got turned down."

"Why?" Archie asked.

"Couldn't really tell you," she said. "They always just fed me a bunch of legal gobbledygook."

"Preposterous," scoffed Archie.

"In one of the cases they said the company wasn't liable because I was under the influence of alcohol." She chortled again.

"Were you?" I asked.

"No," she said. "I don't drink."

"Then why did they accuse you of that?"

"I don't know," she said. "My boss said I looked drunk. I guess I look drunk when I'm running on four hours' sleep."

"What happened? I mean, how were you injured?"

"I fell off a second-floor balcony. The rail was loose."

"Jesus Christ!"

"Broke my leg on that one," she said, almost wistfully.

"Where did that happen?" I asked. "Here?"

"Yeah. That was the first claim I put in here."

"The first of how many?"

"Three."

"So the same insurance carrier rejected three claims by the

same worker?"

"Yup."

I shook my head, my shock no longer make-believe. "Why didn't your boss fire you if he really thought you were drunk on the job?"

"Because," she said, "that ain't grounds for immediate dismissal. Not necessarily. It's at the... what's it called? The 'employer's discretion.' Says so in the handbook."

"Convenient loophole," Archie muttered.

"And Sandy said he'd let it slide if I withdrew my claim."

"Did you?"

"I was going to," she said, "but it got rejected two days later."

"That's outrageous," I said. "You weren't even intoxicated!"

"I know. But I didn't have another job to go to, and I sure as hell couldn't afford no lawyer!"

"Well, why didn't you start looking for one? Another job, I mean?"

"I got a twenty-cent raise two weeks later."

"Was that standard? I mean, had you been expecting it?"

"No."

I glanced at Archie. *Are you listening to this?* I asked him with my eyes. *Can you believe this?* Going by his expression, he was,

415

and he couldn't. "What was their excuse in the other two cases?"

"In one it was gross negligence again," she said. "In the other, I was in violation of company policy."

"How so?"

"I used a chair to dust off a ceiling light. You're supposed to use a ladder. Sandy said I put myself in 'wanton danger' by creating an 'unnecessary hazard.' He told me I shouldn't even bother filing a claim for that one, because it'd just be a waste of time. But I went ahead and did it, anyway, on account my ex was laid off at the time and we were pretty hard up for dough."

"Wow," I said. I meant it. "So that one was another fall?"

"Yeah. Banged up my hip pretty good."

"Why'd you use a chair?"

"I was trying to save time," she said. "We get paid by the room."

"Is that common?" Archie asked.

"Yeah," she said. "I think so. I have a friend who works at the Super 8 in Franklin and it's the same thing over there."

"How much per room?" he wanted to know.

"Three bucks. But I started at one-eighty, so I'm doing pretty good."

"You're doing pretty good," I echoed. I was dizzy with

outrage and pity and disbelief. I felt queasy and shaky, impossibly tired. I desperately needed sleep, but it was imperative that I get a drink first.

"So how many rooms do you clean each day?" Archie pressed.

"Fifteen, twenty if they're already pretty clean."

"And that's with someone else helping you?"

"Yes."

"So you make... what, forty-five to sixty bucks a day, less tax?"

"Somethin' around there, yeah."

I cleared my throat. "Archie," I said. "How much cash do you have on you?"

"Um." He reached into his back pocket, removed his wallet, sifted through the bills in it. "Six hundred," he said.

"Give it to Irene, please," I said.

He offered the money to her. She made no move to take it. "Why?" she asked me.

"To cover a doctor's visit," I said. "And any medication you might need."

She still didn't take the money, just went on looking at me with big, bewildered eyes. "I don't know," she said. "You already

417

gave me so much."

I took the bills from Archie's hand and placed them in Irene's. "And yet," I said, "you're owed so much more."

I dug four hundred out of my own wallet (every note I had on me) and gave it to Carlita. "To help with the baby," I said.

"To help with the baby," Irene translated.

"*Grazias*," said Carlita. "*Utilizaré algo de él para pagar un boleto que apresura que conseguí.*"

"What was that, Irene?"

Irene sniggered. "She says she has a speeding ticket she needs to pay for. I think."

"Oh," I said. "Well, that's fine."

"*Mucho gracias*," Carlita said, and stood and kissed me on the cheek. "*Usted es un buen hombre.*"

"I'm a good man?" I asked Irene. I was probably blushing a little.

"That's what she said," said Irene. She was laughing.

Carlita now went to Archie and kissed *him* on the mouth. "*Usted es un buen hombre, también,*" she said, "*pero usted no debe ser tan triste.*"

Archie looked at Irene.

418

"She says you're a nice guy," said Irene, "but that you ought to cheer up."

So I got drunk. I didn't mean to, exactly; I seldom did anymore. I had intended just to have a couple of drinks, to quiet my jitters and settle my stomach, and, of course, to slake my awful thirst. But come seven o' clock I was working on my fifth whiskey and soda and feeling tremendously better. Ravenously hungry, to boot.

I ordered a basket of chicken wings and a bottle of Bud Light. Archie, as far as I knew, was up in his room on the fourth floor, snoring his head off. He'd no doubt be up in an hour or so and asking if I was ready to perform some more Random Acts of Kindness. Naturally, I would not be. By the time he was up and showered, I would be good and ready for bed.

Oops, I thought, and just then a young man in a gray flannel suit, well-tanned and strikingly handsome, entered the bar. He sat down on the stool next to me and ordered a Miller Lite draft. As he sipped it he stole discreet glances at me, as if trying to decide whether he knew me. I lit a cigarette and pretended not to notice him. But it was, of course, to no avail.

"You look familiar to me," he finally said.

I closed my eyes. A lump formed in my throat. For some very obscure and perhaps unanalyzable reason, I dreaded the idea of having a conversation with this man. "Oh, yeah?" I said, as casually as I could.

"Yeah. Weren't you on the news yesterday? With that guy?"

"Um."

"That really rich guy who's giving away all the money?"

I drank deeply of my medicine. "Rich guy?"

He laughed. "Yeah, that CEO. He runs a coal company or something. I read about him in the paper this morning. You were on TV with him, weren't you?"

"Maybe. Why?"

He put his hands up, I guess to indicate that he came in peace, and laughed again. "No, no, I wasn't going to criticize you or anything."

"Oh," I said drowsily, "what a relief."

"Just the opposite. I totally support what you guys are doing."

I raised my glass to him in a half-hearted toast. "Appreciate that."

He sipped his beer with a maddening absence of urgency. He was, I concluded, one of Them: people who drank booze as if it were iced tea, as if its potential to intoxicate them were as incidental as the weather. "So tell me something," he said.

I stubbed out my cigarette. "What's that?"

"How'd you get him to do it?"

For the first time in the conversation, I looked him in the eye. "What do you mean?"

He'd been smiling, but now his smile waned. "Well... how'd you persuade him to give away all that loot?"

I stared at him, hard. "What makes you think it was *my* idea?"

"Because," he said, and now there was a trace of alarm in his voice. The notion that I might be dangerously insane, I think, flashed through his mind. "Your friend said so."

"My friend?"

"The CEO guy."

"When did he say *that*?"

"Yesterday. On TV."

"He did?"

The young man nodded. "Yes."

"I don't recall that," I said.

"Well."

I polished off my drink and ordered another.

"Let me get that for you," the man offered.

"No, thanks."

He shrugged. "Whatever floats your boat, pal."

My drink came. I raised the glass, put it to my lips, and lowered it. "Who are you?" I asked the man.

"Who am I?"

"Yeah. And don't bullshit me."

He laughed, a bit nervously, I thought. "My name is Rod," he said. "And yours?"

I arched an eyebrow. "You mean you don't already know it?"

"No," he said. "I don't think I caught it."

"Terry," I said, and immediately regretted telling him.

"Short for 'Terrance,' I guess?"

"Dude," I said, and thought longingly of Winston, realized how desperately I missed him, "who the fuck *are* you? Are you with the press?"

He shook his head categorically. "No, man," he said, "I'm a real estate agent."

"Here in Indianapolis?"

"Yeah."

"Business or residential?"

"Both."

I nodded, anything but convinced. "Okay. So is there anything else I can help you with, or...?"

"Well," he said, "there was *one* thing I was wondering about."

"Oh? What was that, Rod?"

He sipped his beer. "You got some kind of dirt on him?"

With a monumental effort I quashed the rage building inside me. "No," I said. "Of course not." And then the rage broke through the dam: "Goddammit, what *is* this? Who *are* you?"

"Whoa," he said. "Calm down, man! You think I'm an undercover reporter or something?"

"I don't know *what* the hell you are," I said, and now I sounded as drunk as I did riled.

"I told you -"

"Yeah, right, a real estate agent. So why don't you go sell a house or something?"

Abruptly, he pushed his beer away, stood, and dropped a five-dollar bill on the bar. "You oughtta get your head checked out," he said. "'Cause somethin' ain't right with it."

"Yeah, yeah." I did an admirable job of concealing my self-doubt, I must say.

"You're paranoid, buddy."

"Pays to be paranoid," I muttered stupidly.

He started off, then stopped, put a hand on my shoulder. "One more question, if you don't mind."

I turned and glared at him. "Get your hand offa me!"

He removed his hand, but kept his eyes trained on me. "When thousands of people quit their jobs because they just won the lottery," he said, "are you and the sugar-daddy gonna bail out all the businesses that go under?"

I blinked, swallowed, tried to speak and couldn't. I was dreaming, surely. At last I found my voice: "I thought you supported what we were doing?"

"Oh, I do," he said. "I think it's great, loads of fun. It's like the wild party the teenager throws when his parents go away for the weekend. Problem is, the party has to end sometime, and when it does, when Sunday night rolls around, there's gonna be a lot of damage to answer for."

"Well," I said. "We'll worry about that if and when it happens."

"Great," he said, and summoned a big, plummy smile. "Glad to see you've thought this thing through."

"You're an asshole," I said, but he was gone before I got the first word out. From my bar stool I called to him: "The party only has to end if we let it! It's up to us to keep it going, to keep the confetti flying! It's in our hands, do you hear me? It's..." I trailed off, brooded over my drink.

Mercifully, there was no one else in the bar, and the bar maid was in the kitchen, fetching my basket of wings.

Soon thereafter, my tummy full and thoughts obliterated, I slept.

34

I did not hear Archie's knock at eight-thirty. I was, of course, asleep. Or in a drunken coma, to be precise. I did not stir until quarter of five the next morning, by which time Archie had long since returned to bed.

In the interim, he told me later, he had eaten dinner and then prowled the streets, giving away sixty-five thousand dollars to such diverse laborers as customer-service representatives for a credit card company, a computer technician employed by a major Internet company, a night watchman at a chemical plant, a truck driver from Minneapolis whom he had met at the Chili's where he'd dined, and a bouncer at a bar at which he had stopped around midnight for a couple of barmy thirst-quenchers.

"Busy night," I said from my perch on the end of my bed, my

head in my hands. A near-empty glass of water, having been refilled for a third time a moment earlier, sat on the dresser.

"Not as exciting as yours, evidently," he said, raising an eyebrow. His air was waggish, at least superficially, but I detected a hint of real disapproval buried under the joke. Or maybe it was concern; I am now tempted to believe that. He was, after all, no teetotaler himself.

I looked at him, wondered if he could sense the awesome pressure behind my eyes. "Did you use the contracts?" I asked him.

"On some of them," he said. "The phone jockeys."

"Okay."

"Is that all right?"

"Yeah." I sighed.

"That bad, huh?"

"That bad," I said.

"You want to go back to bed for a few?"

I shook my head. It was already nine o' clock, and I had lain sleepless in bed for over four hours. I hurt too much to sleep. My hangover had let up as much as it was going to until I had fully re-hydrated and nourished myself, and allowed it to run its course. "No," I said. "We need to get moving. Let me get a shower and a shave and I'll meet you in the lobby."

426

"Ten minutes?" he said.

"Make it fifteen."

He started for the door.

"No, twenty," I said.

It was Wednesday, June 22, the last day on which Archie and I would manage to operate under even the flimsiest veil of secrecy. By the next morning, it would be almost impossible to go anywhere without being harangued or cheered or otherwise severely diverted from our business. Consequently, I have come to deeply regret doing the interview; for all the good it likely did in the way of raising awareness of domestic indigence and opening minds to the feasibility of economic justice, it dad far greater and more lasting harm to the purity and facility of our endeavor. It made everything a lot more complicated and tedious, in short.

Four of Dacey Energy's half-dozen spokespersons received interview requests, over the transom, from at least one of the country's major news networks, and together they received such requests from every news organization in the United States. Everybody from Diane Sawyer to Bill O'Reilly to Mike Wallace to Katie Couric to Wolf Blitzer wanted a piece of the CEO-turned-relief-worker. It was, of course, the biggest story since German troops waltzed into Poland in the dead of night, if not the Biggest Story of All Time.

Three of the spokespersons had passed on word of the requests to the company's vice president, Tim Ballmer, who had in turn relayed the news to Archie via telephone. Archie asked me what I made of the offers, and I told him the only thing that seemed fair at the time: "It's your call." But his indecisiveness proved unrelenting, and so, mostly just to settle the issue, I decreed that he would grant CNN a ten-minute interview in primetime, provided I was allowed to join him. (I was never told whether any of the networks had requested an interview with the both of us.) Archie seemed satisfied with this plan and directed Tim Ballmer, which poor bastard was probably on the brink of insanity by then, to confirm the details with the network.

And, with that two-minute conversation, we sealed for ourselves a mighty turbulent if sensational fate.

In the morning, before the requests came, we gave away a couple hundred thousand and encountered little resistance from either the recipients (most of whom recognized us or at least had heard of us) or the folks we saw on the streets. The donees consisted of refrigerator repairmen, department-store clerks, house-builders, glaziers, shopkeepers, haberdashers, railroad engineers, school teachers and custodians, barbers, librarians, florists, the employees of bowling alleys and jewelry boutiques. To many of these, surprising me yet again, Archie gave twenty thousand dollars each. At his behest, we used only seven contracts all day. So far as I knew, he had yet to mail any of the hundred or so completed forms to Kenneth Stevens, his lawyer. Clearly, as much to my bemusement as to my delight, he was rapidly losing interest in the things.

The lingering after-effects of my ill-begotten bender the night before slackened little till mid-afternoon, dwindling gradually thereafter. Nevertheless, with a couple of beers after dinner, I estimated (with an aplomb which I then found only mildly worrisome), I would be well-fortified for the evening's big gig, the accursed Interview. I did not share this rumination with Archie, of course; I feared he might find it rather distressing that I meant to ply myself with booze before appearing on a live global broadcast. *A fortiori*, I would need to conceal my consumption from him, somehow or another.

I never bothered to ask what I had gotten myself into, why I had apparently elected to use the realization of my chimerical nostrum to develop full-blown alcoholism, and, fortunately or not, the issue was soon rendered moot.

My chance came when we stopped at a gas station near the border of Indiana and Michigan, and Archie went around back to use the restroom. I went inside, paid for our gas, and purchased a six-pack of Coors Light. This I then smuggled into one of my dirty-laundry bags before Archie got back to the car.

We checked into a hotel near the news bureau and I went directly to my room, where I took a quick shower and gulped three of the beers in half an hour. My nerves were steadied at once, my mind gorgeously cleared of ugly, burdensome clutter. Freed of the ponderous shackles of sobriety, my thoughts could now soar unfettered to marvelous intellectual heights.

So revivified, I was ready for prime time.

We went on at eight o' clock, via satellite from Lansing, Michigan. It was the closest city to us with a CNN affiliate capable of supporting a live satellite broadcast. Furthermore, the studio was situated quite harmoniously with our route, which was to take us through western and central Michigan before doubling back and sweeping us into Illinois.

I will now present what is essentially a transcript of the

interview, editing it only for brevity and clarity. Keep in mind that Archie and I heard everything through ear-pieces and could not see the anchor. We were shut away in a cramped, poorly air-conditioned studio on hard chairs characteristic of waiting rooms. How much bearing that had on the course of the interview I can't say, but it seemed important that I disclose it.

Here, then, is the interview:

ANCHOR: Mr. Lancaster, Mr. Farmer. Welcome, gentlemen.

ME: Thank you. Good to be with you.

ARCHIE: Good evening.

ANCHOR: Let's start with the obvious question, if we could... what exactly is it that you two are doing?

ME: Well, in a nutshell, we're criss-crossing the country, giving out money to working people.

ARCHIE: That's about the sum of it, yes.

ANCHOR: All right. Let me ask the next most obvious question: Why?

ARCHIE (chuckling): Well, that's a good question. Mostly it's to repay those with whose help, directly or otherwise, I've achieved such incredible financial success.

ME: And to level the drastically lop-sided playing field the average American faces today, to tip the scales a little more in their favor. Give them a leg up and all that jazz.

ANCHOR: So how much have you given away?

ARCHIE (looking at me): How much would you say, Terry?

ME: Probably around ten million dollars. Maybe more.

ANCHOR (visibly stunned): You've given away ten million dollars to random people?

ME: Everybody's random.

ANCHOR: Mr. Lancaster, how does your company feel about what you're doing?

ARCHIE: I honestly don't know. I haven't asked them. Why should they feel *anything* about it? It's not the company's money that I'm giving away.

ANCHOR: Well, what about the stockholders?

ARCHIE: What about them?

ANCHOR: Mightn't this sort of thing make them nervous?

ARCHIE: I don't see why it should. It's not as if what I'm doing is any reflection of the company's handling of their money. None of Dacey's policies has changed in the least.

ANCHOR: Has Dacey's stock indeed suffered as a result of this?

ARCHIE: Not to my knowledge. The last time I checked, it

was actually up four points. (ANCHOR laughs.)

ANCHOR: Whose idea was this? Yours, Mr. Farmer?

ME (looking at Archie): It was mutual, wouldn't you say?

ARCHIE: I'd say that, yes.

ANCHOR: Mutual?

ARCHIE: Terry - Mr. Farmer - approached me a few weeks ago with the idea. He thought it would make a wonderful human-interest story.

ANCHOR (interrupting): Well, it's certainly *that*, gentlemen!

ARCHIE: As well as help a lot of people, of course.

ME: Yes, I want to make it clear that what we're doing isn't about *us*. It's about all the hard-working American men and women who forever get the shaft in this country, forever come up short no matter how many hours they put in or how much they do without. It's despicable, just revolting how low the average wage is, in almost any industrial sector.

ANCHOR: Are you a working journalist, Mr Farmer?

ME (pausing): No, I'm currently on hiatus.

ANCHOR: From?

ME: I'd rather not say, if it's all right.

ANCHOR (flustered): Mr. Lancaster, how much do you intend to give away?

ARCHIE: I'm really not sure. Substantially more than I already have, certainly.

ANCHOR: As much as a billion?

ARCHIE: I really don't know. I haven't thought that far ahead.

ANCHOR: Really?

ARCHIE: Really.

ANCHOR: Mr. Lancaster, some political insiders speculate that what you're doing has some connection to a citizen-action group you helped found, a 507 called "And For the Sake of the Kids," which in the last few months has contributed almost two million dollars to the campaign of a candidate for the Supreme Court of your home state of Pennsylvania. Is there any truth to those allegations?

ARCHIE (irked): I wasn't *aware* of those allegations, sir.

ANCHOR: Do you deny them?

ARCHIE: I certainly do.

ANCHOR: So what you're doing isn't in any way politically motivated?

ARCHIE: Um.

ME: Of course it's politically motivated. The abominable treatment of labor in this country is very much a political issue.

434

Archie's acting out of sympathy for those people, and to that extent is making a political statement, but he sure isn't using all this as some kind of launchpad for propelling Ben Grent into office.

ARCHIE (uncomfortable): Actually, what we're doing is totally *apolitical*. It's a humanitarian thing, not a political thing. Those who read anything more into it do so at their own peril.

ANCHOR: Well, forgive me, Mr. Lancaster, but you can't exactly be *surprised* by the public's skepticism.

ARCHIE: I don't know that the public *is* skeptical. It's bureaucrats and journalists you're talking about, not average people. Not the kind of people we're helping.

ANCHOR (obstinately): Others suggest that all of this is some kind of elaborate facade, a diversion from some sort of illegal or unethical activity in which your company is involved... perhaps an attempt to deflect attention from Dacey's long history of questionable environmental policies. Or possibly from a personal shortcoming that you'd rather the public not know about.

ARCHIE: All of that is completely unfounded.

ME: Did you bring us on here to ask about what we're doing, sir, or to ask about Dacey Energy?

ANCHOR: Well, both.

ME: Well, we're here to discuss the former exclusively.

ARCHIE: Dacey Energy has nothing to do with any of this. And I don't appreciate people trying to smear its good name because they're too hardened to believe someone like me capable of such widespread generosity.

ANCHOR (smoothly): What do you guys suppose this is going to do for incentive?

ME: How's that?

ANCHOR: What reason are these people you're doling out all this money going to have to keep working?

ARCHIE: We're only giving them five or ten thousand apiece. It's quite nominal. Nothing they could retire on.

ANCHOR: Do you worry that their employers will lower their wages, having learned of the gifts?

ME: Lower them to *what*? Less than minimum wage?

ANCHOR: You're only giving money to minimum-wage workers?

ME: Practically.

ANCHOR: Some economists argue that the key to improving workers' standard of living isn't increased wages but increased productivity, which makes the workers more attractive and valuable both to present and potential employers. The more valuable an employee, the better he or she is paid and the greater his or her professional options. Isn't that what a free market is all about? Workers striving to be the best they can be, and getting compensated accordingly, all in an environment of healthy, spirited competition?

ME: That's the most ridiculous thing I've ever heard, sir.

ANCHOR: Pardon?

ME: You think the kid working for six bucks an hour at Burger King is going to get a raise if he works harder and faster than everyone else? Gimme a break. They'll just give him more work, and secretly wonder how they got so lucky, if maybe he's mentally retarded or something. That's idealistic conservative claptrap right there: the notion that ambition somehow translates into wealth, that those who bust their butts will eventually strike it rich. Nothing could be further from the truth. Unless you already hold an important position where people notice what you do and don't do, where even your most mundane decisions significantly affect the bottom line, nobody's going to pay any attention to the details of your work. No manager of Wal-Mart has ever called one of the cashiers or pantyhose-sorters into his office to remark on how well they're doing their job and offer them a raise. It just doesn't work that way. Unless you're doing something wrong, nobody cares. Nobody cares what your attitude is like, or that you always show up on time, or that you never call in sick, or how much care you take in what you do. Raises, and for the most part evaluative measures themselves, are as standardized and bureaucratized as the hiring and firing processes, as the application form, as job duties and wages and health benefits. Employer discretion died a long time ago, subverted by corporate control. So, if Bob's the VP of marketing for Coca-Cola, it might benefit him to exceed his superior's expectations. However, if Bob spends eight hours a day gluing little pieces of plastic together alongside a hundred indistinguishable cogs in a blindly running machine, he has little reason to go above and beyond the call of duty.

At this point the station manager ordered a commercial break, that the program's sponsors might inform our audience of their fine products. The moment we were off the air, Archie turned to me and said, "What the hell is this?"

"You mean the questions about Dacey?"

"No," he said, his ears aflame, "I mean that flattering introduction. Of course I mean the questions about Dacey! And the 507! How the hell did these people..." His sentence fell away. It was a naive question, and he knew it.

"I wasn't expecting this," I said truthfully. "I thought they'd be so fascinated with the experiment that they wouldn't probe much into its origins. With a present so interesting, who cares about the past?"

His eyes narrowed. He leaned forward a little, sniffing. "Is that beer on your breath, Terry?"

I shook my head. "No, it must be my cologne."

"Thirty seconds," a producer said into our ear-pieces.

"It's beer," Archie said, shock rising in his features. "You were drinking at the hotel, weren't you?"

"Don't be ridiculous, Archie."

He shook his head in disgust. "Jesus Christ."

"Twenty seconds," said the producer.

"I wasn't drinking!" I said.

"Liar!"

"This really isn't the right time to discuss the matter, is it?"

"You're out of control," he said flatly.

"Look, I had a couple of beers before we left, okay? I was nervous!"

"Nervous my ass," he sneered. "You were hungover, is what you were."

"Ten seconds," chimed the producer.

"It's time to focus," I said. "Let's focus."

439

"Sure you're lucid enough for that?"

"Have I said anything stupid thus far?"

The producer now commenced with a countdown: "And five... four... three... two..."

We were back:

ANCHOR: My guests tonight are Archibald Lancaster, president and CEO of Dacey Energy, and Terrance Farmer, a freelance journalist. Before the break we were discussing the possible motivations for the enterprise which the two of you have undertaken in recent days.

ARCHIE: Motivation. Singular. It's for charity.

ME: Only the people we're helping don't qualify for regular charities.

ANCHOR: What sorts of people are they, exactly, whom you're giving all this money to?

ME: Laborers. Mostly manual laborers.

ANCHOR: Blue-collar types?

ME: For the most part, yes.

ARCHIE: Anyone who makes a modest wage.

ANCHOR: An unfairly modest wage?

ARCHIE: Well...

ME: Yes, that's right.

ANCHOR: Who decides whether a wage is fair? Is there a formula of some kind?

ME: Of course not.

ANCHOR: Then how -

ME: It's common sense, really. Somebody who slaves in a restaurant or a factory or a garage all day shouldn't have to scrape clams out of the floorboards, scrounge loose change from under the couch cushions. They shouldn't be living below or barely above the poverty line, is what I'm saying.

ANCHOR: Well, let me just play devil's advocate here... these are unskilled laborers, no?

ARCHIE: Traditionally speaking, they would -

ME: There's no such thing as an "unskilled laborer." Every job requires skill of some sort or another.

ANCHOR: But they aren't professionals, in the strict sense? I mean, these people aren't lawyers or doctors?

ARCHIE (frustrated): No, they aren't.

ME: What's your point, Pat?

ANCHOR: Well, some would argue that jobs pay what they're worth. Meaning, the rarer and more valuable and specialized one's skills, the better he or she is compensated. Isn't

441

intelligence something that society should reward? Shouldn't *entrepreneurship* be rewarded?

ME: I agree that brain-power should be amply rewarded, and in any just society it is. It is indeed rare and exceedingly valuable. Being a doctor or a lawyer requires an enormous amount of intellectual exertion and dedication. But that hardly justifies a meritocracy, if merit is going to be defined in terms of economically viable talents. Why should we prize mental agility at the exclusion of less cerebral dexterities? Just because everyone *can* do something doesn't mean that everyone *wants* to, or that it's pleasant. It might not be mentally challenging, but physically it's arduous. And in many cases extremely dull.

ANCHOR: Yes, but -

ME: In fact, you hit on part of the problem in what you just said a moment ago, about how not everyone can be a doctor or a lawyer. That isn't by choice, isn't it? I mean, one doesn't *choose* to be inadequately mentally equipped for such professions, does one? So we're basically punishing stupidity, if you define "stupidity" as ineptitude at intellectual pursuits. And that's what capitalism ultimately does, Pat: it punishes those who are born with unprofitable genes.

ARCHIE (beet-red): We're not opposed to capitalism.

442

ANCHOR: It sure sounds like Mr. Farmer is.

ME: No, no, I'm not opposed -

ANCHOR: You just said -

ME: Let me finish, please. I'm not opposed to capitalism *per se*. What I'm opposed to, sir, is *unchecked* capitalism, such that wealth is concentrated in massive amounts at the top of the pyramid. That's not a truly free market, a truly democratic society where everybody has an equal opportunity to succeed. The deck's rigged, the dice are loaded, the rules are carefully drawn up to advantage an elite few. It's a kind of *laissez-faire* fascism, in other words, a Paleozoic hoarding mentality which one would hope human beings as a civilization would have grown out of by now. And you know what? It isn't intelligence we really reward in America, anyway; it's *shrewdness*. The guy who invented the whoopee cushion or the cheese in a spray-can sure as hell didn't need a lot of intelligence to come up with it, but I imagine he or she is now living comfortably in the Caribbean. So let's not fool ourselves, please. America doesn't value intelligence in itself, or knowledge in itself. It's not like the four-day champion on *Jeopardy* is the most widely venerated person in the country. We don't revere the geeks and the geniuses, the kids who spend all day with their noses in the *Encyclopedia Brittanica*. No, we deify athletes, musicians, movie stars, and – to a lesser extent – business-minded innovators. Anybody who entertains us or devises a clever means of making a buck. *Those* are the people we really look up to, at least as far as the media would have us believe. Those are the people we admire most and whose so-called "skills" are the most exploitable, and the market reflects it by wildly overcompensating them. So, it's worse than just that doctors and lawyers make ten times more on average than bricklayers and carpet-cleaners. It's that people who fake emotions, hit balls with sticks, strum guitars, and think to add vanilla flavoring to coffee *make a thousand times more on average than the doctors and lawyers!* Now how screwed up is *that*, sir?

ANCHOR (highly annoyed): So are you -

ME: Shouldn't one's income be at least partly proportionate to the desirability of his job? I mean, who wouldn't want to be an actor or a writer or a professional athlete? Not only is that stuff fun - hell, many of us act or write or play sports in our spare time - but it's glamorous, as well. That some of us should get rich doing stuff that for many people is a mere hobby is... well, it's ludicrous, to be perfectly frank. You think Bill Gates wants to work at McDonald's? You think Archie here does? Do you think Bill Gates would rather do his job for thirty bucks an hour or work at McDonald's for sixty? Yet, in reality, Bill Gates could buy and sell every McDonald's employee without even dipping into his bonds. That's insanity, sir!

ANCHOR: It sounds to me like you're talking about the redistribution of wealth.

ME: Yeah? So?

ARCHIE: That's not exactly how I'd describe it.

ANCHOR: How would you describe it, Mr. Lancaster?

ARCHIE: Um.

ME: What's so necessarily wrong with redistributing wealth which is at present unfairly distributed?

ANCHOR: Well, one could argue that you're tampering with a very delicately balanced system. You're throwing in a variable that doesn't arise naturally out of the inherent economic forces. You're breaking the rules of the game.

ME: Yes, that's the whole point, Pat. To violate the natural economic order.

(At this point Archie was squirming in his chair, as if suffering from chest pains. The anchor, meanwhile, was smiling at us with a strained civility, probably thinking us both a couple of nut-jobs.)

ANCHOR: I'm reminded of Bastiat's parable of the broken window, in which the community celebrates a shattered pane in the bakery because it means more work for the local window-fitter.

445

But what the townspeople fail to realize is that the money the baker has to shell out to replace the window could have been used to buy a commodity of which he now must be deprived, which in turn deprives the manufacturer of said commodity of profits he might have used to expand his business and thereby create new jobs. So, at best the business procured by the baker is offset by the business lost to the tailor or the butcher, and at worst radically outweighed by the long-term cost to the greater community. Are you familiar with the analogy? Either of you?

ARCHIE: I am.

ANCHOR: Do you see the application, Mr. Lancaster?

ARCHIE: Well, honestly, no. The point of the analogy - well, it's an economic fallacy, actually, according to Bastiat and Henry Hazlitt - is that seeming good fortune is often bad news in disguise. What at first blush appears to be a windfall for the glass-cutters and window-installers at the minor expense of the baker is in reality a major blow to the local economy. He, Bastiat, was trying to throw light on the problem of hidden costs. So I guess what you're getting at is that, by giving away all this money, we're depriving merchants of profits which would be better funneled directly into commerce and job-creation. But that isn't so at all.

ANCHOR: Isn't it?

ARCHIE: No, because I never intended to spend nearly the amount I will have given away by the time all of this is over.

ME: Besides, look at all the "ifs" in the analogy, the so-called fallacy. *If* the baker would have spent the money on new shoes or a new hat, *if* the vendor of the purchased item were then to pour the profits into something widely favorable, and so on. That's a lot of places where the theoretical trickle-down you're alluding to could evaporate faster than a puddle in Phoenix. What if the baker would have simply *hoarded* the cash he had to cough up to pay for the window? Then he would have stayed as rich as he already was while the rest of the community would have suffered, according to the very logic of the analogy itself. Since, remember, the money he would have spent on the new suit would have miraculously sparked a chain of events leading, eventually, to increased prosperity for all. And that's the intrinsic flaw in trickle-down economics: the presupposition that the rich are actually going to *spend* their money rather than, as they largely actually do, dump it into in an off-shore, tax-exempt bank account and let it collect interest for their grandkids. But even if they *did* spend the bulk of their incomes, who's to say that the resulting profits for the patronized businesses would be used in the desired way, that is, to expand operations and create jobs? What seems more likely is that most or all of the merchants would simply keep the lion's share of the money for themselves and invest the remainder on a limited scale, and perhaps not in job-creating products or services but rather in stocks and bonds. Certainly we couldn't count on them to put the capital toward an increase in wages, God forbid! Besides, when these right-wing supply-side crackpots talk about job creation, they're usually referring to service-sector jobs that pay crap money, not the good jobs that are all but reserved for the kin of current owners, or, in today's crude vernacular, "power-players." Ever notice that it's the same old white guy who's been running all the corporations since the dawn of industry? Ain't no coincidence, I assure you.

ANCHOR (exasperated): Well, is that what *you* had planned to do, Mr. Lancaster? Accumulate as much wealth as you could and then leave it to your children and grandchildren?

ARCHIE (pauses): That's honestly hard to say. I'd kind of hoped to live forever. (ANCHOR laughs quietly.)

There was one more segment to the interview, but those were the highlights. Those were, I should say, all I think it necessary to share.

35

As I said, in the wake of the interview everything changed. No longer were Archie and I two relatively inconspicuous money-storks changing lives *a la* Publishers' Clearing House. Now we were making what were almost regarded as scheduled stops at the workplaces and stamping grounds of the economically underprivileged. We were expected now, and caught few by surprise. That is not to say that our recipients thereafter were any less grateful than those who had preceded them; it is just to explain that much of the magic was now gone. Consequently, albeit quite slowly, playing Santa Claus to the impoverished masses became as much a chore as it did a thrill.

At least, it did for me. Archie, I must say, seemed to grow increasingly pleased with the venture, and increasingly gratified by its seemingly tremendous impact on its beneficiaries. For all he had said about its being "lame on the whole," his enthusiasm for the project seemed to increase in almost perfectly inverse proportion to my own. There were days, in fact, when he made the rounds alone, as he had that night in Indianapolis while I was sleeping off a particularly brutal binge. Did I feel guilty on such occasions? Maybe a little. But so lost did I become in an alcoholic fog that there was little room within me for anything like a definite or deeply-felt emotion. Most of the time I was just numb, or passed out.

In the week following the interview, we traveled to Detroit and surrounding areas, Kalamazoo, and then Chicago and its myriad suburbs. Along the way we gave out probably three or four million dollars, sometimes as much as fifty thousand to one worker. This was Archie's idea. It was also Archie's idea to effectively jettison the contracts. I think we used maybe another thirty or forty during the remainder of our journey, for a total of perhaps one hundred and fifty. At first he claimed that he had come to find them more burdensome than useful. Then he basically just admitted that, with recipients as poor as ours, it was rather insulting to restrict their use of the money, to presume that we knew better than they how best to spend it. I did not object; I had devised the things simply to mollify him in the first place.

It was in the second week of July, in Duluth, Minnesota, that I came up with a way to further streamline the transactions. I presented it as a practical, time-saving measure, and indeed it was that. In reality, though, I am ashamed to confess, I had simply grown lazy and apathetic and perhaps even a little cynical about the whole scheme. No doubt my drinking was chiefly to blame for that.

"I have an idea," I said to Archie as we pulled into the parking lot of a Duluth Microtel.

"You often have ideas," he replied. There was a skepticism in his tone that suggested he was growing weary, if not of my company, then at least of my conduct. It had been erratic lately, of course, and I think he had begun to distrust me. At times, as now, I saw my disintegration reflected in his eyes, and fought at once to arrest it, reverse it, but found my reserves of willpower utterly depleted.

"Do you want to hear it or not?" I had struggled to remain sober all day, mostly for Archie's benefit, and now endeavored to steady my hands.

"Once we get inside," he said. He gave me a quick, pitying lookover. "I imagine you could use a drink."

"Fuck you," I said. I didn't mean it.

"Right." He cut the engine and opened his door. "C'mon, let's go in."

I was determined not to let Archie see me go to the bar. I had resolved to check in, go to my room, take a couple swigs from the pint in my suitcase, and hit the sack. I could wait, I told myself. *Anyone* could wait ten minutes. There were people who spent that much time with eyeballs hanging out of their sockets and bullets buried in their vital organs. There were people who had tolerated all sorts of unimaginable agonies for all lengths of time, and I could damned well tolerate this minor discomfort for ten little minutes.

"Go ahead, Archie," I said. "You check in first."

"You sure?"

"Yeah."

He stepped up to the desk and greeted the clerk. Like everyone else on the planet, she was delighted to see him. He might have a present for her.

As I waited I looked around the lobby, surveying the scene. There were a few people sitting on the couches and chairs, one of them doing a crossword puzzle in a newspaper. Whether they had noticed our arrival was unclear. The bar was off to my left, a little slice of Duluth night-life called The Micro Tavern. It appeared to be empty. I tore my eyes away and looked at Archie and the clerk. She was typing something into her computer. I looked at the clock. One minute had passed.

I looked back at the assortment of travelers on the lobby furniture. One of them made brief eye contact with me and I averted my eyes. I looked back at the clock and saw the two-minute mark approaching. I ran the back of my hand across my forehead, mopping up a copious accretion of sweat. The man doing the crossword folded his newspaper in half and the crinkle of the pages was deafening. Underneath it, the droning chatter of the clerk's keyboard resounded like a car bomb. The room darkened, tilted.

I leaned forward. "Archie?"

He spoke without turning around. "Yes, Terry?"

"I'll be in the bar," I said.

"Naturally."

"Gin and tonic," I said to the bartender. "Please."

"What kind of gin?"

"Doesn't matter," I snarled. "Just... gin and tonic, please."

He frowned and fixed my drink, passed it across the bar to me. "Four-fifty."

I presented him with a credit card. "Start a tab," I said. I drained the glass in my hand, passed it back to him. "And refill this."

A hand fell on my shoulder. I turned and saw Archie standing behind me, his face working with pity and disappointment and exasperation. "I checked you in," he said.

"Thanks."

"May I join you?"

"Please do." I gestured at the stool next to me.

The bartender returned with my drink and took Archie's order: dry martini, shaken. Politely, Archie waited until the fellow was out of earshot to ask me the question I guess he'd been pondering for some time now: "You're losing it, aren't you?"

I burped. "Losing what?" To my surprise I managed to sound at least remotely offended.

"Your grip," he said.

"My grip?"

"Is there an echo in here?"

"I'm not losing anything, Archie." I paused. "Except maybe my natural charm and dynamism. But I'll get those back. I just need to slow down a little."

"You need to slow down a lot."

I slugged down my drink and registered dimly how much better I felt. Five minutes, I reflected, and I was as good as new. "Do you want to hear my idea or what?"

"Sure," he said, leisurely sipping his martini. "Let's hear it."

I lit a cigarette and summoned the barkeep. "Then listen up."

We started in Duluth and worked our way south to the Twin Cities. We started, specifically, on what might as well have been

454

called Main Street, so completely and idyllically American was it, and so centrally situated in the town. The day was bright and sunny but unseasonably cool, drawing out thousands to patronize the sundry restaurants and shops.

Most of them, as plainly evidenced by their dress and the names of the stores on the plastic bags they carried, counted themselves among the nation's working class. Of course: Duluth was and always had been a working-class town, a major producer of coal and iron ore, bursting at the seams with underpaid blue-collars. It was a state of affairs so sublimely charming in its every facet that only my hangover kept me anchored in reality. But at least I felt some vigor again, I reflected, knew some genuine zeal for the creation I had nursed from young. This latest twist on the mission, initially designed simply to expedite the tedium of career philanthropy, now seemed to infuse it with a fresh appeal.

"This is perfect," I said to Archie as we parked the car. "Look at 'em, man. They don't suspect a thing."

He released his seatbelt from its buckle and looked at me. "Why would they?"

I nodded, as if to concede the foolishness of my remark. "True." I took a deep breath and opened my door. "Okay, let's do this thing."

We got out, each holding a large brown paper sack. I glanced into mine, as if worried that an invisible thief had filched its contents. If such had transpired, then either his conscience had compelled him to return the loot or else an invisible hero had intervened. *Archie's right*, I thought. *You're going mad.*

"You want the street," I asked him, "or - " I shot a glance at the tallest building in view, the nine-story corporate headquarters of a regional banking chain, perhaps five blocks to the east. "Or the roof?"

"I'll take the street," he said, gazing upon the throngs. "I want to have a clear exit when pandemonium breaks out."

"There won't be any pandemonium." I smiled. "There will be only a glorious frenzy of spiritual manumission."

He unfurled the top of his bag. "Just as long as the fat ones go after you," he said.

I looked for a staircase on the outside of the bank, wanting to draw as little attention to myself as possible. There wasn't one. I sighed, scanned the street to see if anyone was watching me, and, satisfied that I had not been noticed, stuffed the bag down the front of my shirt. Then I flattened it with my hands as best I could, minimizing the protrusion.

I entered the bank and made a beeline for the stairs. I made no eye contact with the tellers or customers, and prayed silently that nobody would recognize me or, still worse, attempt to detain me. I felt a little like Lee Harvey Oswald must have when he had stolen into a book depository on that fateful day in Dallas so long ago, if indeed he had committed the act for which he incurred the wrath of a nation and a second assassin. Of course, unlike Oswald, I carried no rifle on my person and had not murder but tender notions of social harmony on my mind.

I made it to the roof without being spotted, emerging into the warm, bright day with the bag still firmly ensconced in my shirt. I removed it, walked to the edge of the roof, and gazed down at the multitudes of cheery Duluth townsfolk, scuttling to and fro, howlingly oblivious of their impending good fortune.

I reached inside the bag and scooped out eight or nine thousand dollars in crisp, neat bundles. I clasped the bag under my arm and quickly tore the ties off the stacks I'd removed. Then, currency in fist, I stepped up onto the ledge, into plain view of the crowds below. "Citizens of Duluth!" I cried. "Hark! Behold! The heavens have opened, and now give forth in abundance the manna you crave!" I proceeded to launch bills into the air, whereupon they fluttered to the earth, and into the clutching hands of famished, clamoring souls. "Be like the Israelites of yore! Know thy salvation! Reclaim thy dignity!"

Archie waited for my signal ("Hark!"), and then commenced to distribute his own treasure. People dashed madly every which way in frantic pursuit of paper riches, first jostling and then, as the full import of what was happening sank in, outright trampling each other. Within seconds I realized my grave error, how treacherously I had misjudged human tendencies in circumstances such as these.

The scene unfolding before us was sickening and tragic, cinematically grotesque, exemplifying in bold, vivid, indelible strokes of color the lowest and most ignoble impulses of man, the ugliest face of our peccant kind. A thickset man, in his effort to snap up three hundred-dollar bills which had landed on a sewer grate and were poised to escape, lunged forth and knocked a woman into a lamppost. Another man picked up a child and literally hurled him into a storefront. A mother looked on helplessly as another woman collided with her baby stroller and sent it rocketing down the sidewalk. When we had first unleashed the money, cries of jubilation had swept through the street. Now, as total chaos erupted, howls of pain and alarm multiplied rapidly. People began to tackle each other, to push and punch and kick and trip each other, to do basically anything they had to to gather up more bills. Archie and I watched it all play out in untellable, gradually mounting horror.

"People!" I shouted, but knew at once that it was useless. "Easy does it, people! There's plenty for everyone! Just... hey! Hey! Settle down, for God's sake! There's... I said there's plenty for everyone!"

An awful, guttural moan escaped my lips. My consternation swelled furiously, like a star before it implodes. I was the perpetrator of a nightmare, the instigator of a greed-fueled feeding frenzy which might well leave several of the mob dead. I held my stomach, certain that I was going to vomit.

This is a dream, I thought, *just a crazy dream, and when you wake up you'll be back in Pittsburgh, still working for the newspaper, still living a normal life in a modest apartment on an ordinary street, and the mere thought of knowing Archibald Lancaster will be laughable.*

Oh, to dream that life's worst moments are themselves unreal!

"Will you concede," asked Archie, as we embarked for St. Paul , "that that could have gone better?"

I laughed. What else could I do?

His eyebrows went up, as they always did when he was mildly appalled. "You find it amusing, I guess, that your brilliant idea resulted in dozens of injuries?"

I laughed harder. And then, incredibly, Archie began laughing, too. "Did you... did you see..." Now the tears started rolling. "Did you see that one dude body-slam that guy in the hat?"

Archie nodded, trying valiantly to squelch his laughter and re-assert his displeasure, and failing miserably. Soon his whole frame was shuddering, his belly joggling voluminously with each new defiant gale.

"And that... that lady trip over the curb and smack into the fat kid with the ice-cream cone?"

"I think I heard the splat," he said, and then we both lost it completely.

By the time we got to St. Paul it was almost dusk. We had stopped for dinner along the way, sharing a few more laughs over the course of the meal. And then our moods had darkened, Archie's growing almost obscenely somber, as the reality of what had transpired set in completely. Few words passed between us on the second leg of the journey.

When we got the hotel, a LaQuinta in the east end of town, Archie checked in and went directly to his room. I, of course, went to the bar.

I had some thinking to do.

And so, over countless gin and tonics and a couple of beers (to wash down the gin), with the sleepy folk ballads of Al Kooper and Woody Guthrie to spur my soul-searching, I arrived at some tentative conclusions which were to be solidified by the events of the next twenty-four hours. I decided, first of all, that I had lost all sense of my reasons for taking part in the endeavor with Archie, that I was now merely going through the motions and deriving little if any pleasure from it. Yes, I still enjoyed seeing the looks on people's faces when we handed them a check with three or four zeroes on it or a wad of cash, and yes, I still felt it a hugely important service, but my enjoyment now was somehow clinical, mechanical, at times almost obligatory. It had lost all of the raw, immediate, gut-centered appeal which had impelled me to undertake the excursion in the first place.

Second, I acknowledged to myself, for the first time with unflinching and dispassionate candor, that my drinking was hopelessly out of control, and that, as a direct and inexcusable result, the whole enterprise was in serious danger of collapsing. I was its engineer and primary executor, and without me it would inevitably perish, whether in a matter of days or weeks. Thus I was compromising through my reckless behavior my own vision, my own invention, the actualization of which I had not long ago come to believe perhaps the only decisive justification for my existence. And yet here I sat, hammered again, the hours draining away as the booze drained more of my soul, Archie soundly asleep somewhere in the hotel.

The bottom line, I realized (and I think I may have actually winced), was that I had been disgustingly and unforgivably selfish. I had held Archie prisoner for almost a month now, and except for the first couple of turbulent, difficult days, he had been a wonderfully good sport about it. I had never expected that. Maybe I had even quietly hoped for the opposite, so that I could continue to feel self-righteous about what we were doing, as though I had some kind of monopoly on kindness. Maybe I was falling apart precisely because Archie had it so well together. But, in any case, I owed the man much more than what I had recently found myself giving him. And, of course, I owed myself much more, as well.

When I went to bed that night, I resolved that I would find some way to put things right, to make everything okay again, and for the first time in weeks I felt almost like myself again.

36

"Archie?" I said, knocking again. The desk clerk had told me
what room he was in, after I had proved my identity to him. It was
almost noon, and I doubted that he would be in there - probably he
was already out further shrinking his fortune, or eating lunch - but
it was worth a shot. "Archie, it's Terry."

At last I heard movement from inside, and then I heard
Archie talking to someone. When he answered the door, he had his
cell phone pressed to his ear and gestured for me to come in. He
closed the door behind me and went to the chair at the table in the
corner, sat down. I sat on the end of the bed, waiting for the aspirin
I had popped five minutes ago to kick in.

"We're in St. Paul, Minnesota," Archie said into the phone.
"At a LaQuinta... we got here last night... yes, probably for one more
night... well, I don't know, Winston."

My ears pricked up immediately. His name had cut through
my headache like a blade through bone, penetrating the deepest
recess, perhaps the sole vestige of my former self. When had I last
thought of him? What would he think of me now, if he were to see
me in this wretched state? *Winston*, I thought. *Oh, Winston.*

"I'm going to try to get home soon," Archie said, "for a visit... I don't know for how long... I'll need to talk to Terry about that." He cast a glance at me, then looked away. I said nothing.

"I have to go now, Winston... Terry's going to be here any minute... yes, I'll tell him... all right, Winston, take care of yourself, and take care of the house... okay, I'll deal with that when I get home... good-bye, son." He hung up.

I looked at him through my half-open bloodshot eyes. "Why?"

"Because you have nothing to say to him, Terry, especially not in the condition you're in."

I wanted to explode, to demand an apology, to insist that he call him back and let me talk to him. He had no right, I wanted to say, to stand between me and his son. "You're right," I said. "Yes, you're right."

He sized me up from his perch in the corner. There was a cigar butt in the ashtray on the table. He wore a tangerine shirt and violet silk tie and tan trousers. I couldn't remember exactly when he had taken to wearing such unconventional attire, but I had a vague idea that it had been going on for a while now. Still, he looked better, I realized, than he had in weeks. Rested, serene, easy in his posture. "Terry," he said.

464

"Archie."

"What are we going to do with you, buddy?"

I shook my head. "I don't know, Archie."

"I don't know, either."

I rubbed my eyes, looked around. The sirens in my head were screaming, the hatchet buried deeper than ever. My muscles sang low dirges of angry protest; my throat was a column of gravel, my thoughts the swirling contents of a mad, violent blender. The world was caving in, and all I could do was watch. The pain was marvelous. "How is he?" I asked.

"He's fine."

"What's he been up to?"

He cleared his throat, tapped his fingers on the table. "He's been playing the piano. And painting."

"He's so good at those things."

"Yes, he is."

"I want to stop," I said.

"Good."

I looked at him, and a dam inside of me broke, and all the fear and doubt and disquiet that I had bottled up for weeks surged through, and I felt it all at once, everything at once, all the knotty and haunting and complex emotions in a single, jolting instant, as one terrifically muscular punch. I felt the tears rushing up, the sad, feathery hitching in my chest, and I despised it, how small and vulnerable I felt. But I knew it was necessary, that without it there could be no change, no healing. "Will you help me, Archie?"

"I'll do what I can, yes. If you're serious about stopping."

"I am."

"All right, then." He pursed his lips. "Why don't you go get cleaned up and I'll meet you in your room in an hour? I want to get some lunch."

"Okay."

"155, isn't it?"

"I don't know."

"It is," he said. "Go on, go get showered."

"Okay."

I went, marveling at how strange the encounter had been, how little it had resembled what I had intended to take place, and how, lately, most everything I did felt strange and unintended.

There was a pint of whisky in my suitcase, and I poured it down the bathroom sink. I made sure to do it right away, before I could reconsider, before my wild thirst woke from its transient slumber and hijacked my will. Then I took a very long, hot shower, trying desperately to think about nothing at all. I mostly succeeded. Except for one thing: another idea, similar to that which had occasioned disaster just yesterday, only far more cunning. This one, I thought, would work. This one *had* to work. And it would serve to redeem me, to help me reconcile with Archie and make peace with my demons.

I got out of the shower and looked at myself in the mirror, at my ghostly visage and weedy frame, and at the twinges of a smile at the corners of my mouth.

Archie came by an hour later, as promised. I was ready for him, shaved and dressed and looking at least superficially human. I was quite jittery, but when he offered me a cup of coffee I took it.

"Thank you," I said.

"You're welcome." Now, when he appraised me, he did so without the faint piety and disapproval I had seen in his eyes on previous occasions. He did so now only with sympathy and concern. "Will you need something, do you think?"

"Something?"

"Pills. Valium. Something to bring you down."

I shook my head. "No, I think I'll be all right. I'll just have to grin and bear it for a few days, sweat the alcohol out, get some decent sleep."

"Yes," he said, "you do look tired."

I sipped my coffee. "I am." I lit a cigarette with a trembling hand. "Very tired."

"Then take a nap. I can attend to things without you."

"No," I said. "I had an idea."

He nodded, worked the muscles in his shoulders. "So did I, actually."

I had an ashtray on my knee, and now set my cigarette in it. "Oh?"

"Yes," he said. He flicked his tongue across his lips, took a seat on the bed. We had reversed spots, I noticed dimly. How quaint. "I thought we might go home."

"Oh."

"You heard me on the phone, I suppose."

"Yeah."

He looked at me. "Well?" he said. "What do you think? We could fly there and back. It would just be for a couple of days. I figure you could use the break, anyway. A familiar environment would be good for you right now." He looked away. "I really miss him, Terry. I haven't been away from him for this long in years. And with his mother being so far away already..."

"Winston, you mean?"

He looked up again. "No," he said, completely deadpan, "Juan Carlos."

"I see." I took a draw on my cigarette. "Okay."

"Wouldn't you like to see your own family?"

"They live in Rhode Island," I said. "And New York."

"You never see them?"

"Rarely."

"What about your ex-wife?"

"New Hampshire. And no, I never see or hear from her."

"No doubt they're itching to talk to you, now that you're famous. Your family, I mean."

"Is that what we are, Archie? Famous?"

He shrugged.

"You're probably right, though," I said. "I *should* give my parents a call. And my sister."

"Do that, Terry. It may be just what you need. Contact with people close to you."

I nodded. "Yeah. Maybe you're right."

He steepled his fingers, propped his elbows on his knees, and rested his chin on his hands. "Anyhow, about what I said... your thoughts?"

I puffed on my cigarette, watched the smoke spiral up to the ceiling, hazily transfixed by it. "We could go home, I guess."

He favored me with a wan little smile. "I appreciate that, Terry."

"When did you want to go?"

"As soon as possible. Tomorrow, the day after."

I nodded. "Okay."

Just end it, I thought. *Call the whole thing off. Enough is enough. To hell with your idea. It's stupid, anyway. Go home and stay home.*

"So," he said, "what was *your* idea?"

And I heard myself say this: "I'll show you later. Let me sleep a little first."

He nodded. "All right."

He started for the door, then stopped, turned around. "Oh, before I forget..." He trailed off, as if unsure whether the thought were worth sharing.

I leaned forward expectantly. "Yeah?"

"I saw a man today. On my way to lunch. He was sitting in his car in the parking lot, as if waiting for someone."

"Oh?"

"Yes. And he followed my cab to the restaurant."

470

I put my cigarette out and lit another. "Did you get a good look at him?"

"No, not really. Dark hair. Tanned. I'd guess about thirty or so. That's all I can say." He looked at me, his eyes narrow and probing. "Ring any bells?"

I shook my head. "Not right off, no. But I'll keep it in mind."

"You haven't seen anyone suspicious-looking lately? Nobody's followed you? Nothing like that?"

"No." I thought then of the man at the Sheridan in Indianapolis, the fellow who had joined me at the bar. What had he called himself? Rob? Ron? I couldn't remember. My memory of the occasion was fogged by inebriation, and, somehow being sure that it was an alias, anyway, I had paid little attention to the name he had given me. I looked at Archie, and shook my head again. "No, nothing like that."

He nodded. "Okay. Just keep your eyes peeled."

"I will."

"See you in an hour."

So he went off, I guess to spread a little more wealth before supper, and meanwhile I slept. I dreamt that we were back in the pit mine, Archie and I, but this time we were miners ourselves, and Jimmy Reynolds was our boss. In some vaguely and perversely prophetic way, perhaps, I dreamt that *his* boss was none other than John Friedman, who threatened to fire us all if we didn't mine enough coal to fuel a certain rocketship bound for a distant star. The star, he told us over a bullhorn, had been christened "Inez-466," in honor of the town's sacrifice.

When I awoke the evening was well along, and Archie was still not back.

I paced. Back and forth I paced, racked with nervous energy and an absurd indecisiveness about what course to pursue until Archie's return. I needed to eat, I knew, but I wasn't hungry. What I wanted, desperately wanted -

No. I cut the thought off in midstream. *You don't do that anymore, remember?*

Right. Of course. I had taken the pledge, sworn off the sauce, put the plug in the jug. Those days were behind me. I had called it quits for good. It was time to clean up my act, straighten myself out, walk the straight and narrow.

Just one. You could drink just one.

But when had I ever done *that*?

Do what you said you were going to do. Call Denise.

I went to the phone on the desk, picked up the receiver,

began to dial her number. I was on the fourth digit when I hung up. I couldn't talk to her right now. My thoughts were too jumbled, scattered. I was too keyed up.

A beer would be nice.

I drove my foot into the wall and winced at the bolt of pain that shot up my leg. I reeled backward and collapsed on the bed, clutching my foot. At last the pain subsided.

"This is ridiculous," I said to the ceiling, out of breath.

I found my room key and went downstairs.

I almost didn't notice him. I almost walked right by him - and did, in fact, although a moment later I went back. I had set my mind on carrying out my idea on my own, and was ruminating over it when I got out of the elevator, so lost in my thoughts as to be almost completely incognizant of the people and things around me. And he was anything but conspicuous, sitting as he was in a lobby chair with his legs crossed, a newspaper splayed across his lap, the very model of a bored business traveler. Had he not been doing a crossword puzzle, I almost certainly would have paid him no heed. And if Archie hadn't mentioned what he had seen on his way to lunch that afternoon, I may have written off that detail as but a coincidence. And had I been drunk, as per custom, I should not

473

have been there at that moment in the first place, but rather in the hotel bar or passed out in bed. Call the merging of these three facts a mere fortuity. Call it fate. It doesn't matter what you call it; ultimately it came to nothing, anyhow.

I got as far as the lobby entrance when I stopped cold, something clicking in my head. *Crossword puzzle*, I thought. *Where have I seen that before?* I turned around slowly, a kind of weird trance washing over me, and gazed back at the man in the plush lobby chair.

Rod, I thought clearly, and then the identification was complete and beyond question, a polished crystal pulsating with light. He saw me, and for a split second we made eye contact. Then the elevator doors opened and a group of women in business skirts poured out, perhaps nine in all. I started back, and the second I did he rose from the chair and scrambled into the mix of women, who were burbling stupidly about some idiot man, presumably their boss. Now I moved faster, almost running, and almost colliding with the flock of women. "Watch out!" one of them protested.

"Rod from Indianapolis!" I shouted, and over the heads of the women he looked right at me, and I back at him. There was total recognition in his eyes. Recognition, and guilt.

He reached out, pressed one of the buttons on the control

panel.

"Get out of the way!" I barked at the women, whose movements, I remember, seemed almost choreographed to impede my advance. Their bodies parted with the agonizing slowness of geologic ages.

And by the time I was able to pass between them it was too late: the doors had closed, and Rod the real estate agent had vanished behind them.

There was, of course, no sign of him anywhere. I scoured every floor, square foot by square foot, and every nook and cranny and closet and stairwell. I even checked on the roof. In the rooms, of course, I could not look.

I went back downstairs, dumbly hoping he might be back in the chair, having resumed his crossword puzzle. Of course he was not, but his pencil and newspaper were there. I picked up the latter, inspected it. It was the morning edition of the St. Paul *Star*. Either Rod the Undercover Agent was not terribly bright or else he had not spent much time on the puzzle, for only five of the word-spaces were filled in. (Incredibly, as if the writer of the script of our lives had a particularly keen sense of irony, one of the words was "espionage.")

I dropped the newspaper on the chair and looked around. Not even the desk clerk was present.

"Rats," I said.

For want of an alternative, I proceeded with my plan, though of course my thoughts kept turning to what had just happened. I did what I did with little joy or enthusiasm, which I guess was fitting, since that was how had I done most things lately. I did it, mostly, to keep myself occupied until Archie got back, to keep from drinking.

I started in the parking lot of the hotel itself, methodically lifting windshield wipers and pinning twenties or fifties or hundreds under them, in rough accord with the expensiveness of the vehicles, making sure to wrap the bills tightly around the wipers so that only the rightful owners would be likely to discover them. I did that with about twenty or thirty cars there in the LaQuinta lot, then decided to move on to the cars parked at the meters along the street. This was more difficult, because there were people milling about and I knew if they saw what I was doing they would snatch up every bill I planted the moment I was out of sight. So I was discreet, crafty, and cautious. I was prudent and circumspect.

But not so much, apparently, as to evade detection, because after planting the last bill I turned around and saw a tall man excitedly teasing a bill from one of the wipers. He had taken up the hunt some cars back, evidently: he was clutching a wad of money in one of his fists.

I called to him: "Hey! Hey, stop that!"

He froze in mid-act, the note on the verge of liberation. He appeared to debate for a second whether it was worth trying to free it completely, and then he bolted. I chased him for a couple of blocks, not really sure what I meant to do if I caught him, whether I would actually resort to force to reclaim the money or not. Mostly I was just pissed off, and wanted to put some fear into him.

When it became clear that I was never going to catch him, I let my sprint taper to a jog and then gave up entirely. I stood on the sidewalk, bent at the waist with my hands on my knees, panting as I watched the thief turn a corner and disappear behind a building.

When I finally righted myself I saw a homeless man on the other side of the street, sitting on a crate at the mouth of an alley, smoking a cigarette and watching the scene play out with vapid interest.

"Hi," I said to him. He did not reply. I reached into my pockets and felt around, but of course they were empty. Of course I had nothing to give the homeless guy. His money now belonged to an ungainly opportunist who had vanished into the Minnesota night.

"He stole my wallet," I said, and winced at how lame it sounded to my own ears.

I walked back to the hotel with my head down, asking why, asking why.

The pencil and newspaper remained where I had left them, on the lobby chair previously occupied by you-know-who. The desk clerk had returned, and I went to her, thinking I might wrench out of her some information on my unwelcome traveling companion.

"Excuse me," I said.

She smiled. "Hi. Can I help you?"

"Maybe," I said, leaning into the desk. "There was an incident in the lobby earlier. I don't know if you witnessed it. A fellow -"

"An incident?"

I nodded, very deliberately. "Right."

"What kind of incident?"

"I was going to tell you."

She became, as they say, discombulated. "Oh. I'm sorry, sir. I didn't mean -"

"It's quite all right. Anyhow, someone's been following me. I mean, there's this person who I think might be following me."

She blinked. "Say, aren't you that guy from TV? The guy who's been on the news lately? You travel around with that big-wig coal-company guy and give out money to people?"

Oh, Jesus. Trying to remain cordial I said, "Yes, that's me. Terry Farmer. Anyway-"

"Oh, my God! This is amazing! Are you staying here at the hotel?"

"Ma'am, please."

She blushed. "Oh, right. Sorry. You were saying?"

"Somebody's been following me."

"Who? Why?"

I thought of a million different answers, and none of them seemed satisfactory. "I don't know," I said.

"Oh." Her eyes said: *Then what do you expect me to do?*

I sighed. "His first name is Rod. I don't know his last name. He's about five-ten, five-eleven, dark brown hair, tanned, good-looking. Have you seen anyone like that around the hotel? Do you remember checking him in?"

"No, sir, I'm afraid not. When did he check in? Do you

know?"

"No."

"Hmm."

I glanced at her computer. "I don't suppose you could do much with just his first name, huh?"

She shook her head. "No, sorry. And we're not supposed to -"

"Give out such info. Right. I know." I smiled. "Well, thanks, anyway."

"No problem, sir."

Just then the lobby door glided shut, and I turned to see a man going through the outer doors - or, really, less a man and more the briefest flash of a brown coat, and a swath of black hair above it. Simultaneously, one of the elevator cars arrived in the lobby. A husband and wife and their three small children emerged. I looked back at the lobby entrance, and saw nothing through the glass doors but a few cars lit by the platinum glow of hallogen lamps, and the damp shine of the blacktop.

"Sir?"

I looked back the clerk, my mind swimming. Her eyes were wide and hopeful, the same buttery, unctuous smile still carved on her face.

"I was just wondering," she ventured timidly, "if you guys

were still... doing that."

"Doing what?"

"You know... giving away money."

"Sorry," I said, patting my pockets. "I'm fresh out. Can you just add a hundred bucks' gratuity to my bill or something? I'm in 155."

She scoffed and stalked into the back room. I headed for the elevator, and had just pressed the button for my floor when something occurred to me.

I turned around, stood still, clicked my teeth together, musing and debating. I did not notice when the elevator doors opened and then closed again.

Get them, I thought. *Now.*

Have a drink first.

I went outside, to my car.

The sky was spitting down a misty drizzle. Distant thunder growled faintly, dusk giving way to twilight. I took my keys out of my pocket, looked around, saw no one. I opened the trunk, and then the suitcase, holding my breath.

There was a bad moment when at first I didn't see it, thought it was gone. But my eyes had simply seen what I had apparently expected them to, had feared they would. They had played a nasty trick on me, and for that second or two my heart seemed to sit perfectly still in my chest, my breath caught in my throat. And then I saw it, the shoebox, and looked inside and saw that the photos and negatives were all there, untouched, and my heart commenced to beat again with a hard, heavy thud, and my breath rushed out in a long, shuddery exhalation. I thought I might cry again, worried I might be on the brink of a nervous breakdown. The whole day had been an emotional roller coaster, and the peaks just kept getting higher and the valleys lower. I felt in grave danger of getting drunk at any moment.

I collected myself, replaced the lid on the shoebox, and carried it inside, up to my room.

The evening's suspense, it turned out, was far from over. After hiding the shoebox in the closet, burying it under a pile of dirty clothes, I took the elevator to the fourth floor, Archie's floor.

I was about three rooms away when I stopped dead in my tracks. I wanted to believe it was another momentary hallucination, akin to what had happened a moment ago in the parking lot, but I knew in my gut that this time my eyes were telling the truth.

The door to Archie's room was ajar.

Instantly, to my horror, my mind conjured a series of varied and gruesome images, in one of them Archie's lifeless, bloodstained body prostrated across the crumpled sheets of his bed, face-down, a lazy helix of fresh smoke trickling from the bullet hole in his back. The one that predominated, however, and inspired in me an awesome terror, was of Rod crouching in the bathroom (dark, of course) adjacent to the entryway, lying in wait with a loaded pistol and poised to fire.

I knocked once, twice. "Archie?"

No answer.

I knocked again. "Archie, are you in there?"

Still no answer.

I reached out with a quavering hand, one eye shut tight, and gently pushed the door open. Stepped inside.

"You in here, Archie?"

Someone flushed the toilet. I stood quietly outside the door, listening, sweat coursing down my cheeks. I glanced into the room and saw a suitcase lying open on the bed. The faucet came on.

My voice was tremulous, a child's voice in a dark and unfamiliar bedroom: "Archie?"

"Terry?"

The bathroom door swung open, and there he stood, blond hair tousled and blue eyes shimmering, in a charcoal-colored tweed jacket and paisley shirt and loose-fitting jeans, his face a flawless, shining, authentic miracle, his presence a bright, brilliant light from heaven, a deafening thunderbolt of exquisite operatic majesty.

"Winston?" I gasped.

"Terry!" he cried, and threw his arms around me.

I thought: *Well, Je-sus Christ.*

37

"You... you flew here?"

He laughed. He had been laughing almost nonstop for the past five minutes. "Yeah."

Oh God I love him.

"When? How'd you find us? When'd you get here? How..." I shook my head, rubbed my eyes, gawped at him. That got him going again. "Winston, what the fuck?"

He clapped me on the shoulder, grinning that big shit-eating grin of his. "C'mon," he said, jerking his thumb at the door. "Let's get a drink while we're waiting for my dad to get back. I've been thirsty all day."

I cringed, overcome by a sudden, terrible panic. Sweat broke out on my palms and on the nape of my neck. "A drink?"

"Yeah. There's a bar across the street, isn't there?"

"I'm not sure," I said. I could not bring myself to look him in the eye.

"What's the matter, Terry? You all right?"

"Uh." I tried to inject some conviction into my voice, to reassure him. *Could your timing be any worse, old buddy?* "Yeah. Yeah, I'm fine."

"Good. Then let's go."

He brushed past me, stopped again when I made no sign of budging. "Terry?"

"Okay," I said, and felt some power return to my legs, the last of my willpower crumbling. "Let's get a drink."

He opened the door, and standing in the hallway was a broad-shouldered Hispanic man in a white cook's smock, holding a tray with a covered dish on it. "Are you Mr. Lancaster's boy?" he asked Winston.

"Yes. Oh, is that the food I ordered?"

"Yes, it is. I wanted to bring it to you myself and tell you what a good man your father is. He changed my life today."

"He did?"

"Yes, he did. Will you please tell him, when you see him, that

I said thank you again?"

"I will."

Winston took the tray and set it on top of the mini-fridge. He tried to give the cook a tip, but the cook refused. "After what your father gave me," he said, "that won't be necessary."

"Are you sure?"

"Yes, sir. I am very sure." He nodded at Winston, and then at me. "Good evening, gentlemen."

"Same to you."

He closed the door. "I'd totally forgotten I even ordered that," he said to me.

"Do you want to eat before we go?"

"Maybe just a couple of bites."

While he ate I used the bathroom, and as I did it dawned on me why the door to the room had been ajar: so Winston wouldn't have to get up and answer it when room-service brought his meal.

It was a Friday night, and the bar was brimming over with thirsty, rowdy patrons. There was smoke, and noise, and men playing pool, brawling men with chesty voices which rose obnoxiously above the din. There was a jukebox. There were old men hitting on young women, and middle-aged men drinking alone who had probably spent most of their lives in bars just like this one, drowning unarticulated fires with oceans of ethanol. The fires were never quite extinguished but only retarded, and so those within whom they burned were compelled to return to the well again and again, and drink of its slow poison. Goddammit, I would be one of them no longer; let my own fire burn, I thought, and ravage what it would, that I might then build anew upon the ashes.

"Winston," I said as we took our stools, "I have to tell you something."

"Shit, Terry," he said, "I expect you have *lots* of things to tell me."

I nodded. "That's true, but there's something I need to say right now, right up front."

He looked at me, and I became lost in his eyes. "What is it, Terry?"

I opened my mouth to say it, to declare it incontestably and irrevocably: *I don't drink anymore.* But nothing came out.

"Terry?"

My ears in that moment were deaf: the music, the clinking of bottles, the voices of the people around us, the clacking of billiard balls and even the frothy ejaculations of the apes who held the cues - for me they were all muted. I stared hard into Winston's eyes,

487

hoping to convey with my own the gravity of what I needed to say, silently urging him to accept it for what it was, without comment or question. And then, as all the sounds resumed at once, I said: "Your father's not the way you remember him." *No*, I thought desperately, *that's not it. That's not what I meant to say.*

"What do you mean?"

"Um. Gee, you know... I'm not really sure." I grimaced, disgusted with myself, ashamed of myself. I ran my fingers through my hair, lit a cigarette. I was exhausted, frazzled.

"What's wrong you with, Terry? You've been acting really weird ever since you walked into that room."

"How'd you get in there, anyway?"

"The girl at the desk gave me a key. I told her I was Mr. Lancaster's kid. You guys have been all over the news, you know."

"I know."

The bartender came over. "Get you guys somethin'?"

"Heinekin," Winston said without missing a beat.

The bartender turned to me. "How about you, buddy?"

"Uh..." Only Winston and the barkeep were looking at me, but I felt like the whole world was watching. And I knew with an awful, helpless certainty that the decision had already been made for me. I heard myself order a Crown and Coke, and felt my

488

stomach twist itself into a knot. I was sure I was going to be sick long before the drink even hit my lips.

Tomorrow, I thought, *you can try again tomorrow.*

Physically it was heaven. It was precisely the medicine for which my brain had been clamoring all day. Every neuron soaked it up like a sponge, and the pleasure thereby delivered was orgasmic. "Oh, God," I said. "Jesus."

"Terry?"

I looked at him, half-smiling, delirious with relief and guilt and dread. No doubt he interpreted this delicate play of emotions as simple lunacy. "The drink," I said. "It's fantastic."

"Good." He patted my shoulder comfortingly. "I'm glad."

I guzzled the rest of it and called for another. Winston made equally quick work of his beer and likewise ordered a replacement. "I hadn't had a drink all.. in quite a while."

He smirked, then laughed. I laughed, too. The alcohol was already starting to color my thoughts, and I could almost believe that the two of us were back home, whooping it up at The Carousel, just like in the old days of but a month ago. Part of me began to wonder if maybe I were still back in my room at the hotel, fast asleep in my bed, the whole bizarre evening but a dream. But the drink tasted and Winston's face looked too real for me to believe it.

489

It was true, I realized: he was here, sitting beside me in a bar in St. Paul, Minnesota.

"Winston," I said, massaging one of his shoulders, "you sly little bastard!"

"Terry," he said, relishing my delight, "it's been a while."

I shook my head, still in awe. "So what the hell? Tell me again how it is I'm looking at you right now. I was sort of distracted when you told me earlier."

"Okay: I spoke to my dad this morning on the phone. He told me you guys were spending tonight at a LaQuinta in St. Paul. Turns out there's only one."

"No shit?"

"Not one turd. So I figured, 'What the hell? Why not take a little trip? You've got nothing better to do, with school being out till August.' Then I called American Airlines and booked a flight from Pittsburgh to Minneapolis. There was one to St. Paul, but the other one got me here sooner. I almost called my dad to let him know I was coming, but I liked the idea of it being a surprise."

"So that's it? You just flew out here? What time did your plane arrive?"

"Ten to seven."

"And you took a cab from the airport to the hotel?"

"What a sleuth you are, Terry."

"Holy shit. You're pretty resourceful, man."

He chuckled and swigged his beer. "Known to be, time to time."

You promised him. You promised yourself. The thought came hurtling out of nowhere, intruding on my buzz like an axe. I pushed it away, doused its flames with my fresh Crown. "So you've been following it on the news? All that's been happening with your dad and me?"

"Most of it," he said. "Coverage has kind of waned these past couple of weeks, ever since the interview. Have you guys slowed down or something?"

"Sort of. You saw the interview?"

"Yeah."

"What'd you think?"

He smiled. "Not bad. Not bad at all."

I savored his approbation almost as much as I did my drink. "Thanks."

"So how much have you given away?"

"You know," I said, "I honestly couldn't tell you."

"Over a hundred mill?"

"I'd say so, yeah."

"That's a lot of money."

"Yes, it is."

"I bet it's driving my dad nuts."

"Nope," I said, finishing my drink. I flagged the bartender. "Not at all."

He arched his eyebrows, bearing an uncomfortably close resemblance to his father.

I laughed. "It's really not, Winston. What I said before is true: he's different now. A new man, you might say."

He sneered. "My ass."

"No, it's true. Hell, ours has pretty much been a one-man operation for the last week or so. Your dad's been shouldering the whole thing by himself."

"Really?"

"Yes, really. Why would I lie?"

He sipped his beer, appeared to ponder the question. "I guess you wouldn't. So... do you mean he's *glad* now to be on the road with you, helping people?"

I shook my head. "'Glad' isn't the word for it, Winston. The man's on a mission. He's got religion."

"Wow." He seemed to pale a little. "I'm... shocked."

"Not half as much as I am," I said.

"How long's he been like this?"

I shrugged. "Hard to say. Ever since the interview, at least. Maybe before that. This past month's been kind of a whirlwind, you understand. It's hard to... you know, it's hard to remember anything all that clearly." The bartender served me another Crown and Coke, half of which I slugged down immediately. I was almost drunk again. It was glorious. "You've spoken to him on the phone, haven't you? Weren't you able to detect a change in him? Hasn't he shared anything with you about his new... his new outlook on things?"

"I guess not." Tension was now rampant in his features. I think without realizing it, he had begun yanking at his collar. He pointed to my pack of Malboros. "Do you mind?"

"Help yourself. You all right, man? You seem a little... anxious."

He lit the cigarette, tried a smile. It was wholly unconvincing. "I'm all right." He paused, smoked, chewed on his lower lip. "Terry?"

"Yeah?"

"Let me ask you something."

"Shoot."

"Do you think..." He let out a deep breath, took another draw on his cigarette. "Do you think that my father would be doing what he's doing even if you didn't have those pictures? Even if you weren't blackmailing him?"

"Winston," I said, "I think it's been a long time since your father counted himself a victim of blackmail. What he's done these last few weeks, he has done entirely of his own volition. You can rest assured of that."

"You're certain?"

"Positive."

He nodded, still gnawing on his lip. "Terry, there's something I'm not telling you."

I burped, looked at him. "Huh? What?"

"I'll tell you later, when there's time." He stubbed out his cigarette in the ashtray. "Come on, we need to go."

"Huh? Why? Where?"

He pulled on my arm, and I realized he was entirely serious. "Just... trust me on this. I'll explain it later. Let's go."

"Okay, okay."

I took another quick draw on my own cigarette, crushed it out, swilled down the last of my drink, and followed him out of the bar.

By the time he got to the parking lot he was running. He did not slow down as he crossed the street. I remember thinking for a moment that he was going to get run over, and that I would have no answers when Archie asked me why his son had been dodging cars in the first place. Angry drivers blared their horns. He ignored them. I maneuvered the traffic as best I could, calling to him, telling him to slow down, asking him what the fuss was all about.

"Come *on*," he kept saying. I complied. When we got into the hotel he told me to give him my room-key.

"To *my* room?"

"Yeah."

"Winston, why?"

He admonished me with his eyes. "You're costing us valuable time, Terry."

I fished the plastic card out of my wallet and gave it to him. "Here. Now, what the hell do you want it for?"

"Tell you later." He reached into his pocket, removed another card, and thrust it into my hand. "Go up to my dad's room and tell him what's going on. I'll meet you there in a few minutes."

"But I don't *know* what's going on."

It was too late. He was already in the elevator, and before I could say anything further the doors closed.

As Winston's elevator began to ascend, another car arrived in the lobby. I waited for its doors to open, meaning to humor Winston and go to his father's room. But Archie rendered that unnecessary, at least presumably, by materializing before me.

"Terry?"

"Archie?"

"What the hell's going on?"

"I don't..." I looked around, I think half-expecting Napoleon's ghost to be stretched out on the lobby sofa, maybe skimming a copy of the day's *Le Monde*. I turned back to him. "Archie, I don't have the foggiest fucking clue."

"Why is there a suitcase on my bed? Is it yours? And where did that tray of food on the fridge come from? Were you charging things to my room?" His eyes narrowed. He stuck his nose out, trying to sniff my breath. "Terry, are you drunk?"

"No." Lying, at least where alcohol was concerned, had become second nature to me. It was fairly troubling. "I might have had a couple."

"Where? When? There's no bar in this hotel."

"Across the street," I said. "With Winston."

He blinked. His face was blank, uncomprehending.

"You know... your son?"

"What are you talking about, Terry?"

"Come with me," I said.

We got into the elevator and went to the fourth floor. Winston wasn't there, so we went to my room on the first floor. There we found him, sitting on the bed with his face in his hands, weeping softly to himself. The room was ransacked, drawers jutting out of the wardrobe and bedside table like uneven teeth, clothes and papers strewn across the floor, one of the chairs overturned. Even the bathroom looked as if a tornado had swept through it.

But, of course, all I cared about was the closet, and what was buried under the pile of clothes in there. Or, more accurately, what *had* been buried under the clothes in there: a casual inspection revealed the shoebox to be missing, along with its contents.

And my young friend had quite a story to tell, too.

"I don't believe you," I said. My buzz was effectively dead, annihilated by brain-numbing shock. Archie stood beside me, ostensibly mute, his face ashen and queasy. "You can tell me again, if you want, but I'm still not going to believe you."

Winston blubbered some more, tears streaming down his face in great, Oscar-worthy rivulets. I felt no pity for him. I felt nothing for him. If I had been able to believe what he'd told us (or what I *thought* he had told us), I suppose I would have murdered him right there and then. Nothing fancy or dramatic - just a swift, clean blow with something heavy, *voila* and *finito*.

I looked at Archie. He looked away.

"I'm sorry!" Winston shrieked. "Oh, God, I'm so, *so* sorry!"

I shook my head, paced, lit a cigarette. I looked at Archie again. His eyes were still trained on the floor. I walked in circles, looked at the closet again and again, praying each time that the heap of clothes would be arranged as they had been when I'd left, that the shoebox would have magically returned. No such miracle took place. "Winston?" I said.

He just looked at me with his watery, bloodshot eyes, which plead feverishly for some nominal mercy.

"Where is he now?" I asked.

He sniveled. "He wouldn't tell me."

That's when I lost it. I lunged at him, and if Archie hadn't restrained me I honestly think I might have killed him, or at least hurt him badly. "Calm the *fuck* down, Terry!"

"Calm down?" I screamed, rolling my hands into fists so tight I drew blood from the palms. "Calm *down*? Some motherfucking real estate agent is walking around right now with pictures of you fucking some big-shot judge's wife, maybe even jacking off to them while he gets his bank on the phone, and it's all this little shit's fault!" I scowled at him, my bottom lip quivering. "Well, *almost* all his fault. Maybe if you could learn to keep your dick in your pants, we wouldn't be in this situation to begin with."

He grabbed me by the collar with both hands and shoved me backward. "That's enough, goddammit! I don't think they're gonna put a white collar around your neck anytime soon, either!"

"This isn't about me, Archie! So don't try to *make* it about me!"

Groaning, he picked up a lamp and hurled it at the wall. The whole room seemed to reverberate with the impact. Winston gasped. "*Bullshit!* This is as much about you as it is about him, or me, or anyone else, and you damned well know it! Why are we out here, Terry? Why are we standing in a hotel room in goddam Minnesota in the first place? Because of *you!* Because of your fucking egocentric fantasies, that's why! You've had a God-complex from the first dollar we doled out and you know it as well as I do! And what have you been doing, pray tell, these past two weeks, while I've been throwing my money at every Tom, Dick, and Jane with an empty pocket and a sad story to tell? Drinking yourself into a filthy, shameful stupor and feeling sorry for yourself, that's what!

And why? Because they haven't put you on the cover of *Time* yet? Because the Pope hasn't called to personally thank you for being such a rare child of God? You're pathetic, man! If it weren't for me this whole thing would have fallen apart before it even got started! So don't give me that holier-than-thou horseshit, all right? I know you'd just love to think of yourself as the innocent bystander in all this, Terry, the unimpeachable man of vision and infinite mercy whose pure intentions were perverted by the moral shortcomings of others, but it just ain't so. Come on down from the cheap seats, buddy, because believe me, your ticket's for a front-row seat!"

"At least," I said, my rage boiling over now, my hands paper-white from the strain, "my vice doesn't hurt anyone else. At least I don't go around acting like a goddamned saint while I'm fucking everyone but my wife in hotel rooms when I'm supposed to be out helping people! At least I can satisfy my ego without sticking my dick in any whore who opens her legs for me!"

He growled and shoved me again. "I said that's *enough*! You will *not* speak to me like that in front of my son! For that matter, you won't speak to me like that at all!"

I stared at him, gritting my teeth, seemingly all the blood in my body rushing to my head. For a moment I wanted to kill him as much as I wanted to kill Winston, and perhaps wanted to kill myself. Things had been bad enough before. Now my Grand Scheme to Save the World had backfired on me with one almighty, colossal report.

None of the good we had achieved, and I mean none of it, seemed even remotely worth the anguish of that moment. Maybe that's the thing I'm ashamed of more than anything else, that in the hours and days that followed I allowed Winston's betrayal of his father and me to negate the value of what we had done, the kindness we had shown to strangers in need. That I allowed him to pollute all that, even to erase it, with his one enormously cruel and thoughtless deed, and make me regret for a time having met him. The only thing that might shame me more is that I had grown so vulnerable and frail and preoccupied with selfish cares as to expose us to such treachery in the first place.

"I'm sorry," I said quietly, relaxing my fists.

"He's not a real estate agent," Winston offered. "The guy who took the pictures, I mean." He wiped snot on his sleeve, spoke to the floor. "I told you, he's a private investigator."

Archie and I both looked at him, saying nothing. Then I darted into the bathroom and closed the door behind me, needing to be alone for a minute, needing to cry.

Here's the story Winston had relayed to us, ramblingly and disjointedly, with the details filled in that he did not divulge until later:

A few days after our encounter with him at the Inez strip mines, and one day after his article was published in the Charleston *Daily Mail*, John Friedman phoned Winston to pump him for further information regarding his dad's humanitarian collaboration with me. Winston told him the truth: he knew no more about it, really, than what was being disseminated by the media. He did omit to mention, however, that he was privy to the endeavor's unsavory origins.

Incredulous that Winston was telling him everything he knew, Friedman persisted in calling the house several times a day for almost a week. (Winston said Friedman had never disclosed the source which had supplied him with Archie's home phone number, but I speculate that it was probably a disgruntled board member at Dacey or someone with an axe to grind against the company, perhaps a former business competitor.) Eventually, bowing to the pressure, mostly wanting to shut the man up but also, he confessed, resenting the adulation being lavished on Archie by the press, Winston had blabbed that he thought his dad might be doing it to cover up something nasty or embarrassing in his personal life - a possibility suggested, you might remember, by the CNN anchor who interviewed us.

When he heard this, Friedman pounced like a dog on a steak, or, more literally, a journalist on a titillating lead. If Archie felt it necessary to go to such astounding lengths to keep a certain skeleton shut safely away in the closet, the fellow reasoned (quite plausibly), then it would have to be one of the world's ugliest and most sordid affairs. Learning this fact redoubled his determination to learn Archie's secret, evidently, because after that he began calling Winston three or four times a day instead of just once or twice. Most of the time Winston didn't answer the phone, knowing it was almost certainly Friedman again and already starting to regret having spilled the few beans he had.

In the midst of all this the CNN interview was aired, and watching it, Winston said, made him hate his father all over again, or at least the saintly image that he was projecting to the public. Because he *wasn't* a saint, Winston told us. He was a liar and a cheat, and the fact that he was now sharing his money with poor people, under duress, didn't change that. In fact, he said, in a way it made it even worse, made a mockery of fairness and justice. To atone for a sin under the cloak of compassion, he said, to engage in such systematic deception at the undeserved gain of one's

503

reputation, was unconscionable. Yes, he was glad that people were benefiting so much from Archie's transgression, but no amount of good deeds, he reiterated, could erase it. Perhaps Friedman sensed these feelings in Winston, and the ambivalence with which he regarded his dad's bogus transformation, because thereafter, with a brilliantly calculated delicacy and sophistication, he began to work on the boy, goading him to aid the cause of exposing our philanthropy as a sham and Archie himself as a fraud.

"I have a man following them," he told Winston during one call. "A P.I. from Detroit. He's specially trained in these kinds of things. In the art, you might say, of unmasking those who would show the world only their prettiest faces." He claimed that this man (whose name he never revealed but which Winston later learned to be Rod Morrow) had witnessed Archie and me engage in all sorts of lewd and depraved acts, even had a few on celluloid, including such delightful eye-poppers as the use of narcotics and group sex with prostitutes. When Winston suggested, shrewdly, that if Friedman were telling the truth then there was no reason for him still to be digging, looking for dirt, Friedman replied with total conviction that his goal wasn't to destroy Archie, but only to extract for the world the truth about why he was doing what he was doing, why he suddenly felt it his responsibility to single-handedly cure poverty.

Friedman also insisted that ethically I was no better than Archie, my motivations for helping him aside, since obviously I knew the truth and yet nevertheless had chosen to assist him in perpetuating such a shameless and massive lie. He did not ask Winston many questions about my involvement in the enterprise, perhaps because Archie was the focus of his investigation and I was but a mere accomplice to the great hoax, but he made it plain, Winston said, that there was no lost love between us.

And then came the bombshell, the unholy nuke that reconfigured the moral map of the whole crusade, that redefined my view of Archie and of the new, outwardly virtuous manner of living he had professed, at least by his conduct, to have embraced: Friedman told Winston that Morrow, the private investigator, had photographed Archie going into a hotel room with a young woman at a Sheridan in Indianapolis. And *these* photos, he added, he would be only too happy to share with Winston, if Winston cared to see them.

"'You were doing it again,'" Winston had muttered through one of his sobs. "That's all I could think when he told me that: that cheating on Mom with one woman wasn't good enough for you, that you'd might as well do it again since the last time you got caught the world made a hero out of you. And the very idea of it, of you taking advantage of that status just to get into some naive woman's pants, made me sick to my stomach." He had looked at both of us then with big, mournful eyes. "That's when I knew they couldn't be true, all the things I wanted to believe about you. That you really *had* changed, for one. And maybe that you were actually sorry for what you'd done, that you'd begun to understand how selfish it was and what you'd put me through, even if Mom never found out and even if she wouldn't care. That's when I knew it was all bullshit, and when I decided I'd help Friedman any way I could, so long as it meant that you'd pay, that you'd get your comeuppance."

Of course, I knew that Friedman must have lied. Archie never could have done something like that right under my nose without my knowing about it. And he wouldn't have kept it from me even if he had. He and I shared a bond now, sacred and powerful in ways that the rest of the world would never understand. He was - God help us both - my friend now, and friends don't keep such secrets.

"Right, Archie?"

He looked at the wall, said nothing. Winston looked at him, then back at me, his bottom lip working, eyes still damp with tears.

"Archie?" I laughed. "Oh, *come* on! You've gotta be fucking

506

kiddin' me! It's true?"

"Yes," he said softly. "It's true."

I shook my head. "I don't believe this. I don't believe any of this. This is a goddamned *nightmare!*"

"Well," he said, "don't bother pinching yourself, Terry, because you're already awake."

"Who was she?"

"Does it matter?"

"I'm just curious."

"She was one of our extended family, okay? A donee. A single mother."

"Nice," I said, still convinced that someone was pulling my leg, that this whole thing was just one big, juvenile prank. "Real nice."

Friedman had mailed copies of the photos to Winston the next day, explaining that he would have sent the others as well but he was unwilling to jeopardize his plan by distributing such sensitive documents to anyone. Winston hadn't believed him, of course, had rightly surmised that the other alleged photos were a pure fabrication on Friedman's part, but that he had told the truth about *these* particular photographs was enough to persuade Winston that the man was serious about exposing Archie. And that, however unpalatable the likely ramifications for everyone involved, Archie *deserved* to be exposed.

So, the next day, Winston had divulged to Friedman the true basis for Archie's and my endeavor, and had agreed to cooperate with Morrow in his efforts to procure physical evidence of the offense underpinning our design. Winston, of course, had known precisely of what such evidence actually consisted, and had related all the pertinent information to Friedman. Friedman had then gone to work with Morrow on constructing a more detailed plan, and imparted it to Winston by phone a few days later.

Winston hadn't been sure if it would work: for one thing, even if he managed to locate us, it was unclear whether he would be able to obtain access to the photos; he suspected that I was as much on Archie's side now as Archie himself, and would be unwilling to surrender them even if he showed me the photos of Archie with the woman in Indianapolis. (He had been correct in this conjecture.) And for another, he doubted that he *would* be able to locate us, as there would be no way to request a street address and room number and all that without arousing suspicion. Needless to say, the two of them had managed to iron out such minor kinks.

Later on I would wonder why Friedman hadn't been content

simply to publish the photos Morrow had taken of Archie with the woman in Indianapolis. Such images, though inestimably less devastating than those which Morrow had pilfered from my hotel room, likely would have sufficed to permanently tarnish Archie's reputation and to kill what was already a fledgling enterprise. (I never saw Morrow's pictures, but from Winston's description of them I inferred that they did not exactly admit of varying interpretations.)

I guess the answer - and I can only assume that Archie would agree, as I saw no point in broaching the question to him - is as primitive and immune to intellectual analysis as is greed itself: why settle for a mere nugget of gold when you can just as easily raid the mine? Friedman smelled an opportunity to ruin Archie's career and in the process turn the entire world against him, and he was hell-bent on seizing it, notwithstanding the comparably feeble weapon already in his arsenal.

I imagine that, to the extent that he tried to justify it to himself at all (beyond the purely selfish benefit it would confer on his career in journalism), such a vendetta struck him as righteous, perhaps even divinely sanctioned, inasmuch as it would Expose the Truth. It would behoove my more ambitious and less scrupulous former colleagues, I here hasten to opine, to consider the possibility that the costs of exposing the truth sometimes outweigh whatever inherent virtues it might rightfully claim: that something is true does not automatically render it suitable for public consumption; and there is perhaps a special place in hell, if such a realm exists at all, for those who would blithely transgress the boundaries of common decency under the guise of political freedom. (Not, of course, that Friedman and Morrow confined their investigative methods to those permitted by law; had Archie been so inclined, I've no doubt that he would have won any lawsuit he might have brought against the reporter and his camera-toting hitman.)

There seems no better evidence, to me, for the randomness that ultimately governs our lives than the chain of events by virtue of which Morrow gained access to my hotel room. Even with Winston's help, had those events been altered even slightly, it seems probable that the photographs I took of Archie and Vanessa Grent never would have fallen into his hands.

You'll remember, I am sure, that "flash of a brown coat" I saw in the lobby of the LaQuinta while pressing the desk clerk for information about Morrow. The coat, of course, was Morrow's, and he had, while concealed somewhere in the vicinity, heard at least the tail end of my conversation with the clerk. And so gleaned what was for him the factual equivalent of a million-dollar jackpot: my room number. After I'd gone outside to retrieve the shoebox from the trunk of my car, he had gone to the front desk and summoned the clerk, who, disgruntled by my refusal to present her with a cash gift, accepted his facade as an assistant to Archie and me and cavalierly furnished the man with a key to my room. And why not? How could he know my room number if he weren't telling the truth? It probably didn't hurt that he tendered to her a generous gift of two hundred dollars on behalf of Mssrs. Lancaster and Farmer.

Rats.

"Get him out of the hotel," Morrow told Winston over the phone. "I know what room he's in, and I saw him get something out of his trunk and take it inside. I think it was a shoebox. The pictures must be in there. All I need is twenty minutes, if that."

By showing up at Archie's room a few minutes later, I made Winston's job much easier. Had I not, and gone instead to my room and waited for Archie to get back, I suppose I would have caught Morrow red-handed. What might have happened then is anybody's guess, but it sure wouldn't have been pretty. Perhaps, then, in some highly circuitous way, I owe Winston, if not my life, then at least the full use of my legs.

When I emerged from the bathroom a few minutes after seeking refuge in there, I found Archie and Winston exactly as I had left them: Archie standing, still pallid and numb with shock, and Winston sitting on the bed with his head drooping and his hands in his lap. I don't think they had spoken a word to each other in my absence. They had no more to say to each other than I had to say to either of them. The heroic Samaritan empire which Archie and I had erected was over, finished, toppled in the course of a single evening, never to be revived.

I looked at them. "So which one of you broke into my apartment? I suppose you'll tell me the truth now, since you've no longer a reason to lie."

At first neither of them acknowledged the question, and then, slowly, Winston raised his hand. "That was also me," he said.

I nodded, biting my lip to stifle the growl in my throat. "I thought so." I looked at him. "Why'd you do it, Winston?"

"I wanted the pictures," he said, without looking at me.

"Then why didn't you just ask for them?"

"I didn't think you'd give them to me."

512

"Why didn't you try asking before you jimmied my door with a crowbar?"

He shook his head. "I don't know."

"For that matter," I said, "why didn't you just take the pictures yourself? You could have swiped my camera when I wasn't looking."

Finally he lifted his head and looked at me. "I didn't want to have to see it," he said.

I nodded again, still gnawing on my lip, bridling an urge to grab him by his hair and knock a hole in the wall with his head. I shifted my gaze to Archie, and then back to Winston. "You guys are a real piece of work, you know that?"

"Terry," Archie grumbled, as if to warn me not to push it. Winston went back to staring at the floor.

I lit a cigarette, slumped into one of the chairs at the table in the corner. "Why don't you guys run along now?" I said, my voice queerly steady, assured. "I need some time alone. To think."

"I could use some of that myself," Archie said, and gestured for Winston to follow him. To me he said, "Why don't we sleep on this, Terry? I'm sure we'll be able to approach it more constructively in the morning, once we've calmed down and had some rest."

"Sure," I said. I took a long, deep draw on my cigarette, gazing vacantly at the wall. "Of course we will."

And with that they left.

And where did I go, five minutes later, but a liquor store three blocks from the hotel, where I purchased a pint of whiskey?

I drank all of it, naturally, and when I passed out in my bed that night, I had pretty much decided that suicide was the only dignified solution to my troubles.

38

The phone woke me up. I could tell by the state of my head that I had not slept for more than six hours. I slid an aching arm out from under the covers and fumbled for the receiver, shakily pressed it to my ear. "Hello?"

"Terry." Archie, of course. "Sorry to call you this early, but I think we need to move fast."

"Move fast?"

"Yes."

"Okay."

"Are you all right?"

"No."

"Did you get drunk?"

"Yes."

"Go back to sleep. I'll be there in one hour."

"Okay." Then, before he could hang up, I blurted, "Where's Winston?"

"With me. Why?"

I cleared my throat, in which a river of mucus had formed overnight. "Never mind."

"One hour, Terry."

"Bye."

I fell back to sleep almost immediately.

And woke up again when he knocked on the door. Getting up to answer it proved a monumental effort, requiring a full two minutes. Each time he knocked I called back, "Coming!" When at last I opened it, I saw him standing there, alone, through bleary eyes, unshaven but with most of his color back. What struck me most of all was that, for the first time in a month, the man was dressed in blue jeans.

I, of course, clad only in my boxer shorts and the bedspread which I had wrapped around myself like a robe, surely looked cancer-stricken by comparison. Without our exchanging a single word he came inside and I closed the door, immediately stumbled back to my bed and collapsed on it in a heap of sweaty flesh and ornamental fabric. I truly wanted to die, and honestly thought I might.

"Terry," he said. "Do you need to go to a hospital?"

"Uh huh."

"Seriously?"

"No."

"Can you talk to me?"

I tried to nod, but apparently, my head concealed by the spread, the gesture was ambiguous.

"Was that a yes? I couldn't tell."

"Yes! Yes!" I poked my head out from under the spead. "Sorry. Please just... sorry."

"I wish this could wait," he said, "but it can't."

"Just talk."

He lowered himself onto the end of the bed, and for a moment I recalled a Saturday morning from one of my teen years. I had gotten ludicrously smashed at a party the night before, and my father had come into my room and lectured me while perched on my bed, precisely as Archie was now. *I can't teach you a lesson any better than your hangover can,* he had said. He had been right, but that had not stopped him from proceeding with the censure, anyway. What Archie said was this: "I'm going to the press."

I threw back the bedspread, dug my knuckles into my eyes - the lids were like concrete slabs with thorns protruding from the backs of them - and tried to bring the man into focus. "The press? Why?"

He hesitated, caught, I think, between a sigh and a sob. "Because I want to end this."

"Do you mean...?"

"Yes. I'm going to reveal everything. I want this to be over."

I ran my tongue over my lips, but could summon no moisture. My heart thumped sluggishly, arduously, and even the slightest movement in my muscles produced dazzling pain. "Archie, maybe... maybe you're being a little hasty here. Has what's-his-face even called you yet?"

"No," he said. "Not yet. But he will."

Incredibly, the phone on the bedside table began to ring.

As Archie talked to Winston on the phone, I pieced together what had happened: Morrow had called Archie's room, wanting to talk to the man. Wanting to discuss business. Evidently he had issued a pretty strict ultimatum, because before he hung up Archie said, "Five PM?"

He replaced the receiver in the cradle very, very slowly and sank onto the bed again, regarding me with exquisitely dour eyes. "I've got nine hours," he said.

"He called?" At last I was somewhat awake, though my mind was still profoundly cloudy. A pot of coffee and a few gallons of water would fix that. *And maybe a beer or two.*

"Yes. Winston spoke to him." He chuckled quietly, ruefully. I did not like the sound of it; it brought to mind such words as "touched" and "unhinged." "Gave him a tongue-lashing, actually. How sweet."

"Are you really going to do this?"

He sighed and brushed his hands over his thighs. "Yes." He looked at me, and there passed between us thoughts which I cannot quite articulate, even now, thoughts without any definite shape or form but pulsating with raw emotional weight. There were things communicated too fine in their edges and too sharp in their contours to be translated with a pen. And I knew then that he meant to do as he had said.

"You're a good man," I told him. "In the ways that count."

At three o' clock on the afternoon of July 15, 2004, Archibald

518

Lancaster held a press conference in one of the reception rooms at the LaQuinta in St. Paul, Minnesota.

News organizations were permitted to send one ambassador each. Every local television station and newspaper deployed its finest field reporter. Every major cable news outlet was represented. A few Internet-based outfits also participated. There were in all perhaps two dozen vampires in attendance, armed with pens and notepads and cameras and microphones they didn't need. They were prepared, by God, and hungry - nay, ravenous - for the tastiest, most succulent meal of their professional lives.

Shortly before noon, Archie had placed a telephone call to Rod Morrow, in which he had expressed his intention to convey the sum Mr. Morrow required to suppress the photographs and spare Archie a lifetime of humiliation and universal estrangement from his peers. Just how much did Morrow want, you ask? Why, but the fiddling figure of one billion dollars (a goodly chunk of which would no doubt be funneled to Friedman). Morrow cautioned that a lawsuit against him would result in no less and perhaps even more embarrassment and ill will toward Archie than if Morrow simply went ahead and published the photographs. Archie had conceded this, and demanded that Morrow meet him in person to exchange the money for the pictures. Morrow had suggested that they meet at a restaurant in Minneapolis at five o' clock. Archie had agreed, and then gone to work on drafting the brief remarks he would deliver to the world three hours later.

Before his call to Morrow, Archie had made another: to his wife of twenty-two years, Evette Carolyn Compton-Lancaster. She was in Chicago, where she spent virtually all of her time. He had not spoken to her in almost three months. He told her about Vanessa, about me, about our crusade, about Friedman and Morrow, about Winston's involvement in the thing's demise. And then he told her what he meant to do, how he planned to atone for his sundry misdeeds. Incredulous beyond description, she had told him that he would be hearing from her divorce lawyer, warned him never to contact her again, and hung up. He had expected nothing less, he'd told me, and would grant her a divorce. She had long deserved one, would probably have requested one eventually, anyway. His marriage had been effectively defunct for years.

A little after two, with the speech written, Archie and I took Winston to the airport so that he could catch his three-thirty flight to Pittsburgh. Archie wanted him to be in the air when the conference was broadcast, a wish to which Winston dutifully submitted. It was awkward, saying good-bye to him. I was still torn between hating him and revering him, between wanting him and wanting to kill him.

But such feelings did battle only on the surface of my heart. Beneath them, in the far heavier and more constant chambers, I felt only an old and innocent affection, tempered by disappointment which I knew time would assuage. I guessed that things would never be the same between us, and that, probably sooner than later, our relationship would dissolve altogether. Maybe that was for the best, I tried to tell myself. Maybe the two of us had exhausted all the secret, torrid magic that was ours to create.

As he disappeared into the crowd of travelers beyond the gate, a great, bittersweet sadness washed over me, and I smiled ever so faintly, wondering that where there once had been unrequited lust there was now but fondness and pity, relieved that my long and stubborn fever had finally broken.

Probably anyone reading this not only watched but remembers with excruciating clarity the three-minute speech that Archie delivered that day. Nevertheless, I here reproduce it to the best of my ability, tweaking it only slightly for enhanced dramatic effect:

"Good afternoon. Five months ago, I commenced a professionally inappropriate and adulterous relationship with the wife of a close friend and business associate." He was here assaulted by a torrent of camera flashes; pens were put to paper with crazed, frenzied delight; the reporters leaned forward in their chairs, thrusting their microphones at him, exploding with almost carnal anticipation. Archie's voice did not waver, and he proceeded with rather unfamothable aplomb:

"With this friend I shared certain political interests in whose furtherance I sometimes acted unethically, in ways that were mutually advantageous to our respective ends. But I wish to state emphatically at the outset that this friend, whom I shall not name, engaged in no similarly questionable conduct. He is a decent and honorable man in impeccable public standing, and highly regarded by his colleagues, political foes as well as allies. I mention our personal and professional ties not to embarrass him, and certainly not to implicate him in any of the misconduct I have described, but only - *only* - to underscore the seriousness of my betrayal of his trust. To him, I extend my sincerest and most heartfelt apologies, while recognizing their gross inadequacy as a remedy."

Here he paused, and looked at me. I was seated in the front row, having been virtually ignored by the media gathered to witness this hideous funeral. I encouraged him with my eyes, and after a moment he continued:

"When a certain individual came into possession of evidence of this inappropriate relationship, he proposed that, to make amends, I engage in the sort of humanitarian enterprise which has unfolded, largely before the eyes of the world, over the past four weeks." Heads swiveled immediately in my direction. I stared straight ahead, at Archie, and again prompted him to go on. "Of course the idea struck me as ludicrous, not in small part because I could find no rational explanation for what might have motivated it. What did this man have to gain from my undertaking such a venture? What selfish interest might it serve? None was apparent to my cynical mind, because, quite simply, none existed: he had no grudge to appease, no agenda to satisfy, no money to make or ego to inflate. He suggested it, and helped me to realize it, purely because he felt it was right, and good, and just.

"I ask you, ladies and gentlemen: how often does such a thing happen? How many such benevolent souls does the world contain? Tragically few, I am afraid. Which is precisely what has made this journey so remarkable, so rewarding, and so thoroughly instructive. In the space of a single month, I have learned more from my friend about what it means to live a virtuous life than I had in all my preceding forty-eight years on this planet. I ask you to consider that, and to respect it, and to spare it the harsh lenses of your journalistic microscopes. There are things in life, as painfully few as those who still care about what is right, too sublime to bear dissection, things whose beauty shrivels before an examining eye, flowers whose petals wilt upon the icy touch of the intellect. I implore you, then, to leave it alone." He paused, regarding his captive audience, fighting back tears. "Leave it alone."

He concluded: "It is irrelevant what prompted me to choose this time and this occasion to divulge the truth behind our recent endeavor. Perhaps, in the days ahead, you shall learn all the sordid, juicy details that will make readers plunk down their change and viewers tune in in record numbers, that will triple your circulation and double your ratings. If that should happen, so be it. I suppose all of that is well beyond my control. As for me..." He swallowed, looked at me. The pause could not have lasted more than a few seconds, but to me, and I imagine to him, whole years elapsed within it. "As for me and my friend, we're going home."

The sun was setting. I heard the engine on the wing outside my window roar to life. A moment later the plane began its slow taxi down the runway. Archie was asleep in the chair beside me.

Tired myself, but too jittery to sleep, I reached into the pocket in the back of the seat in front of me, removed the newspaper wedged inside it. It was a *USA Today* from July 13. On page 2A ("the runners-up page," we'd sometimes called it at the *Post*), the following headline appeared: "Mid-West Sees Sudden Rise in Overqualified Job Applicants."

According to the story, people in Wisconsin, Minnesota, Iowa, and Missouri, with yearly salaries as high as fifty thousand dollars, had begun applying, in massive numbers, for menial, even mininum-wage jobs. Almost invariably, these applicants sought only evening or weekend positions, sometimes willing to work a maximum of ten hours per week. When asked why they wanted such jobs, they all gave a variant on the same answer: "I'm looking to supplement my regular income." Several economists and experts in labor relations had noted that the areas to which the phenomenon was confined seemed to be those "where you might guess there's a high probability of an impending visit to such businesses from Archie Lancaster and his cohort." Coincidence, asked the author of the article? Maybe, he said, but he wouldn't bet on it.

I stuffed the newspaper back into the pocket and looked at my friend, deep in slumber, as our plane lifted off the runway and began its slow climb upward, toward the clouds. "Me, either," I whispered. "Me, either."

When, a half-hour later, a stewardess came by with her cart and asked me if I'd like a beer or a glass of wine, I couldn't help but laugh. "No, thanks," I said. "A Coke will be fine."

She did not ask for a tip.

EPILOGUE:

Home Again

39

When I reflect now, six months later, on my adventures with Archie and Winston and the thousands of strangers whom I met in the course of my travels, it all seems impossibly remote and surreal, a distant fantasy as improbable as it is charming.

I have been asked by my family and friends and former colleagues, more times than I have cared to answer, whether the experience was worth all the turmoil and the eventual disgrace that marked it. I have always replied in the same way: "It was worth a hundred times the turmoil, and what disgrace? When push came to shove, and the cards were on the table, Archie conducted himself with more dignity and honor than most of us are privileged to witness even once in a lifetime." And I always mean it, every time.

So am I now biased in the man's favor, as I was once biased against him? Am I too close to him to form a fair and impartial judgment of his character, as I was once too unfamiliar with him, and too blindly hostile to his very existence, to render such an assessment? Perhaps. But I would also be the first to condemn his mistakes, to acknowledge his moral failings. I do not condone his infidelity. Far more importantly, I denounce unequivocally the greed and indifference to human suffering which he displayed for the better part of three decades. But I am a man strongly inclined to forgive wherever there exists even the flimsiest warrant for it, and Archie has provided me with much better than that.

We live in a world, remember, where the richest and most comfortable human beings were once applauded for sharing even the tiniest fraction of their wealth, as if such generosity exceeded all bounds of rational and civilized behavior. Fortunately, Archie and I changed that. Beginning as early as a day after the CNN interview, and increasing steadily ever since, scores of wildly affluent people - other CEOs, politicians, prominent lawyers and doctors, even a few dozen athletes and entertainers - have followed Archie's lead by donating as much as twenty or thirty percent of their liquid assets to such worthy charities as the Salvation Army and the Christian Children's Fund.

These are noble and touching gestures, and I am deeply grateful for each and every one of them. But it is important to remember that the vast bulk of those in need are far less visible than the homeless man in rags and the malnourished child on TV. In the modern world, the price one pays for escaping such a miserable fate, it seems, is a kind of social and economic obscurity. And once you have been assimilated into that class, and have ceased to draw by necessity on society's emotional and financial resources, you are pretty much stuck there, left to drift

531

interminably in a leaky life-raft alongside billions of others in their own rotted, sinking vessels. And the best you can hope for, day after day, year after year, is that you'll somehow stay ahead of the water, that you can shovel it out fast enough to stay afloat. One had might as well live his entire waking life with a gun to his head.

But now I'm just stating what I have spent hundreds of pages showing, I suppose, and so shall heed Archie's advice to the press: I shall leave it alone.

I guess it would be unfair not to tell you what happened to John Friedman and Rod Morrow, and what became of the photos that the latter filched from my hotel room. I am pleased to report that, enraged by Archie's ruse and subsequent vindication at least in the eyes of a few prominent observers, Mr. Morrow released copies of the photos to the New York *Times*, which for legal reasons declined to print even censored versions of them. In fact, after consulting the company's lawyers, it declined to do more than run a short, three-paragraph article describing in very little detail the pictures and, in far greater detail, how the paper had obtained them. Its editor-in-chief then relinquished them to Archie, who burned them in his kitchen sink. Presumably Morrow has retained the originals and the negatives, though to my knowledge he has done nothing more with them.

A few weeks after the *Times* article was published, Vanessa Grent filed suit against Morrow on invasion-of-privacy grounds, and was awarded several hundred thousand dollars in an out-of-court settlement. Friedman has maintained an extremely low profile in the days since, turning down myriad requests for interviews and making no public comments whatever regarding the photos, Morrow, Archie, or anything of the like. As far as I know, he is still employed by the Charleston *Daily Mail*.

I am tempted to call him sometimes, late at night, and ask him if he's excited by the prospect of going to hell. But I never do. I've a hunch that, even with the fire and smoke and that razor-sharp pitchfork poking in his ass, such anguish could never compare to the torment he suffers every day, right here on earth.

Back in October, mostly as an amusing afterthought, Archie asked his lawyer, Kenneth Stevens, to investigate how many of our hundred and fifty or so promisees had actually met the terms of the contracts they'd signed. Remarkably, all but sixteen of them had: twenty percent of the monies we had donated to the rest of them remained securely embedded in their bank accounts, wholly untouched. When Archie called me with the news, I jokingly posed the question whether we ought to sue the handful who had reneged.

"Wouldn't the press," he replied, "just love me *then*?"

In the first week of September, Archie and I founded an organization called And For the Sake of Us All. It now has offices in all fifty states, which are operated almost exclusively by volunteers. Folks of limited means are invited to visit these offices and submit, along with their tax returns for the previous year, a simple one-page form asking for their name, mailing address, marital status, number of children, and yearly household income. If they qualify (and nearly all of them do), a few weeks later they receive checks in amounts suitable to their circumstances, just as they would have if Archie and I had donated the money to them personally.

So far the system appears to be working extraordinarily well, filtering out fraudulent claims with far greater efficiency than the two of us could have managed on our own. We both agreed that we could not have gone on much longer doing things as we had, even without Morrow's unwelcome intervention, both on account of our limited energies and the unfortunate realities of human nature: people lie, especially where money and sex are concerned. Perhaps the best part of the whole thing, this new program we've instituted, is that it can function with almost total autonomy, requiring very little oversight and attention. That leaves Archie free to pursue his new career (he and Winston run an art gallery in the city), and me to write this book. Which, of course, is now almost finished.

The second best part, I guess, is that the gloomy predictions of certain nay-sayers in the media, as well as a seemingly endless array of stodgy, pipe-smoking economists, have all been decisively refuted: the American marketplace has not collapsed, McDonald's is still a thriving, multi-billion dollar corporation, Marx's ghost has yet to rape a schoolchild, and the country itself seems to be running as smoothly as ever.

But slowly, very slowly, more and more people are finding it possible to live without constantly worrying about bills, skimping on necessities like food and clothing, sacrificing even the most modest luxuries, leaving grave illnesses largely untreated, going days at a time without seeing their spouses or children, and dragging through the workday on five hours' sleep. Finally, they have a little joy in their lives, a little fun, a little freedom.

And the feeling that gives me... well, I wouldn't trade it for all the eternal riches in all the sparkling coffers of heaven.

40

Christmas is just two weeks away, but I got the only present I could ever want all the way back in August. It arrived at my door quite unexpectedly, and at just such a moment that, if I had read of such a thing in a book or seen it in a movie, I would have balked and dismissed the storyteller as an untalented hack, a contriver of gimmicks, an abuser of artistry. But it happened to me, and besides, of late I have grown rather inured to seeming implausibilities.

Just ten minutes before the knock came, I had found myself rummaging through my wallet, discarding all the junk that had been weighing it down for months. And I came across Susan's letter to me, the one she had left at the front desk of the Inez Sleep Away. I pored over it for a long time, my eyes returning again and again to the letterhead, which contained the telephone number of her boss's office. At one point I even had my hand on the phone, meaning to dial the number and try to get in touch with her. But something had stolen my nerve - the passage of time, maybe, and the way things had ended for Archie and me - and I had lowered the receiver with a heavy feeling in my stomach, a kind of wistful resignation.

I was just lying down to take a nap when I heard the knock. I got up to answer it, grouchy and irritated, figuring it was a door-to-door salesman or a Girl Scout peddling cookies.

But it was not. It was Susan. Susan Reynolds, from Washington, Pee-A.

She stood on my doorstep in faded jeans and a cherry-red tank-top, her hair in a ponytail, open-toed sandals on her feet. Smiling as she was, drenched in waning, pale sunlight, she might have been some gorgeous apparition. Until she spoke.

"Still want that second date?"

"Susan," I said, dizzy with surprise and delight. "Is that you?"

"It's me," she said, laughing. Oh, the way the sun played on her hair, and danced in her eyes, and rendered her face an ageless portrait, majestic in its every angle! Oh, the way the sun played on her hair, and in her eyes.

"Come in," I said, stepping aside. "Come in, come in."

She came in.

"This is amazing," I said. "I'm... I'm amazed."

She laughed again, and I gestured for her to take a seat on the couch. "Thanks." She sat and crossed her legs, settling into the cushion. "Well, yeah, I guess it *is* pretty incredible, huh?"

"It is," I said. "I'm honestly still wondering if you're real."

"I'm real. It's me. I'm here."

"How... how did you find me?"

She smiled. "You're in the book, remember?"

"Ah."

I just looked at her for a second, still reeling, and then, unsure what else to do, offered her a drink.

"Sure," she said. "A beer would be nice, if you've got one."

I almost told her I didn't, then remembered the stray bottle of Bud Light that was kicking around in the snack bin. I had been meaning to pour it out, but had never quite gotten around to it. Or, perhaps, had not quite been willing to. "Sure thing," I said.

I went to the kitchen, fetched the beer, poured myself a glass of Pepsi, and carried the drinks into the living room. I handed her the beer and sat down in the rocker by the window, across from the couch.

"You didn't want one?" she asked.

"Nah," I said. "I gave up drinking."

Her eyes widened a little as she sipped her beer. "Really? Why's that?"

"Well," I said, smiling, "it turns out I'm allergic to alcohol."

"You know," she said, "I doubted that you'd even live here anymore."

538

"Oh? How come?"

"Well," she said, averting her eyes, blushing a little. "You know... just with your being so close with Mr. Lancaster and all, I figured..."

"That I'd be able to afford something a little bigger? One of those mansions on Penn Avenue like his, maybe?"

She laughed with relief. "Yes. Exactly."

"Well," I said, "it's true that Archie and I are pretty tight, but the only money I have is what I saved from my job at the newspaper, a few stocks and bonds, and a small portion of the million dollars I extorted from him. The rest of it I returned."

She chuckled and swept her bangs out of her eyes. I felt a flutter in my chest, a pleasant tickle in my stomach. "So what he said on TV was true? The only reason he did what he did was because of... your arrangement with him?"

"At first," I said. "But then he did it because he wanted to."

She nodded, musing. "Hey, maybe people really *can* change."

I smiled at her and sipped my Pepsi. "Maybe so," I said. "Maybe so."

At one point I inquired how her brother Jimmy was doing.

"Much better, actually."

"I'm glad to hear that," I said.

"Thanks to you, of course."

"Thanks to Archie," I said.

"To the both of you."

"The both of us, then."

The evening wore on, and with it, our conversation. One subject wove gradually into another, and we chased each tangent with increasing exuberance and ease, until the words flowed as effortlessly as are these words now, as a stream down a steep hill, yielding to a warm and lovely gravity far beyond its grasp or control. The words were still flowing happily when the clock on my mantlepiece chimed nine o' clock.

"It's late," she said, glancing at her watch. "Terry, we've been talking for almost four hours!"

"Have we?" I had lost track of the time myself.

"Yes."

"Well," I said, "if you need to go..."

"No," she said. "Not just yet." She smiled. "I like this."

"Me too."

I moved to the couch, put my arm around her. "I'm glad you came," I said. I leaned in slowly and pressed my mouth to hers. She kissed me back, and did not pull away until I did.

And then, for a long moment, I simply looked at her, and marveled at her beauty, a thing too sublime to bear dissection, a flower whose petals would surely wilt under all but the softest gaze.

January 1, 2005 - January 16, 2006

Hurricane, WV
Morgantown, WV

Made in the USA
Coppell, TX
29 July 2020